Shot Through the Heart

Cat Lindler

Shot Through the Heart

Copyright © 2013 by Cat Lindler

Book Design and Cover Art by Marion Sipe

ISBN 13: 978-0-615-91751-1
ISBN 10: 0-615-91751-8

Published by Two Toes Press, San Antonio, Texas

Printed in U.S.A

Dedication

To Frodo, who passed away in 2009. I miss your input, my big, hairy friend. And then there were two....

Acknowledgments

Thanks to Chalene (as always) for her copious and insightful comments, and to the writers and readers of western romance who inspired me. Thanks also to the Library of Congress librarians for their assistance in locating factual, period information about Mexico.

Other Adventure Romance by Cat Lindler

http://catlindler.com

Kiss of a Traitor
Starlight & Promises

*"You're a loaded gun—there's nowhere to run.
No one can save me—the damage is done.
Shot through the heart, and you're to blame . . ."*
-Jon Bon Jovi, 1986
"You Give Love a Bad Name"

Uno

1885
North central Mexico

A wolf is relentless in pursuing its prey, and the female is the most tenacious.

The Ghost Wolf surveyed her territory, gaze alert to her surroundings and the life it harbored. Nothing missed The Wolf's notice, not the hard-plated armadillos that nosed across the sand or the lizards that scurried about on mysterious missions. Roadrunners spun out small dust storms in their wake, chasing the lizards. On the occasional updraft, the buzzards, ever-present harbingers of death, circled and observed from a panoramic vantage point with sharp eyes.

She took in a deep breath, and cold, dry air bathed her lungs, the clean taste coating her tongue. At the sheer, stark nature of the desert, her chest tightened, heart beat faster, not with anxiety but with a sense of awe, as though she were but a grain of sand in this immense land.

The Wolf's hunting grounds, the Mexican *altoplano*, sloped downward from the western Sierra Madre

Occidental to the eastern Sierra Madre Oriental, north
to the Rio Bravo del Norte and south to San Luis Potosi.
The high plateau consisted of mostly barren, rocky desert
spotted with bristled-gray vegetation and the *ejidos* of
campesinos. She turned a cheek to the twists of a breeze
that slipped down the mountainside, flinging sand and
tossing tumbleweeds across the tracks of long-eared
jackrabbits and the deeper oval imprints of white-tailed
deer.

A coyote's yip rolled through the silence then melted
into the sand. Life on the high-altitude plain had its own
pattern, a constant cascade of predator and prey. The
roadrunner watched the lizard. The buzzard watched the
roadrunner. The coyote watched the armadillo.

The Wolf watched them all.

As a gold-plated sun slid toward the western
mountains, spreading a layer of crimson, magenta, and
purple hues, a rider pounded across the sand, waving his
arm and calling out, "It's coming!"

At the shouted words, The Ghost Wolf turned from
her perusal of the desert and swiveled about in the
saddle to peer down the tracks, far beyond the curving
dunes and dusty mesquite brush to where the horizon
dwindled into a lilac haze. A ribbon of smoke ascended
like a reata to heaven, sucked upward by the ghostly
breeze and curling into the flat silver expanse.

High overhead, a warmer wind tore apart the train's
breath into ragged shapes and pulled her gaze to the
sky. Images formed, and her eyes narrowed. She tried to
retreat, to hold back the memories, but in the scudding
clouds created by the train's smoke, the past welled
up. The clouds coalesced into one face—one hateful
countenance. As though detecting the scent of death, her
nostrils flared.

"Chaz?"

The voice came from beside her and brought her
back—back to the high desert and sandy plain, back to

slanting sunlight glaring off rock and distributing long shadows through the depression to swallow up the hooves of the horses. Chaz gasped in an alkaline-tainted breath as though the train's approach had pressed the air from her chest. *Seventeen years.* Seventeen years she had borne this. Her hand hurt, and she lifted it, glanced down. In the grip of her preoccupation with what she could not change, she had drawn her pistol. Her hand now clutched it so fiercely her palm sweated, welded to the wooden butt. She forced her fingers to relax and holstered the gun.

As she gazed at the young man on the white-footed bay, a smile came to her lips and dispelled the last bitter taste of the past. A length of auburn hair tumbled over his forehead to obscure one eye, and she had to restrain herself to keep from smoothing it back. At the advanced age of sixteen, he wouldn't appreciate the motherly gesture.

"Are you ready?" Excitement brightened his voice. "Remember your promise. I may enter the cars this time." The smoothness of his face betrayed his age, but the blue eyes held a maturity far beyond his years, forced on him by their circumstances, by her seventeen-year obsession. Her heart ached for his lost childhood.

"Yes, Raúl." She lowered her eyes and brushed the coating of grit from her leather duster, hiding her underlying fear from him. "I remember. You are too impatient. Impatience will be the death of you."

The breeze picked up sand particles from the sides of the depression, splattered the side of her face, and spooked her horse. Chaz quieted the animal with a hand on its neck and checked her companions. Fuerte lay like a sandy boulder, nose twitching, fringed tail wagging like a clock pendulum, painting curves in the dust. Raúl's exuberant expression. Salvatore's patient look and slow nod at her perusal. Alec's lazy, handsome grin. Her cousins and uncles and the other men of Asilo, all arrayed behind the screen of mesquite and agave cactus. They were here for one reason…because they loved her and followed her lead, even into death.

Was it worth it?

Worth it and more.

Worth every drop of her blood and that of her family.

To a Yaqui, honor was everything. Violation of respect dictated only one response—vengeance. Vengeance was a duty—a holy quest. Even had she told her family she was through with this settling of scores, that they had done enough, they would carry on the vendetta without her.

Her jaw hardened, steel stiffened her spine, and her gaze returned to the dying rays of the sun glinting off sand and sparking glitters from the quartz grains. The color of silver. Hard, shiny silver. The lifeblood of Mexico. A blessing for the *Americano* mine and railroad owners and a curse on the poor people. For The Ghost Wolf, silver represented more…much more. Silver was the coin of her revenge.

The train crested the hill, a dot of black growing into a smudge, slowing down as it approached the curve. Chaz tightened up on her reins, and that unique tingling, one of nerves and anticipation, raced through her blood.

It happened this way every time.

The car rocked like a cradle, and he would have dozed on if not for the squealing of metal on metal, jerking cessation of movement, and absence of clattering wheels. Voices, once softly droning, rose to a tumult. His muscles bunched, fueled by the gut feeling the train hadn't paused to allow a herd of deer to move off the tracks. Dillon West thumbed back his hat and shifted his weight on the hard wooden seat.

"*Por favor*, gringos. Raise your hands, and do not move! Turn out your pockets." The words, shouted in

Spanish by a husky, youthful voice, shifted Dillon's taut body into full-blown rigor mortis. He released a harsh breath and squirmed upright. *Damn! After riding Thorne Railroad for months with no sign of* La Lobo Fantasma, *the banditos caught me napping.* Justus Thorne would not be pleased, but then, Thorne was far from pleasant under any circumstances, or so Dillon had heard from numerous sources. Of course, the great man hadn't dealt with Dillon directly, only through an intermediary, a distasteful lawyer by the name of William Giles. At their last meeting, along with the envelope of money, Giles handed out a warning: "Results, West. Mr. Thorne expects results."

With chagrin, Dillon recalled his reply: "He wants results, he'll get 'em."

Nope, Mr. Justus Almighty Thorne would be ass-kicking mad and howling for blood. His ten thousand dollars in silver hadn't bought much of anything. However, there was plenty more where that came from.

Spurs jingled behind him, the clink of coins, and the muffled squeaks of passengers as they protested relinquishing their costly possessions. Cold steel prodded his shoulder, and Dillon looked up into a pair of dark eyes set in a swarthy face with a drooping mustache. Dillon dropped a battered gold pocket watch and a slim purse into the outstretched hand. The man was an *indito*, Yaqui. *Too old to be the one with the youthful voice.* Other voices rumbled, deeper voices, all accented with Yaqui dialect. A serape bushed his shoulder as the bandito moved down the aisle to the next passenger. Dillon chanced a quick glance over his shoulder, saw a tall, wiry, black-clad figure exiting the car through the door to the pass-through.

With one eye on the mustachioed bandito and his compadres making their way up and down the car aisles, Dillon leaned sideways and peered out the soot-stained window. A slim man in dusty gray leathers, mounted on a tall gray horse, was nudging it toward the rear of the train where the silver-mine payroll and a slew of silver ingots rested in a heavily guarded safe. An enormous, shaggy-coated animal, the same dingy gray as the horse, trotted at the heels of the mount. *A dog...or a wolf?* Sure enough, he'd hit pay dirt, and the handle fit. *La Lobo Fantasma,* The Ghost Wolf. As elusive as a ghost and traveling with a wolflike dog. After three months, Dillon had uncovered only one other piece of information. The man had a younger brother, or protégé, who rode by his side. *The youth who'd entered the train?*

Dillon's speculation fled with a barrage of gunfire from the baggage cars. Undoubtedly, *Capitán* Carterá Manzanita's *rurales* were fighting back, their jobs, and most likely their necks, on the line. In the war against the train robbers, the mestizo ex-banditos proved more hindrance than help. *El Presidente* Porfirio Díaz formed the *rurales* from the deepest dregs of the barrel of Mexican bandits and cutthroats. The police force was Diaz's effort to curb such threats as *La Lobo Fantasma* posed to the lucrative relationships *El Presidente* enjoyed with American investors and rich Spanish *hacendados.* However, the very *rurales* he relied upon to guard his investments proved corrupt and incompetent, and ultimately, impotent in bringing the robberies to a halt.

The shooting stopped. The *rurale soldados* hadn't stood a chance against the superior firepower of the train robbers. *No surprise.* Dillon wondered how many died and what the hell he was going to do next, now he'd lost Thorne's silver shipment. Under the watchful eyes of the armed men in the car, he surreptitiously observed The Wolf's men unloading the silver bars and coin onto waiting pack mules.

Their leader sat astride the gray with the wolf lying on the sandy ground beside the horse's hooves. What with the grimy window and a Mexican desperado breathing down his neck, Dillon noted fewer details than he'd like, but at the sheer number of attackers, close to fifty, he whistled silently through his teeth. A dozen men, as well armed as a military troop, surrounded *La Lobo Fantasma* like a presidential honor guard. The Ghost Wolf was a study in silver — shirt, vest, trousers and chaps, long duster coat, and wide-brimmed sombrero. Soft afternoon sunlight streamed around him, making him a pale smudge against the backdrop of the silver-gold chaparral- and sagebrush-covered hills. Dillon suspected that from a distance, the gray horse and clothing would blend into the silvery sky, rendering the bandit all but invisible.

He found his gaze drawn to another figure, smaller, slimmer than the others and dressed in black, who sat astride a white-footed bay not far from The Ghost Wolf. *The youth?* A flatbed wagon with low slatted sides and pulled by an octet of mules was situated off at one angle, a manned Hotchkiss gun mounted in the rear of the wagon bed and aimed at the baggage cars.

The sound of boot heels tapping on the wooden floor brought Dillon's head around and his attention back to the bandits. With a wave of a sun-browned hand and a flash of white teeth beneath a coarse mustache, the last man darted through the door at the end of the car. Dillon snapped his gaze back to the window, watching the man leap from the platform between the cars to the back of a rangy roan, whose reins the bandito in black held. The sun shone on the face of the man in black, and Dillon caught a glimpse of shaggy auburn hair — marking him as a gringo, not a Yaqui — and the features of a half-grown man. A bandana circled his throat, and a sombrero dangled down his back by the chin string around his neck. A grin only a youth could summon up in the midst of a train robbery split the boy's face. The leader in gray turned his horse, urging it upward to position himself on the ridge crest above the tracks. The youth and other riders soon joined him, leaving only the Hotchkiss gun wagon behind to guard their escape.

The train inched forward, and Dillon feared he was rapidly losing his chance—perhaps his only chance—to follow the banditos. He swore and bolted from his seat to tear from the car onto the platform. With a rat-a-tat burst from the Hotchkiss, bullets sliced the air above his head.

Smart move, West.

Dillon hit the metal grate between the cars, invectives spilling from his mouth, and ripped out the knees of his new worsted-wool trouser suit. Damn thing cost him fifty dollars in Denver. His twenty-dollar hat, caught by a bullet, sailed out over the railing to land in the dust and cinders beside the track. As the locomotive gathered speed, streaming vapor from the coal car stung his eyes and made them tear. He waited until the train traveled beyond range and sight of the Mexican gang, then pushed himself to his feet and rushed through the cars to the engine.

He stormed through the open doorway, flashed his railway authorization at the startled engineer, and pointed to a pair of hills about a mile distant. "When you enter the pass at Tecalas, slow the train to a crawl until you see me riding alongside," he ordered. "Then make tracks for Zacatecas. Keep your mouth shut about my presence here."

Mouth agape, the engineer nodded. Dillon turned and ran back through the cars toward the cattle car at the rear, pausing only long enough to check on the health of the payroll guards—alive—and the status of their safes—empty.

In the cattle car, Dillon tore off his suit, grimacing at the damage to the expensive garment, and pulled his riding clothes from his saddlebags. He crossed the bandoliers over his chest, ducked his head into the opening of a woven poncho, and slapped a wide sombrero on his head.

Victory, his chestnut stallion, saddled and waiting,

pawed an iron-shod foot against the boards of the car while snorting air from his nostrils.

The train slowed, and Dillon hauled open the cattle-car doors to view bristly cactus and thick mesquite brush whizzing by. He mounted Victory then backed him against the wall of the car and away from the moving scenery. Muscles knotted beneath the mount's glossy red coat, and when a clear space emerged, Dillon dug his heels into the horse's flanks. Victory leapt forward with a surge and soared through the air, landing hard on the sandy ground and wobbling for a moment. Once the horse steadied beneath him, Dillon pushed Victory into a ground-eating gallop.

Dos

More a rude outpost than a bastion of civilization, the
pueblo boasted a sprinkling of low adobe huts, rough
walled and mud stained, which hunkered along a rutted
track. A mean-looking cantina with a half-dozen horses
hitched outside to a peeling rail anchored the far end.
Pigs wallowed in dry washes, and scrawny chickens
pecked at the ground. A few women, heads swathed
in rebozos, moved lethargically along the street, skirts
sweeping the ground and stirring up dust. No sign of
pistoleros, wolves...or ghosts.

Dillon had followed the tracks of the Mexican
banditos for three days. Dust coated his throat and
clothing, and his muscles ached like the devil. At first,
he wondered why the banditos had proven so difficult
to capture in the past, as they seemed to take no pains
to disguise their escape route to confuse pursuers. He
chased The Ghost Wolf across desert and rocky shale,
through stands of skeletal mesquite and into and out of
dry washes. When the tracks reached a plain of volcanic
rock, they disappeared as though he'd been chasing
spirits. Dillon was good. He'd tracked murderers and
Mescalero Apaches, Army deserters and bank robbers.

You'd think he could stay on the trail of a full mule team. With a wry smile, Dillon shook his head. *Seemed not.* He'd never seen the like, had no idea had they'd done it. *Ghost, indeed.*

The thought was but one prickly spine in the cactus field Dillon was coming to see as Justus Thorne's empire. He'd done his homework. Thorne owned twelve silver mines and ran cattle over thousands of acres. His railroad stretched from Guanajuato to Zacatecas and hooked up with the Mexican Central running to El Paso. Another line ran to Veracruz and lucrative amethyst mines. Under the friendship of Porfirio Díaz, Thorne and other rich Americans faced no opposition in continually expanding their realms south of the United States border. Though The Ghost Wolf had plenty of trains from which to choose, Giles said the bandito robbed only those owned by Thorne Enterprises. In the back of his mind, Dillon wondered why, but it didn't really matter; Thorne was the one who was paying him.

Dillon was no stranger to Mexico. As a former bounty hunter, he'd retrieved wanted criminals from across the border numerous times. He understood the culture and the politics. Couldn't say he agreed with Díaz's methods, progressive on the surface, hard as shoe iron underneath, but Dillon had to grudgingly admit Díaz had cleaned up his country to attract foreign investment. Mexico had a long history of lawlessness, and *El Presidente* had taken a hard stand to combat his country's unsavory image. While expanding the railroads and improving the infrastructure of cities, he also erected gallows at every crossroads and cracked down on the banditos. But at the same time, although Mexican justice was swift, it was also merciless; courts were circuses, and political opposition was not tolerated. Díaz was in for the long run.

With Victory's reins in his hands, Dillon squatted on his heels atop the slight rise above the pueblo and examined the horses at the cantina. Plagued by flies, the animals shook their heads and stamped their feet in the dusty street. One horse in particular caught Dillon's attention—a white-footed bay. "Huh," he grunted. Seemed one ghost wandered away from the celestial world and into the land of the living. Dillon mounted Victory and followed a goat track down the slope into town.

Once inside the cantina, he propped a scuffed boot on the bar rail and dropped a silver coin on the scarred wooden surface. "*Aguardiente,*" he said.

The man behind the plank-board counter looked at Dillon as if he'd descended from the heavens and ordered nectar of the gods. With a scowl, he shook his head.

Dillon tried again, hoping for something more approaching bourbon than turpentine, and a reasonably clean glass. "*¿Bebidas alcohólicas?*"

The bartender, if he could be deemed such, plunked a smudged, chipped glass on the bar and slopped a clear fluid into it. Dillon picked it up and sipped the fiery drink, recognizing the distinctive taste of tequila, bitter and potent, made from the blue agave plant. Turning at the waist, he surveyed the room. Peasants, campesinos in gray-white trousers and tunics, hunched about tilting tables. In the far corner, a card game was in progress. Six men, rough and nasty-looking mestizos, gun belts, wicked knives in sheaths at the waist, battered sombreros canted forward to hide their eyes…and one slim young man in black leathers. Dim, smoky light in the cantina picked up the auburn highlights in his hair and the beginnings of a mustache—more fuzz than whiskers— that lined his upper lip. As he crouched over a handful of grease-spotted cards, sweat pearled on his forehead, and his knuckles gleamed pale with the strength of his grip, as if the cards held the answers to life itself. With a shaky hand, he threw a card on the table and looked up. Dillon caught the glint of blue eyes.

"*¡Bastardo!*" the man across the table shouted, leaping to his feet and drawing a skinning knife. The mestizo had a good sixty pounds and four inches on the youth and clearly no scruples about using the weapon to carve out the boy's heart. As the mestizo lunged forward and the other gamblers scattered like tumbleweeds in a hard prairie wind, the boy shoved back from the table, scrambled to his feet, and backed up to the wall, eyes wide, limbs trembling.

Dillon smoothly slid the Navy Colt from its holster. Gun in one hand, drink in the other, he took three quick, silent steps across the hard-packed dirt floor and nudged the mestizo's kidneys with the point of the barrel.

"*¡Basta!*" Dillon said. "*¡Tome asiento! ¡Ningún argumento!*"

The larger man apparently hadn't had enough, he didn't sit down as ordered, and by all accounts, damn well wanted an argument. He spun around as though he had a death wish, the knife headed for Dillon's stomach. Dillon tossed the liquor into the man's eyes and swung his gaze to the frozen young man. "*¡Vaya pronto!*" he yelled then turned his full attention to the mestizo, who was rubbing his burning eyes with the back of one hand and slicing the air with the knife. Dillon ducked under the wild flailing and planted a fist in the man's gut. To his dismay, the boy left the wall and drew his gun.

"*¡Vaya!*" Dillon shouted as the mestizo expelled a pained breath. "*¡En seguida!*"

Not only was the boy not going—*now!*—but his features reflected youthful rebellion at being ordered about by a stranger. When he holstered the gun with noted reluctance and pushed his way through the onlookers to disappear out the door, Dillon released a heavy breath. He could now finish off the man trying to kill him. With a kick to the man's groin, which elicited a strained, "*¡Mula!*" the man dropped the knife, doubled over, and clutched his testicles.

Dillon loosely translated the obscenity in his mind, which implied impotency, and responded in kind. "*Chilito*," a kind of Mexican slang for "little cock." Dillon credited his university education for his mastery of vocabulary. Bringing down the butt of the Colt onto the man's head, Dillon sent him to the floor. He flung away the glass and backed cautiously toward the door, gun covering the other mestizos and any others who might want to join the party. Everyone edged away as though they had no more concern for the man with his face in the dirt floor than they did for the cockroaches scurrying across the rough adobe walls.

When his back hit the tattered cloth that served the cantina for a door, Dillon swung around to sprint to the hitching post. Victory was no longer tied to the mesquite pole, and the boy, atop the white-footed bay, waited in the street with Victory's reins in his hand. Dillon shoved his revolver in his holster and ran for the horse, springing into the saddle with a leap. Sounds of the mestizos gathering their courage came from inside the cantina. As Dillon and the boy put heels to their mounts, shouts and gunshots came from behind them, singing above their crouched bodies.

They stormed out of the pueblo like a pair of desperados with gold in their saddlebags and a posse breathing down their necks, and charged up into the hills. The boy pumped a clenched fist in the air and yelled, "*¡Caramba!*" Dillon cut him a scowl, though the same ripple of adrenaline sped through his veins. Had he been fifteen years younger than his current thirty-five, he'd probably have done the same.

With the mestizos on their heels, Dillon followed the boy's lead, galloping along tracks no wider than jackrabbit trails leading into the Cold Mountain range. They climbed higher, the boy weaving back and forth along switchbacks, traversing ledges that would give a mountain goat vertigo, and slipping through blind canyons that turned out not to be so blind. After two hours of hard riding, the youth slowed the bay and turned into a rocky chute. Near sheer walls of exposed rock soared on either side of Dillon, and boulder rubble from some avalanche event littered the narrow pathway. Sickly looking hickory clung to fissures, accompanied by the occasional splash of bright red paintbrush peeking out from behind jagged cuts. The chute, no more than a dozen yards across, narrowed even more as it approached a small meadow with a trickling stream that spilled down in a silvery spray from somewhere high above. There, the boy halted and swung down from his horse.

Victory's sides were heaving; sweat foamed on his neck where the reins had rubbed against it, and around the edges of the saddle blanket. Dillon was as winded as the horse as he slid out of the saddle. Before taking the thirsty horse to water, he pulled off the bandana around his neck and wiped Victory's wet, trembling hide. He loosened the girth but left the saddle in place. Though they seemed to have left the angry mestizos behind, he'd learned from past experience to be prepared for a hasty escape. He hadn't made it this far in his dangerous line of work by being careless. Nonetheless, his move in saving the boy's life had been a calculated one. Sure as shootin' the boy had to be *La Lobo Fantasma's* young companion, brother, cousin, or whatever. A little gratitude thrown in his direction could go a long way in finding and capturing The Ghost Wolf. He figured it wouldn't hurt to milk the boy's appreciation for everything it was worth.

"Who are you?"

Dillon turned his attention from the horse to the business end of a .45. The milk of gratitude he'd expected curdled. He lowered his gaze again and rubbed the bandana in circles over the horse's sweaty side. "The man who just saved your hide," he said in a steady voice.

He wasn't surprised the boy spoke English, seeing as he was a gringo like Dillon. With Dillon's blond hair and blue eyes, eyes the same color as the boy's, he stood out in a crowd of Mexicans like an antelope in a herd of longhorns.

When Dillon checked the boy again, the gun barrel had dipped, and though distrust ran across the boy's face like a Texas twister, he returned the pistol to its holster.

"*Sí*," the boy said. "Guess I owe you."

"*De nada.* It's nothing. Just two men in a bar fight and a swarm of liquored-up mestizos. You were outnumbered. I'd have done the same for anyone."

A crooked smile slipped across the boy's mouth. "*Gracias.*" He extended his hand. "Raúl Gutierrez. I appreciate your help."

Dillon took the hand, shook it firmly. "Dillon West." He arched a brow. "You make a habit of playing cards with the local pistoleros?"

An easy grin tugged at Raúl's mouth. "No. Chaz would have my hide."

Dillon took Victory's reins and walked alongside the boy and his bay to the stream. The horses lowered their heads and began to drink. "Chaz?" Dillon asked casually.

Raúl's grin disappeared, and his brow contracted in a frown. He remained silent as he stared at the ears of the horse.

Dillon refrained from pressing, and silence settled like drifting dust around them, the only sounds the mournful call of an Inca dove from the ocotillo shrubs, the horses slurping, and water tumbling into the stream.

The boy's head came up, and he regarded Dillon with a look of curiosity. "What were you doing in Flores? It's far from the well-traveled routes."

Dillon chuckled. "Flores, eh—flower. More like prickly pear cactus." Then his mouth thinned. "Why do you ask? A man could make a mistake butting into another man's business."

A light kindled in Raúl's eyes, and he ignored the implied warning. "Are you running from the law?"

Dillon shrugged and spread his hands. "Depends on what law you're talking about. I found it practical to leave Texas for a while. Seems I parked my boots beneath the wrong bed. Her protector objected. Unfortunately, he turned out to be a Federal judge and a railroad owner, richer than Leland Stanford himself. Course the fact that I sweet-talked her into giving me information I used to take five thousand dollars off one of his trains didn't exactly endear me to the man." He caught Raúl's gaze, held it, and winked. "You're a man. I'm sure you understand."

Raúl flushed and stood a little straighter. "Sure. Then you'll be moving on. Where are you headed?"

Victory had drunk his fill, and Dillon pulled up the horse's head. He moved to the saddle, tossed the stirrup leather over the seat, and cinched in the girth. "Don't rightly have a destination in mind. Thought I'd just wander about a bit till the heat cools down and see if I could pick up some work in the meantime." He peered over the horse's back at the boy. "Don't know of any ranchos hiring that could use a good gun, do you?"

When interest entered the boy's eyes, Dillon held an expectant breath.

"Don't know," Raúl said. "Not many ranches around here are owned by locals." His voice turned bitter, and he turned his head to spit on the ground. "Díaz took most of the land away from the *inditos* and gave it to his rich *Americano* friends and the *hacendados*. But maybe Chaz could use you," he mumbled, hesitation creeping over his features, and shuffled his feet in the tough grass. "After all, I owe you."

Dillon waved a dismissive hand. "Don't worry about it, Raúl. It's already forgotten."

"No. A man always pays his debts."

Dillon folded his arms over the saddle, his gaze on

the boy. "Okay. If you insist and you think your boss can use me. I don't want you doing something you'll get into trouble over. I promise I can carry my own weight."

Tres

Chaz rested her shoulder against the rock at the cave entrance and watched the two riders climbing the mountain trail. Cool, moist air pressed on her back and the side of her face with icy fingers, and she absently rubbed the old scar on her cheek as though it still ached. The habit was one she could not seem to break. Fuerte, shaggy gray back rising taller than her waist, leaned against her legs. An hour ago, when the lookouts spotted the horses, Salvatore had brought word. The icy digits dug deeper, provoking a shiver. Raúl knew better than to go into the valley on his own. Though the local *inditos* were friendly to her and her family, Manzanita had spies everywhere. The *rurale capitan's* lust to bring *La Lobo Fantasma* to justice was second only to Chaz's desire to see Thorne Railway come to ruin and tweak *El Presidente's* nose in the bargain. Her visceral reaction came from what she now saw: Raúl had picked up a companion. At the thought that one of Manzanita's bloodthirsty *soldados* had forced Raúl to lead him here, her shivering ran into shaking, and she gritted her teeth to gain control over her body. Fuerte sensed her agitation and growled low in his throat.

She gestured to two men standing beside her, rifles gripped tightly in their hands across bandoliered chests. With silent nods, they slipped down the trail. When footsteps echoed on the rock behind her, she cast a backward glance.

"He's a man now," Salvatore said, laying a gentle hand on her shoulder and squeezing.

She shook off his touch, not wanting him to sense her weakness. "No, he is a boy, a foolish boy with a death wish. I should have left him in Asilo with the women and *niños*."

Salvatore took hold of her shoulders and turned her toward him. "You could not have kept him there. His heart burns as hotly as yours. He is a man in all but years."

Chaz sent him a black look. "If he continues along this reckless path, he'll never see those years. I am alive only because I have been careful."

A sigh sifted from him. "A man must be free to do as he sees fit."

"A man!" she spat. "I know better than most the nature of men. I will never think of Raúl as becoming one of that detestable race."

"And you have some magic by which you can prevent that?" A tick fluttered over his cheekbone. "You have been with us for many years. How long will you allow the past to poison your mind and soul?"

Her brows hiked upward. "How can you ask me that?"

"I had hoped you would have learned much from the love of your uncles and cousins—men all. But you refuse to accept that some men are better than others. You are wiser than this, Chaz. Sometimes I think you revel in your hatred, delight in it."

Wind sang through the cave with an eerie voice, and overhead, a thousand bat wings fluttered; sharp little claws scrabbled for purchase.

Chaz spared a glance for the multitude of small, furry bodies stirring on the cave ceiling and released a deep sigh. "My apologies, Salvatore." She returned her gaze to him. "Truly, I do accept what you say. But the men you speak of are family. I still cannot trust any other. I do not know if I ever will. I die each day to think that Raúl may eventually inherit the evil from which he was conceived."

"You speak nonsense, *Sobrina*. A man is a product of his upbringing, not of his blood. Raúl is an honorable boy, and he will be an honorable man. The sooner you accept that, the sooner you can rid yourself of the pain that eats away at you. In the meantime, you must allow Raúl to grow up. You cannot protect him forever. He will be a man, and men must do as they wish."

"*Pinche machismo*," she swore, turning about to watch the riders once again.

"*¡Alto!*"

Dillon pulled Victory to a halt, dropped the reins, and raised his hands. His gaze flickered to the rock sentinels sloping upward, seeking out the glint of a rifle barrel. There, above him to the right, where harsh rays bounced off metal like sun off a mirror. He'd expected a reception. The Ghost Wolf wasn't going to let just anyone wander into his territory without a proper introduction. With a bit of luck, Raúl's presence would vouch for his credentials.

Raúl waved an arm, and one man came out from behind a boulder on his left. Rocks skittered downward beneath the man's feet, but his rifle never wavered from Dillon's head. He was large, bearded, and dressed similarly to the pistoleros in the Flores cantina. They could have been cousins.

The man came to a sliding stop in front of Raúl. "*¿Qué pasó?*" he asked the boy.

Dillon mentally translated the ensuing conversation. "Who is this man, and why do you bring him here?"

"I met him in Flores," Raúl said. "He saved my life."

The man snorted. "What were you doing in Flores, little flea? Chaz will take a willow switch to you, and you know better than to bring a stranger to this place. He could be a spy."

"He's no spy. He rides with me, and I'm taking him to Chaz."

"He could ride with the devil for all I care. He must be tied and blindfolded. No one other than family can know of these paths."

Raúl nodded and dismounted. "I was going to do that when you appeared." He pulled the reata from his saddle, walked over to Dillon, and smiled, switching to English. "I am sorry, señor West, but I must tie you and place a cloth over your eyes. Chaz demands it."

Dillon canted his head toward the man with the rifle. "Is that Chaz?" He knew it wasn't but hesitated to let the boy know how well he understood Spanish.

Raúl laughed and repeated Dillon's question. The man smiled but didn't relax his vigilance. "No," Raúl said, coming back to Dillon. "He is Largo."

Dillon held his hands together in front of him and lowered them so the boy could loop the rope around his wrists and lash the bindings to the saddle horn. The result effectively kept him from reaching his revolver on his hip or the rifle in his saddle scabbard if he wanted to, which he didn't. When the boy whipped off the bandana around his neck, Dillon closed his eyes and leaned to one side. The cloth was positioned over his eyes and knotted behind his head.

A creak of leather came as Raúl mounted his horse, and Dillon gained an impression of the boy leading Victory by his reins. The sound of shoe leather on the left rock face painted a vision of the older man climbing back up to his hidden position behind the boulders.

They traveled upward for hours, with numerous twists and turns. Victory stumbled occasionally on the rocky path but soon recovered his footing. The sun grew more intense, the air cooler and thinner, and at last, the way leveled out. Sudden damp cold caressed his cheeks, and Dillon sensed darkness, a tremendous weight of rock above and about him, the sharp ammonia odor of bats. *A cave in the mountainside.* After what seemed like an eternity, when claustrophobia threatened to overwhelm him, they broke out into the sun again, a gentler sun, soft warmth rather than the fiery heat of the plain. At the scents of green grass and the clean blue of water, Victory nickered, and his steps became more urgent.

They must have forged on for at least a mile before Raúl brought the horses to a stop. The water ran closer to them, gurgling and splashing on rock. Dillon waited patiently for Raúl to remove his blindfold, but the boy soon became involved in a heated argument and seemed to have forgotten about his trussed-up companion.

"What is this?" a low-pitched, husky voice asked in Spanish. Some quality in the tone made Dillon frown, but the voice was unfamiliar. He didn't think his man was with the group on the train. *La Lobo Fantasma?*

"He saved my life in Flores," Raúl said. "Sanchos accused me of cheating at cards and tried to gut me. This man took out the pistolero and allowed me to escape."

"How do you know he does not work for Manzanita? He could have set you up and then rescued you to gain your confidence."

Dillon smiled inwardly. The Ghost Wolf was shrewder than Raúl…and less trusting. Though he hadn't precipitated the situation in the cantina, he would have if he'd thought of it.

"He didn't." Raúl's voice was indignant. "And even if he did, I didn't have to bring him here. I could have easily lost him in the mountains."

The grass muffled any sound of footsteps, but Dillon

felt the person he suspected of being The Ghost Wolf
walking toward him, circling his horse, assessing him
with suspicious eyes. The scrutiny made his scalp itch.

"And why *did* you bring him here?" the voice asked
in a softer tone. The words poured over Dillon in a caress
and sparked a fire in his blood. He shook his head to
dispel the sensation. *Must be the thin air at this altitude.*

"Since we lost Luis and Xavier, we've been in need
of sharpshooters," Raúl said. "He's a pistolero on the run
from the law in Texas. We can use him. You know we
can."

"Leave me now," the voice said sharply. "See Delicia
for some food. We will have a serious discussion later.
You still have not explained what you were doing in
Flores on your own in a card game with one of the most
dangerous men in the territory."

Dillon didn't need his sight to sense the boy's
hesitation at leaving him to the mercy of The Ghost Wolf.
But he received confirmation.

"Don't you dare hurt him! He saved my life."

"So you said. Now *váyase!* Go! I will take care of your
companion."

"But..."

"*¡Váyase!*"

"You understood every word, did you not?" the
voice asked in English from the vicinity of Dillon's left
stirrup.

When he declined to answer, the man removed
Dillon's revolver from the holster on his hip and slid his
rifle from the saddle boot.

Hands touched his and loosened the knots about
his wrists. When they were free, Dillon raised his
hands and pulled down the bandana. His gaze swung
immediately to the face of the man beside him, and for
the next few moments, the fierce thrumming of his pulse
overwhelmed all his senses.

A pair of dark blue eyes, nearer black than blue,

stared back. They set off a face of exquisite beauty framed by hip-length, wavy black hair. Dillon's lips pursed in a silent whistle. *A woman. And what a woman.* Who was she? High cheekbones and a knife-blade nose revealed her Yaqui ancestry. The golden hue of her skin, the slim shoulders rising above the white peasant *camisa,* and the delicacy of her facial proportions proclaimed her Spanish blood. The eyes spoke of mixed European descent. A mestizo, what they'd call a half-breed in Texas, but like none he'd ever seen, excepting for the marks of violence she bore, which were common among the mixed race. A thin scar bisected one dark eyebrow, pulling it up into a permanent arch. A second scar ran from the corner of her left eye, curved around her cheek, and ended at the left edge of her mouth, giving her a cynical look. In some unique way, the scars added to rather than detracted from her beauty. She was no mere girl but a woman, early or mid-thirties, probably close to his age, and the years showed on her face. Like the scars, they gave her a mature beauty.

"Howdy," he said, feeling an idiotic grin spread across his face. He swept off his hat and bowed low. "Dillon West. Pleased to meet you, señorita."

She slapped away his hat and hand and stepped back. As her gaze bore into him, hands went to her slim, full-skirted hips. "Get down, señor West," she said sharply with an imperative gesture of one hand.

He tore his gaze away from the enchanting sight of her and glanced around. Two men, bristling with weapons, stood off to one side. One held Dillon's rifle and revolver. He let his gaze drift past them. A green valley surrounded by towering mountains stretched out in all directions, and thick grass spotted with low-growing mesquite bushes flowed beneath the hooves of his horse. Pines, Encino oaks, birches, and Tejocotes hickory lined the lower mountain slopes, and a wide stream chased over the rocks beside him. A substantial adobe-walled *aidea* crouched off in the distance next to the ruins of an ancient city marked with rock pillars and rubblework walls.

"I ordered you to dismount," she said.

Dillon brought his gaze back to her and smiled. "Perhaps that's the problem, *querida*. I don't take kindly to orders from someone who doesn't even have the manners to introduce herself in a friendly manner."

Her face colored to a shade of puce, and she turned to the two men and spat out, "*¡Dispárale!*" Rifles swung toward his head.

"Whoa, there," he said with a little laugh and raised his hands. "Let's not be hasty. Sorry if I ruffled your feathers." He slung a leg over Victory's neck and dropped to the ground, hands still held up in front of him.

The hint of a smile lifted one corner of her mouth. "So you do understand Spanish."

Dillon shrugged one shoulder. "Only the important phrases…like 'shoot him.'"

"Put him *en el bote*." She gestured with an arm.

Dillon exhaled on a sigh. Getting close to The Ghost Wolf was going to be more difficult from a jail cell, nigh on impossible. He glanced about, looking for the man he'd taken as the leader of the banditos during the train robbery. This woman must be *La Lobo Fantasma's amante*, his mistress, or his wife.

"*Sí, Jefe*," one of the men, the larger, meaner looking of the two said and moved in Dillon's direction. Dillon backed away.

"It is only until I speak with Raúl," she said. "You will be well treated. We are not *monstrous*."

Dillon capitulated, not that he had a choice, though he had less than a burning desire to be thrown into some dark, airless prison. He'd spent time in Mexican hellhole jails, and the experiences were less than agreeable. Not to mention that Thorne was as edgy for results as a greenhorn sitting on an anthill. But he'd already wasted months, and he couldn't afford to lose his advantage now. This was the closest he'd come to The Ghost Wolf, and the closest he'd likely get. As the men led him away toward an adobe hut on the edge of the *aidea*, Dillon looked over his shoulder at the woman. "Do you have a name?" he asked. "I'd like to know the name of my jailer in case I decide to apply for mercy."

She smiled faintly. "You may call me Chaz."

So this was Chaz.

The jail was no hellhole. Dillon had a clean bed with a thick, horsehair-stuffed mattress, heavy woolen blankets for the cold nights, two barred windows for light and fresh air, and all the food the full-figured, older woman named Delicia could induce him to consume. With all the *tortillas enchiladas, nopales* tamales, pig *carnitas*, chicken, and goat cheese, Dillon began to worry more about his waistline than fear for his life.

His incarceration lasted no more than a week before Raúl came to his rescue. The boy showed up at his door one morning as Dillon lay on his bunk, hands stacked behind his head, and watched the lazy flight of a red-tailed hawk above the mountain range. His stomach was still digesting the *huevos* omelet, *frijoles*, and fried *cebollas* and *papas* Delicia had brought him for breakfast.

"*Hola,*" Raúl said, a grin lighting up his face as he swung open the door. "Chaz wants to see you."

Dillon let a sigh leak from him and returned the grin. "It's about time. In another week, I'd have been too fat to fit through the door."

They found Chaz beside the stream in conversation with a handsome man with thick black hair and snapping dark eyes. He had a touch of Spanish arrogance about him, in his stance, the elegant tilt of his head, his whipcord leanness, and the silver-concho-studded trousers and short jacket he wore. Dillon pegged him as pure Castilian descent and wondered what he was doing in this mountain den of thieves. Perhaps *he* was The Ghost Wolf.

When Dillon approached, Chaz's gaze lit on him in sharp appraisal. He rubbed a hand over his bristly jaw, conscious his face hadn't come close to a razor for some time. While she scrutinized him, he looked her over. Off-the-shoulder ruffled *camisa*, plain white but alluring in its soft draping across her bosom. Full, ankle-length skirt of some crimson cloth, which clung to her hips. A multicolored striped sash wrapped about her small waist and flowing down the side of her leg. A gun belt with a revolver in the holster hung low about her hips. *Huraches* on her bare feet, and a bright yellow scarf tying back her long black hair, barely managing to confine the heavy mass in the breeze kicking up from the foothills and teasing the tendrils. His groin reacted with heat and a surge of blood. Whoever's mistress she turned out to be, he wouldn't mind getting closer to her. That is, if he didn't have a job to do.

"*Buenos días*, señor West. *¿Cómo está usted?* I trust your confinement was not too unpleasant," she said.

Dillon smiled and shook his head. "Not at all, señorita Chaz. In fact, the hospitality has been more than satisfying." He patted his full stomach.

"Señora," she returned somewhat stiffly.

So she was married. Dillon appraised the man beside her, whom he assumed to be her husband, and offered his hand. The man ignored it, and his eyes burned into Dillon like branding irons on a maverick's hide. Dillon couldn't blame the prickly señor. His body's automatic reaction to the alluring Chaz was all but impossible to hide.

Chaz waved a graceful hand at the man. "This is señor Cazadore. He is family." She sent Cazadore an admonishing look. "Do not be impolite, Alec, señor West is our guest."

Alec took Dillon's hand with obvious reluctance

and shook it. At the same time, he circled his free arm about Chaz's waist in a universal possessive gesture. A little frown appeared between her brows, and she adroitly pulled away from the embrace, not making her movement too obvious but conveying an unspoken signal to the brooding señor Cazadore.

That was interesting. Perhaps she wasn't the arrogant Spaniard's woman after all. That or they were at odds with each other. Dillon wondered if he could be the subject of their disagreement and inwardly hoped he was. He'd pump Raúl later for information. Why it mattered he couldn't say, but he felt the need to pursue the idea. The more he knew about this nest of thieves, the more likelihood of success.

"Quite a spread you have here," Dillon said, looking out over the lush valley. "But it's kind of out of the way, don't you think?"

Her eyes narrowed. "Let us talk business, señor West. Raúl tells me you seek employment and you claim some competence with a gun. He also mentioned you were wanted in Texas."

"You could say that," he said with a direct look. "But a man's business is private, if you know what I mean. If you're angling for a reward, think again."

"If you wish to work for me, you will provide the information I request."

Work for *her*? Dillon could think of many things he wanted to do with her, but working for her didn't rank high on the list. *Anyway, who's in charge around here?* Playing along for the moment to see where it would lead seemed sensible. "Say, you aren't connected with the *rurales*, are you? Justus Thorne's a friend of Díaz's, and I understand *El Presidente* doesn't bother with trials of guilt or innocence. My only transgression was to delay a few trains. Thorne shouldn't even miss the silver. After all, how much money can one man keep track of?"

When Dillon mentioned Thorne's name, Chaz drew

in a sharp breath. A flush covered her face, and her eyes
sharpened into blue ice.

"You have taken silver from Justus Thorne?" she
asked, spitting out the man's name as though she'd taken
a bite of *chile* pepper.

"A bit here and there. A man has to survive, and
when he's deprived of honest work—"

Chaz made an abrupt gesture, clearly dismissing
him. "Go now. See to your horse. Raúl will show you to
the remuda." Her eyes narrowed in warning. "Do not try
to leave. Even if my men failed to gun you down before
you left the valley, you would never find your way out of
these mountains."

Her men, again. Dillon began to believe he'd
stumbled across the wrong gang of banditos. If not for
the boy and that familiar white-footed bay… His mind
spinning, he allowed Raúl to lead him away from Chaz
and Alec toward the far end of the *aidea*.

With a thoughtful frown, Chaz studied Dillon as
he departed with Raúl. What did the man want? Why
had he saved Raúl's life? Was he being honest, or was
he one of Manzanita's spies? She could not envision the
easygoing American as the sort who would work for an
animal like the mestizo *capitán*. However, money was a
powerful lure for any man. The fluttering in her stomach
when she had first seen him, his yellow hair, blue eyes,
and finely made face, made her body warm and her
jaw clench. It was not a reaction she was used to or
welcomed, a reaction she did not understand. For a long
time now, the only men she could bear to be around were
those of her family. Why did Raúl bring this stranger into
their midst? Nonetheless, to reject the man who saved
Raúl's life would require explanations…explanations
she could not give voice to. Even after all these years, the
pain and fear were still too great.

"Why do you keep him here?" Alec asked, breaking into her thoughts.

At the look of jealousy on Alec's face, Chaz let out her breath on a sigh. Broad streams of sunlight gilded the mountains, and clouds cartwheeled in a cool breeze that murmured through the valley. When it played with a long strand of her hair, blowing it across her face, Chaz secured the loose tress behind her ear.

Why couldn't Alec accept that she wanted no man, not even him? He had pressed her for marriage many times, and she had turned him down. Apparently he believed persistence would gain him what he desired. He was wrong. She would never take a man to her bed. She loved Alec only as a cousin, as one could be expected to love their blood relatives.

"Why not?" she said at his hooded eyes and sour expression. "We are short on gun hands. If this man turns out to be what he claims, why should I not hire him?"

Alec crossed his arms over his chest. "What he wants is *you, corazón*. Make no mistake. If you take on this man, allow him to get close to you, he will destroy all you have worked for. He will tear apart your family and break your heart."

Her mouth flattened. "I will not allow him to do so. And do not call me *corazón*. I am no man's heart, nor will I ever be."

"Do not pout so, my little cousin." He smiled and tweaked her nose. "It makes you look like a naughty child." He took her arm and led her toward the stream. "Let us stroll to the shallows. I shall catch frogs for you and see if I cannot restore your good disposition."

She laughed. "You need not wet your boots on my account, Alec. I am perfectly happy with my disposition, just as it is."

Cuatro

"So I reckon Alec is Chaz's husband," Dillon said as he walked shoulder to shoulder with Raúl toward the remuda where the horses wandered about inside a pine-pole corral.

"*¿Esposo?*" Raúl laughed. "Alec may wish it so, but Chaz treats him like a brother."

"Then I haven't met the husband, or is he that Largo who held me at the point of a gun?" Raúl stood only a few inches shorter than Dillon's six foot two, and Dillon placed his age at around sixteen or seventeen. Old enough to consider himself a man without the years of experience to back it up—a volatile, dangerous time, prone to reckless actions, as witnessed by the debacle in the cantina.

Raúl dropped his gaze to the dusty toes of his boots. "No. Her husband died. He was a revolutionary."

"I see," Dillon said. So much for his theory of her being married to The Ghost Wolf. She must be his mistress. "And you, Raúl. What's your relationship to Chaz?"

The boy's head came up, astonishment on his face. "You do not know?"

Dillon shook his head. "No one's said much to me other than to ask how many tamales I could eat in one sitting."

Raúl chuckled. "Yes, Delicia can be as much a dictator at times as Díaz."

"Chaz?" Dillon asked, raising a questioning brow to bring the boy back to the subject.

"She's *mi madre*, my mother."

Shock slammed Dillon in the chest. *His mother?* He'd have thought her too young to have a son the age of Raúl. Why, she must have been a child when she gave birth. Who, then, was The Ghost Wolf? Raúl? No. The Wolf had to be one of the other men.

Dillon mulled over what Raúl said before, about Chaz's husband, the man who was Raúl's father. It held as much water as a spittoon full of holes. Raul's father wasn't Yaqui or even a Spaniard; he was white. Was the boy lying to protect someone? Was The Ghost Wolf his father and an *Americano?* Might be an avenue to amble down.

When Dillon approached the corral, Victory whickered for his attention. However, another horse drew his eye — a leggy gray mare, the same one he'd seen at the train robbery, the one belonging to the leader of the banditos. Victory swung his head to one side to nip at the mare and trotted to the rails, hanging his head over the top one.

Peeling red-gray pine poles banded the corral, a generous area with the ground beaten into dust from the hooves of many horses over a long time. Several hickory trees spread branches over the poles and provided a dappled shade. Fresh water dribbled into a trough from some underground aquifer. The space was free of stones and burrs, testimony to the care the men of the *aidea* gave to their mounts.

"Hi, fella," Dillon crooned as he rubbed his palm over the chestnut's broad forehead. "Missed me, did ya?"

The horse snuffled and tried to take a bite out of Dillon's shoulder. Dillon thumped him on the nose then stiffened when the sensation of being watched crawled over his skin like a sidewinder slithering across sand. He raised a hand to sooth the prickling on the back of his neck, looked over his shoulder, and spied the wolf, one hell of an imposing animal, three and a half feet at the shoulder if it was an inch, and had to weigh over a hundred pounds. Hound ancestry showed in the long neck and muzzle, deep chest, and strong legs, but a sense of the feral lurked about its face. A crossbreed, Dillon decided, some kind of wolfhound mixed with local wolf.

The eyes were all wolf, yellow and wary. Dillon came down on his haunches and held out a hand. "Nice doggie," he said in a soothing voice that wanted to stop up in his throat.

"That's Fuerte," Raúl said from over his shoulder. "It means—"

"Strong," Dillon murmured. "Is he friendly?"

"Well, you still have your hand."

Dillon tossed the boy a glance to see if he was serious. Raúl was. He brought his gaze back to the dog, and gradually withdrawing his arm, patted the side of his leg. "Come here, Fuerte," he said low and steady. When the dog took a few steps forward, Dillon praised him. The long, fringed tail slowly wagged, and soon, Dillon had a lapful of wolf-dog and a lolling tongue slavering his face.

"Wait till Chaz sees this," Raúl said with a grin and a chuckle. "Fuerte seldom takes to anyone, and he hates Manzanita's men. If you were a *rurale*, he would have smelled it on you."

When Fuerte knocked Dillon onto his ass and tried to lick him to death, he laughed. He was in. With both Raúl's and Fuerte's approval, he couldn't miss.

The day passed with no more sign of Chaz or her gloomy lover. In fact, the *aidea* became strangely quiet, except for Delicia and the other women, and even Raúl had disappeared. It didn't take Dillon long to conclude that another of Thorne's trains was being stopped and relieved of its burden of silver. He searched the *aidea*, looking for Chaz, but she also seemed to be missing. Surely The Ghost Wolf didn't take women along during his raids.

With the sun dipping its head behind the western snowcapped peaks, Delicia shoved a length of cloth and a bar of soap made from soaptree yucca into Dillon's hands, pinched her nostrils together with her fingers, and pointed in the direction of the stream. Okay, he supposed he smelled a bit like horse and dust and sweat. He hadn't bathed for several weeks, though he shivered at the thought of exposing his skin to the coldwater stream and nippy evening air. Once beside the fast flowing water, Dillon figured he might as well wash his clothes while he was at it. He stripped off his belt and boots, and waded into the water until it reached his thighs. His teeth chattered from the rush of cold.

"Most men have the sense to remove their clothing before they bathe," a voice said from farther along the bank. *Chaz.* Somehow, he wasn't surprised.

"You know of a better way to wash everything?" he asked while rubbing the cake of soap over his shirt.

Chaz laughed, a low, throaty sound. That laugh sent another kind of chill bumps across his skin. "Yes," she said as she stepped out from beneath the concealing shadows of a small grove of Encino trees. "You give your clothing to Delicia or one of the other women to wash."

The muscles in Dillon's face froze. Chaz was dressed head to toe in dusty gray leather—skintight trousers, silk shirt, long duster coat, bandana, sombrero hiding her eyes, holster riding low on her hip and tied down to her thigh like a pistolero's. Fuerte glided silently beside her and moved to the stream to lower his head and drink. Dillon could swear a gong clanged in his brain. He felt like smacking himself silly. *The Ghost Wolf. Chaz was La Lobo Fantasma.*

When Dillon could force himself to speak, he managed to keep the surprise from his voice. "And you? You're a woman. Would you wash my clothes?"

Chaz shook her head. She broke a twig from the tree overhead and tapped it against her leg. The movement mesmerized him, made him sweat despite the iciness of the stream rushing over him and tugging at his legs. He thanked God for the water that lapped against his waist. "I'm no woman," she said. "I don't wash, cook, sew, or carry out any of the other duties assigned to the women in this *aidea.*"

She tipped back her sombrero and let it fall against her back. Lines bracketed her mouth and furrowed her forehead. His gaze moved up to her eyes. Was that pain he saw? What did she mean about not being a woman? She was more woman than he'd seen in a long time. Sudden warmth replaced the ice in his veins. Had she looked into a mirror lately? No, Dillon doubted anything as frivolous as a mirror existed in this isolated outpost. He let the subject die and unbuttoned his soapy shirt. "Want to join me, *querida*? I'll scrub your back," he said softly. Dillon stripped the shirt from his shoulders and draped it over a rock where the water could stream over it. When he moved on to his pants, he looked up. The bank was empty. As silently as a ghost, Chaz had disappeared. Cold seized him again, and as quickly as his frozen limbs would allow, he finished his ablutions and laundry.

Chaz stormed through the grass, taking increasingly longer strides, feet kicking up sparrows and quail, and Fuerte trotting at her heels. Piñon jays dropped their bounty of pine nuts, screaming *krawk-kraw-krawk*, from needled branches, and a horned lark swept through her

vision. It lit on bush sage and scolded her with *tsee-ee,
tsee-ee.* At any other time, she would have stopped to
observe the birds, for every living creature was a guest
within her asylum. But not today. Today, she dwelled on
Dillon West.

Why had she felt compelled to track down her guest?
Delicia had directed her to the stream, and Chaz knew
he would be bathing. Regardless of Raúl's acceptance,
there was something about the gun hand she did not
trust. He had a secret. It coiled in her gut like a sleeping
serpent, but she could not catch a glimpse of it. On the
surface, Dillon was charming and well favored. Not
that his face did not have its faults. Taken one by one,
nothing about his features spoke of classic beauty. Taken
all together, they melded in a pleasing way that made
one forget he had a rather large nose and bottom lip, and
shaggy wheat-blond hair that looked as if he had cut it
with a skinning knife. The dreamy, little-boy quality of
his clear blue eyes made up for those imperfections. Yes,
even Chaz admitted she could admire him in a purely
abstract way, the way she assessed good horseflesh.
Nonetheless, what lurked beneath that slick exterior, that
wide, golden-pelted chest that had burned her eyes when
he took off his shirt, and those guileless blue eyes? She
could all but imagine his strong hands gripping her arms,
his mouth taking possession of hers...

She shivered. What was she thinking? She would
never, *never* allow another man to touch her. Old
memories crouched like a hunting puma behind the wall
Chaz had erected in her mind after Raúl's birth. No man
would ever corner her again, hurt her again, not even a
silver-tongued, slumberous-eyed, golden-haired stranger
who had stolen the trust of her son.

She would test his skill with a gun and his sincerity
about working for her. Then, then...then what? Then
nothing. She would take advantage of his services while
she needed him, and one day when he decided it was

safe to return to Texas, Dillon would vanish from her life as suddenly as he'd entered it.

In the hacienda, Delicia was cutting fresh wildflowers for the table. When Chaz walked in, the older woman looked up. She studied Chaz for a moment then smiled, one of those knowing smiles that so unnerved Chaz. At times, Chaz believed the woman to be cursed with second sight.

"You have feelings for him, for this man," Delicia stated with her normal degree of certainty when the subject concerned Chaz and the course of her life.

Chaz picked up a knife and began chopping the ends of the stalks off crimson paintbrush blooms. "I have feelings for no man," she said. "I am incapable of such feelings. You, of all people, should know that."

Delicia gave a sharp shake of her head, saying in Spanish, "Nonsense, Charissa."

Chaz turned quickly, the knife in her hand. "Do not call me by that name!"

Delicia's lips tightened into a pursed line. "Your mother gave you that name."

"My mother is dead."

"So she is, but you are not. You are a woman, and a woman needs a man—for love, companionship, to accompany her through life's journey. That is God's will."

Chaz let loose with a bitter laugh and set down the knife when her maniac chopping of flowers threatened to slice open her fingers. She sank into the wooden chair beside the table and tugged at her boots. "For that, my dear *tia*, I have Raúl and Salvatore and Alec, and all the other men of the family. I have no need for another man in my life, especially this one. Had God wished for me to love a man, he would not have sent me the devil when I was a child." She grunted with the effort of pulling off the boot.

Delicia moved over to her and helped with the boots.

Soon, the footwear thudded to the wooden plank floor. "Do not mock God, Charissa," Delicia said and went back to her flower arranging. "We all meet the devil at some time, in some form. It is God's way of testing us." Chaz snorted.

"Cast the devil from yourself and look at señor West with your heart, not your memories." Delicia released a gusty sigh. "This one, he is different."

"You mean because he has that yellow hair and speaks clever words in a Texan drawl? Many men like that have come across my path. He is no different from any other."

Delicia's smile dimpled her ample cheeks. "He is different, and you feel it, as do I. I believe he can give you what no man in our family or of your acquaintance can. He is the one, Charissa. I feel it."

Chaz sprang up from the chair and stalked across the room to the hearth to throw on more logs, even though the room's heat made sweat prickle at her temples. Nothing annoyed her more than Delicia's precognition. Chaz refused to believe the Yaqui woman had the ability to see into the future, but she had to admit that, at times, Delicia's "feelings" proved to be more than fancy.

"There is no *one*, not for me. I will send him away tomorrow."

"No, Charissa, you will not. You will keep him."

A lazy breeze whispered as it crept through the pine shakes on the roof of the hacienda and slipped around the corners of the adobe walls. The dusty gray and blue and tan shirts and canted black sombreros of the onlookers crowded the railing of the *pórtico*. Boots scuffed and shuffled on the wooden planks. Overhead, sun struck sparks off silver.

"I could think of a better use for silver," Dillon said, putting one foot on the steps of the porch and bracing his forearm on his thigh as he tracked the glinting silver coins flipping through the air above his head. Almost leisurely, he drew his revolver with his right hand. Fanning the hammer with his left palm, he sent six bullets through the center of six coins. "Next," he said, holstered his gun, straightened, and turned toward Chaz with an insufferable grin.

"Are you as accurate with a rifle?" she asked, unable to keep a grudging admiration for his skill from her tone.

"Well," he said as he accepted the Winchester from Salvatore, "I reckon I'm a mite better. A friend once said I could clip the wings off a fly at a hundred yards. Course, he'd been drinking at the time."

"And could you, could you shoot the wings off a fly?"

That engaging grin flashed again. "Naw. Hit the fly every time." His hands a blur, he whipped the rifle up to his shoulder and squeezed off two shots. The first one took off the top flower from a yucca plant about a hundred yards out on the meadow. The second severed the stem, and the waxy yucca toppled over. "See," he said and lowered the rifle, "Missed with the second shot."

A frown gathered between her brows. Señor West was entirely too sure of himself, too competent to be the reluctant train robber he claimed. Only a full-fledged gunslinger shot that well...or a lawman. Earlier, he'd proved his skill with a shotgun. A well of suspicion swirled in Chaz's gut.

"You are too good," she said, voicing her reservations.

"Too good?" A blond brow arched up. "Didn't know such a thing was possible. Where I come from, if a man's not good enough, he's dead."

"You are no simple, bumbling train robber," she said with an accusing look.

Dillon hooked his thumbs in his belt loops and tilted

his head to one side. "Naw, guess I'm not. I was a Texas Ranger ten years ago, during the Mason County War. In seventy-five, when Scott Cooley killed John Worley in cold blood and scalped him, I'd had enough. Major Jones knew I was friends with Cooley at one time, and he came after me when I deserted. Texas became too hot for a while, so I wandered down into Mexico, joined up with what was left of Juárez's liberals. When Díaz took over, I knew it was a lost cause and time to skedaddle again. Went back to Texas and the opportunity offered by trains loaded with silver crossing the border. Could have done the same in Colorado, I suppose, but Texas, being my old stomping grounds, was familiar and closer to the border in case I felt a need to" — he grinned — "you know, suddenly change my address."

"That's a lot of information for a man who has remained closed-mouthed about his past until now."

"Pardon, ma'am," he replied, sweeping off his hat and bowing like a courtier. When he straightened, he was smiling. "I thought you asked. Just trying to be sociable here, you know, get along, be one of the boys."

Chaz threw a questioning look at Salvatore, her uncle and Delicia's husband. He was her second in command, and she respected his instincts. At his shrug, the corners of her mouth winged down into a scowl. Salvatore could have been more help to her, if he had wanted to be, but he seemed to like Dillon, as did everyone except Alec, and she suspected the Spaniard based his reservation more on the charisma of the man rather than his background.

"*A bien.* You begin tomorrow," she said with a tight smile. "You may ride with us, but Alec will ride behind you."

Dillon returned her smile with a slow one of his own, and her stomach jumped. "Only if you ride beside me, *querida,*" he said in a voice too low to be heard by Salvatore.

Blood rushed into her face. "You call me *querida* one more time, and the only person riding beside you will be the devil," she hissed.

"Promises, promises," he said softly and clucked his tongue against the roof of his mouth.

Steam from the locomotive's coal boiler rose above the pines, Encino oaks, and Tejocotes hickory dotting the arid hills of the high desert plateau of the Sierra Gordo outside Guanajuato. A herd of white-tailed deer behind them ran for the cover of a grouping of tall mesquite bushes, and a pair of turkey vultures spiraled overhead in the dry air.

Aware of Alec nudging up his behind, trying to goad him into making a stupid move, Dillon sat atop a jittery Victory. He tossed a don't-mess-with-me look at the Spaniard and noticed the gold watch fob peeking out from the man's vest pocket. *Drat!* The watch was the one Dillon gave up during the train robbery, though this wasn't the man who took it from him. The watch belonged to his father, who fell at Gettysburg. Before Dillon left this band of desperados, he'd damn well retrieve his watch.

Alec returned a smirk to Dillon's dark look and gestured with the rifle for Dillon to turn back around. Chaz, mounted on her gray mare, rode beside Dillon, knee to knee, and Raúl crowded in on his other side. Ahead of the horses, the dog, Fuerte, lay in the dirt like a hairy, granite rock.

Dillon had declined to shave, figuring the scruffy growth of beard lent him more of the air of a pistolero. He'd never truly robbed a train, but he had enough familiarity with the procedure. If he accidentally shot one of Manzanita's *rurales*, well, he'd still sleep nights. From what he knew of the tactics and mercy of the mestizos, the *capitán* and his band of cutthroats were long overdue for permanent residence in pine boxes. Few banditos made it to trial; most made it no farther than the closest live oak.

Dillon had accomplished his first goal: finding *La Lobo Fantasma*. His next move was to learn where The Ghost Wolf and her banditos stashed the silver they took from the trains. Thorne wanted his property returned, and in returning it, Dillon would merit a bonus amounting to ten percent above the balance of the ten thousand owed him for the leader's capture. Of course, as they left their sheltered valley, The Ghost Wolf's men blindfolded him again, but if he hung in there long enough, gained their trust, he had no doubt he could discover the hideout's location.

Chaz sat loose and relaxed on her horse's back, as though she was anticipating a cotillion rather than a shootout with throat-slitting *rurale soldados*, and Dillon marveled at her composure. Dressed in her gray leathers, gaze fastened on the approaching train's smoke, she looked as cool as a mountain breeze. When Alec cleared his throat in a meaningful way, Dillon turned his gaze from the woman. The Spaniard panted after her like a stallion in rut. *Didn't want her* amante *to get an itchy trigger finger*. With that preening stud continually sniffing at her heels, getting her alone and away to Thorne could prove as difficult as stealing a deer haunch from Fuerte.

Dillon's attempted flirtation was going nowhere fast. Either the woman was immune to his charms, which other women had assured him were irresistible, or she simply didn't like him. Either way, Plan A died a hard death. Time to roll out Plan B, which he hadn't quite worked out yet. However, he couldn't do anything until he uncovered the location of the valley and the cache of hoarded silver. Dillon had a suspicion that simply absconding with The Ghost Wolf wouldn't stop the robberies. Through Raúl, he learned the majority of the gang were related to Chaz in some way or another, and a deep-seated hatred of Justus Thorne ran through the entire family like a mother lode of gold. Thorne was a distasteful man, no doubt about that, and Dillon, himself, held no fond feelings for the man, but the railroad giant lived in Chicago, for God's sake. What Thorne could have done to gain the animosity of this family eluded him.

However, that wasn't his problem. The Ghost Wolf and the silver were.

Chaz had positioned her men in the basin of a dry riverbed, the high, sloping sides testimony to gullywashers during the wet season. The front men were stationed a few hundred yards up the track behind the cover of low-spreading piñon. They would take the locomotive and overcome the engineer. The wagon carrying the Hotchkiss gun sat on a level area beyond Chaz and the main portion of her band. She knew exactly how long it would take to stop the train, and situated the greatest firepower where she most needed it.

Dillon's presence beside Chaz made her wonder what this trial by fire would reveal. She was aware Alec hoped the gringo would slip up, reveal he was a spy for the railroad, the *rurales*, or even Díaz. Chaz wasn't as certain of the man's motives. That uneasy feeling still nudged her, but she found herself gradually relaxing around him. Raúl's easy trust still bothered her, and Fuerte's complete acceptance, even fawning, puzzled her. Manzanita had tried to penetrate her band before, but never had anyone gotten this close.

That other feeling also persisted, that itching beneath her skin, that annoying tightness in her groin whenever Dillon came near. It beset her now, and a frown tightened the corners of her mouth. She forced her attention to the approaching train. She had a job to carry out. If Dillon was a wolf among the sheep, he would soon reveal it, and she would deal with him. No one would stop her from ruining Justus Thorne and putting a silver bullet through his heart.

Chaz had moved her attacks from place to place, night to day, dawn to dusk, so Manzanita never knew when or where to expect The Ghost Wolf. With hundreds of miles of track from which to choose, she held the advantage and continued to surprise the trains and their *rurale* guards. The mines produced such large amounts of silver that nearly every train leaving the area transported some portion of the earth's bounty. From originally stockpiling the silver in the towns, which were even less secure than the trains, Thorne's strategy recently changed to saturating the routes with silver-bearing trains in the hopes a few would make it past The Ghost Wolf's bandits. With any luck, Chaz's spy network among the campesinos had provided accurate information. This train, their target today, carried purely freight, no passengers, other than the *rurales* who guarded the silver shipment.

Brakes squealed on the tracks, which indicated the advance group had boarded the train and taken control of the locomotive. As the train neared, the ground trembled, the screeching of metal on metal swelling when the brakeman tightened the brake shoe against the rail wall. The V-shaped smoke stack came into view, and an acrid smell of burning soft coal permeated the air. Streams of soil cascaded down the slopes of the dry wash, and a dusty brown horned lizard scrambled away and over the rim when its sandy cover collapsed.

The train jerked to a stop, and the horses charged up the sides of the wash and onto the plain below. The Hotchkiss gun opened up, spraying a wide arc of bullets into the wooden doors of the freight cars. Above the stuttering gun, men shouted inside the car directly behind the coal box and waved an arm toward it.

Her men tugged open the doors, where the *rurales*

lay on the car bed, flat on their stomachs with their
hands laced behind their heads. After her men tied
them and shoved them into the corners of the car, the
boxes containing ingots and the safe stuffed full of silver
coins were dragged out and loaded onto the wagon.
The operation went as smoothly as honey dribbled on
cornbread.

Cinco

Dillon acquitted himself well during his first experience at train robbery. When one of the *rurales* reached for a gun hidden beneath his prone body, Dillon shot it from the *soldado's* hand, taking with it a few fingers and a bit of palm flesh. He then wrapped the wound with his own bandana before securing the man and moving on to the silver. As Chaz directed the removal of the loot, she threw him a considering look.

The next few robberies ran as efficiently as the first, and Dillon made himself useful. Her men accounted him a superb gunman, and he began to feel as if Chaz's defenses were slowly dropping. Of course, she still blindfolded him on the way into and out of the hidden valley, and he still didn't know what she did with the silver she took from the trains. However, he did discover she wasn't hiding it in her sanctuary. In each instance, Chaz left with the wagon and a group of her men to ride off in a different direction before his blindfold was secured.

On the fourth raid, Dillon solidified his position with the banditos. When the train came into view, it snaked across the low hills like an endless, fat black viper. It was longer than any they had taken so far and pulled six passenger cars in addition to the freight and cattle cars. The men moved restlessly aboard their horses. Leather creaked, bridle bits rattled, and low, nervous whispers flew back and forth.

As they waited under cover beside the tracks for the train to stop, Salvatore leaned toward Chaz. "I have a bad feeling about this, *Sobrina*," he said in a low, tense whisper. "The train is too large, and our forces are split. We are too few in number today."

Chaz studied the oncoming train. Salvatore had a point. She'd divided her band today to hit two trains on different routes in a tactic to pressure Justus Thorne, enrage him, force him to make a personal visit to inspect his trains and the extent of his losses. Her plan was to bait the hook with lost silver until he bit. Chaz glanced at Dillon, who shrugged and gave her a lopsided smile. As her gaze roamed over the charming gringo, the hatred hardening her heart at the thought of Thorne melted a bit. With the beard and his dust-covered poncho and chaps, Dillon looked every bit the bandito, if not for his blond hair, which was too distinctive. She would talk to him about dying it darker so he could more easily blend in. Due to Díaz's fondness for their money, *Americanos* were common in many areas, particularly in the wealthier cities, but they were rare out here in the high desert.

"Leave it, Chaz," Salvatore pleaded. "Let us turn around and go home."

Chaz gave a sharp shake of her head. "No. We are here. To retreat now would betray our presence and bring the *rurales* on the train after us. With the wagon, we cannot move quickly or silently enough to elude them. We are committed to incapacitating them, at the very least. I will not leave the big gun behind and risk losing it."

When the train stopped, the doors on the five cattle cars flew open, and a river of mounted *rurales* flowed out. Chaz motioned for the Hotchkiss gun operator to fire into the horde. Bullets spewed forth, downing horses and soldiers. The cavalry scattered in a pincer movement to avoid the bullets and surround the banditos.

Dillon remained by Chaz's side, squeezing off rounds from his Winchester lever-action repeating rifle. Every bullet found a target, but his aim was to wound and incapacitate, not kill. Despite Thorne's blessing to gun down anyone who got in his way of neutralizing The Ghost Wolf, slaughter wasn't in his blood or nature, and he never killed unless provoked. However, when Dillon saw they were outnumbered by at least five to one, he suspected the slaughter was likely to go the other way. The *rurales* weren't as particular about where they deposited their lead. When a bullet creased Chaz's shoulder, Dillon grabbed the reins from her hands, spun Victory about on his hind legs, and got the hell out of the way of any further fire. He rode in front with Chaz, and the other men charged along behind them. When they reached a spate of low hills separated by natural depressions, the *rurales* hot on their trail, Dillon signaled for the band to split up and circle around. They understood his orders and seemed to accept his leadership, peeling off one by one into wide, sweeping circles.

Chaz tugged on her reins, and Dillon released them. He looked back at her. The color had drained from her face, paling her golden cheeks to a creamy white, and blood flowed in a steady stream from her shoulder, but she rode securely in the saddle, swiveling at the waist to fire on the soldiers running behind them. Dillon sent her a grin and swerved wide to the left, heading for a stand of mesquite trees. With Raúl protecting her back, Chaz followed. Fuerte flew in front of them, picking the easiest, safest path. They charged through the trees and swerved around a field of barrel cactus. Up ahead, the ruins of an *aidea* sat beside the edge of a dust storm rising up out of the blustery wind like a brown fog. *Perfect.* Here they could make a stand. As the dust enveloped them, Dillon pulled up Victory behind the ruined mud wall of a hut and threw himself from the saddle. Even before Chaz and Raúl joined him, he was picking off soldiers who rode blindly forward and burst out of the dust cloud.

This time, Dillon didn't bother with placing his shots carefully; he simply placed them wherever they landed. A quick look at the other two revealed Chaz was weakening, though she still handled her rifle with competence, and Raúl's marksmanship hit its target more times than not. When the final two soldiers spun about and fled, Dillon turned to Chaz. Her legs gave way, and he caught her about the waist, holding her on her feet. Her lashes lifted, her gaze meshed with his, and only for the space of a heartbeat, he wished he'd met this señora in some other place, at some other time. The warm weight of her against his hip sent a tingling through his body and straight to his heart, warming it.

Hoof beats shook the ground, and Dillon swung up his head. At the same time, he drew his pistol and pointed it toward the disturbance. The horse emerging from the dust was familiar, as was the prickly man riding it. *Alec.*

"I'll take her now," Alec said. He slid his horse to a halt and reached out his arms for Chaz.

"Finders, keepers," Dillon replied with a grin, though he really wanted to plant a fist in the center of the man's aristocratic face.

Raúl stepped forward. "Where were you?" he asked the Spaniard with accusation in his voice.

"With Salvatore," Alec said and withdrew his arms. "We met up, all but you three, at the arroyo, where we backed the *rurales* against the edge. After relieving them of their weapons, horses, and boots, we set them loose to walk to the next *aidea*, which should take them about four days."

"Good work," Chaz said to Dillon's annoyance; he couldn't recall seeing Alec at any point after the cattle cars opened up. "Did you go back for my Hotchkiss and the silver?" she asked.

"*Sí, chiquita.*" His voice caressed the endearment and caused Dillon to grit his teeth. "I retrieved your big gun. The *rurales* killed Lopez but did not touch the gun. Unfortunately, the train left by the time we arrived and took the silver with it."

"*¡Mecachis!*" she swore and shifted to pull away from Dillon.

His arm tightened around her waist. "Whoa, *querida*, take it easy. You're wounded."

"*De nada*," she said and yanked herself free of his grip, though she sucked in a sharp breath.

Alec curled his fingers in a beckoning gesture. "Come ride with me, Chaz."

Dillon stepped in front of her. "If she's riding with anyone, she's riding with me. I brought her here safely, and I'll be taking her back."

Alec's brows hunkered together in an ominous scowl. "You go too far, gringo." He made a move for his pistol, but Dillon's Colt was already in hand before the Spaniard cleared leather.

Chaz stalked away from them. "Stop now, the both of you. This isn't a bullring, so cease your snorting. I ride my own horse. Niebla!" At her name, the gray pricked her ears and trotted toward Chaz.

While Dillon and Alec shot frowns at each other like bullets from dueling pistols, Chaz mounted Niebla with only a small groan and reined the horse around.

Dillon strode toward her and seized the horse's bridle. "At least let me dress that wound before you lose more blood and fall out of your saddle."

Chaz gave him a scathing look. "Let go of my horse. A waterhole lies not far from here. We will stop there and care for the wound. I am not the only one wounded." She put her heels to the gray and took off before Dillon could make it back to Victory. Raúl and Alec were directly behind her, and Dillon took up the rear, cussing and choking on the dust of the other horses.

The waterhole lay in a depression that pocked the land like a sinkhole. Thin Mexican piñon pines, in bunches of three, ringed the shallow, sandy water, roots greedily soaking up moisture as if to take advantage of such a rare commodity in this part of the *altoplano*.

Chaz removed her coat and vest and lowered the shoulder of her shirt. The deep, ugly crease oozed blood—more blood, Dillon told her, than he would have liked to see. As he dipped his bandana in the water and gently dabbed at the injury, her mouth firmed. Fire streaked through her arm and neck. It was all Chaz could do to keep from flinching away, but she set her jaw and endured it. When Dillon pried open a couple of bullet cartridges and poured black powder into the palm of his hand, she gave him a bewildered look.

He smiled and winked. "Learned this in Texas. It's crude medicine but should stave off infection until we can return you to the *aidea*." Then his brows hunkered together, and he pursed his lips. "Course, it could hurt a bit."

As he sprinkled the powder on the wound, Chaz clamped her teeth on her bottom lip. Then he scraped a match across his leathers and lit the gunpowder. It flashed and then smoked. The flesh burned like he'd taken a flaming brand to her, and she sucked in a harsh breath.

After making sure her injury was not too serious,

Raúl and Alec moved off to water the horses at the other end of the shallow depression.

Dillon canted his head, slid his hand over her shirt, and slipped it back onto her shoulder. "Six inches to the right, and the bullet would have caught you in the throat."

His touch did more to unsettle her than the burning wound, and she averted her eyes. "Then I suppose I am lucky."

"More like reckless and foolish, I'm thinking."

Her gaze came back to his face. "Listen, señor West, I'm thankful for what you did out there, but these are my men, this is my—"

"Vendetta? I'm not stupid, you know. There's a reason you want Thorne's silver."

Chaz held back the sharp words that came to mind, and for a long moment, only the high, rasping squeal, the *keeer—r-r* of red-tailed hawks, and the sputtery mutterings, low snorts, and soft brays of a covey of Gambel's quail beneath the cover of the mesquite brush broke the silence.

Dillon folded his arms across his chest, and his eyes peeled away at the layers of the past and delved into her soul. "Why Thorne? Why not one of Díaz's dozens of other *Americano* cronies? What did Thorne do to you to garner your undivided attention?"

"What makes you believe I have any particular interest in Thorne? I assure you, Thorne Railway is simply convenient. Were some other gringo operating in this area, I'd take their silver too."

"Why?"

"Why?" Chaz rounded on him, fisted hands rising to waist level. "Because this is *Méjico*, not *Los Estados Unidos*. The silver belongs to the *Méjicanos*, the campesinos, the dirt-poor farmers and laborers, not the rich Spanish *haciendos*, Porfirio Díaz, or especially the wealthy *Americanos*. Have you seen the conditions at the silver mines? Have you offered solace to the widows whose husbands and sons die daily while extracting silver for Díaz and his friends? Have you buried the bodies and prayed over their graves?"

"No. But you have to admit Díaz has made improvements in the country. Perhaps he relies too heavily on foreign investment, but he's trying to rule a country founded on conquest, revolution, and bloodshed.

Chaz turned her head and spit on the ground. "Díaz is a pig."

"I can see your point about Díaz, but not Thorne, who's taking advantage only of what's been offered to him. Are you after him because he's an American? Doesn't seem enough of a reason to me. After all, you have gringo blood in your veins, and Raúl is more *Americano* than Yaqui."

As Chaz stared at him, the blood left her brain, leaving her light-headed. Dillon knew about Raúl? *How could he? What had Raúl said to him?* He had an innocent though earnest expression, as if he was carrying on a debate at the *universidad* rather than speaking casually about her bastard child. Her muscles gradually relaxed. Perhaps he did not know. One had only to look at Raúl to see he was of mixed blood, and Dillon missed nothing. Chaz also supposed Raúl mentioned she was his mother, but even Raúl did not know the entire truth. Turning away from Dillon, she walked briskly toward her horse and said over her shoulder, "Unless you wish to eat my dust again, I suggest you mount up."

"Where are we going? I suppose you have some prearranged meeting place for when you become separated from your men."

"Yes." She swung her right leg over the gray's back. "Then we stop the train again when it slows for the foothills of the Western Mother."

"Again?" Dillon shook his head. "Give it a rest, lady. Haven't you wreaked enough mayhem for one day?"

Chaz stiffened her back and turned Niebla to the west, where the sun was drowning in a cauldron of crimson. "The silver cannot escape me, señor West. I have a reputation to uphold."

Dillon blew out a noisy breath. "Chaz, you're one loco señora, and I've met my fair share."

Night had fallen by the time Chaz rendezvoused with her men and caught up with the train again. This time, it held no large body of *rurales* to make the robbery difficult. Dillon reckoned the guards were still walking barefoot toward civilization. The train was ambling along as though the engineer knew *La Lobo Fantasma* would return, and he'd accepted the futility of running. He seemed almost grateful to Chaz for taking the silver off his hands, and the banditos quickly unloaded it.

As they rode away, the moon ascended, silvering the cactus. When they headed in an unexpected direction, into unfamiliar hills, Dillon grew thoughtful. He urged Victory to catch up with Chaz and leaned sideways to speak to her.

"Where are we going?"

She assessed him, as though assuring herself she was doing the right thing, and the moon's light reflected silver in her midnight-blue gaze. "You have asked many times what we do with the silver. I thought it was time you found out."

Alec twisted around in his saddle with a glower. "I still believe you are making a mistake. You do not even know if you can trust this man. He is a gringo. How can he understand the motives for what we do?"

"I do not recall asking for your permission," Chaz snapped. "I make the decisions for my family. Have you allowed your jealousy to cloud your mind?"

His lips came together in a pinched line, and he fell silent.

Dillon also remained quiet. Chaz was offering him one of the two pieces of information he most needed. What's more, she'd handled the arrogant Spaniard just fine on her own.

They rode through the night toward the mountains, and the desert stars shone brightly in a cloudless heaven, flinging cold light on the organ pipe and grandfather cactus. The cacti held up their arms and marched into the distance like a surrendering troop of Mananita's *rurales*. Far away loomed the black shadow of the Western Mother range, thick with juniper, piñon pine, and cypress. At last, when the mules pulling the wagon showed signs of fatigue, Chaz called a halt, and they huddled in their bedrolls without even the warmth of a fire to take the chill from the air.

Dillon awoke to the smell of creosote and coffee. He rubbed the sleep from his eyes and peered over at a smokeless fire made from greasewood. A pot boiling over the flames flung out the stimulating odor. The sun had yet to clear the eastern horizon, and embryonic light tinted the sky with a soft gray blue. He dragged himself from the bedroll and over to the fire. Hunkered down on his heels, he warmed his hands by the heat of the flames and inhaled the coffee aroma.

Chaz's voice came from over his shoulder. "We leave in ten minutes. If you are not ready, I will leave you behind."

Dillon straightened his legs and jerked around. He'd taken about enough of her stinging words. "Good," he said. He grasped her elbow and propelled her away from the fire and the other men. "Then we have time to air our lungs."

Chaz shook off his grip and stopped, facing him with anger carving lines in her face. "We have nothing to talk about, señor West. Your only job is to follow my orders and keep your mouth shut."

Dillon reined in his irritation with difficulty and

softened his tone. "What's wrong, *querida*? What did I do to put a burr under your saddle blanket?" When she puffed up like a horned toad, a light went on in his head. "Is it what happened back at the train? Your having to retreat? Is that what's eating at you?" Color flamed her face, and Dillon knew he'd struck a nerve. He cupped her shoulders in his hands. "For God's sake, Chaz, we were outnumbered. You couldn't have known about the *soldados*."

A shiver went through her body, and she dropped her gaze. "Never have I run from Manzanita." She reached up, clasped his wrists, and broke his grip. "Never!" When she tried to walk away, he caught her, bringing her back around.

"Leadership involves more than bravado. If you hadn't run, you and your men would be dead or dying, bleeding out into the sand right now. No one has any reason to question your courage, but blind courage is plain stupidity."

"How would you know? Have you ever fought for anything you believed in? Have you risked your life for anything other than your own selfish pleasures?"

Dillon stopped himself from reminding her that robbing trains wasn't the noblest of pursuits. His mouth kicked up in a smile, though inside he bled from the memories she stirred up, memories of blood and war. "You have me pegged right, señora, but I know what sacrifice means. My father fell at Gettysburg, slaughtered for following what he believed in. My mother never recovered from his loss and wasted away, becoming a shell of the strong woman she was."

Her features relaxed into a rare expression of pity, and her hand came up, palm cupping his cheek for a brief caress then lowering. "*Lo siento mucho*, I'm sorry. *Dispénseme*, forgive me. You must miss them terribly."

He locked his gaze on hers. "Yes. I reckon about as much as you miss your husband."

Dillon could swear she flinched, and something surfaced in her eyes, something hidden in their dark depths that gave him pause.

Chaz lowered her lashes and veiled that puzzling emotion. "No, I do not miss him."

Okay. She wasn't a grieving widow. "How old was Raúl when his father died?"

Her lashes whipped up. "Raúl was not yet born."

Dillon pressed, even though he sensed her reluctance to carry this conversation further. "How'd he die?"

A muscled flexed in her cheek, and her mouth thinned out. "I killed him."

"I see," he said, but he really didn't. At the look on her face, the obvious anguish and pain, a wave of tenderness washed over him. Dillon did what came naturally. He took her chin in his fingers, lifted her face, and brushed a soft kiss across her lips.

For a second, the length of a blink, Chaz relaxed against him before the sharp point of a knife pricked the underside of his chin. Dillon held very still, and Chaz jerked away as though he'd slapped her instead of kissed her, and shoved the knife back into the sheath at her waist. Her eyes snapping with fire, she spit out, "Saddle your horse, señor West, and do not ever touch me again."

"It was only a harmless kiss," he protested.

"No kiss is harmless." She spun about on a heel and stalked away.

Dillon noticed Alec standing by the horses, his smoldering gaze fixed on them. The Spaniard was too far away to have heard their words, but he couldn't have missed the kiss. Clearly, he was in a snit over what he saw as Dillon's encroaching on his territory. As Chaz approached Alec, he closed the ground between them in angry strides and gestured sharply. She held up a hand, shook her head, and moved off to her gray.

Dillon barely managed a quick gulp of the strong, bitter coffee before he mounted Victory and rode out.

Giving Chaz some space, he trailed along beside the wagon. He couldn't sort out why she'd reacted so intensely to his innocent kiss. It was barely a peck, but she'd acted like he'd ravished her. Chaz wasn't a virgin; Raúl was testimony to that, and Alec displayed all the signs of a jealous lover. Dillon didn't get the feeling she disliked him. Perhaps she didn't quite trust him, but the look in her eyes before he closed his own eyes and touched his lips to hers had been far from dislike. Maybe he'd simply embarrassed her in front of her men. Dillon convinced himself that was the reason for her pulling away. Why it bothered, he couldn't say. Nonetheless, it did.

The sun climbed high, and the heat kicked up a touch of hell. The landscape changed from cactus, thorny bushes, and sand to tough-grass meadow speckled with low acacia and tall madrone bushes. Up ahead, a small *ejido* shimmered on the horizon. Dillon mulled over what he knew about this land. During the Emperor Maximillian's reign, the *ejidos*, which had sustained the campesinos for centuries, were broken up and distributed to his French friends. After defeating Maximillian, Juarez set up the communal farmlands for the peasants. Now, Díaz, though once a soldier for Juarez, followed in Maximillian's footsteps. Only this time, he granted the peasants' lands to Spanish landowners and foreign investors whom Díaz could call on for favors. Few *ejidos* remained, and of those, only the smallest.

Dillon supposed these poor people saw The Ghost Wolf as a hero. After all, she took silver from the gringos and Díaz. Were they hiding it for her? They came up to the first rude dwelling, and a gaunt older woman hobbled out the door, flapping her apron at the riders. At the woman's heels swarmed a regiment of barefooted urchins, like chicks following a mother hen.

"*¡La Lobo Fantasma,*" the woman said in a breathless

voice, "*bienvenido!*"

The grin spreading across Chaz's face represented the first genuine expression of pleasure Dillon had seen on her. She swung down from her horse and took the woman's work-worn hands in her own. Leaning forward, she placed a kiss on each of the woman's weathered cheeks. "Maria," she said, "*¿Cómo está usted?* And the *hijos*, the children, they are well?"

"*Muy bien, gracias.* Juan no longer coughs since you brought the medicine."

Chaz released Maria's hands and squatted down. She held out her arms to a small, thin boy of about six, who hurtled forward and flung himself into her arms. Dillon watched in silence while the fierce Ghost Wolf embraced the boy and smoothed a hand over his dark head. At squeals coming from beside the house, Dillon turned to see Fuerte gamboling with a group of older boys and girls. The animal dwarfed the children, but they showed no fear, and the wolf-dog's tail wagged vigorously as he darted in and out amongst them.

Raúl dismounted and made his way to the wagon. With a small bag of silver coins in his hand, he approached Maria and passed the bag to the woman. A brilliant smile lit her face, and she clutched the pouch to her chest.

With one last pat to the woman's cheek and a few softly spoken words, Chaz and Raúl climbed back onto their horses, and the band rode on. The same scenario played out at every stop within the *ejido*—grateful, haggard women and children of all ages. What the *ejido* seemed to lack were men.

"Where are their husbands and fathers?" Dillon asked Raúl as they rode toward the final house.

"Those Manzanita did not kill have been taken to the mines. Díaz's *soldados* made a sweep through this area two years ago and took all the able-bodied men from their families. They now work as slaves in the foreigners' silver mines."

Dillon's brow puckered in a perplexed frown. "How can he do that? These are free people. Slavery is illegal in Mexico."

Raúl gave him a sad smile. "That may be so, but imprisonment of revolutionaries is not. He declared the men traitors, tried them in absentia, and took them for the mines."

"Are they revolutionaries?"

A cocky grin materialized. "A few were. The people here hate Díaz and wish to see him fall. But most of those who joined the insurgents escaped before Díaz's men could take them."

Dillon became thoughtful. He knew Díaz was not loved by all his people. Dillon had heard rumors of a populist movement, but that these poor, malnourished people could carry out a successful uprising seemed impossible.

By the time they made their way through the *ejidos* on the high plain beside the mountains, they had distributed among the women and children all the silver coin taken from the train. The wagon now held only silver ingots from the mines. Chaz turned the men toward the mountains, and they climbed upward. The track stretched out broad and gradual; even so, the mules strained against the heavy load. Once they reached a plateau covered in grass and acacia bushes and rimmed with juniper and pine, Chaz called a halt. The men dismounted and began to set up camp.

Seis

Chaz questioned once again the wisdom of her decision to trust Dillon as she watched him loosening the cinch on his saddle and lifting it from the chestnut's back, his arm and shoulder muscles bunching and flexing beneath his shirt. She could be placing her men in danger and threatening the cause of the revolution. The *Americano* had proved his worth several times and given her no reason to mistrust him, but a tendril of unease still plucked at her nerves. She supposed she would find out soon enough whether he was what he claimed to be or had ulterior motives for joining her band.

His kiss returned to her, the gentle sensuality it expressed. That thought brought to mind the prick of wanting that arose in her, the strange sensation that so unsettled her. At times, when Chaz witnessed the tenderness between Delicia and Salvatore, and the other men and their wives and sweethearts, her heart yearned for something more, something she knew she couldn't have. A sigh whispered past her lips, and she turned away to tend to her horse. She needed no man. She still had Raúl, and there was always Alec. He loved her, wanted her, but her feelings for the Spaniard ran tepid.

They roused no fire within her, no longing for intimacy. Chaz valued his friendship and loyalty, but she could never love him as a woman was supposed to love a man. Chaz told herself she had good reason for her inherent distrust of men. Sometimes she grew maudlin, questioned if it was not time to overcome the fears of childhood. Was she to live the remainder of her life without the love of a good man? And where, exactly, did one find a "good" man? Not this man, certainly, but one had to start somewhere. She shook her head at the turn of her thoughts.

With her horse cared for and grazing on the tough grasses, Chaz extracted a cake of soap and a length of cloth from her saddlebags and headed for the small stream that ran beside the live oaks and willows along one edge of the hills. The wound had stiffened her shoulder, and the thought of soaking it in the cool water brought a smile to her lips. She was becoming self-pitying, and it was all the fault of Dillon West.

Chaz had removed her shirt when a rustle of movement came from the grasses behind her. Her breath suspended in her throat. She whirled about, the cloth held against her breasts with one hand, her other hand moving to the gun on her hip.

Dillon emerged from the long shadows cast by the trees as the sun westered. He raised his hands to waist level, palms outward.

"Easy, *querida*. I came to check on your wound."

"Then check," she snapped out, and turned her back. Her heart pounded against her ribs in an alarming manner. Dillon moved toward her, boots snapping twigs and rustling against the grasses. When his warm palms settled on her upper arms, she jumped.

"What's got you so spooked?" he asked as his hands smoothed slowly up and down her bare arms. His voice descended to a low, soothing level, the way he might speak to a nervous horse. "You're as jumpy as a longhorn in a thunderstorm."

A quiver shot through her, and she inched away from his touch. "I am not spooked. You should have announced your presence."

He chuckled. "Then you would have run away."

Chaz whirled about with an angry rejoinder on her tongue. Dillon caught her words in his mouth, and his hands dropped away from her arms. He did not hold her, restrain her in any way, other than his mouth clinging to hers. Chaz began to pull away in reflex, but his gentle assault weakened her knees. When her taut muscles relaxed, his arm came around her waist, urged her up against him and held her loosely. She could break away at any time, and that knowledge kept her from doing so.

His tongue eased her lips apart and dipped inside, and his hand described soft circles on her lower back. *Why are you letting him do this? Why are you letting him touch you? You know what he wants.* Chaz didn't have the answers to those questions, and in her conflicted state, she allowed him to continue. She played no active part, did not kiss him back. In all honesty, she did not know how. No man had kissed or held her since...

Panting, chest heaving, Chaz yanked back her head and stumbled backward a step. She brought up her hand in a hard slap to the side of his face. His hand slipped away from her waist, fell to his side, and Dillon tilted his head to regard her with a questioning look.

"I told you not to do that again," she said; the words emerged only as a shaky whisper.

"Okay. I won't. Not until you tell me you want me."

"You'll never see that day, gringo. I dislike being touched."

His smile was seductive and a touch sardonic. "Perhaps you enjoy it more than you're willing to admit."

Chaz shook her head. "No." Pain cinched her chest, and she breathed slowly, deeply, as she fought against it.

"Why?"

The pain eased, and she said, "That is none of your business, señor West."

Dillon made a sound halfway between a sigh and a groan. "Will you at least allow me to tend the wound? I promise I won't touch you any more than necessary."

"No. Leave. I can care for it myself."

He dipped his head and laid the salve and bandages on the ground. "Then I'll cut and run."

When Dillon departed, disappeared into the gathering darkness like a wraith, Chaz allowed her emotions to spill over. Her body shook, not only with the painful memories he'd unearthed but with her reaction to his kiss. What was she thinking?

Dillon paused behind the trunk of a water oak and lowered himself to the ground. Fuerte slid up beside him, stretched out on his belly, and nudged Dillon's hand. Dillon scratched the dog's head while his gaze rested on the woman beside the stream.

The words spilled out of him in a whisper: "I was under the impression The Ghost Wolf was a man. Boy was I wrong. A woman, and not just any woman, but a mother." He shook his head as if he couldn't quite believe his words. "Perhaps I was also mistaken about Alec being her lover. She doesn't react like a woman who's used to a man's touch." Again, he was jumping to conclusions. Of course the Spaniard considered himself her man. Dillon could see it in the man's eyes every time Alec looked at her.

Dillon's gaze shifted to the dog, who cocked up one ear and gave every impression of listening to and considering Dillon's words. Dillon grinned and ruffled the dog's ears. "Okay, my furry friend, you may not have an opinion on that, but perhaps you can explain this to me. She gives the poor campesinos the silver coin taken from Thorne's trains, keeping none or very little, as far as I can see, for herself. But she still has the silver ingots, the bulk of the wealth taken from the trains. So her motives can't be as pure as they seem on the surface. What does she intend to do with them? Ingots aren't easily spent currency like coins. She must be storing them somewhere in these mountains. Hopefully, within a few days, I'll have the answer to that question."

Fuerte gave a soft woof and laid his head on his paws.

When Chaz tugged down her trousers and stepped out of them, Dillon's hand stilled on the dog's head. The light had dimmed, and he could see only her pale silhouette against the darker shadow of the trees on the opposite bank of the stream, but his mind filled in the details. She was slender and long-legged, scrawny he would have thought had she been any other woman. He knew that beneath that trim frame lay hard muscle. He'd felt it in her arms and along the small of her back. She was as lean and finely toned as an antelope. Nothing soft about her other than her small breasts, which he'd felt briefly when they flattened against his chest. His shaft filled and pushed against the seam of his trousers. He all but got to his feet to wander back down to the stream, when Fuerte lifted his head with pricked ears, whined, and a man stepped out of the trees along his right side. Dillon's hand went to the butt of his Colt, and he rose silently to a crouch.

"*Hola,*" the man called out. *Who else but Alec Cazadore?* Dillon straightened his legs and patted a hand to his thigh to call the dog. "Let's go, boy. She doesn't need us to watch over her any longer." Fuerte lumbered to his feet and attached himself to Dillon's heels, and they walked quietly away.

* * *

Chaz looked toward the voice and dropped down in the water until only her shoulders remained above the surface. "Alec," she said breathlessly, ashamed to admit she had hoped it was Dillon.

Alec leaned back against a tree and folded his arms in front of him. "The puma prowl close to the mountains tonight, *chiquita*. You should have posted a guard. If you had asked, I would have come with you."

Chaz bristled at his implied censure and extended an arm. "Throw me the cloth, Alec, then leave while I dress. I do not need a guard. Fuerte is guard enough."

He bent over and retrieved the cloth from the pile she had made of her clothes. Rather than tossing it to her, he kept it in his hands. "I do not see your dog."

"Well, he must be somewhere about." Her mouth crimped at the stubborn gleam in his eyes.

"You have avoided me for the past few days," he continued. "I wish to clear the air between us, and since I have you captive, so to speak, you will tell me what weighs so heavily on your mind."

"*Por Dios*," she said with a harsh breath. "I have nothing on my mind other than passing on the silver to Venustiano so he can use it to strike at Díaz. But if you keep me in this water much longer, I will consider shooting you in the *ayotes*."

A smile crept across his mouth. "Ah, Chaz, such language. Were I a lesser man, I would believe you. However, I know you would not waste one of your silver bullets on me."

"*Por favor*," she said in a plea. "Throw the towel, Alec."

His face sobered, and a crease pleated the skin between his brows. "Do you care for him, Chaz?"

"Who?"

"The *Americano*, of course. I am not a blind man. I see the way you watch him."

Heat flared in her face despite the cooling of the

water. "I watch him because I do not trust him."

"I do not believe you, *chiquita*. What makes him so different from me? Why will you not give me a chance to show you what it can be like between us? I have loved you since you were a frightened, little *niña*. At the time, I could understand why you so feared me and the other men. Now you are a woman. You no longer have reason to be frightened. You are a woman made for love, Chaz, and I want so much to give you that love. Why will you not trust me?"

Chaz shivered, the cold pebbling her flesh. "Please, Alec. Not now. I am freezing."

Alec sailed the towel out over the water and into her hands. "That is the problem," he said, his words harsh. "You are frozen inside and refuse to do anything about it. If you do not allow yourself to love, some day you will be a lonely, bitter old woman." He turned abruptly and stalked off.

Siete

Dillon settled on the ground beside the campfire.
He still couldn't puzzle out why they'd camped in
this meadow, why they hadn't moved on to stash the
silver. The plateau they occupied extended as flat and
featureless as a tortilla, stretching out to a boundary of
tall mountains in only one direction. Sitting out in the
open with the booty on them seemed a bit reckless for a
band of train robbers pursued by the *rurales*.

By the time lights flared above them on the
mountainside, the silver disc of a full moon sailed across
the black backdrop of the sky. The lights on the mountain
slid downward in a smooth golden rope, undulating like
a river, and moved out onto the plateau. Soon, as the
visitors quickly crossed the meadow, the pounding of
horses' hooves transferred vibrations to the log on which
Dillon had parked his bottom and on the ground beneath
his boots. He set down the tin cup, came to his feet, and
drew his Colt. Across the glow of the fire from Dillon,
Chaz rose at the same time and motioned for him to
holster the weapon.

Individual torches separated out from the stream
of light, and their flickering illumination picked out the

features of the riders. They were a rough-looking lot, clothed in short jackets and serapes or ponchos, and wide sombreros, rifles held across their laps and pistols on their hips, all done up like banditos, that is to say, exactly like Chaz's men.

A large, bearded man led the horsemen, which numbered around a hundred. He looked like every other desperado Dillon had run across since crossing the border into Mexico: clad in dark leathers, sombrero, and bandoliers crossing his chest, serape draped across one shoulder. When Chaz moved forward to greet the visitors, Dillon held his breath.

The large man dismounted, caught Chaz up in a bear hug, and swung her around. "Tino!" she said breathlessly, laughing, the first time Dillon had heard the delightful sound escape her severe demeanor. It was full throated and hearty and tingled along his nerves like lightning in a storm.

The man pointed at Dillon. "*¿Quién el gringo?*"

Chaz replied too softly for the words to carry, then taking the man's hand, led him to where Dillon stood with the hairs on his nape rising and puckering the back of his neck. When they stopped in front of him, Chaz said in Spanish, "Tino, I wish for you to meet señor Dillon West, an *Americano* pistolero. He recently joined our number." She switched to English and turned to Dillon. "This is Venustiano Carranza. He is a revolutionary and a friend to my family."

Dillon sized up the other man like they were two roosters in a flock of hens. Carranza was in the prime of life, somewhere in his thirties, tall and well built. The proprietary hold he kept on Chaz's hand told Dillon The Ghost Wolf had another *macho hombre* vying for her affections. He saw his position becoming stickier as the pathway to her door grew more crowded. Soon he'd have to elbow the men aside.

Dillon pasted a smile on his face and stuck out

his hand. Carranza took it with what looked like reluctance, and both men squeezed...hard, a mockery of a handshake. Dillon was pretty sure he'd pull back a mangled stump. When Venustiano let go, Dillon winced and flexed his hand. Chaz frowned, and Carranza tilted back his head, laughing.

"He's as weak as a flea, *chiquita*," Carranza said in Spanish. "I cannot understand what you see in him."

She shook her head. "I see nothing in him, Venustiano, other than another gun, and quite a good one, the best among my men."

Dillon deliberately gave the man an idiotic grin, nodded his head like a mule on loco weed, and rested a hand on the butt of his Colt. "*Bueno pistola*," he said in an atrocious accent.

Chaz sent him a scowl.

He replied with a shrug of one shoulder.

Chaz and Carranza walked away to the wagon, where the revolutionary's men had begun unloading the silver ingots and packing them in sacks on the mules that trailed the group into the camp. When Dillon saw his ten percent about to ride away, he quickly made his way to Chaz.

"Since I'm only a pistolero," he said, "I expect to be paid for my services."

Chaz snatched up an ingot and tossed it at him. It hit him in the chest, knocking the breath from him with an "Omph!" Dillon juggled the ingot to one hand and swept an arm around at the rest of Chaz's men. "Don't they get a cut?"

Her eyes turned to him. In the illumination from the torches, their normal blue appeared as black as the night sky. "My men do not expect pay for what they do." Venom coated her words. "We work for the downfall of Díaz and his foreign friends. If you have a problem with that, señor West, I will point you in the direction of the nearest *cuidad*."

This was a development Dillon hadn't anticipated. The Ghost Wolf was an outlaw, a train robber. She was supposed to keep the silver, hoard it like a miser, and assuage his conscience about bringing her and her men to justice. This scenario wasn't in the script Thorne had handed him.

Dillon struggled with that little devil on his shoulder, who told him to keep the silver—seeing as it was all he was likely to get—lost the battle, and returned the ingot to the wagon. Chaz gave him a puzzled look, and he smiled somewhat sickly. "*Viva la revolución*," he said.

Her answering smile was worth it...almost.

Okay. The fearsome Ghost Wolf gave the silver to the oppressed campesinos and the revolutionaries. She wasn't a dirty, flea-infested, mustachioed desperado who robbed and killed indiscriminately and ran off with the loot to an expensive hacienda with marble floors and silver-plated walls. Did that make her actions any less criminal? Not in Thorne's book. As Thorne's employee, Dillon still had a job to do, regardless of Chaz's motives. Thorne was paying him good money for results, and he'd never run away from a job because he didn't agree with the principles behind it, despite his infrequent charitable nature.

When Carranza and his men departed, Dillon sat beside the fire to nurse a cup of coffee and a plate of beans and figure out what he was going to do now. The silver was gone, and he doubted he'd have any luck finding the revolutionary and his men and taking it back. By the time he tracked down the band, they would have converted the ingots into rifles, pistols, and ammunition. Somehow, he had to put an end to The Ghost Wolf's depredations on Thorne's railway. Now he had to come up with a way to carry that out.

Chaz was warming up to him. She had defended him to Carranza. Perhaps fanning those embers and developing her trust further would be the most productive. She might even spill secrets regarding her revolutionary friends. Surely more than one had a price on his head. If he couldn't get the silver, he could make it up in bounty.

Dillon tossed the dregs of his coffee on the fire, laid the tin plate on the ground for the ants, and sought her out. Chaz had bunked down behind a low hill, and the moonlight limned her form rolled up in blankets and the black braid of her hair draped across the saddle pillowing her head. She looked vulnerable and harmless, and his heart gave a little hitch. Dillon reminded himself of her true nature. *A ruthless train robber. A crack shot.*

As though Chaz read his thoughts, she came up on one elbow in a blur, blankets flying and a rifle in her hands. Dillon tilted his face into the moonlight, and she slowly lowered the rifle. A shaky hand smoothed the hair escaping her braid back from her face.

"You are determined to get yourself killed, aren't you?" she said.

"That wasn't my intention." Dillon sank to the ground and crossed his legs Indian-style.

Chaz shifted to sit upright, mirroring his position, and laid the rifle aside. "Then what was?"

He lifted his gaze to her eyes. "My intention?"

She nodded.

"Tell me more about Carranza. How you met him and why you're involved in his activities."

"Why should I? You once said a man's business was private. That goes double for a woman's."

"Then he's your lover."

Even in the pale wash of moonlight, Dillon detected the blanching of her face. He took a chance, reaching out and placing a hand on her wrist. She didn't pull away. That was a step in the right direction.

"Carranza is not my lover," she said. "His father and mine were friends."

"Were?" he asked softly.

"They are both dead. My father, Vito Gutierrez, was an *indito* rebellion leader. When my mother was pregnant with me, General Quintin Hidalgo shot and killed him. The general had spread rumors my father was a traitor."

"Hidalgo rode as Díaz's aide during Juárez's War of Reform, didn't he?"

Her eyes narrowed. "You are well informed on Mexican politics."

"I told you I joined the liberals for a while." He smiled. "I'd heard of Hidalgo."

It looked as if she was fixing to lie back down. "What happened after your father was killed?" he asked. "Did your mother raise you alone?"

"No. Hidalgo forced her into marriage. She was *muy bonita*, and some say Hidalgo accused my father only so he could have her."

"So you grew up with the man who killed your father. That must have been a bleak existence."

"Hidalgo died of *vomito prieto*, the yellow fever, when I was four. My mother and I were then freed of his presence."

"I can understand now why you have no love for Díaz and his men."

"I already told you my actions stem from Díaz's treatment of the campesinos and his love of the gringo investors. My personal life plays no part in what I do."

Dillon snorted. "*Querida*, our personal lives affect *everything* we do—good or bad."

"Did I not tell you that you were not to call me *querida* again?"

"*Querida*," he said and leaned in toward her with a grin. "*Querida, querida.*"

The muscles of her face twitched, and a smile slowly appeared. "You, señor West, are as incorrigible as an unbroken colt."

The grin left his face. "But I'm not a colt, *querida*. I'm a man, and it could be the moonlight, but I think I'm crazy about you."

Chaz flattened her hands on his chest and straightened her arms. "I assure you, it is the moonlight."

Slowly, Dillon shook his head and covered her hands with his. "You're wrong, Chaz. I'm pretty sure I'm crazy about you. I know you don't like being touched, so I'll ask this time. May I kiss you, real soft like?"

Chaz drew in a breath, and he started to move away, but then she grasped his hands and tugged him back. He had no intention of spooking her off so early in the game, but he also didn't want to give her too much time to think it over and change her mind. So he moved right in.

Her mouth had softened, as though she'd expected a proper kiss. *Easy, Dillon, little bitty steps...baby steps.* Dillon lifted her hand and placed a gentle kiss on the back. Then turning it over, he hissed her palm, lingering a bit. "I'm a patient man. I can wait."

"Ha! You wait for nothing."

"No, señora, I wait for you." He kissed her hand again.

A flash of anger swept across her face. "You mock me?" she hissed. "You slobber on my hand like Fuerte, like a dog?" Chaz yanked her hand away and swung at him. He laughed and caught her wrist.

"Missed, darlin'," he said with a grin.

Chaz shoved so hard on his chest he toppled sideways, landing on the sharp spines of a prickly pear cactus. She leapt to her feet, stepped over him, and stomped off.

Fuerte had been lying beside her and now lifted his head from his paws. "Guess she's pissed at me," Dillon said, cocking a brow at the dog, relived the animal liked him and hadn't taken out his throat yet.

Fuerte yawned, laid his head back down, and closed his eyes.

While Dillon picked the spines out of his butt, he felt eyes searing his back. *Alec again?* Honestly, the man was more annoying than a screw fly. When he looked behind him, Raúl stood there with his legs braced apart and his hat canted back on his head to reveal his auburn hair and the glint of blue eyes. Dillon hoped the youth hadn't witnessed the scene between his mother and him.

"Did she tell you about the bullets?" Raúl asked as he strolled over to Dillon.

The question seemed to come out of thin air and, thankfully, have no relation to Dillon's conversation with Chaz. "What bullets?" He flinched, grimaced, and plucked another spine from his hide. "Ammo isn't exactly in short supply around here."

Raúl settled down on a hunk of granite poking up above the scrub grass. "You've asked her about the silver, about why she gives it away."

"Yeah, well, she explained that to me. She supports the campesinos and the rebels for the downfall of Díaz."

Raúl picked up a branch from the ground and stripped bark from it. He lowered his eyes to the task. "She kept some."

Dillon's ears pricked up. So she *did* hoard away some of the silver. His bank account suddenly looked better. "Where does she stash it? In the valley?"

A rueful smile lifted the edges of Raúl's mouth, and he shook his head. "In her revolver."

Confusion swirled like a whirlpool inside Dillon.

"When she took the first train," Raúl said, "she set aside a small amount of silver and melted it into bullets. Six to be exact. She loaded that revolver of hers with them, and the gun never leaves her hip."

A germ of an idea formed in Dillon's mind like a bank of gathering thunderheads. "They're for Thorne, aren't they?"

Raúl nodded. Fuerte lumbered to his feet and walked over to the boy, plopping down atop his boots. Raúl scratched the dog behind its ears.

"Why?" Dillon asked, the pain in his behind forgotten. "Why Thorne? She can't possibly know the man. What did he do to her to make her hate him so much, enough that she wants to put silver bullets in him?"

Raúl slowly shook his head. "I don't rightly know. She won't speak of it, but it's like a mesquite thorn under her skin. I'm worried about her. Salvatore often cautions her about taking unnecessary risks, but she accepts no one's counsel. Lately, it's as if she's challenging Justus Thorne to come down here in person to stop her. I'm afraid she'll get her wish, and instead of her killing him, he'll kill her."

Dillon gripped the boy's shoulder. "Rest easy, son. As long as I'm here to protect her, Thorne won't get the chance." At the hollow vow, Dillon's conscience needled him. What would he really do if Thorne showed up and demanded he hand over The Ghost Wolf? Wasn't his mind still as set on ending the train robber's ravaging of Thorne's trains? On collecting the rest of his pay and his share of the silver?

As night wore on and the moon cast its light on the meadow, Dillon and the boy, each buried in thought, sat in silence, side by side with the great dog at their feet.

Ocho

The sun had barely stolen over the mountains when Largo banged on the door of the hacienda, the rapid and forceful knocking telegraphing his impatience.

"I am coming!" Delicia called and shuffled forward in worn carper slippers. She pulled her wrapper tightly about her generous figure and knotted the sash at her waist. "Cease that noise! I am not deaf!"

When she swung open the door, Largo brushed past her.

"Chaz!" he called out. "Chaz, I must speak with you. News comes from Sonora!"

"Wipe your feet," Delicia spat. Fog rolled in with the dawn, and a misty rain settled on the plateau. Water dripped from Largo's hair, and his booted feet tracked muddy prints across the wide planks.

Largo mumbled an apology, backed up, and scraped his feet on the brightly colored braided rug that lay at the threshold.

Chaz emerged from her bedroom, hopping on one foot while she pulled a boot on the other. Her tangled hair streamed down her back, and the tail of her white shirt hung loose about her hips. "What?" she asked. As she looked down the staircase at Largo and Delicia, she still struggled with the boot. She sat on the top step and tugged the boot home, then standing, trotted down to the main floor.

Largo removed his wet hat and twisted it in his hands. "It is Cajame. He sent word to all the Yaqui. Díaz's military have him bottled up in El Añil."

Chaz had feared this time would come. Cajame was a cousin, as were many of the Yaqui. When Díaz centralized the government, he brought all Mexicans under his domain. This meant the Yaqui as well as the city dwellers in Mexico City. His courting of the foreign investors meant capital for railroads, mines, and agriculture. But the most fertile of Mexico's lands lay in Sonora along the Yaqui and Mayo Rivers, the ancestral lands of the native Yaqui, who still maintained their regional caudillos, spurning Díaz's centralization efforts. Díaz's plans for the region included diverting half of the Yaqui River to a valley for irrigation and displacing the *indito* residents. Those without homes then became available for working on the railroads or in the mines.

Cajame, a revolutionary leader, had emerged among the Yaqui and formed a rebellion. He'd built a fort named El Añil between Pótam and Vícum in an impenetrable forest that stretched from the Yaqui toward the Mayo.

"Díaz has attacked the fort without success," Largo said. "He offered the Yaqui life and property in exchange for surrender. Cajame said he would end the rebellion only if the troops would leave the river. Díaz's soldiers now surround El Añil, and Cajame sent out a messenger from his citadel, calling all Yaqui to come to his aid."

Chaz slipped her arms into her leather jacket and turned, tucking in her shirt at the waistband of her pants. Her gun belt already hung about her slim hips.

Those who saw her daily often wondered whether she slept with it. "Well, Largo," Chaz said, "do not stand there and drip water all over my floor. Gather the men." Delicia moved behind Chaz and quickly braided her hair.

Trees closed in around them, tall quaking aspens with slender boles and the sturdy trunks of water oaks with dry, rustling leaves. The abundant, fertile environment was as different from the barren expanse of the *altoplano* as a Chihuahua was from a wolf. Dense thickets of thorny acacia appeared impassable other than the faint deer path the group followed. When Dillon glanced away into the dusk of the forest for only a second, his eyes became incapable of picking up the path again. If not for the horses ahead of him, he would have lost his way. They'd wrapped the feet of the horses in sacking to deaden the sound of hooves and masked their nostrils to forestall any inadvertent nickering. The wheels of the supply wagons were wrapped similarly and well greased to prevent betraying squeaks and creaks.

They rode in pairs, Alec and Largo out front, followed by Raúl and Salvatore, then Dillon and Chaz, a dozen more strung out behind them. Chaz remained silent for a long time, her gaze on the forest ahead and to either flank. When she turned sideways, whispering words, they seemed to come out of nowhere.

"Do you have a wife, señor West?"

"Me, married?" Her question struck like a copperhead, and he swallowed to relieve the taste of venom in his throat. "Once I did."

Her look was one of curiosity at the hesitance of his reply, and she pressed for more. "Only once?" she asked dryly.

"Okay," he said slowly, already regretting what he was about to say. But he had relentlessly quizzed Chaz;

seemed about time he answered some of her questions... truthfully. "I was married once, a long time ago. Patricia was a Texican, one of those tough, enduring women who could grow corn where there's no rain and coax water from a dry well. We had a daughter, Grace, all spindly legs and arms and a mouth that was never still, with hair as golden as prairie grass and eyes like cornflowers."

"What happened to them?" she asked quietly, as though she'd picked up on his despondent mood.

"Mescalero Apaches. I'd been away for a few days, hunting, and when I returned... Well, nothing was left but charred wood. The Mescaleros had taken my family. I tracked the band for months. By the time I caught up with them, it was too late."

"What did you do?"

"What do you think I did? I killed them."

Chaz reached over and laid a gentle hand on his arm. "You must have loved your wife and child very much."

Dillon sent her a rueful smile, shaking off the painful memories. "Yes, well, as I said, it was a long time ago, and I was just a kid. We both were."

Alec dropped back. "We need you at the back of the column," he said to Dillon. Dillon sent a questioning glance at Chaz, and when she nodded, he pulled aside, into the trees, and let the riders pass by. Then he anchored the rear guard behind the wagons. They were some one hundred thirty strong. During the long ride, they passed through the town of Guatimapé and across the Sierra Madre Occidental to San Dimas and up the narrow strip of land between the ocean and the eastern edge of the mountains. Then through Casala to Culiacán on the Tamazula River, and on to Pótam. Small, isolated Yaqui rebel bands dibbled in along the way to join them, all eager to go to Cajame's aid. Now this ghostly horde, led by a ghost in gray on a gray horse, a wolf at her heels, flowed silently through the forest, trying desperately to reach the fort with food, medicine, ammunition and rifles, and men to wield them.

Some of the men were bloodied already, and six had died, victims of a skirmish with *rurales* on the banks of the Tamazula River outside Culiacán. After a mad scramble across the shallow river, they jogged east to lose their pursuers in the forested foothills of the mountains then swung back northwest when they were sure of safety.

Since he'd awakened at dawn days ago and learned of their destination, Dillon had continually bounced ideas off the corners of his brain. This trip seemed to be fate intervening. Their objective was about three hundred miles from Nogales and the U. S. border. A bit more than a week's hard riding. A fair piece, but closer than Asilo. Unwittingly, The Ghost Wolf had allowed her men to escort her in exactly the direction Dillon wanted her to go. If he could spirit her away from Cajame's fort, out from under the noses of her men, he'd have her in Thorne's hands before they knew she was missing. But was that really what he wanted to do? Not for the first time in his life, he questioned his motives. *Damn*, but the woman was beginning to grow on him and muddy his thinking. However, other than their brief conversation, throughout most of this journey, Chaz remained out of his sight.

His musing fled in shouts coming from ahead and the crack of gunfire. He swung around the men in front, and for the next few minutes, chaos reigned. Men running in all directions, as much as the thick foliage allowed, shots echoing in the trees, coming from God knew where. Dillon barreled past a rider, nearly unseating him. In the same moment, he whipped his revolver from its holster and another from his belt. A rifle was no good in this arena; couldn't tell in what or in whom a bullet would land. Victory's reins in his teeth, hands free and full of iron, he forced his way forward. Thorns reached out and ripped his trousers, drawing blood. He cursed and urged the horse to do his best. *Chaz on his mind.* What if Chaz was killed? *No Ghost, no silver, no bounty.* A bit mercenary, and he should have been ashamed of his thoughts. Inexplicably, he was, more than he wanted to be. After all, he was here only for the silver, wasn't he? Nevertheless, something deep inside his chest tightened and coiled at the thought of that beautiful woman lying dead on the trail. No, it was more than that. Something inside him wept for her, tears that had nothing to do with the silver or her beauty.

Then horses crashed through the forest behind him. *What the hell?* Meaning came in a bolt of understanding. *The wagons.* They were after the wagons. The men would be useful to Cajame, but not without provisions, arms, and ammunition. Cajame's plight was a siege situation not a test of barehanded men against men.

By the time Dillon got Victory turned around and headed back toward the wagons he'd passed before, everyone had the same idea. A bottleneck of men and horses tangled along the trail. With no clear path through the thorns and dense trees, it seemed to take forever for everyone to sort themselves out and string out in a galloping line.

The drivers lay in the leaf litter, shot all to damnation. The wagons were gone, back down the same trail they'd used to traverse the forest.

"What happened?" Chaz's voice came from behind a couple of dozen men blocking her view of the site. When she made her way through them, she dismounted, went down on one knee, and cradled the head of one of the drivers in her hands. "Rafael, he was only seventeen. He begged to come along, drive a wagon, and I allowed it." Chaz looked up with despair glistening in her eyes. "What will I tell Rosita, his *madre*?"

Alec laid a hand on her shoulder. "Chaz, we can still catch them and retrieve the wagons."

"No," she said. She straightened and swept back the

braid from her shoulder. "They will expect us to pursue.
The *rurales* will have set an ambush along this trail." She
pointed to the bodies. "Carry them into the trees and
cover them with leaves. We do not have time to bury
them. This forest must be their cathedral."

A priest from one small village had joined them
days ago, and he knelt beside each body, giving them
last rites. The men then carried the dead off the trail into
the dimness beneath the tree canopy. As they passed
Chaz with the body of Rafael, she reached out and gently
caressed the smooth cheek of the boy.

An hour out from the fort, one of Cajame's men met
them and acted as a guide. He led them along twisted
paths a turkey couldn't have found. They soon broke
free of the forest and entered a cleared area of perhaps
fifty acres. Once more, sunlight bore down on them.
Cajame had built his fort of logs and sharpened saplings
taken from the forest that protected him, and from that
fortress, the revolutionary leader himself rode out to
meet them. He was a short, wiry man of unprepossessing
appearance, a well-trimmed mustache and the snapping
black eyes of a Yaqui Indian. He wore the white trousers
and shirt of the peasants, and *huraches* on his dusty feet.
His complexion was darker than that of Chaz, but then
Cajame was pure Yaqui, while Chaz had some Spanish
and white blood. If Dillon saw this man on the streets of
Zacatecas, he would have taken the Yaqui leader for a
peasant farmer.

Cajame jumped from his horse, swept Chaz from
her saddle, and embraced her in a tight hug. She stood
inches taller than him, but he lifted her easily and swung
her around. His laugh echoed out across the clearing.
"Chaz, *mi sobrina*, but you have grown up so. It has been
many years. I do not know why I expected a wild *niña*
with bare feet and flying hair." He flipped the end of

her long braid, from which much hair had escaped its confinement. "But you still have the wild hair, I see." Then he kissed her on both cheeks and tucked his arm around her waist for the walk into the fort. Fuertes trotted along at her side, head high, nose working, wary and alert.

Dillon pulled his horse into line behind Chaz, managing to come up alongside Alec, and eavesdropped on the conversation between Chaz and Cajame.

"We lost the wagons," Chaz said to the rebel leader. "The *rurales* attacked us on the trail through the forest and killed eight of my men."

Grimness tightened the muscles of his face. "Then that path is no longer safe. Day by day, they draw the noose tighter around us."

Chaz pivoted in place and looked out over the clearing. "But where are the soldiers? I expected them to be pounding on your door."

Cajame chuckled, saying in Spanish, "No, *mi sobrina*. They have pulled back to the edges of the forest while I *think over* their terms for peace. And do not worry yourself about the wagons. We have other, more serious problems here at El Añil."

As they entered the gates of the fort and a man directed Dillon to one side to tie up his horse, he lost the thread of their words. The fortification contained a larger area than it appeared from outside. Low, rambling log houses filled the stockade, and a remuda, within which perhaps thirty horses milled about. Ladders led to a planked walkway that encircled the walls, and men with rifles paced along their length, fewer men than Dillon had expected to see. The fort certainly seemed to be undermanned, and how they'd held off the Mexican army for this long was beyond his comprehension.

Chaz and Cajame had disappeared into a small cabin that sat at the back of the fort. Dillon hitched Victory to a pine pole, removed his saddle, and rubbed him down.

Then he collared a passing rebel and asked where he could find some vittles. He figured he'd first eat, and then he'd check out the fort and find the back door. Every castle had a back door.

"¿Vomito prieto?" Chaz said, repeating what Cajame had told her of his dire situation. She eased into a wooden chair and declined with a wave the glass of *aguardiente* Cajame's man offered her. "But how many men are left?"

Cajame settled into the chair across from her and poured a generous measure of the fiery liquid into his glass. "Less than four hundred. And I have food for only half that. I fear I will have to agree to terms soon."

Chaz's mouth twisted. "The supplies in the wagons we lost would have helped."

"Perhaps," he said with a smile, "but they would not stop the fever. Perhaps they would have given us another month or two, at best." He took a sip of the drink, grimaced as he swallowed, and shook his head. "No. I must try for the best terms I can get from the government. Last month, some Yaqui and Mayo wanted to sue for peace and leave. I had their leaders executed to assert my authority. I cannot have desertions. There can be only one leader in a struggle such as this." He sighed and looked down at the scarred surface of the wooden table. "Now I fear they were right. Only their timing was wrong."

Chaz reached across the table and took his hand in hers. "You are right, of course. A leader must retain authority, else all is anarchy. What you are trying to do here will benefit all the Yaqui and the Mayo."

His deep brown eyes met her gaze. "At tremendous cost. But all wars have tremendous cost, do they not? Fortunately, the government is unaware of our precarious situation. I managed to bring in some food and rifles, but now I'm forced to close some roads from the river. I allow only those I trust to leave to buy arms and ammunition."

Chaz squeezed his hand. "We are with you. My men can help, give you more time."

"*Sí*, Charissa. And I thank God you made this effort." Cajame thumped hard on the tabletop, causing the glasses to bounce about. "Pedro! Food! My *sobrina* is hungry, as is her *lobo*." Fuerte, lying beneath the table on Chaz's feet, banged his tail on the floor.

"Yellow fever?" Dillon shook his head and backed away from the door of the largest cabin, which turned out to be an infirmary filled to the gills with sick and dying men. Raúl was on Dillon's heels, and Dillon bumped into the boy.

"Don't go in there," he said to Raúl. He grabbed the boy's elbow and hustled him away from the building. *A yellow fever epidemic.* That explained the lack of men in the fort. They'd walked right into a contagious nightmare. Alec stood across the way, talking with Salvatore. Hauling Raúl with him, Dillon strode up to the two men.

"Do you know they have yellow fever?" Dillon asked.

"Along with little food and no medicine," Alec said with a nod. "Cajame has less than four hundred men, and half of those are too sick to fight. His food stores will last no more than a few weeks."

"Well," Dillon said, "that tears it. We have to get out of here before we catch the fever or starve. A hundred-odd extra men with no provisions ain't gonna help this Cajame."

"I agree," Salvatore said, "but Chaz will never desert and leave Cajame to his fate."

"Then we'll take her," Dillon said. "Once the

government troops overrun this stockade, it won't take them long to figure out who Chaz really is, what with that damned wolf-dog and all. Then they'll hang her. They may make peace with Cajame, but they'll never let *La Lobo Fantasma* slip through their fingers."

Raúl scrunched up his face as though he'd processed only part of what Dillon said. "Take her?"

"You know, hogtie her, throw her across a horse, and beat leather for Asilo."

Alec tossed up his head with a short laugh. "And is this something *you* will do, señor West?"

Dillon scowled. "If I have to. But I'm hoping I'll have some help."

"She will kill you," Alec said.

"Maybe," Dillon replied, "but not before I get a rope on her and get her shed of this place."

"I will speak with Cajame," Salvatore said. "Perhaps he can make her see the sense of her leaving. Any men who wish to remain behind may stay. The rest we will take with us."

When he began to walk off, Dillon called after him, "Keep our plan under your hat. Don't let her know what we have in mind. For this to work, we have to take her by surprise."

After Salvatore left, Alec said, "You realize, do you not, that she will never agree."

Dillon responded with a slow nod. "I'm thinking the same way. Better go get my rope."

"Leave? We only just arrived. I am no coward to desert my friends and family at the slightest sign of trouble." The men, Salvatore, Cajame, Raúl, Alec, and Dillon surrounded Chaz, and she bristled at their stiff postures and rigid jaws projecting an intimidating front. But they were crazy if they thought she would simply turn about and leave Cajame and his rebels to be taken prisoner by General Carbó. If the rebels were fortunate, the general would force them into labor in the mines owned by Díaz's foreign investors. If they were not as fortunate, they would swing on ropes at the crossroads alongside murderers and thieves.

"Slightest provocation?" Dillon said in a comeback, hands planted firmly on his hips, body leaning forward aggressively. "Yellow fever? Your only son, Raúl, in danger of dying from disease or a bullet to the head? Over five thousand government soldiers holding this flimsy fort hostage? No medicine, no weapons, no ammunition. Any of this make sense?"

"He is right, Charissa," Cajame said more calmly than Dillon had expressed himself. Still, tension radiated from his stiff body and voice. "I am grateful for your attempt at assistance, but it is too little too late. We are running out of food. I cannot sustain even my men. Now I have over a hundred more mouths to feed."

Frustration ran like a river through her. "We will get more food. You said you kept open several paths to the river. I'll take out a small patrol and bring back food."

"Charissa?" Dillon said. Confusion tangled in his voice and expression. "Your name is Charissa?"

Chaz made a small, dismissive movement with her hand. Dillon could ask such irrelevant questions at times.

"That will not solve the problems here, Chaz," Salvatore said. "The men also need medicine, guns, and ammunition."

"And," Cajame added, "although you might get out, you could never get safely back with wagons."

"You must listen to him," Alec added. "We cannot chance your capture by government troops."

Chaz could no longer countenance this mutiny. "I will not discuss this any further. We stay. That is my decision. I will choose the men to make a foray for food, medicine, guns, and ammunition. If we cannot use wagons, we will use horses." She pushed past them and

burst through the doorway into the waning sunlight
outside the cabin. Dusk was coming swiftly on the heels
of afternoon, and a late-day breeze brought in the scents
of the river, pine trees, and sage growing on the plain
beyond the forest. However, it failed to dispel the odor
of sickness coming from the infirmary. Perhaps the
men were right, and she should leave. *No.* She'd fought
hard for her status as leader of Asilo. She could not now
allow others to make decisions for her. After assessing
the situation, she could reverse her order if necessary
without losing her leadership position.

Days passed, then a week. Three of her men came
down with the fever, and Chaz did not change her
mind. In spite of the losses and deprivation, she saw her
numbers making a difference in the defense. If not for her
men, Cajame would have lost the fort by now.

As Chaz checked on her men, Dillon emerged on
the edge of her vision in the pale light of dawn, but she
was in no mood to argue again with a hired gun hand.
Then the sharp report of rifle fire came from the walkway
above her, and the scent of gunpowder mingled with
the aroma of horses, sickness, and the forest. Two bullets
sailed over the wall and chipped the bark from the log
house beside her. General Carbó had pulled back his
main force to the edges of the forest and the far bank of
the Rio Yaqui, but snipers continually reminded the fort's
defenders they were under siege.

"Don't you ever duck?" Dillon said, drawing closer.
"The Roman gods might have been immortal, but you're
not. Have some sense, Chaz."

"*Silencio*, pistolero," she said as she turned and faced
him. "I have felt the sting of lead before, and I am still
alive."

"For now," he said glumly. "But if you stay here, that
government general will be stretching your neck before
long." He tilted his head to one side and peered intently
at her. "*Then* how will you rob Thorne's trains? Is it all

over, Chaz? Have you given up because of some damned
stubbornness?"

Jesu, the man was infuriating. "You talk too much,
pistolero. And you speak of what you have no
knowledge. If you wish to leave, then leave. Go! *¡Salir!* I
do not need you."

When Dillon stepped closer, she felt the urge to take
a step back, but she held her ground. "Stop there," she
said. "You have turned my men against me and tried to
coerce me into doing what you want. I will not stand for
it."

Dillon shook his head, rested a hand on the gouges
made in the log wall by the rifle bullets, and his voice
grew soft and silky. "You're wrong, Chaz. It was a
mutual decision. We asked Cajame to speak to you alone,
but I think he's a bit intimidated by you, as are most men.
I apologize if we've made you uncomfortable."

"And you, señor West, are you intimidated by me?"

"No, darlin', I'm fascinated by you." He moved away
from the wall and drew closer.

His words left her speechless, and something cracked
inside her, a part of that icy casing around her heart. She
fought it to no avail.

"Damn," he said suddenly. He dropped his gaze and
examined the palm of one hand. "I caught a splinter from
those logs." He whipped off his bandana and wrapped it
about the hand. "I'm gonna need your help getting this
out. Come here." His words were a low plea, almost a
whisper.

Chaz shook her head to dispel the enchantment his
voice weaved about her like silken ropes. "Why? You are
perfectly capable of tending your own wound."

One corner of his mouth kicked up in a wry smile.
"Come on, Chaz. It's your fault I'm wounded. The least
you can do is fish out this piece of log. I swear it must
be six inches long. Makes me queasy just to look at it.
Please." Dillon held out his hand.

"This is ridiculous. What would my men think to see us holding hands?"

"To hell with your men."

Chaz reached out and allowed him to enclose her slim hand in his larger one. "This is loco," she mumbled. "But I can see nothing with this bandana covering it."

"Now closer," he said and slowly pulled her toward him.

Chaz busied herself in trying to unwind the bandana. The edges were caught between her hand and his. "You must let go if you want me to tend to this."

"It was just an excuse, *querida*," he whispered. "You were right. I wanted only to hold your hand."

She resisted at first then allowed herself to be drawn into his embrace. Dillon did not kiss her, which she expected and might have rebuffed, but pressed her against his broad, warm chest. What was it about this man, above all others, that had her quivering so, that made her want to be in his arms? Why could she not fight this feeling? His breath felt moist on her neck, and his hands moved her arms behind her back, pressing her body against his.

"I'm surely sorry about this," he said on a sigh.

"For what?" she whispered, relaxing into the embrace.

"This." Cold iron clicked on one wrist, then on the other.

Nueve

Chaz howled with outrage, and men came running from all parts of the fort. She lashed out with her feet, and when Dillon crushed her to his chest, she tried to take a chunk out of him with her teeth, so he pushed her away and backed up.

Fuerte came like a bullet out of the torchlight. *Damn*, Dillon had forgotten about the dog. Seemed Fuerte's loyalty to him didn't extend to manhandling Chaz. "Raúl!" he shouted. "Grab that animal!"

Chaz hissed like a cornered panther. "Trust you? You son of a *puta*! Just when I thought I... I could... I will pluck and split you like a prairie chicken, Dillon West!" She threw a desperate look at her men, who now formed a semicircle around her and Dillon.

"I am *La Lobo Fantasma*, The Ghost Wolf, your leader, your family. This man is nothing!" She spat in his direction. "Release me at once. I command it."

Several men looked unsure and began to step forward. Then a man pushed his way through the circle. "No, Charissa!" Cajame said, his voice a hurricane of sound. "This is my fort, my stand, and *I* am the leader of all within it. Señor West is not at fault. I gave the order to have you restrained and removed from the fort. I provided the irons for your wrists, and señor West carried out the deed because…because we felt he could take you by surprise and secure you without harm. In three days I will make terms with General Carbó. You must be far from this location by that time. I will not allow him to hang you. If you are here, more blood will be shed, and we have little of it left."

Cajame approached and took her chin in his fingers, lifting her face to him. "Will you go peacefully, *mi sobrina*, or will you be tied to a horse? The decision is yours."

"Here is where you will leave," Cajame said. They stood side by side on the walkway overlooking the wall. When Chaz's army first arrived at El Añil, it had appeared as if the fort occupied an isolated island in a sea of cleared forest, only bare ground leading up to the walls. But in Dillon's initial inspection, he found an impenetrable thorn thicket spreading outward from the rear of the fort and pressing against the logs. Why the defenders left the thicket intact made obvious sense. No army could penetrate its dense tangle and piercing thorns. With the thicket guarding the rear wall, in the event of an all-out assault, Cajame's men had only to defend the front and sides. Now Cajame pointed out beyond the thicket.

"The river lies in that direction, just past the line of cottonwoods. General Carbó does not bother to station men on this bank of the river because of the thorn thicket. He knows it is as impossible for us to negotiate as it is for his men."

"I'm with the general," Dillon said. "I don't know how you expect us to make it through those thorns with our hides intact."

Cajame wagged a finger and smiled. "Ah, *mi amigo*,

that is because you do not know my secret. You will not go through the thorns but beneath them."

Dillon braced his hands on the wall and looked down on the thicket. The logs rose to a height of twenty feet or so, and the thicket came to three-quarters of the way up. The thicket was so dense he couldn't make out the ground beneath it.

"You have a tunnel under the thorns?" Salvatore asked, voicing Dillon's thoughts.

"Only a few of my most trusted aides know of this route," Cajame said as he nodded. "We still have those within our army who wish to make their own terms with the general. This tunnel is of my own devising. I will make peace with Carbó, for the sake of my men, but I will not allow his *Federales* to take me. When the time comes to open the gates of El Añil, I will leave through the tunnel. This war is not at an end, and I will carry on from another location."

Dillon looked into the man's swarthy face, "If you're not among the prisoners, won't Carbó take revenge on those who surrender? Seems to me he'll turn the surrender into a massacre."

"No." Cajame shook his head. "The general may be a *Federale*, and we have fought on opposite sides, but he is an honorable man and no *rurale*. If he promises safe passage for my people, he will keep his word."

Cajame showed them the entrance to the tunnel. It lay beneath the dirt floor of an unremarkable shack that held hogsheads of lard. They helped him roll the barrels to one side, revealing an enormous trapdoor that appeared to be simply another section of flooring. Once they opened the wooden flap, instead of steps leading downward, a wide dirt ramp sloped at a gradual angle into the darkness below. The opening in the floor and the ramp were large enough to accommodate a horse. Cajame lit a torch and disappeared into the earthen-walled passage. When they reached the bottom and moved out into the air, weak sunlight filtered through the chinks of logs that formed the sides and roof of the tunnel, separating it from the thorns. A few tendrils wormed their way through, grabbing at their clothing, and Cajame pulled out his machete to chop away at these encroachers.

"Nature seeks always to gain entrance," he said, "so vigilance is ever necessary to keep the way open."

"What does the other end look like?" Dillon asked when they halted but a few feet into the domed tunnel.

"You will find a door close to the point where the thicket ends. The branches grow up and around it, and it opens inward. You will have to use the machete to carve a path the last few feet into the trees." A brief grin flashed across his mouth. "It is good, no?"

The men exchanged grins. "It is good, *sí*," Salvatore said.

Chaz refused to speak to Cajame or any of her men, but to Dillon's relief, she seemed resigned to leave peacefully. Her silence served as a rebuke to all who'd usurped her command, and she reserved her coldest manner for Dillon, the man who'd betrayed her. He accepted it as a small price to pay for her safety, Raúl's, and his own.

They departed that night under black mountains of clouds rising up and obscuring the moon. When the horses balked at the tunnel, they blindfolded them. Once again, the mounts wore sacking about their hooves and muzzles to prevent any inadvertent noise that would betray them to stray patrols. Cajame assured them that soldiers eschewed the riverbank along the thicket, but Salvatore would take no unnecessary risk. After cutting their way out of the thorns, they piled the branches up in the hole they made, thus disguising the exit once again. On foot, they led the horses in an easterly direction beneath the cottonwoods. They passed as silently as the owls and bats dipping as blacker shadows through the night sky, trolling for unwary mice in the leaf litter and night insects on the wing.

A mile or so from the fort and the site of the siege, they mounted up and galloped through cultivated areas and onto the plains. Two days brought them into the foothills of the Sierra Madre Occidental, and they passed out of Sonora into the state of Chihuahua. There they veered south, following the edge of the mountain chain.

Dillon had argued with himself from the time they left the thicket. United States territory beckoned, and the thought of spiriting The Ghost Wolf across the border continued to seem like a viable option and an end to this messy affair. He figured he would find it relatively easy. Chaz always laid her bedroll off at a distance from her men. He could have silenced her in the night soon after leaving the fort, lashed her to a horse, and headed out north. He'd spent a goodly amount of time in Sonora and knew the passes and shortcuts. Chaz and her men had traveled through the area only a few times. By dawn, he could put twenty miles between them. Even though Dillon still didn't know the location of her hidden silver — and he convinced himself there *was* hidden silver — he could collect the remainder of his bounty…if he wanted to.

So why don't you? Why do you hesitate? Was it related to the mystery of the woman herself, why she became The Ghost Wolf and why she robbed only Thorne's silver? He couldn't quite unravel that knotted mystery. At this moment, his desire to understand his reluctance to carry through with his commission and figure out Chaz's connection to Thorne weighed more than the lure of Thorne's money and the silver. He could afford to wait a while; he could put off his dream of a ranch in Colorado — a few more weeks, or months — until he fed his curiosity about why she'd singled out Justus Thorne for financial ruin. At least, that's the excuse Dillon gave himself for his lack of action.

Chaz continued her seething in silence, a silence so uncharacteristic of The Ghost Wolf, that Salvatore, Raúl, and Dillon wore perpetually concerned frowns. But waves of anger rolled through her like thunder on the plains, and none dared approach her. Then a week after they entered the foothills, Raúl fell ill and reeled in his saddle. Chaz rode up beside him and steadied him with a hand.

"What is it?" she asked, her first words to any of the company since leaving Cajame's domain. "Are you tired? Would you prefer that we camp here?"

Without answering, Raúl toppled off his horse. Chaz reached out to catch his arm to prevent him from hitting the ground and failed. Although she screamed inside, the vocalization came out only as a strangled cry. She threw herself from Niebla, ran to her son, and dropped on the ground beside him. Panic clawed at her guts, and she rested her hand on his forehead then looked up, searching for the others, who spurred their horses toward her.

"He is burning with fever." Her heart drummed hard and threatened to escape the confines of her chest. "What have I done? It is the *vomito prieto*! I know it is. I have killed him!"

Fuerte was the first to her side, and he hovered over Chaz and Raúl, licking the boy's face. If a dog could have a worried expression, Fuerte's drooping eyes and the whine in his throat reflected just such an emotion. Alec arrived closely on the dog's heels, as he had ridden just ahead of her and Raúl. Coming down on his knees beside her, he briefly examined the boy for telltale signs of the onset of the yellow fever. "I do not think this is *vomito prieto, chiquita*. He has fever but no vomiting. It

more resembles the *tres-días* fever." His words told her
nothing; the three-day fever was a catchall name that
covered every incidence of short-lived fever of unknown
origin.
    "No!" Chaz shook her head violently. Her braid
unraveled, and the strands flew wildly about her head
and into her eyes. "It is *vomito prieto.* He caught it from
Cajame's men at the fort. I have killed him." *Life without
her son?* A fist clenched her heart, tears sprang to her
eyes, and her sorrow seemed bottomless. She had
willingly exposed her only child—the only child she
would ever have—to the deadly sickness. And when
Salvatore and Dillon, even Cajame and Raúl, had applied
to her to leave the fort, she'd refused them. Now, for her
arrogance, God would take her only treasure from her.
    "No," Alec said, trying again to make her listen to his
words. "Release him, Chaz, and let me see to him." But
she would not. Alec did not know what she knew, that
God was not a loving presence in her life but a vengeful
one. She shoved Alec away and pulled Raúl into her
arms. The tears remained trapped in her eyes, but a dry
sobbing burst from her throat. She rocked back and forth
as she cradled her dying son tightly to her chest. *¡Por
Dios! How could I have let this happen?*
    A stinging slap to her cheek took her by surprise and
jerked back her head. Hands clutched her shoulders, tore
her away from Raúl, and hauled her to her feet. Chaz
spun about, breaking the hold, one hand half-drawing
the skinning knife from its sheath at her waist, the other
balled into a fist. Dillon stood before her, his feet braced
apart, his body drawn up to its fullest height, which
at best, was only a few inches more than hers. His face
held a wary look, as well it might, seeing as she planned
to carve it from the bone. For a second, in her rage at
Dillon's interference, her thoughts left Raúl.
    Dillon held up his hands, palms facing outward.
"Take a breath, Chaz. Let Alec do what he can for Raúl.

You're hysterical, and in that mood, you can't do the boy any good."

Chaz glanced back at Alec, who had dragged Raúl beneath the shade of a hickory tree and was stripping off the boy's clothing.

"Sorry about the blow," Dillon added, "but I had to get your attention. You weren't of a mind to listen to reason."

Her tongue cleaved to the roof of her mouth. When he slanted his head to one side, his eyes asked the question as to what she planned to do with the knife. Chaz drove it home in the sheath and turned her back, walking over to Alec and Raúl, and Salvatore, who had now joined them.

Calmness settled over her nerves, her *hysteria*, as Dillon called it. Chaz would have used the word *demencia*. But it was the same. In believing she'd caused the death of her son, she'd experienced a temporary madness. Dillon was right in striking her. Had he not, she would have held Raúl in her arms until he died. Although she still assumed Raúl had contracted the yellow fever, she reined in her terror and willed herself to see what Salvatore and Alec could do for him. Some survived the fever. *One in a hundred.* Had she lived such an exemplary life God would spare Raúl? *Of course not.* She stole and killed, and no matter the weight of the penance the priest gave her to complete, her sins lay too gravely on her soul to forgive. Inside, she died, while outwardly, she remained silent and let the men go about their work.

"Look," Alec said, turning to Chaz. "The bite of the hairy spider, a tarantula." He pointed to a swollen red area on Raúl's calf. "This bite is not deadly but painful and explains the fever."

To Chaz, the tarantula was a familiar denizen of the desert. A shy creature, it seldom bit. But if trapped inside a bedroll... No, a bite was too convenient and too unlikely. Anyway, the puncture more likely came from a thorn Raúl picked up in the thicket tunnel. A more plausible answer was the yellow fever. She struggled to focus on Salvatore, who had already gathered some leaves and was chewing them into a mass. Her inner turmoil and racing thoughts screamed through her like a sharp wind, made her doubt, proclaimed his efforts would be useless, that she would lost her son through her careless actions. She could barely restrain herself as he placed the leaves over the wound.

"To draw the poison," he said. "We will rest here for a few days until the fever is gone."

"Yes," she answered. The words sounded wooden to her ears, and surely she was going mad to pray that such a simple remedy would cure her son. It could not be so. While Salvatore and Alec wrapped the leg, Dillon came up beside her and rested a hand on her shoulder, squeezing lightly. "He'll be fine," he said.

"Yes," Chaz said. She made a small dismissive move with her hand and battled the wave of dread that swept over her and threatened to pull her under.

"I'm worried about Chaz," Dillon said to Salvatore when they halted to rest in a meadow buried in the shadow of the mountains. All about them, piñon jays and bobwhite threw their songs into the still air.

"Ah, you noticed," Salvatore said. "I thought you oblivious or perhaps in a stupor."

Dillon's shoulders stiffened. "Of course I noticed. It's as plain as the spots on a pinto. Didn't see any sense in bringing it up before now. I thought she'd come out of it once Raúl recovered. Even Raúl's teasing her about mistaking a spider's bite for yellow fever hasn't made an impression. She's eating next to nothing and getting as thin as an aspen. It occurred to me maybe she's sick."

"Sick at heart, not yet in body," Salvatore said with

a frown. "You must understand what she has been through. When Charissa came to us, she was fifteen and frightened of her own shadow. She had to overcome many obstacles to gain her leadership and the respect of the men. She is family, but she is also an outsider, a mestizo. Her blood is mixed—Yaqui, Spanish, and American. Her son is also of mixed blood. The Yaqui value pure blood. For a long time, many would not accept her. She is not as confident or hardened as she appears on the outside. Now she feels we have taken control away from her. It is a betrayal, more egregious because it comes from family. Then Raúl's sickness made her realize what she had done in taking her son into that fort."

"Hell, that's a hairbrained idea," Dillon said, shaking his head. "None of us knew the fort had yellow fever, and anyway, Raúl didn't catch it. Chaz knows we did what we did for her safety and that of Raúl. How can she hold it as a betrayal?"

Salvatore let out his breath on a long sigh. "Nonetheless…" He nodded to where Chaz sat alone at the base of a pine, her head pillowed on her crossed arms over bent knees. Clouds scudding across the sun made her image flicker, as though she were only a figment of Dillon's imagination. Fuerte sat beside her, as still and silent as his master. "Speak with her, Dillon. Raúl and I have tried, but she seems not to hear us."

"And you think she'll listen to me? Hell, she hates me as much as she loves silver."

Salvatore's features creased into a smile. "Hate is a complicated emotion, señor West. Try. I believe she will listen."

Dillon strolled over to where Chaz sat. "Mind if I share your tree?"

When Chaz looked up, her blue eyes appeared dull, lifeless, and she gave a careless shrug. "Why?"

"Why not?"

She frowned and scooted over.

Dillon settled on the ground on the opposite side from Fuerte, his back against the tree, his knees drawn up. "Chaz—"

She stopped him. "I will not talk about what happened. This is a private matter."

"Okay, then let's talk about something else."

"I am not certain I want to talk at all, especially with you."

Keep pushing, Dillon. He had to convince himself that eventually she would open up. Perhaps if he ambled instead of galloping head-on, he could pierce that armor surrounding her in a roundabout way. "What do you want to do after all this?" he asked, lifting his arm with a sweeping gesture.

Her head turned toward him, and this time, he detected a subtle spark of life. "After all what?"

"All this—robbing trains, stealing silver, consorting with the likes of Cajame and Carranza. When the mines run dry and the trains stop running and the rebels no longer need you. You know Carranza's winding down his frontal attacks on Díaz and turning to politics. Someday he'll be *El Presidente.* Raúl's fast growing into a man, and he'll be leaving you, searching for a woman who's not his mother. What will you do then?"

Chaz looked thoughtful, and Dillon had hope that, in some small way, he'd gotten through to her. "What will I do then? I hadn't really thought about it. It will never really be over, even after I… And you are right about Carranza. His political ambitions now outweigh his revolutionary fervor. However, I suppose I will remain at Asilo, pick jalapenos when they are ripe, and make tortillas with Delicia. And some day I will grow old and lonely, because by that time, those I care about will have passed on or left me. Also, I will pray often for my soul, beg God to forgive me for what I have done."

"Do you need all that much forgiveness?"

"Do you not think so? I have killed many men."

"Well, I suppose you could say a few prayers for me, too. I'm not really the praying kind, and I haven't exactly led a saintly life."

Her small smile warmed his heart. "Yes, señor West, I will also pray for your soul. And what will you do, after all of this?" Chaz mirrored the sweeping gesture he'd made.

"After all what?"

"All this — robbing trains, stealing silver, and consorting with the likes of the notorious Ghost Wolf. What will you do when I need your services no longer? Will you move on to some other employer? Will you meet your end by the gun? As you know, that is the fate of gun hands."

A grin tugged at his mouth, and he allowed it access. "Unlike you, I have a plan, had one for a long time. I bought a piece of the prettiest land you ever did see in a valley in Colorado, near Boulder. Sweet water, lush meadow for horses and cattle, and a thick stand of spruce on a rise that overlooks the stream and the valley. I'll build my house there and settle down, create an empire."

"Alone?" Her voice sounded wistful, but her expression remained neutral.

"Naw. I'll want a wife, naturally, and a passel of children. An empire makes no sense if I can't pass it on to family."

"I see," she said quietly. "And have you picked out señora West?"

"Well, there's this red-haired schoolmarm I ran across in Tucson in '79. But she's a mite short for me, comes only to my collarbone. Thought she was a dwarf when I first saw her. Course, height don't matter much when you're lying down, belly to belly. Her hips are kinda narrow, not built much for child-bearing. And she has this sharp, turned-up little nose that always makes her look like she's smelling a skunk. Don't know if I can go through the rest of my life not knowing if my wife's expression is a result of her unfortunate nose or if I oughta wash out my socks and union suit."

Chaz laughed and rose to her feet, brushing off the leaves from the seat of her pants with one hand. The dog rose with her and shook his shaggy coat. "She sounds as if she is perfect, this red-haired schoolmarm with the sharp nose. When we are through here, I hope she is still waiting for you."

He reached up and grasped her hand, keeping her from walking off. "When *will* we be through, Chaz? What are you really up to? I don't swallow for a minute this silver-for-rebellion act. Sure, that's *what* you do, but it's not *why* you do it. Somehow, Thorne's at the bottom of whatever you're looking for. Why, Chaz? What's the last act of this deadly little play of yours?"

Shutters closed over her face. She pulled her hand from his grasp and walked away without answering. With one longsuffering look at Dillon, Fuerte followed her.

After speaking with Dillon, Chaz emerged from her shell a bit, like a turtle testing the air for the presence of a hunting coati. She still retreated into black moods, times when an unutterable despair seemed to claim her, but she did speak, and her appetite picked up.

As Chihuahua State gradually gave way to Durango, the riders closed in on the trail that would turn west and cross the pass in the mountains. The morning before that change in direction, they came within a couple of miles of a large *aidea* where they planned to stop for a day or two to buy provisions for the arduous trek across the Sierra Madre. They were strung out in a line, and Angelo and Raúl rode ahead to greet the *aideanos* and assess the village stores.

In a scattering of dust and brush, Angelo suddenly

exploded over the hill ahead at a dead run. He sawed on his horse's mouth and came to a sliding stop beside Chaz. Fuerte, who was loping along at Niebla's side, released a surprised bark and jumped out of the way to keep from being trampled by Angelo's horse.

"*Rurales*," he panted, as winded as his horse. "Two, three hundred, heavily armed. They are burning the *edificios*."

Chaz's heart dropped to her stirrups. "Raúl?" she said, looking eastward to where a dark smudge stained the sky. Originally, she'd taken it for thunderclouds. Now she envisioned her child lying dead in a pool of blood.

"He is safe, watching from the shelter of an abandoned estancia along the road. The *rurales* have gathered up the strong men and are holding them in a corral at the far end of the town. The young women and children are kept separate, locked in the hacienda of the local *jefe*. The old ones..." Angelo choked and gasped for breath. "The old ones, they already shot and piled in the square."

The drought that had afflicted Chaz since they left Sonora lifted. Like a blossom soaking up the first rains of spring, she came to life, the fierce Ghost Wolf once more.

Sweeping her arm in a wide arc, she said, "Alec! Take your men and approach from the left. Salvatore, go right and into the cottonwood grove that bounds the creek bed. Dillon, stay with me. We will ride right up the middle. When you hear our gunfire, come in from the sides. Do not allow any of these dogs to escape. They will pay for the dead with their own lives."

The men complied, split off from the main body, and thundered across the rocky ground to their ordered positions. Chaz checked the men left behind her—about thirty hardened fighters, good men all. Regardless of what had happened in El Añil, she realized she still had their loyalty, and their fierceness made her heart beat

faster. With such men at her side once again, she could
not fail.

"Rifles as we move in, and then pistols. Be careful
you do not shoot those we are to save."

The men nodded, a few calling out, "*Sí, Jefe.*" Reins
tightened, horses danced in the dust, and rifles slid from
saddle scabbards. The prospect of a battle against a larger
force brought out grins on mustachioed faces.

Chaz pulled out her rifle, checked the load, and
urged Niebla into a gallop. Dillon's horse pounded right
behind her. She twisted at the waist to look back. The
ends of Dillon's serape fluttered and streamed in the
wind, and a worried expression sat on his face. If she
had taken the time to do other than give him his orders,
he would have argued, said, "Two or three hundred?
That's three to one odds." However, what worry had
she for odds? Every one of her men was worth at least
three *rurales—rústico,* cowardly swine who fought only
for plunder and ran when faced with a real fight. When
Dillon raised the hand clutching his rifle in a little wave
then settled his hat lower on his head, a smile played
on her mouth. She faced forward to the smoke from the
burning buildings that billowed into the heavens ahead,
forming a pall over the *aidea.*

The main road snaked past the adobe estancia
where Raúl waited. He swung out from behind a line of
tumbled walls and spurred his horse into a run, angling
into the column behind Chaz. Fur flying, Fuerte streamed
off to one side and out of the way of the horses' hooves.

"Let's get them!" Raúl shouted. He swept off his
sombrero and swung it in the air.

Chaz dropped back beside him. "Caution, *niño.* You
will kill no one with that hat. Either drop it or put it back
on your head. Fight with your guns instead. Follow my
orders and stay behind me and Dillon."

"Of course, *Madre,*" he replied with a wide grin.
He slapped the sombrero back on his head and yanked

his rifle from the saddle boot. "But another chance to kill *rurales*! *¡Qué divertido!* I wager I kill more than you, Emilio!"

Emilio, a bear of a man in his mid-fifties, with a barrel chest and a long, thick mustache that drooped to inches below his jowls, had fought with Chaz since she took on the name of *La Lobo Fantasma*, long before the child, Raúl, could even sit a horse. Exposure to the harsh sun and wind of the *altoplano* had etched a map of lines and sculpted hollows across his face. At Raúl's taunt, Emilio scowled and smacked his rifle across the rump of Raúl's horse.

" *¡Silencio, niño!*"

Raúl's horse hopped sideways, and he had all he could do to stay in the saddle.

Chaz laughed, kicked Niebla, and she leapt ahead of the others, taking the lead.

The smoldering ruins of casas on either side of the road told the story of the *rurale* raid. Chaz had seen many *aideas* such as the one they now entered. The people who lived here would lead a peaceful life, mostly farmers, with a few businesses in the town district. Their deep reverence for the religion brought to Mexico by the Spanish showed its roots in a beautiful church, a catedral dating back hundreds of years and lovingly tended, which anchored the eastern end of the settlement. The *jefe's* sprawling hacienda, a long, low adobe house of graceful elegance, sat at the western end. The main area of destruction lay between the two distinctive structures.

Flames consumed the adobe buildings from the inside out and sent a rain of sparks upward that ignited additional blazes when they landed. Spreading smoke impeded the progress of Chaz's men, and cinders dropped about them like burning hail, spooking the horses. Chaz stayed steadfastly in the lead. When the first *rurales* came into view, she raised her rifle and put down two men. The loot they had taken from a store spilled from their arms, and boxes of canned goods and barrels of flour bounced and rolled across the street. Niebla vaulted over the obstacles and landed with a jarring thud on the other side. Chaz never stopped firing. She switched to pistols and found flesh with every shot. Behind her, Dillon's and Raúl's pistols spit lead in a regular pattern, and drove back those they failed to kill or wound. Chaz ignored the bullets spinning past her, tugging at her jacket, and she dimly heard Dillon shouting at her to get down. However, this was a holy battle, and an invincible power filled her.

The corpses of the village elders lay ahead in a grisly pile of sprawled limbs and bloodied bodies. Fury rose up in her blood. *God forgive those who did this, for I cannot.* That the lives of good, innocent people should be wasted in such wanton devastation, as though they were no more than offal to be tossed into a refuse heap.

Her pistols empty, Chaz grabbed her rifle. She dropped from Niebla's back while the horse was still galloping down the street, and darted into the shelter of a doorway. Behind her, fire raged inside the building, and the heat of the blaze baked her back. She slapped at a cinder that dropped on her arm and smothered the flames. Quickly, she loaded the pistols and the rifle, glanced about for Raúl and Fuerte, and spotted them together farther into the *aidea.*

Dillon suddenly appeared beside her and threw his back against the door. With nimble fingers, he fed bullets into his pistols and put them away, one in his holster and the other wedged beneath his belt. The remainder of her men had ridden past them, and Salvatore and Alec and their riders were closing in from the sides.

"Any ideas?" Dillon asked while loading his rifle with cartridges from the bandolier that formed an X across his chest.

"Yes," she replied and slewed her gaze to his grim-set face. "We go from house to house toward the hacienda and kill anyone who gets in our way. The other men will take care of those left out in the open. The *rurales* will not murder the women and children unless they realize they are losing and have no hope of escape. They will hold them as long as possible to bargain for their own lives."

Dillon raised a brow. "*Are* they losing?"

Chaz ducked, pulling Dillon down with her when a bullet flew out of nowhere and nearly took off her hat. It buried itself in the wood door behind them. "Of course. And now you owe me for your life."

"A kiss for luck?" he asked as he still crouched on one knee, his eyes on hers.

She stared at him with arched brows, incredulous. "Now?"

"No time like the present." Taking her chin in his fingertips, Dillon pulled her face to his and drank from her lips. When he released her, a grin spread across his mouth. "Like hate and love, danger and passion stir up the same emotions."

"You are loco," she said and grinned in spite of herself. But he was right. His kiss ignited a sudden fire inside her that blazed as fiercely as the ones consuming the *aidea*. Chaz forced herself to stop smiling like a lovesick calf and composed her features. "Come," she said. "We have much to do and many men to kill."

Progress toward the hacienda involved slipping from doorway to doorway. Many *rurales* had taken refuge inside buildings the fire had not yet reached, and Chaz and Dillon shot through windows and burst through doorways, rolling across the floors and ducking behind furniture and store shelves. Their fierce assault left a trail of bodies behind them, and Chaz exulted at each *rurale soldado* she sent to hell. Dillon muttered in a continual monologue behind her, so close he crowded her and bumped against her.

"Give me room," she hissed then fell to the floor,

shoved from behind and covered by a large, heavy weight. Bullets whipped over their bodies.

"I'd do that, *querida*," he said in her ear, his hot breath searing her, "if you'd watch what you're doing and what's behind you. Those *soldados* ain't firing tamales, ya know."

"Get off me, you *zote*. You are crushing the breath from me."

The weight eased then slowly lifted from her back. Dillon caught her elbow and pulled her to her feet. "Now careful," he said gruffly. "Slow and easy will get us where we're going in one piece. You barge ahead again, like a blind pig through a burning barn, and I'll tie you up and stash you in a dark corner. Come back for you later. And now you owe me."

Her silent, searching look examined his face, the taut muscles in his jaw and the hard line of his lips. "Is that concern I hear in your voice, señor West?"

Dillon seemed taken aback, and then his stern expression returned. "Hell no, señora. It's purely survival instinct. With your guns backing up mine, I have a better chance of getting out of this alive. So just…just be careful." His face relaxed again, and a tender look surfaced in his gaze.

"*Sí*," she said softly. "I will be careful. I would not want to lose a good gun hand." Silently, Chaz admitted she wouldn't want to lose Dillon. He was nothing to her, other than a dead shot with pistol and rifle, but the thought of his death brought a strange, dull pain to her chest, a tightening to her throat. She pulled herself together. "We have to move on."

"Yeah," he said with a nod. "Me first. You guard my rear."

Chaz shook her head. "No. I will take the lead."

With no further argument, he accepted her lead.

With Dillon behind her, Chaz passed the square where a battle waged between her men and the *rurales*.

Bullets flew like bats on a summer night, and the odor of expended gunpowder burned her nose and overwhelmed her senses. The screams of men and horses and guns spitting fire scorched her ears. Chaz turned away. She would not search again for Raúl among the combatants. For once, she must accept him for the man he nearly was and fix her mind on her own progress rather than his safety. The insight had come to her gradually that she could not protect him forever, especially after confronting his mortality when the tarantula had bitten him. The thought pained her, made her heart ache, to admit he was no longer a boy in need of mothering. But to become fully a man, Raúl must prove himself, gain confidence in his abilities. For him to do that, she knew she must learn to let go.

The hacienda of the *jefe* lay before them, no more than several hundred yards away. Guards paced along the long veranda and craned their necks toward the commotion coming from the square. Sunbeams pierced the parting clouds above and glinted off rifle barrels held tightly across chests.

A grove of spare-needled piñon pines swept around the west side of the hacienda and crept up nearly to the adobe walls. Rambling bougainvillea climbed the posts of the veranda, brilliant purple and red floral bracts spreading onto the roof and spilling over the eaves in a fiery cascade that mimicked the flames devouring the town. In a garden that filled the eastern side and circled around the front, plots of *chile* peppers, maize, tomatoes, and beans on wooden frames shared space with native red paintbrush and bright yellow cosmos.

Chaz and Dillon moved toward the trees. There they sat on their heels on the dry grass beneath the concealing branches that filtered the sunlight and threw lacy patterns on the ground. At shadowy figures creeping up on them from the other side of the grove, Chaz bolted up, rifle pointed toward the intruders.

"*Hola,*" a familiar voice whispered from behind the shelter of a tree.

"Raúl," Chaz said on an expelled breath. When Raúl approached, Furerte beside him, she restrained from gathering her son in her arms to assure herself he was uninjured. A bloody scrape creased his brow, and somewhere in the fight, he'd lost his sombrero. He appeared well enough, and excitement danced in his eyes. Largo lagged behind Raúl, his gaze scanning the area behind them. He took up position beside a tree and leaned his shoulder against the trunk.

"How goes the battle for the *aidea?*" Chaz asked, fighting hard to keep her voice calm.

With a grin on his youthful face, Raúl dropped onto the ground, crossing his legs and resting his rifle across his thighs. Fuerte collapsed too, clearly exhausted, a bit of the fur on his tail singed. He released a sigh and rested his head on Raúl's legs.

"As expected," Raúl said. "Only three of our men have serious wounds, Emilio among them. A bullet in the leg. He's being tended by Alec at the far end of this grove. The others penned up about fifty *rurales* in the church and are holding them at bay. Many fled, deserted like the cowards they are. Those who stood their ground in the square are dead."

She nodded. "*Bueno.* Then we have only to rid ourselves of these." Chaz pointed her rifle toward the hacienda. "But we will need more than four to get the hostages out alive. We must somehow convince the *rurales* to surrender, unless they wish us to kill them."

"I will bring some aid," Raúl said as he got to his feet. "Largo can stay here with you."

No! Not Raúl! Not now that he was safe here with her. Chaz fought the urge to say that Largo should go. He was more experienced than her son. In spite of this, she squelched the thought and held her tongue. "Go, then," she said instead. "Quickly. I wish to end this as soon as possible. Every minute we delay, the women and children come closer to death. When these men learn the battle is lost, they will threaten to kill those they hold. If we wait too long, they may decide the situation is beyond hope and will begin the killing."

Raúl slipped off into the darkness, and Dillon rested a hand against the small of Chaz's back. "What will you do with those *rurales* in the church?"

"I want to shoot them the way they executed the elders."

Dillon cocked a brow. "You won't, will you? You'll let them get away with their lives."

Will I? A vision arose of the bodies of the elders in the square. Chaz wanted nothing so much as to execute every living *rurale*. However, The Ghost Wolf had a reputation for mercy as well as charity, and deep inside, Chaz knew she could not simply murder them. Her soul had many sins to answer for; she could not add wanton killing to that burden. And if she did, what kind of example would that act set for Raúl?

"No." The word left her on a ragged sigh. "I will not. If those in the hacienda lay down their arms without harming the hostages, I will allow all of them to go," she said firmly. "As much as I wish for vengeance for what was done here this day, I cannot kill in cold blood. If they surrender, I will take their weapons, horses, and clothes, and set them to walk back to wherever they came from. Another day will come when I face them again. Then, when they have guns in their hands, I will kill them" — she paused for a harshly drawn breath — "but I will execute five of them, beginning with their officers, for every hostage they kill."

When Raúl returned with sixty men, Alec among them, Chaz stepped out from behind the trees, in view of the hacienda but out of pistol range. Alec stubbornly took up position beside her. Dillon brushed up against her other side, and the two men exchanged challenging glances. She sighed at their unspoken hostility and determination to be her sole protector, but her gaze quickly returned to the hacienda. The guards could still take her down with a rifle, but the sixty guns pointed at them emphasized the stupidity of any rash action. They immediately retreated inside the structure.

"You in the hacienda," Chaz called out. "I am the woman of *La Lobo Fantasma*. My *marido* has you surrounded with more than ninety pistoleros. Your compadres, those who are still alive, are in the church. If you throw down your guns now, we will release you. If you harm one woman or child, we will set this casa on fire and shoot anyone who tries to flee. Then we will fire the church. I swear to you that not one man will escape our wrath."

After a few minutes of silence from the hacienda, rifles and pistols flew out of windows and doors, littering the ground. Then the *rurales* exited, hands held high. As Chaz promised, the men were stripped and set out on the road. The women ran from the house, clutching the hands of small children and holding babies in their arms. Cries of " ¡*Mucho gracias, Salvador! ¡Los queremos, La Lobo Fantasma!*" poured from their throats. One woman, swathed in a rebozo and cradling an infant against her chest, ran to Chaz and threw herself to her knees. She looked up with an imploring look in her eyes.

"Please," she pleaded as tears bathed her face, "where is *La Lobo Fantasma*? I wish to kiss his hand in gratitude for coming to my rescue and that of my son."

Chaz raised the woman to her feet. "I will convey your thanks, señora. *La Lobo Fantasma* is occupied still in releasing the men from the corral and dealing with the remaining *rurales*."

With the women safely hidden in the grove and guarded by two of her men, Chaz moved to the church, where the same scene played out. Of the original three hundred *rurales*, fifty-two survived the day. Chaz lost only one man, who died from his wounds two days later as the band traversed the mountain pass across the Sierra Madre.

The battle for the *aidea* wrought a sea change in Chaz. Her confidence returned, and the spirit of The Ghost Wolf once again took up residence.

Diez

"Zacatecas?" Dillon shouted, so shaken his hands trembled. "You're actually thinking about going into Zacatecas for a raid on Thorne's silver stores?"

Lines of determination etched Chaz's face. "I am not thinking about it, I am doing it."

He opened his arms wide. "You're insane, lady. Zacatecas is filled with troops, and the silver is bound to be heavily guarded. If you have a death wish, at least consider the lives of your men and your son."

Chaz hissed an oath. "Unlike you, my men trust my judgment and follow my lead. You are free to go if you do not wish to accompany us."

Dillon noticed she made no mention of her men overruling her orders at El Añil. She seemed to have put it permanently from her mind. Couldn't blame her, he supposed. He'd probably have done the same. *But Zacatecas?*

He stepped closer and placed his face right in hers. "Perhaps I would if I knew my way out of this damned valley."

Chaz snapped her fingers. "Santiago, blindfold señor West and escort him out of the mountains. He is leaving us."

When Santiago moved toward him, Dillon shot a glare his way. He seized Chaz's wrist and pulled her up to him. "The hell I am. Like it or not, I'm now part of this band of desperados. You may not care about Raúl's welfare, but I do. I didn't save his life so you could throw it away. If you're set on going to Zacatecas and committing suicide, I'll be there to see that the boy gets out alive."

Color still sat high in her cheeks, but relief flickered in her eyes. For a second, the hard angles of her face softened. The reaction was so brief, if he'd blinked, he'd have missed it. Then a mask came back down over her features. "Then you will follow my orders," she said, "and you will now release my hand."

Dillon hadn't even realized he was still holding it, and he dropped her wrist. With an oath beneath his breath, he strode away to saddle Victory.

Chaz stared at Dillon's stiff back as he exited the hacienda. His words had wounded her more deeply than he would ever know. If she admitted the truth, in her blindness propelled by vengeance, she had thought little about putting Raúl and her men in danger. They faced danger every day and emerged nearly unscathed. She had lost a few men, but what would she do if she lost Raúl? Was Thorne's demise worth the life of her child? She could accept death as a testament to her Yaqui honor, but the death of her son? Could she live with that on her conscience? Chaz supposed she *had* thought about it on some inner level, but Raúl's death in a gun battle was no less terrifying than Thorne showing up some day to take her son away from her. And as long as Thorne was alive, that possibility existed.

The years had been hard, and Raúl the only light in her dark existence. Chaz did this for him—everything she did, she did for him. The campesinos and the revolutionaries benefited from her raids on Thorne's trains, but her motivation was Raúl, always Raúl...and Thorne. Her need to erase the past through striking back at the man whom she hated more than anything. Her robberies of Thorne's trains had failed, so far, to pry the man from his Chicago mansion. This raid on Zacatecas was a last attempt. If it did not bring the great man south to guard his silver, she would leave Mexico and confront the lion in his den.

Chaz could not express her gratitude to Dillon for promising to look after Raúl. For so long, she'd lacked a man's protection…did not want it. Now, when Dillon rode by her side, unfamiliar emotions welled up inside her. Her pulse accelerated whenever she looked at him and he gave her that slow, sexy smile. She felt safe with him, a feeling that engendered both annoyance and elation. Nonetheless, nothing had changed. She needed no man's protection, no man's advice, no man's love. She had Raúl, and when Thorne lay dead, she would have all she'd ever wanted. However, merely to kill Thorne was not enough. She wanted him to suffer, to be ruined, emotionally and financially bankrupt. That desire motivated her to rob the trains. Then when she determined he had suffered enough, the silver bullets in her revolver would deliver the final justice. At last, he would pay.

A soft, velvety night descended on their journey. In the starlight and the radiance of a half moon, the road to Zacatecas glimmered, leading down out of the mountains, which Dillon learned were the Sierra de los Organos, the Valley of the Giants. For the first time, he left the valley unfettered and without a blindfold. Soon after descending from the heights, they came upon a sombrero-shaped hill with a small city at its base, Sombrerete, a center noted for silver mining during the time of the Conquistadores. The veins had quickly given out, and now the city was a sleepy, dusty settlement with soaring, ancient stone architecture built on the silver's bounty, sitting on one small branch line that linked it to the Central Railway.

Chaz's men entered the main thoroughfare in small groups from different directions to seek out simple lodgings. They'd traded their bandito gear for the rough leathers favored by *rancheros*, who were a common sight in every town on the *altoplano*. Chaz wore a dress and had covered her braided hair with a mantilla. Even in the modest, aristocratic clothing, the gun loaded with silver bullets hung at her hip.

Dillon flat-out refused to ride with Salvatore and displaced Alec as companion to Chaz and Raúl. Dillon and Alec nearly came to fisticuffs before Chaz defused the situation with a sharp word. Now as Dillon and Chaz rode stirrup to stirrup, Dillon noticed Raúl's interest drawn to the bright lights and rowdy guitar music coming from the doors of a cantina. He spurred Victory ahead and urged his horse closer to Raúl's mount until their knees bumped. "Not on my watch, you don't," Dillon said low.

Raúl sent him a cheeky grin. "But I feel lucky tonight."

"You're lucky I don't lock you in the hotel. If you make one move toward that cantina, I will."

Raúl's grin grew wider. "Don't worry so, Dillon. I already received a lecture from Chaz. I will behave."

"I reckon you will," Dillon said with a curt nod. When he dropped back alongside Chaz, she said, "Raúl is merely high-spirited. I spoke with him. You need not watch him like a hawk."

"High spirits are likely to get him killed," he murmured. "I would have preferred we camped out in the bush. I still don't know why you insisted on our exposing ourselves by coming into town."

"I want a bath."

Dillon snapped his head to her, mouth agape. "A bath?"

Amusement gleamed in her eyes. "Yes, señor West. You know, with heated water and soap bubbles?"

His gut churned. Chaz was hiding something. They hadn't come into town for her to have a bath. The corners of his mouth winged down. "What's the real reason, *querida?*"

The amusement fled her face, and she turned away. "I am meeting with someone."

By now, Dillon knew better than to ask if that "someone" was a lover. "Does it involve Zacatecas?"

"Perhaps." She offered no additional information.

"You won't be going alone," he said as he pulled up Victory in front of the livery stable that sat beside a substantial hotel. He dismounted, circled around Niebla, and held up his arms. When she glared, he lowered his arms and stepped back. Chaz swung out of the saddle, her blue skirt belling like a bright parasol.

"I will go alone," she said. "You will remain at the hotel with Raúl, and you will not follow me."

Dillon offered his arm, and she placed her hand on it, though this womanly movement was hesitant, reluctant. "Try and stop me," he said. He stretched out a hand and unbuckled her gun belt. "And get rid of this, for God's sake. You look more like Belle Starr than a highborn Spanish señora." He removed the gun belt and tossed it to Raúl.

She frowned. "What do you —?"

"He's right, *Madre*," Raúl said with an unrepentant grin. "Ladies don't wear gun belts."

She seemed to swallow her protest, and with a lift of her brows, asked instead, "Who is this Belle Starr?"

"A cattle rustler," Dillon replied, "and I was under the impression our objective was to keep a low profile."

As Raúl buckled the belt around his slim hips, she cast a glance at her gun. "I suppose you are right about the gun, but I will not allow you to accompany me tonight."

"We'll just see about that," Dillon said under his breath. He left the horses for Raúl to deal with and steered her toward the hotel doors. He held one ajar and allowed her to precede him into the lobby. The plush, genteel appointments reflected a shabbiness, underscoring the decline in the town's fortunes. Still, it was the best Sombrerete offered and, he supposed, better than a bedroll beside a cactus. With her hand on his arm, he escorted her to the desk.

"We'll require two rooms," he said in flawless Spanish to the *hotelero*, "one for me and the señora, and one for her brother." Her hand tightened on his arm, and when the clerk turned away to retrieve the keys, he faced her, taking in the stricken expression on her face. "Don't get your knickers in a knot. I'll share Raúl's room."

Her lips tightened. "Yes, you certainly will."

The man returned, and Dillon collected the keys and ushered Chaz up the grand staircase to the third floor where their rooms sat next to each other. He unlocked the door to Chaz's room, held it open, and motioned for her to enter. She swept past him, skirt brushing against his legs. He followed her and pulled the door to behind him.

Chaz spun around, a hand raised to her throat, looking like a jackrabbit scared up by Fuerte, who was currently bunking with Salvatore on the outskirts of town. They'd agreed earlier the dog was too memorable to parade into town. Though the townspeople hadn't likely met The Ghost Wolf, they'd certainly heard of the bandito. Even in the backwaters, news traveled quickly.

Dillon hadn't meant to scare her. He tilted his head, considering why his presence in her room could provoke such a response. His bewilderment was no more puzzling than the lady herself. Nevertheless, he wanted to get to the bottom of this meeting of hers and come to a mutual understanding. He shed his gun belt and sombrero and dropped into a deep, upholstered wingchair against the wall.

Chaz inhaled and exhaled deeply a few times, and seemed to get her breath back. She moved away from him to a desk beside the window. A soft breeze came through the open embrasure and fluttered the lace curtains. As she pulled the combs from her hair, slid the mantilla from her head, folded it carefully, and laid it on the desk, her hands shook.

"Come over here and sit," he said softly, the way he would talk to Victory when the horse scented a puma. He gestured to a matching chair across from him. "I just want to talk."

She turned her back and gazed out the window. "We have nothing to talk about."

Dillon heaved an impatient breath. "I swear, Chaz, if you don't tell me when and where you're meeting this man tonight, I'll stay in this chair and keep my eyes on you until we both grow beards and gray hair."

Chaz looked over her shoulder. "Is that all you want to know?" she asked, surprise in her voice.

"Unless you also want to tell me why Thorne is so important to you."

"No." Shaking her head, she swung around to face him. "No. That I cannot tell you. It is my business, not yours."

"Then sit and explain to me why you have to meet this hombre alone tonight. Let's have a civilized conversation for once without any threats of death and mayhem."

Chaz shrugged her shoulders and crossed the room to the chair. Her hips naturally swayed in the dress. Somehow, she managed to suppress the feminine action when clad as The Ghost Wolf. *A shame. It suited her.* She settled into the chair, crushing the delicate fabric of her skirt beneath her, and eased backward as though she expected to encounter a porcupine. Suddenly, she shot forward to the edge. "Raúl," she said. "How will he get into his room?"

Dillon sighed inwardly at her obvious attempt to change the subject. "I left his key with the *hotelero*. I reckon he has enough sense to ask for it."

"Oh." Again she eased back cautiously.

Dillon met her gaze with what he hoped was sternness. "Now answer my question."

"He is one of Carranza's men. He has the information we need to enter the presidio in Zacatecas. The numbers of guards, their positions, schedules, the combination to the silver vault."

His jaw slackened, and his mouth sagged open. "They store the silver in the prison?"

Her brows came up. "If you were Thorne, would that not be the best place for you to guard your silver?"

Dillon rolled his eyes to the ceiling and tried to catch his breath. "Let me get this straight," he said once his gaze settled on her again. "You plan to penetrate the territorial prison, one of the most heavily defended structures in Zacatecas State, steal several wagonloads of silver, and get away with your lives?" Pushing to his feet, he traveled across the rug and punctuated his words with sharp gestures. "I thought, perhaps, Thorne had built a warehouse out by the mines, some building fifty men might actually have a chance in hell of taking. But the presidio?" He stopped to send her a glare. "This is the most boneheaded expedition I ever heard of. You couldn't slip a tortilla out of Zacatecas Presidio without detection."

"You have been inside it?" she asked quietly.

"Not the one in Zacatecas, but I've seen the bowels of enough similar prisons to know what you're planning is just plain crazy." He pointed at her. "I warn you if you go through with this, the only way you'll be coming out is in a pine box with the padre praying over your corpse."

Her shoulders stiffened, and Dillon came down on one knee in front of her, taking her hands in his and squeezing them. "Forget this, *querida*," he said. "Go back to the trains. If you want to punish Thorne for some imagined slight, then surely taking the silver off his trains is punishment enough."

Chaz shook off his hold. "Nothing but his death is punishment enough, and my motive is not based on imagination but reality. It is a matter of honor."

"And how will your death, as well as the deaths of Raúl and your men, satisfy that honor? Do you imagine Thorne will weep over your grave?"

The color drained from her face, and she stood, causing him to fall back. "No. I will laugh over his."

A sharp knock came at the door, and the corners of her mouth lifted in a smile. "It is Raúl." She stepped away from Dillon to move to the door. Dillon got to his feet, following her and drawing his Colt from the holster he'd laid on the bed. When her gaze flickered sideways to him, he tilted his head, raised the gun barrel level with his cheek, and drew back the hammer with a sharp click.

"Ask before opening," he said.

"*¿Quién es?*" she called out.

"Raúl."

With a sigh, Chaz swung open the door. Raúl waited on the other side, a hand braced against the lintel. He looked past her to Dillon. "I'm dying of thirst. Come to the cantina with me and watch over me as if I were a *niño*."

Dillon gave Chaz a pointed look. "Will you be here when I return?"

"I will." Her frown revealed her exasperation with him. "I plan nothing more strenuous than a hot bath." She held out her hand. "I will take the key and lock my door."

He handed it over, collected his gun belt, strapped it over his hips, and shoved the sombrero onto his head. "I'll be checking that you do. I'll return and escort you to a late dinner, *mi esposa*."

My wife. Though it was only a charade, the words sounded surprisingly sweet to his ears. To someone who'd avoided matrimony since the deaths of his wife and daughter in another life, it was a minor miracle. Chaz shooed him out the doorway, where Raúl stood impatiently, closed the door, and turned the key in the lock.

The cantina was fancier than the one in Flores, the clientele less cutthroat, but the same cigarillo smoke colored the air, and fumes of spilled liquor scented the atmosphere. Dillon rested his elbows on the bar and ordered *aguardiente*, getting it this time. *Thank the god of alcohol.* He sipped the fiery liquid and watched Raúl, who took up position behind a quartet of poker players. First, Dillon had to take care of Raúl; then he had to take care of his own business. A young señorita at the end of the bar looked promising. She was reasonably clean and sober, which was more than he could say for the others within view. He beckoned her over with a silver coin.

"See that young man," he said, motioning toward Raúl. "It's his birthday." He flipped the coin into her outstretched palm. "This should ensure you keep him occupied for the remainder of the evening. I'll collect him after midnight. If he's still with you, I'll double that coin."

She smiled, and her slumberous eyes crinkled, making her look even younger. "*Sí*, señor. For this much, I will keep him until dawn."

"No. Only until I knock on your door. Which one?"

"Six," she said over her shoulder as she made her way to Raúl's table.

Lord, that gal's as swift as a filly and just as eager.

As Raúl followed the girl up the long, winding stairway to the upper rooms, he sent Dillon a wink and a wave.

Dillon tilted up his glass for a last swallow, settled his hat on his head, and left the cantina. He first stopped at the telegraph office where he sent a wire to Thorne's silver agent in Zacatecas. His second stop was a puddle of darkness along the street outside the hotel, where he could watch the front door and the window to Chaz's room. He didn't have long to wait before Chaz emerged from the hotel lobby onto the street. She had changed into black leathers, and he nearly took her for a man. He smiled grimly. So much for her waiting in her room for his return, and her hot bath must have been a hurried one. He'd left her less than an hour ago. When she turned right and slipped into the alley running alongside the building, he trailed her.

Dillon pushed to keep Chaz in sight along the twisted stone-cobbled streets. Narrow, multistoried, stone and wood residences lined the way. The air smelled of *chile* peppers and roasting meat, and sewage in the open gutters between the houses. The cries of sleepless children wafted from open windows, mingling with the husky moans of a couple making love. A pair of amorous cats echoed the couple's cries. If not for a faint moon overhead and the occasional torch along the streets, he would have lost her a dozen times.

At last Chaz halted beside a church Dillon recognized from a previous visit to Somberete—Santo Domingo, an impressive structure made of stone with two rows of the carved effigies of saints framing either side of the large wooden doors. A man separated from the black shadows behind a pillar. When he walked into the moonlight, its illumination fell on his face. *What the hell? Alec.* Along with the churning in Dillon's gut at being excluded from this parlay, questions bounced about his brain. Was Alec the mysterious man she was meeting, or was this puffed-up aristocrat her protection tonight? When the church doors opened to admit the two, Dillon figured he'd find the answers to his questions inside.

He waited until the doors closed again then sped across the street and up to the intricately carved doors. After pressing his ear to the crack between the two slabs of wood, he inched open one door and slipped inside. A trio of conspirators stood by the chancel railing and off to one side in front of a statue of the Madonna, where candles flickered in red glass votives, imparting a faint waxy odor to the air and an ethereal luminosity on the proceedings.

The interior of Santo Domingo echoed Spanish elegance, a familiar theme of Catholic plenty amidst the poverty of the flock. Pale, dark-veined marble floors spread down the narrow aisles of the nave and led to a marble arch at the apse, which rose loftily above the altar. The church held rows of pews, a rarity in Spanish cathedrals, where most often the faithful were expected to kneel during the Mass on bare wooden or stone floors, which resulted in perpetually bruised knees. The pews and chancel were made of rich dark wood, and a ribbed and vaulted ceiling of the same material. Along each side of the church, within the crossing and lining the transepts, ran soaring marble columns, sentinels to more than a dozen niches, each holding a saint's shrine. Colorful, intricate stained-glass windows behind each niche and above the altar let in faint torchlight from the streets outside.

Dillon dropped to his hands and knees and crawled down the aisle toward the meeting. When the voices grew clear enough for him to understand, he entered a row of pews, turned around, and settled down, buttocks on the floor, spine resting on the pew ahead of him. He couldn't see what was going on and hadn't gotten a good look at the man Alec and Chaz had come to meet, but he could hear, and that was enough for now.

"I have a sympathizer inside," a man said in Spanish in a gravelly voice, as though he'd downed a glass of *aguardiente* and hadn't had the chance to clear his throat. The voice was unfamiliar; he wasn't a man Dillon had met among the banditos or the revolutionaries.

"Is the way in prepared?" Chaz asked.

"Yes, but for only four men, and they must be at the door to the east entrance at two in the morning, before the changing of the guard in the Casa de la Moneda."

"I will be one of those three."

The hell you will, Dillon said silently, and suddenly, the man's words registered. "Aw, shit!" Dillon cursed beneath his breath. *The Casa de la Moneda! That damned woman.* She'd lied to him, which meant she still didn't trust him. Thorne hadn't stockpiled his silver in the presidio but in the Royal Mint. The presidio would have been hard, hell, near impossible to penetrate, but the Royal Mint? If they could pull off this robbery, bank robbers everywhere would erect a statue to The Ghost Wolf.

His wire to Thorne's agent in Zacatecas was now as effective as a fart in a windstorm. The troops would be waiting at the presidio not *Casa de la Moneda*. Of course, he'd also planned to spirit Chaz and Raúl away on some pretext, any pretext before the robbery — even by force, if necessary. It seemed Chaz's instincts in not trusting her new gun hand had proved more insightful than she realized. Unwittingly, he'd aided rather than foiled Chaz's plan to relieve Thorne of his silver. Now he wouldn't have the chance to send a second wire, because they were saddling up at dawn for the ride to Zacatecas.

His belly boiled at Chaz's lies, even as he understood her reasoning. But he had a job to do, and he'd held off this long only because of this *goddamed*, inconvenient attraction to her. If he didn't get himself together, he'd lose both her and the silver. *Her* and *the silver?* His gut told him that wasn't a possible outcome to this impossible situation. It would have to be one or the other. He had to make up his mind. The hell of it was, he wanted her, so why was he still thinking about the silver? No doubt about it; he was a louse. *Damn it, why not admit it?* He was one screwed-up hombre, and if he was in her place, he wouldn't trust himself either.

Dillon listened with one ear while fatigue caught up with him and weighted his eyelids. As he strained to pay attention to the conversation, the remainder rang no immediate alarm bells in his brain. The murmuring, echoing softly like the voices of angels among the arches, the effects of the liquor, and the tension in his muscles overtook him. He closed his eyes, and the voices grew fainter and fainter until they faded into nothingness.

When Dillon opened his eyes, near silence and the waxy scent of candles from the shrines swirled about his head. Bats rustled against the roof far overhead, and Dillon thought hosannas wouldn't be out of place in that peaceful space. He rose to his feet and shook his head to clear the cobwebs from his brain. His muscles had grown stiff from having slept with his backside on the marble floor and his spine against the wooden pew, and he stretched to relieve the soreness.

A quick survey revealed the man had gone, as well as Alec, from what Dillon could see. Chaz still remained. She knelt at the chancel rail beneath the statue of the Virgin Mary. In the wavy candlelight, her lips moved, but he was at too great a distance for him to hear her whispered words. He figured she was praying to the saint for the success of her venture. Somehow, he suspected the mother of Christ wouldn't condone this insane plan.

He pulled out the cheap new pocket watch he'd picked up from the small store off the hotel lobby and glanced at the time: one in the morning. He'd slept for almost two hours. Dillon suddenly remembered Raúl. He'd left the boy at the cantina, and God only knew what

trouble he'd gotten himself into by now.
Voices and the metallic echo of rifles being
chambered floated in from the street outside the heavy
doors. Dillon's gaze leapt to Chaz. She remained in the
same attitude, head bowed, elbows on the polished rail,
forehead resting on her clasped hands. The voices grew
nearer, and the hinges on one door protested with a sigh
like a breeze as it cracked open. *Was she deaf?*
Dillon exploded into action. He reached Chaz before
she could lift her head. Seizing her arm, he pulled her to
her feet. "*Federales!*" he whispered urgently. Her eyes
widened, and she nodded.

Dillon towed her toward one side of the cathedral,
where the massive pillars soared majestically to the ribs
of the vaulted roof and the row of sentinels threw inky
stripes across the dark-veined floor. He winced at the
tapping of their boots on the stone surface.

"*¿Quién es?*" The words flew out into the cathedral
and bounced about from pillar to pillar.

Dillon pushed Chaz against the dark side of the
nearest pillar, her back to the rounded marble, his chest
against hers. When she squirmed, he took her hands
tightly in his, holding her arms motionless at her sides.
He pressed his lips to her ear and whispered, "Shh."

The soldiers fanned out into the church, booted feet
clomping down the main aisle and along the sides of
the pews. *Three or four men, and careless at that.* Voices
raised in talk, questions, and laughter bounced back
and forth. If Dillon and Chaz had wanted to add the
soldados' number to those killed by The Ghost Wolf,
it wouldn't have been hard. But this was no night for
killing. Therefore, Dillon didn't dare peer around the
curve of the pillar. The candlelight could quickly reveal
their position if a man was glancing their way. So they
remained motionless, a part of the stone, pressed even
more tightly against each other.

The softness of Chaz's body beneath her leathers,

her small breasts squashed against his chest, made
Dillon's thoughts wander away from the *soldados* and to
their situation. He released her hands and held her face
between his palms. In the blackness of their hiding place,
he couldn't see her eyes. Nonetheless, her breathing
quickened, chest rising and falling rapidly, breath
soughing across his cheek, and the slow lope of her heart
accelerated into a gallop.

Now Dillon had Chaz where he wanted her, at a
place and time where she couldn't back away, couldn't
threaten to geld him. In some way, it seemed fitting. For
once, she feared capture more than she feared the touch
of a man.

"If they see us," he whispered into her ear, "pretend
we're lovers."

Her body trembled, but she nodded.

Would I be a snake to take advantage? A tiny needle of
conscience pricked him. *Ah, hell.*

Dillon slid his mouth slowly across the slope of
her neck, landed soft kisses on her eyelids—closed, he
noticed—and settled in on her mouth. Her head shook
slightly, but her lips were slack, barely parted. No real
struggle, no resistance. Chaz could bite his lip if she
really wanted to. Perhaps she feared he'd make a noise
that would betray them to the soldiers.

Her mouth gradually opened wider, and Chaz
sighed into the kiss. Her rigid body became soft, pliant.
Dillon released her head and skimmed his hands down
the sides of her neck. He unraveled her braid, sifted
through her long hair, and moved his palms across
her shoulders and down her arms. He kept the kiss
light, nonthreatening, more exploratory than ravenous.
However, he couldn't stop his tongue from dipping into
her mouth on a foray to taste her sweetness.

The soldiers moved around the cathedral, discussing
the events of the day and pausing briefly to pray
beneath the plaster saints. Dillon kissed Chaz, no longer

concerned with their predicament, his full attention focused on tasting, feeling, canting his head first one way then another. His head swam in a way it never had before. He was light-headed, weak-kneed, and suffering a painful swelling between his legs, aware only tangentially of the presence of the soldiers, who eventually ceased their search and left through the door, allowing it to slam behind them.

At the dull thud of the wood, Chaz brought her hands up flat against his chest and applied pressure. Dillon broke off the kiss and stepped back, out of the pillar's embrace and into the candlelight. Chaz followed, and Dillon finally saw her expression. Beneath a thin layer of anger lay the dewy softness of a woman well kissed.

"You should not have done that," she said.

"Why? They would have left us alone. Lovers probably often seek out these shadows for assignations."

Chaz lowered her gaze to the floor. "Because the soldiers may not have believed us. How could we have fought…" When she raised her eyes, they now snapped with irritation. The spell his kiss had cast over her had worn off. "Do not do it again," she said harshly.

A grin flickered across Dillon's face. *Because I suspect you enjoyed it too much?*

"And what are you doing here?" she asked.

"I felt the sudden need for absolution?"

A confused expression swam across her face and settled in her gaze. "I do not understand you at all, Dillon West."

Neither do I.

She turned away with a murmured comment he didn't quite hear and disappeared quickly into the bowels of the cathedral.

He glanced at his watch again. *Dang! Raúl!* The soldiers would eventually stop at the cantina. Chaz would whup him with a plow line if Raúl got himself into trouble.

Dillon returned as swiftly as he could to the cantina.
When he asked for the girl, the barkeep told him she was
upstairs with a customer, and he had to cool his heels at
the bar for what seemed like forever. She finally made
an appearance, and he learned the *puta* had sent the
boy on his way, wrung out and satisfied, more than an
hour earlier. Dillon made his way back to the hotel and
took the stairs three at a time, praying all the while Raúl
had managed to find his bed with no mishap. When he
whipped open the door, the boy was sprawled across the
lumpy mattress, softly snoring.

Dillon tossed his hat on the chair in the corner and
unbuckled his gun belt, slinging it over the chair back.
He had stripped off his boots, jacket, and shirt when a
scream came from the adjoining room. *Chaz!*

He snatched the pistol from his holster and darted
out the door into the hallway. At Chaz's door, he used
the extra key he'd requested from the desk clerk. He
swung open the door, rushed in, and went down into a
crouch, panning the gun about the darkened space. The
room held no one other than Chaz, whose slim figure
thrashed on the bed, mangling the covers and tossing
them to the floor.

The monster left, *the door closing as quietly as the ticking
of the mantle clock...*

*Charissa curled into a ball on the bed, pulled her
nightgown over her bent knees and clenched toes to cover
every inch of exposed skin.* I won't cry. I won't cry. I won't!
*Regardless of the litany, silent tears streamed down her face to
wet the pillow beneath her cheek.*

*Even in the face of her screams and struggles, Charissa
knew no one would hear her—and even if they did, they would
be too frightened to come to her rescue. Resistance only made
the monster more vicious. Then he would hit her, hurt her even*

more...perhaps he would even use the knife again, the one he had taken from her hand. With trembling fingers, she touched the scars on her face, wet from her tears. He could injure her, even kill her, but he couldn't quell the fight inside her no matter what he did.

Whimpering came from her dressing room, and Charissa wiped her eyes. She slid off the bed, and winced, stifling a cry. The pain didn't seem as bad now as it was after the first time, though she had no real comparison. She had buried the memory of his first visit too deeply.

She released the dog, crouched down, and flung her arms around his neck. Pepe was only a puppy, but at sixty pounds, a formidable foe. Since the time when the dog first attacked and bit him, the monster had ordered a servant to muzzle and lock the animal in the dressing room. Charissa unbuckled the muzzle and threw it across the room.

She rose to her feet, mouth set in a grim line. Her breast burned, and her stomach knotted. The monster would not touch her again. The knife was her pitiful attempt to kill him. But she'd proved too weak to plunge it deeply enough, and even if she tried again with another knife and succeeded, the police would come. They would hang her. The monster was rich and powerful, and he ruled the police like he controlled the courts and judges.

Charissa stripped off her nightgown and quickly dressed in the clothes stowed away in the bottom of the cedar chest. The shirt, trousers, cap, and jacket she had taken from the rubbish bin when the stable boy discarded them. The boots, her cousin had outgrown. She cut off her long ebony hair and stuffed it into the bottom of the chest beneath her velvet riding habit. Pulling the cap over her hair and tugging on it to shadow her face, she retrieved the ragged carpetbag hidden under the bed. It held more clothing, food, and the jewels she'd inherited from her grandmother. She slipped a stolen knife—not the knife but another one—into her boot and wedged a pilfered gun into the waistband of her trousers beneath the jacket.

Removing the dog's collar, Charissa slipped a noose of

*rope around his neck. She paused for a moment and glanced
around the room, a bedchamber fit for a princess—not a
despoiled indito—with silk bed hangings and drapes and soft
wool carpets underfoot. Graceful Queen Anne furniture flanked
a marble fireplace, and expensive paintings dotted the peach-
colored walls. She felt only relief in leaving it behind. It was
the monster's lair, and since her mother's death, she had known
only pain and despair within its walls.*

*When Charisa reached the foot of the grand staircase, a
stout figure stepped out of the shadows.*

*She pressed a shaky hand to the base of her throat. Her
pulse beat against her skin in a rapid tattoo, abating only with
recognition. "Mariposa, you scared me half to death," she
whispered.*

*The woman's lined Mexican face twisted in anguish. She
enveloped the girl against her soft bosom. "Where will you
go?" the woman asked, pulling back, her gaze searching
Charissa's face.*

*"As far away as is possible," the girl replied with
bitterness.*

*The woman pressed a handkerchief filled with coins into
the girl's small hand.*

"You should not do this." Charissa tried to return the gift.

*The woman closed the girl's fingers over the packet. "You
will need it. You cannot use your abuela's jewels to buy bread."*

*Tears welled up in Charissa's eyes. "I'll always remember
your kindness."*

*The woman unlocked the front door and gently pushed
Charissa out into the night. "Vaya con Dios," she said, and
the girl and dog walked into the mist coming off the great lake,
shrouding the mansions...*

"The monster!" Chaz cried in her sleep and twisted
as though pain wracked her body. "Go away! Stop!
Please, don't!" Her hands came up, curled into claws,
and she pushed and tore at an imaginary assailant.

Dillon swiftly lit a lamp beside the bed and settled
down on the edge of the mattress, taking her wrists in

his hands and pulling them down by her sides. "Hush, Chaz," he said. "You're safe. No one will hurt you."

His touch galvanized her into a more violent reaction, and she flew at him with nails and teeth. "The monster!" she screamed again. "Pepe, help me! Stop him! Kill him! Kill the monster!"

For a moment, Dillon assumed she was awake, but when he secured her flailing arms again and looked down into her face, she was still asleep, still trapped in some nightmare. Fear and pain contorted her features, and his heart twisted. *Damn, if only I could take that pain away.* What dream could have such an effect on a strong woman like Chaz? He pulled her into his arms, against his bare chest, and cradled the back of her head in his palm. "Shhhh," he said. "It's Dillon. I won't hurt you. Wake up. It's only a nightmare."

Chaz wouldn't or couldn't awaken. She whimpered and moaned, repeatedly cried out for Pepe to kill the monster. *What monster? And who was Pepe?* Dillon muffled the wrenching sounds against his chest. "Quiet, *querida.* I just want to hold you." At last her muscles relaxed, and she stopped fighting him. Her breathing deepened, and with a final sigh, the dream seemed to slip away from her.

Dillon leaned down, laid Chaz back on the bed, and tried to release her. She clung to him in her sleep and whimpered when he attempted to remove his arms. He supposed her sleeping mind thought he was Pepe. With a sigh, he swung his legs onto the bed and settled down beside her, and she still clutched him tightly. With her regular breath warming the hollow of his throat and her heart beating against his, he drifted off into sleep for the second time that night.

Once

Dillon woke to the feel of steel against his heart and the smell of gunpowder in his nose. He opened his eyes, glaring at Chaz and the pistol pressed into his chest.

"What in hell are you doing?" he asked.

"What I would do if I found any snake in my bed."

His hand flashed up, quick as the reptile she'd called him, and he snatched the pistol from her. He flipped open the barrel and dumped the bullets out on the floor. They landed in a patter of clinks and rolled beneath the bed. She stared at him as if she couldn't quite believe his hand could move that speedily. That same hand now came up, and he caught her chin between his thumb and fingers, holding it fast.

"I'm getting damn sick and tired of your threatening me," he said. "The next time you point a pistol at me, you'd better pull the trigger, señora, or I'm just liable to retaliate in kind. If you were a man, I'd have been tempted to blow your head off by now."

She jerked back and slipped off her side of the bed, pulling off the top blanket with her and wrapping it about her body. Red flamed on her cheeks.

"You, señor," she said with venom in her voice and

expression, "had better remember for whom you work. If you were any other man, I *would* have blown your head off by now."

He slid up in the bed, crossed his arms over his bare chest, and leaned back against the wall. "What's pricking your hide this morning?"

"This!" she said, sweeping an arm toward the bed. "I wake to find you have crawled into my bed during the night. You wait until I am asleep, break into my room, and sneak into my bed."

He raised a hand. "This? This is what's got your petticoats tangled? You *whoa* right there. I didn't break into your room, and I don't have to sneak into any woman's bed."

"Only the lowest kind of man would..."

Dillon threw back the covers, under which he'd somehow ended up during the night, and swung his legs off the bed, standing. "Look," he said with a broad gesture. "I've still got my britches on good and tight. If I had any intentions other than doing a good deed, I'd be buck naked right now." He came around the bed toward her, bare feet smacking on the wooden boards. As he advanced, she backed up.

"Perhaps I should have left you alone last night," he continued. "But no, I'm a cotton-headed fool. I heard you screaming and thought some polecat might be murdering you. So I let myself into your room with a key, mind you, gun in hand, ready to fill the varmint with lead, and I find you fighting off imaginary monsters. Because I couldn't wake you, I held you to keep you from hurting yourself, and you wouldn't let go. Guess I fell asleep. Excuse me, señora, for caring enough to see what the hell was going on in here."

Her back hit the wall just as Dillon came nose to nose with her. The fingers clutching the covers to her neck gleamed white with strain and trembled. As he crowded her, fear crept into her face, so he backed off. Her shoulders dropped as soon as he put a few feet between them.

"I...I'm sorry," she said, looking down. "I thought..."

"I know what you thought, but I generally wait until I'm asked." He realized the affront in his words and changed the subject. "Who's Pepe? You kept calling for him last night. Is he Raúl's pa?"

Her head came up. "No, he is a dog, a wolfhound."

"A dog? Like Fuerte?"

"He was my childhood pet."

"What's the monster? You were fighting with some kind of monster."

Her frame grew rigid, and her face drained of blood. "There is no monster. As you said, it was only a nightmare." Chaz came away from the wall and walked toward the chair where her riding clothes were draped over the back. "I thank you, señor West. What you did was...kind. I apologize for accusing you of being less than a gentleman." She picked up her blue skirt and bodice and turned toward him. "You may now leave. The night is over and so is my nightmare. We have a long ride before we reach Zacatecas."

"Right, Boss," he bit out. "Next time I'll just mind my own business." He stalked out the door.

Doce

Zacatecas lay a good four days journey by horseback,
around the eastern foothills of the Sierra de los Cardos,
the slopes of which wore clothes of palm, mesquite,
nopales, and governor. Due to the difficult climate,
few flowers grew, and only dusty browns, grays, and
greens receded to the horizon. On the third day, they
approached Fresnillo, a modest town boasting many
platernos, silver mines running through the hills in
twisting confusion. Though Chaz was still disguised as
a Spanish aristocrat on journey, she detoured around
the main portion of the town and turned south. That
night they camped on the plains among the spiny yucca
and huizache, and for the first time since the incident in
Sombrerete, Chaz's nightmare revisited her.

An inability to draw breath, burning throat, and
sharp pain in her chest awoke her. Soft, sandy ground
cradled her body, and once again, she found herself held
tightly in Dillon's arms. Predawn faintly washed the
sky in shades of pink and pale blue. Fuerte lay snoring
next to an ocotillo shrub a few yards away, and the other
men were out of sight beyond a low dune. From past
experience, her nightmares followed a pattern. Once

triggered by some unfathomable incident or situation, they continued almost nightly, sometimes for weeks at a time. Fearing her dreams would wake the others, she'd moved her bedroll to a discrete distance beneath a trio of stunted huizache trees. Alec had protested, insisted she needed to remain in sight, but the demons that visited her at night were her business, and she took pains to hide them. By Dillon's presence, she had not moved far enough away.

His body was warm, his arms strong and soothing, and although the effects of the dream lingered, her tense muscles relaxed and breathing slowed, as though the monster could not harm her here in this place, while this man was holding her close. *A ridiculous notion.* She knew little about him and suspected he carried secrets—like all men—that would cause her pain. Nevertheless, her body welcomed his protection. Other feelings, ones that were becoming more frequent and disturbing, made her limbs tingle.

Without disengaging his hold, Chaz shook her head. She could not want this man or any man. She could not have feelings for him. He would bring her only misery.

Dillon stirred and sighed, and she looked down at where he nestled his face into the crook of her neck. His eyes, heavy with sleep, were now open, and their very blueness warmed her like the bright sky of a summer day.

"You do not listen, do you?" she said low.

He smiled slowly. Not a lecherous smile, but one filled with sincerity and tenderness…and concern. "Guess I'm a slow learner." Then his smile waned. "Tell me about the monster, *querida*," he whispered. "He's frightened you long enough, most of your life, I suspect. Only by acknowledging him can you shed him forever."

His arms tightened, not enough to frighten her, but making her aware of the solidity, the tenderness of his embrace. Her defenses crumbled like sandstone in a flash flood. Perhaps he was right. She had never told anyone about the monster, not even her family. When she'd arrived on Delicia's doorstep those many years ago, the kindly woman took in Chaz and asked no questions. Even through the birth of Raúl, Delicia and Salvatore never pressed her for explanations. And through the years, the monster pursued her at night the very same way she pursued him by day. How did keeping her secret help her? What harm would it do to tell him? Perhaps he had a point. The Church believed in confession to rid oneself of sin. Perhaps in baring her soul, she could purge the pain and end the nightmares. If she was to choose a confessor, Dillon was the perfect one, because he would move on someday soon and carry her secret with him.

"He is a man," she said with hesitance, voice trembling, "or what passes for a man. He shamed me. When I was only a child, he shamed me every night and drove me from my home. I was too small. I could not defend myself."

"Jesus," Dillon said and came up on his elbows over her. His gaze searched out her eyes, but she averted them. Her stomach twisted into tight knots.

"This man, this monster, is Raúl's father," he said, the words a statement not a question.

Paralysis seized her throat, and she could not answer.

"He raped you," Dillon went on. "The bastard raped you and left you with child."

Words trembled on the tip of her tongue, but she still could not release them.

"Who is he?" he asked roughly, angrily. "One of Díaz's men?"

Chaz managed to find her voice. "No. Please, do not ask about him. I want only to forget."

"Like you forget every night, in your nightmares? Oh, yes, you're doing a great job of that." His mouth twisted cynically. "Tell me his name, and I'll put him below ground. *Christ!* To rape a child. What kind of low-bellied weasel would do that?"

"My stepfather," she said, spitting out the words as though they had a bitter taste.

A breath whistled from between his teeth. "His name," he demanded once again.

Her gaze meshed with his. "No. This is my pain, not yours. Never will I reveal his name. Not until he is dead."

Puzzlement ran across his face. "Dead? What? Are you planning to kill him yourself? If he's Raúl's father, then he's an American, not Mexican." He grew still and thoughtful, then sudden understanding surfaced on his face. He sat up as though pulled upright by strings. "Thorne. It's Thorne, isn't it? That's why you're so all fired determined to take his silver. That's why you load your pistol with silver bullets. Does Raúl know?"

Fire kindled in Chaz, and she caught hold of his shirt, twisting it in her grasp. "You know nothing! If you say anything to Raúl, I will kill you. My pistol holds more than one silver bullet."

Dillon tsked. "There you go, threatening me again. Seems like you're the one who doesn't listen."

"Please," she pleaded, "do not pursue this. I…I cannot think about it anymore."

His expression softened, and he lowered his head and body, hands braced on either side of the ground beside her, placing a chaste kiss on her lips, merely a feathering of his mouth over hers. It wrung her heart with a longing she had no right to feel.

"Please," Chaz said again. "I am a shamed woman. I have no desire for a man. I have known only pain and degradation from a man's touch."

* * *

Something cold and slithery crawled about in
Dillon's stomach. He carried his own burden of pain.
And now he wondered: *Does hers run as deeply as my own?*
With a fingertip, he lightly traced the scar down the side
of her face. She tried to pull away.

"Shhh," he said. "Did he give you this too? Did he
scar you outside as well as inside?"

Though Chaz remained silent, he didn't really need
an answer. *That tore it.* The realization of what Thorne
had done to Chaz, to her face, her body, and her mind,
put an end to Dillon's loyalty. Not only was Thorne a
greedy, manipulative man, he was also a child-rapist. His
actions truly merited him the title of "monster." Dillon
was through with Thorne. *To hell with the money.* He could
always earn more.

"I won't hurt you, *querida.* You know that in your
heart, where it really matters. The shame is Thorne's, not
yours." He brushed his lips against her cheek, her ear.
"Now I know why you're so distant around men and
shy away from being touched, but what you experienced
isn't typical of what happens between men and women.
Love is slow and easy, like loping along a flat plain on a
smooth-gaited horse with warm wind in your hair. Love
is nothing to fear."

"I do not fear anything," she said, her voice growing
shakier as his mouth continued its easy assault.

"But you do," he said as he lifted his head. "That's
what puzzled me most, other than your pursuit of
Thorne. I've never met anyone like you. You're the
strongest, most fearless woman I've ever come across."

"I do not fear you. I do not fear love," she insisted.
Even so, her words descended into a whisper of sound.

"Let me show you, *querida.* Let me show you what
it can be like. You've crawled beneath my skin, you
bloodthirsty little bandito, and I'm damned if I can
scratch hard enough to get you out. Let me love you,
querida. Let me love you like you deserve to be loved.

I won't do anything you don't want me to do. You can stop me at any time. Let me love you, because damned if I don't think I'm half crazy in love with you already."

Chaz swallowed, and her heart thudded against the inner walls of her chest. Let him love her? Was that what men called it? That…that thing they did to women? Dillon was right in one respect: she was afraid, but not of love; afraid if she agreed to go through with what he wanted, she would lose all respect for him. Right now, she liked him in spite of her efforts to remain indifferent to his charm. If she allowed this to happen, she would come to hate him, like she hated Thorne.

"Come on, darlin', I'll behave myself. I promise."

Her lips twisted. "You promise? What is a man's promise? I know what men are like."

Dillon seemed struck silent, and his eyes peered into hers with a look of mixed irritation and compassion. "No you don't, *querida*. You know nothing about men, only one man, one who has no business calling himself a man."

"I have every right not to trust your word. I know nothing about you other than your skill with a gun."

"And that I saved Raúl's skin, and I've helped you rob Thorne's trains, and I saved your own skin, and I told you about my wife and daughter, the Apaches…" He leaned over, opened her carpetbag, and rummaged through it. He came up with two of the rawhide strings she used to lace up her leather riding shirts. When he plopped on his back, she jumped to her feet.

"Guess we'll have to do it this way," he said and held out his hand.

She looked at the strings, and her brows came together. "What am I to do with those?"

"Why, tie my wrists to the trees," Dillon said with a grin and wiggled his hand. The strings swayed from his fingers.

"What? You want me to tie you up?"

He released a gusty sigh. "If it's the only way you can be sure you'll be safe from my animal lust, sure. Tie my wrists to the trees."

"You are loco." Chaz slowly shook her head. "I could not do such a thing."

He dropped the lacings on the ground. "Okay. But I can't promise you my passion won't get the best of me next time I end up in your bedroll. I might lose my head and ravish you."

She scooped up the strings as avidly as if they were made of silver and sent him a frown when he laughed. "*Sí*, señor West, I will tie you to the trees, but that is all I will do. I will leave you here for the coyotes, without food or water, while I ride off to Zacatecas."

Dillon laughed again and stretched his arms over his head, resting his hands next to the slender trunks of the huizache trees behind them.

"You will not laugh for long," she said as she looped one of the strings around a tree then around his wrist, knotting it tightly. "I can promise you that." Moving to the opposite side, she secured his other wrist to a second tree. The entire time, his sultry gaze made her warm, warmer than the morning warranted. She turned to face the sere breeze blowing across the wash, drying the sudden sweat that sprang up on her forehead.

"Is it getting hot, *querida*," he said from behind her, "or is it just me?"

She braced her hands behind her against the trunk of the third tree, which grew separate from the other two, and her gaze lingered on him. His face still wore a smile, and he lay deceptively still on the blanket, but energy seemed to ripple through his body. She should leave him here, exactly as she'd said she would. It would teach him not to tease her. She was no simpering señorita with whom he could flirt, at least one who would flirt back.

"Come here, *querida*," he said, his voice suddenly

silky, low-pitched. "Give me a kiss before you leave me to starve and die of thirst. It's the least you can do for a hogtied cowboy."

She pushed off the tree and went to his side, looked down on him.

Dillon was no longer smiling. Instead, the skin stretched taut across the sharp planes of his cheekbones, his blue eyes had darkened into pools of deepest indigo, and his mouth parted slightly, his tongue slowly licking his lips.

"Kiss me," he said again. "Please, *querida*, kiss me."

This time, his words penetrated her skin and seeped into the deepest part of her. She could not believe she was going to do it. She lowered herself to her knees, leaned over, and touched her mouth to his. His lips moved under the light pressure and parted. When he dipped his tongue into her mouth, she pulled back and sat up.

"See, you can take as much or as little as you want," Dillon said, smiling. "I'm your willing slave. I can do only what you'll let me do."

His mischievous smile drew a small one from her. In his helpless position, he could not hurt her, and that made the difference. She could take from him instead of him taking from her. She could explore—something her body had yearned to do since she'd met him—and hadn't dared for fear he would take control and force her into a situation that sparked the old fears.

"I like this," she said, "your being my slave." Chaz kissed him again, lingering longer, allowing the kiss to go on and on, letting his tongue explore her depths. Warmth slipped through her, into her blood and bones to concentrate in the moist valley between her legs. The longer, deeper she kissed him, the warmer she became. Her head spun, and her limbs grew as light as air. Was this desire? Could she truly desire this man, any man?

"Touch me," he whispered when she released his mouth.

Chaz stiffened. *Now it began. He lay on top of her and yanked up her nightdress, roughly parted her legs. His breath rank with whiskey on her face; the hair on his legs rasping like sandpaper against her smooth thighs. The probing... The probing... The touching, brutal and invasive, and then the pain...*

Dillon gazed into her eyes as though he could read the painful images in her mind. "My neck, *querida*, touch my shoulders, arms, chest. That's all I'm asking. Stay above my belt buckle if that makes you comfortable. Only do it before I go plumb crazy from wanting your touch."

She could hardly believe *he* wanted *her* touch, that he would be content with such. Thorne had never asked her touch him, and when she did, scratching and hitting as she fought, he laughed and held her hands pressed to the bed. He'd never asked for anything at all. He simply took. That this man craved her touch and asked for nothing in return, reached into the deepest part of her and opened a door of light.

She gingerly ran her fingers along the side of his neck, across the broad span of his shoulders, and up the sinewy strength of his arms. Beneath her hands, his muscles bunched and released, flexing in response to her caress. The stronger his reaction, the firmer her touch, until touching truly became caressing, until the palms of her hands tingled with the heat from his body and her own muscles clenched and let loose in counterpoint to his.

Curiosity to explore more fully rippled through her. A yearning within her body blindly moved her hands, and she slid them to his chest. It felt wonderfully strong and firm beneath her palms.

"Unbutton my shirt," he said softly.

When she sought out his eyes, their blue depths radiated only pleasure, contentment. They did not burn with lust or glint with cruelty, which she had seen too often in Thorne's eyes. Her trembling fingers moved to the buttons and pushed each one from the holes. She laid her palms on his chest and eased back the edges of the shirt from his torso. Surprisingly silky hair, unlike Thorne's coarse red pelt, tickled her fingers and the heels of her hands as she slid them over his skin to push the fabric out of her way.

Dimly, she heard the call of a whip-poor-will, like a mournful phantom, from inside the ocotillo bushes beside them. She glanced up to see Fuerte flicking an ear at the sound. Toads serenaded each other in deep, throaty bass voices from the edges of the low-lying water hole behind them. The calling of the bird and the courting of the toads echoed the pounding of her heart.

A moan came from deep inside Dillon's wide, marvelous chest, and he said her name, over and over, a mere murmur like satin, like lazy sunshine. He followed with endearments and other words running smoothly into one another, reminiscent of water flowing over stones. Chaz looked back at him and barely registered anything other than her name on his lips, could not decipher the words' meaning. Nonetheless, she felt them, and she drifted further and further into that hazy realm of power and what must have been desire, though she'd never had experience with it before. She was so aware of her body, heart beating faster, blood surging through her veins.

His arms tensed, and his wrists strained at their bonds. In that moment, when he failed to break free — though Chaz was certain he wished to — she knew she was safe. He truly could not take control away from her. That awareness emboldened her, and her hands moved to his belt buckle, unfastening it, and slid down to the riveted snaps on his leather pants.

Dillon raised his head and peered at her with unfocused eyes. "The boots first," he said, his voice as throaty as the toads'. "The boots have to come off first."

The words brought her back to reality, and heat climbed up her neck and into her cheeks. Now he'd made her aware of the step she was about to take. *Can I? Should I?* Chaz returned his look. "I know that, señor West, for I, too, wear boots."

Dillon smiled, lowered his head to the ground, and closed his eyes.

But he was right. In her distracted state, she had forgotten about the boots. She scooted down to his feet and tugged off his boots. Then looking up the long length of his body, she found herself lost, as though her brain had taken flight.

"The snaps, *querida*," he said. "I'm gonna explode if you stop now."

"I could," she replied, "stop now."

His eyes opened, head lifted, and gaze arrowed to her. His eyes held a plea. "Really? *Por Dios*, Chaz. Have mercy." When she remained silent, he sighed, sagged back, and closed his eyes again. "Okay," he said. "If that's what you want. I stick by my word."

Was it what she wanted? Had she gone far enough already, or even too far? Her banked memories said yes, she had, but her body said no. She wanted to see more, for she might not have the chance again. "No," she murmured, "it is not what I want. I think I want something from you, but I do not know what to do. I have never made love to a man, particularly a man who lies flat on his back like a sunning lizard."

His eyes remained closed, but another smile curved his lips. "You could start where you left off. To do this right, we both have to have a might fewer clothes between us."

Chaz managed the snaps on his pants, but when she pulled open the placket, his manhood sprang up at her. She gasped and fell back on her behind.

"It's not a snake, darlin'," he said with a shaky laugh. "It won't bite you."

He was watching her from beneath his lashes, and as he laughed, that formidable staff of flesh shrunk and grew limp. It no longer looked so frightening. She had never actually seen Thorne's body. Throughout his assaults on her, time after time, beginning when she was thirteen, she'd kept her eyes firmly closed and prayed she could have done the same with her legs. Of course, as a mother, she had often bathed Raúl, but the boy's male parts were nothing like Dillon's.

Making the difficult decision to carry on, Chaz came back to him, having to straddle his legs to tug off his leathers. Once she accomplished undressing him fully, other than his shirt, she slid back and sat on her heels to examine him. Shirt open, nude below that, he resembled a splendid amber puma—caught in a snare and tethered to a tree. When he'd ceased laughing, his shaft had grown again, swelled to a wide, proud staff that emerged and stood erect from the nest of golden hair around his groin.

She leaned forward and brushed her hand over its tip. It bucked, and Dillon's hips rose off the ground. The power she exerted over him filled her with a surge of confidence. Grasping his manhood in both hands, she squeezed.

"Easy," he wheezed out. "Easy, darlin', or this'll be over before it begins."

She released him and backed away. Now the time had come to make an irrevocable decision. She would have to undress. Then would come…the rest. Chaz no longer believed it would be as painful as she remembered. Dillon was not Thorne, and she felt different. She was no longer a frightened girl, and her body yearned as if it wanted what she sensed Dillon could give her. Again, she asked herself, could she do it? This time, the answer came down firmly on the side of no. Although she tried to talk herself into it, she could not carry through. The memories remained too raw, too close to the surface.

But she could still do *something*. Fully dressed, she

straddled his hips and allowed his manhood to come up against her. He moved, and sparks of pleasure ran through her. His proud flesh between her thighs grew harder, throbbing through the seam of her pants. When she looked into his eyes, the expression in them worshipped, caressed, respected. Her embarrassment and apprehension slowly fled.

"Now what?" she asked. She made the mistake of looking down, seeing him full and firm between her legs, all but inside her but for her leathers. Unwanted thoughts of Thorne caused uncertainty to trickle through her. She ruthlessly pushed them aside.

Dillon must have seen the trepidation on her face, for he spoke low and gentle, like he was crooning to spooked cattle on a stormy night, and gradually drew her gaze back to his eyes. "Well, this isn't exactly right yet. At some point, we need to get those clothes off you, but for now, lie down on me and give me a kiss. I sorely need one."

His request seemed harmless enough, so Chaz followed his instructions and welded herself to him, breasts to chest, heart to heart, groin to groin, legs to legs. Between her parted legs, his filled shaft rose up hard and bucked when she slid against it. She kissed him, and he kissed her back. Gradually, her inhibitions fell away. She needed something to fill her…but remove her clothes? Stand naked in front of him? Strip as Thorne stripped her? *No!*

"No," she said. She sat upright and struggled to her feet, standing spread-eagled over him. "I cannot do this. I no longer want to participate in this…this game of yours."

"It's not a game, Chaz. Please, untie me," Dillon pleaded with a gasp, the tendons in his neck as tight as a stretch of barbed wire. "I can't help you unless you let me go. You'll never beat this fear if you refuse to face it."

Let him go? Her breath caught in her throat, cinching

her chest again. "I cannot. You said I would not have to."

A look of appeal crossed his face. "I won't hurt you, Chaz. I want to help you."

"I cannot." Stepping off him, she turned away and walked toward the water hole.

Even from a distance, his groan soared out across the sandy ground. "Please, just shoot me," he said, then, "Chaz, I'd really welcome a bullet in the brain right about now. Hey, dog, bring me my gun..."

When Chaz returned an hour later, Dillon lay asleep, the muscles in his face again smooth, manhood quiescent. She smiled and shook her head. The man seemed able to sleep anywhere at any time, even when trussed naked to a tree. She drew her knife and cut the leathers that bound him to the trees, cursing softly when she remembered too late she needed them to lace up her shirts. She covered him with a blanket from her bedroll and left to find coffee and something to fill her belly. Her body ached, bereft and unfulfilled, but she was helpless to understand what she needed to release the tension running through every muscle.

Trece

Chaz looked down at the city reclining below and partway up the steep slopes of a V-shaped valley. Mule trains carrying silver from the mines burrowing into the mountainsides crowded slim, serpentine roads. As they descended to the valley floor, Chaz and her men clung to trails bordered by sheer, breath-stealing drops.

Zacatecas consisted of a main square, the Plaza de Armas, and a labyrinth of winding *callejones*, alleyways that rambled through the city in mazelike confusion. Impressive cathedrals dotted the streets fanning out from the square, along with government houses and wealthy residences. They passed other noteworthy landmarks she recognized: the State Government Palace, the Palacio de la Mala Noche—the palatial home of a silver mine owner—and the Hotel Francis, where they set up headquarters.

Her target, Casa de la Moneda, a long, two-story building of pink sandstone quarried locally from the soaring mountains, sat only two short blocks from the main square. Markets, bustling humanity, and pastel-colored buildings decorated with elaborate wrought iron balconies surrounded it. Constructed in the fourteenth century as the Spanish House of Currency, Casa de la Moneda had become the Mexican Royal Mint in 1845. Soldiers swarmed over the fenced grounds and guarded the ironwork gate, bars shadowed the rectangular windows, and a solid, iron-shod wooden door allowed admittance only with the proper credentials.

Chaz, Dillon, Raúl, and Salvatore stood outside the fence beneath the leafy shadows of a piñon tree and examined the edifice. Furerte leaned against Chaz's legs, and although the enormous dog garnered a few curious looks, dogs of all breeds wandered about at will in the streets, and most glances were only cursory. Alec had left on some mysterious mission, and *dang* if Chaz would tell Dillon where the man was and what was going on.

"Said it before, and I'll say it again," Dillon stated, "you're crazy, señora, if you hope to penetrate this fortress and get out in one piece with the silver in your pockets. I've seen Federal banks with less security. They must have, what, a couple hundred *soldados* quartered on the grounds?"

A fluid smile flowed across her mouth, and that smile made Dillon's heart pound in more ways than one. He recalled the night he'd come to her rescue after her nightmare, and her confession and actions beneath the huizache trees, those small steps she'd taken toward trust and leaving her fears behind. Those earthshaking events had convinced him to deny Thorne warning of the attempted assault on the mint, not that he wanted to have anything to do with Thorne any longer. And even if he did, Chaz had no chance of success. Now that she could see the difficulty of the task, surely she would call it off. Her smile indicated otherwise.

When she walked away from Salvatore and Raúl, farther down the fence, he followed and asked, "Are you listening to me?"

Her voice was faintly defiant. "I heard your words clearly, señor West."

His mouth twisted in a grimace. "Don't you think we're past your calling me señor West?"

A blush rose up her throat into her face. "This is business, señor West."

"Then in the interest of business, why don't you humor me and tell me how you hope to pull off this insane idea."

"You will know when I feel you should know."

Dillon clamped his teeth together until the muscles in his jaw throbbed.

Chaz met with her lieutenants in the salon of her room in the Hotel Francis. As she had no wish to place the authorities on alert, the remainder of her men had spread out into other, smaller hotels in Zacatecas.

Dillon occupied a chair at her right side, his long, lean body sprawled in its depths like a resting panther. Blond hair, mussed from wearing his sombrero, stuck up in angles and tumbled across his broad forehead. It gave him an endearing, mischievous look, like that of a naughty boy. But the eyes and hard planes of his face were all man. *Her man.* The unexpected direction of her thoughts startled her, made her draw in a sharp breath and her heart beat faster. *Was he?* Could she truly say that and mean it? Could she say it about any man, especially this man, a gun hand with a mysterious, and no doubt violent, past?

The waywardness of her mental argument brought heat to her cheeks. *No. Never* her *man.* Notwithstanding the feelings he stirred, she could not let the *Americano* distract her from her vengeance. Perhaps once she finished with Thorne, drove him to desperation and left him bleeding at her feet, she could concentrate on having a normal life. But then, when it was finally over, would

Dillon move on? From what he'd told her of his past, he was a tumbleweed, blowing whichever way the wind carried him. Would it carry him away from her the next time it blew? To Colorado, a place he'd mentioned with fondness. *So far away...*

The door opened, and Alec strolled in, his gaze going immediately to Chaz. "The dynamite's here and stored on the outskirts of the city in a cave."

His entrance and words brought Chaz back to the conversation and the business at hand.

"Dynamite?" Dillon shouted and pushed himself up in the chair until he sat on the edge of the cushion as rigidly as a pine pole. "What dynamite?" His gaze swung to Chaz, and his eyes lit with accusation.

She held up one hand. "Calm yourself, señor West. If you have patience, you will receive the answer shortly."

"No one said anything about dynamite," he muttered but then held his tongue, leaning forward as tensely as if he expected a sudden blast to blow the chair out from under him.

"You see," Raúl said before she could speak again, "we will not take the silver. We will burn the Casa de la Moneda and melt the silver."

"Hush, *niño*," she said.

"Burn it?" Dillon's voice rose shrilly again. "You plan to burn the mint and melt the silver? What kind of damn fool plan is that? I thought you wanted to steal the silver, give it over to the needy campesinos and the revolutionaries. Why would you melt it?"

"Because," she said, turning to meet his eyes, "we cannot steal it. Our men are too few, and we have no wagons to transport it. Even if we did, we could not escape from the center of the city, carrying tons of silver, without the *soldados* catching us."

"Then what's the point of us being here if you can't take the silver?"

"The point, señor West, is to deny the silver to Justus Thorne."

Throughout Dillon's argument, Alec stood calmly by, arms crossed over his chest and a smile on his face. Now he said, "You are merely an employee, señor West. Chaz, Salvatore, and I made these decisions before you were hired."

Dillon sent Alec a look so intense, had the man been standing on a stick of dynamite, his hat and boots would now be halfway back to Sombrerete. Then shaking his head, Dillon expelled a harsh breath and sagged back in the chair. "Said it so many times the words are branded on my tongue. You're one loco lady."

Dillon had a passing acquaintance with dynamite, from the Macon County Wars, enough of an acquaintance to know he didn't like it. The nitrate explosive was touchy and unpredictable, and he was fond of all his body parts, exactly the way they were in their current arrangement. Nevertheless, he found himself among the group whose task it was to get the dynamite inside the mint and set the charges. Raúl had volunteered, but Dillon convinced Chaz to give the boy's spot to him.

A brilliant idea, West, he told himself as he loaded dynamite sticks into a succession of woven sacks. However, it was he or the boy, and he couldn't let Raúl's youthful exuberance get him killed. But, Christ, he hated working with explosives, and thinking about all that lovely silver melting into a useless lump. *I could build my ranch in Colorado with just a small portion of the silver contained in that mint. Damn Chaz. Couldn't he keep just a few bars?* He swallowed his disappointment.

That brought up another thought. What was he going to do about Justus Thorne now? He knew what he wanted to do. He wanted to smash in the man's face, before shoving a cactus up his butt, before depositing a .45 slug in the snake's belly, before staking him out on an anthill, before…

Dillon shook his head. He'd have to settle for making sure Chaz experienced no more disappointments, no more pain or violence from the man who'd once been her stepfather...her rapist...the father of her illegitimate child. If it required stealing, he would steal—and if it required killing, he would kill. Okay, and if it required setting off dynamite, he'd set off dynamite. Never again would that man lay hands on Chaz. He would take his ten percent out of what they stole from Thorne's trains, if there actually was any, and he'd remain by Chaz's side to the end of this, whatever that may entail.

Yeah, what the hell, now you have a plan. How do you figure on carrying it out? How will you manage it with Thorne being none the wiser? Obfuscation. In more innocent times, Dillon had attended a university in Pennsylvania, but it was a word he'd picked up from an educated whore in San Antone. Obfuscate: to confuse, conceal, disguise, and befuddle. He liked the word. It had class. He would obfuscate the hell out of Justus Thorne 'til he had the man chasing his own tail like a rabid coyote. Afterwards, he would let Chaz deliver the fatal blow. She deserved that much.

Then what? He hadn't thought that far ahead.

When Dillon joined the banditos, the night was moonless, with galleons of brilliant stars sailing overhead and noisy crowds pulsing in the streets. Upon entering the square, they merged into the raucous festival and parade of saints. The men in the joyful procession wore white embroidered tunics, and the women, colorful, ankle-length full skirts, dancing feet whipping up the dust. Fireworks exploded off to one side, and Dillon nearly dropped his sack of dynamite. Chaz had planned for this, warned him about the fireworks, but in his rattled state, he'd simply forgotten. He gathered up his shattered nerves, patched them back together. The festival, with its rowdy hordes, bobbing torches, boisterous mariachi music spilling onto the alleyways from numerous cantinas, and firework displays — Chaz knew it would draw the guards' attention away from the gates and hide the activity of the three men creeping up to the grounds of the mint.

A guard at the smaller western gate, who turned out to be on Carranza's payroll, ushered them in through the opening and directed them to a door nearly hidden in shadows at the far corner of the building. They crouched low and ran across the parched lawn, not only to keep from being seen but as a result of the heavy sacks slung over their shoulders. Alec came last, right behind Dillon, carrying the jars of lamp oil that would accelerate the fire.

Dillon concentrated on keeping his footing, trying not to slip and fall and blow himself to hell and back. Meanwhile, he kept his eyes on the forbidding expanse of the sandstone building and the barred windows, alert for the reflection of a rifle barrel in the light of the torches strung out along the length of the iron fence.

All lay still within the dim depths of the grounds, and his gaze drifted to the backs of the guards at the main gate. They smoked and laughed while watching the plaster statues of saints parade by, carried in fancy litters on the shoulders of the campesinos. Monk parrots squawked in the branches of pines overhead, and Dillon's muscles twitched with every screech, adding to the tension in his back and shoulders.

At last they reached the door, where another paid guard permitted them to slip past into the cool darkness. The thick walls allowed little sound from the street to penetrate, and once the door closed behind them, the eerie silence, after so much chaos, roared in Dillon's ears. The heat from the night outside dissolved into a dry cold, and he shivered. His short, light jacket, which had felt suffocating earlier, now seemed barely adequate to keep his quaking bones from coming apart.

Salvatore pulled out a tinderbox and lit a candle, a small, weak flicker of light in a greater blackness. Its glow illuminated his mustachioed face from below and gave him a devilish look.

They couldn't reach the vault, which lay on the lower, underground level down a wide set of stairs and was guarded at the base by a contingent of *soldados*, so they arranged the dynamite in a circular pattern against columns on the first floor. With luck, it would bring down the roof and upper story and ensure no recovery of the vault's contents. The guards below in the vault would not die, if all went according to plan. Chaz was not a wanton killer. She thirsted only after Thorne's blood. Her men, who waited among the crowd outside, would stage a distraction on the mint's grounds. Hopefully, the guards would bite at the bait.

The charges set, Salvatore snuffed out the candle, and the men took their places in the dark corners. There, they waited.

When the front door flew open and calls for assistance along with the sounds of gunfire and shouting blew in from the street, the guards on the vault level pelted up the stairs, boots ringing on the stone floor and rifles held across their chests. The men in the shadows waited until the guards joined their compadres outside. Then candles flared, Alec, Salvatore, and Dillon poured out the oil, and they lit the long fuses linking the dynamite sticks.

Dillon lit the last fuse and sped after Salvatore and Alec, who ran yards ahead of him. He cleared the side door seconds before a deafening blast shoved him in the back and knocked him off his feet. He lay on his stomach on the sere grass, his arms over his head, with an ocean of heat and waves of wood splinters and sandstone chunks pelting his back. A hand grabbed his arm and yanked him to his feet. Alec, of all people, had dropped back and now pulled him into a sprint, and they hauled leather for the gate.

Dillon slipped through the opening into the alleyway

and glanced at the mint. The conflagration seared his eyes. "Thanks," he said, turning to Alec. The man looked at him stoically, said in a matter-of-fact voice, "*De nada.* You cannot help it if you run as slowly as a hog-tied steer. Besides, Chaz would have been most vexed with me had I left you to roast."

"Yeah, well, glad you had a good reason to save my life."

Alec shrugged and smiled as smugly as usual.

Damned insufferable cock, wouldn't I love to return the favor and save Alec's miserable hide, and, of course, humiliate him in the process, preferably in front of Chaz? Anyway, it was the blast and not his speed that led to his falling.

When Dillon turned his gaze back to the mint, most of it still stood, but the roof had collapsed, and flames shot from every window. The guards at the front gate stood petrified, jaws sagging, eyes wide. The parade had halted, and everyone in the street stared at the building. With one voice, a cheer of "*Viva!*" arose from the crowd, drowning out the roar of the flames.

Dillon had never seen Chaz dressed quite this way, and he stared, his mouth open, like a trout catching mayflies. He still wore his smudged clothing from earlier and reeked of smoke, lamp oil, and dynamite residue. Chaz looked like the Queen of Spain in gold satin and lace, and smelled of roses.

"What are you all gussied up for?" Dillon came out of his trance and pulled at the buttons on his soot-smeared shirt.

At the glint in her eyes and her wide smile, his muscles stiffened like the trunk of an oak tree. Much as he admired her beauty and the slant of her mouth, he'd begun to dread it.

"Aren't you packed to leave?" he asked. "You're going to have a heck of a time managing that dress on horseback through the mountain passes."

"We are going to the theater," Chaz said. "The players are performing Rigoletto, and I have not yet seen it. I had a bath prepared for you in the bedchamber and have laid out your clothing."

His brows climbed his forehead. "*Opera?* You want to go to the *opera?*"

"I always attend the theater when I visit Zacatecas."

He threw out his hands. "After you've blown up the Royal Mint and are the most wanted desperado in Zacatecas State?"

Amusement danced in her expression. "You do not like the opera?"

His fingers went back to the buttons. "I've slept through my fair share, but that's hardly at issue here. We need to haul our tails out of town before we get a real good look at the inside of the presidio."

"No one pursues us. The guards saw nothing. No evidence remains to connect us with the burning of the mint. The campesinos despise the *soldados*. They will say nothing."

Dillon gave up on the shirt, his hands still shaking too hard from his nearly being blown to smithereens, and Chaz walked over, taking over where he'd left off. He dropped his arms to his sides.

"Okay," he said, "we're in the clear, for now, but why stick around? Don't we have more trains to rob? Thorne still has loads of silver running about the countryside, waiting for us to lift. We did what we came to do, and now we should get out while the gettin's good."

She shook her head and came to his belt buckle, pulled on it. Dillon grew hard and reached for her, but she pushed him away. "You stink of smoke. A bath first, then the opera, and then" — she glanced up through her black lashes and unbuttoned his trousers — "then we shall see."

Well, that sounded promising, but he wouldn't bet the bank on it. He stepped back and slid his trousers off his hips and down his legs. *Damn, his boots.* He hobbled over to the fainting couch and plopped down on it. *Sexy move, West.*

"You haven't answered me," he said as he pulled off his boots one by one. "You might think you've distracted me, made me forget what I was saying, but it takes more than a little seduction to fog my mind. Why aren't we leaving?"

A frown plowed a small furrow between her brows, and she walked away to pick up a slim cigarillo from a dish on a side table and light it with a match. "We are waiting," she said after she drew on the cigarillo and let the smoke stream out from between her parted lips.

He pulled his trousers off over his feet and straightened up. Still dressed in his union suit, he braced his hands on his knees. "Waiting for what?" He knew he would regret the answer, and he did.

She sent him a look through the fragrant smoke wreathing her head. Her eyes sparkled with pure mischief. "For Thorne, of course."

"Of course," he said with a sigh, feeling like a fool Comanche addled on peyote. "Of course. We blew up the mint not to deny Thorne his silver but to lure him to Zacatecas."

"Of course." Her smile needled him, and she drew on the cigarillo again. "Now will you bathe and dress quickly? The water grows cold, and I grow impatient. I would not want to miss the overture."

The opera house offered a gaudy mixture of Baroque extravagance and Spanish elegance. Gold leaf-decorated columns held up the domed ceiling, from which a heaven of sparkling chandeliers floated like warm yellow suns, gently illuminating the audience and stage.

Painted panels depicting scenes from famous operas bedecked the plaster walls, and heavy garnet velvet drapes, matching the upholstered seats, swathed the areas between the panels and embraced the music within their boundaries. A sea of silks and satins and glinting jewelry about swanlike necks and draping onto sun-tinted bosoms flowed across the boxes and balconies above the common people ensconced below, dressed in their Sunday best with white tunics and brightly colored peasant blouses.

From her box to the right of the stage, Chaz lifted the opera glasses and leaned forward, her attention rapt on the soprano dominating stage center and swelling the air with a sweet aria. Dillon listened with one ear and folded his arms over his chest, his narrowed gaze fixed on the uniformed soldiers stationed at the doors. He had a hunch they were there for reasons other than their love of opera and their desire to hear Rigoletto sung by the Italian company. They held their rifles tensely, respectful of the crowd, unobtrusive but alert, heads continually turning, faces stony, gazes sweeping the audience. Occasionally, one guard would look up at the wealthy boxes as though assessing the patrons within their graceful confines. Each time that occurred, Dillon grew still, held his breath, and his gut churned.

What were he and Chaz doing here, out in the open? One of the campesinos from the festival parade could have passed on a description of the men running from the mint's side gate, and when he and Chaz left the opera, Manzanita's men could be waiting for them.

Chaz laid a lace-gloved hand on his knee, and he turned with a strained smile. "Can we leave now?" he said low out of the side of his mouth, as if the guards could read his lips.

She smiled sweetly with an expression of relaxed bliss. "During the first act? *Por Dios*, Dillon, relax. You are as prickly as a cactus. We are in no danger."

"What about them?" he asked and dipped his head toward the nearest soldier.

"Their presence means nothing. Díaz values his houses of culture, and the *soldados* attend every performance to ensure good behavior." One eye closed in a saucy wink. "Unruly revolutionaries have been known to disrupt the congenial atmosphere."

Dillon attempted a smile, but he suspected it was a bit macabre, and as he looked at her, his heart beat faster. She was so beautiful tonight, more beautiful than a bandito had any right to be. The lace mantilla swept the side of her face and concealed the scar that lay beneath it. Her dark blue eyes gleamed and bright red mouth glistened. As his gaze poured over her, she turned back to the opera. In her concentration, her tongue swept out to moisten her lips. Now Dillon's heart wasn't the only part of him to swell. He leaned sideways and tasted the skin at the base of her neck where it met her shoulder.

She fluttered her fan. "Not at the opera, señor," she said. Her eyes darkening with interest belied her words. "You must behave yourself and refrain from creating a spectacle, or you will draw attention to us."

When the gazes of three of the soldiers focused on them, Dillon could see what she meant. With a sigh, he straightened and returned to the action on the stage. His thoughts wandered to Thorne and his own plans. *If Chaz ever found out Thorne paid me to find and deliver The Ghost Wolf... That wouldn't happen, couldn't happen.* He was now determined to bring Thorne to Mexico and meet him on his own terms without Chaz ever knowing. He would truss up the man like a wild turkey, far from the law and the wealthy miner's bodyguards, in a place where Chaz could not interfere. Once he had Thorne alone and helpless, he would fetch Chaz and let her put her demons to rest. Soon his painful erection eased, breathing deepened, and eyelids drifted closed. Like usual, he fell asleep.

After the opera, Dillon returned Chaz to her room, and she invited him in. His mind, still a bit sluggish from his opera nap, now interpreted her invitation as a sign she wanted his company. He came fully awake, as did the rest of his body, particularly his nether parts. She moved over to a chair, removed her wrap, and dropped it onto the chintz upholstery. He came up behind her, and slowly, almost reverently, eased the straps of the golden gown off her shoulders.

She tugged them back up, turned at the waist, and gave him a look he had difficulty interpreting. *Confusion? Irritation? Get the hell out of my life?* No it wasn't a glare, more as if she were mentally saying: *I think I want you but don't know for sure, and until I do, back away.*

He backed away.

Okay, this was going to require some help, if he even decided to carry on. His conscience was giving his head a mental thumping. This woman, this amazing, complex, exasperating woman trusted him with her life and the life of her son, and he'd crept into her good graces with all the best intentions of a fox creeping into a hen house. She'd put her faith in him, and when all was said and done, he was no better than Thorne.

Every time Dillon dwelled on his duplicity, he felt lower than a mud puppy in a wallow, slinking along on its belly in the muck. To top off the nagging of his somewhat dubious scruples, another persistent thought dug beneath his skin with ever-increasing urgency. If he kept pursuing Chaz—and he knew he couldn't leave her alone—what if he planted a babe inside her? Would she think he, like Thorne, would leave her to raise another illegitimate, fatherless child on her own? *Damned if I would.* Course, having only Thorne's behavior to go on, she couldn't know that.

Dillon walked to the table beside the window and lifted a bottle of champagne. "How about we celebrate, *querida?*" he said as he arched a brow and waggled the bottle.

She shook her head. "I never drink spirits."

"Never?" That someone her age didn't drink liquor, even wine, hadn't crossed his mind, considering she was a desperado. Damn wine cost him thirty dollars, and someone was going to drink it. He pulled the cork from the bottle, poured two glasses, and offered one to her. "Come on, Chaz. Let's celebrate. We just pulled off the greatest non-robbery of the century. Besides, it'll help you sleep."

She looked at the glass through hooded eyes then raised her gaze to him. "One drink," she said, "for a restful sleep."

He agreed with a grin. "One drink."

Dillon's drunks followed a predictable pattern. First, the booze warmed him, and then a feeling of euphoria spread through him. At some point, he became horny. Always, before he passed out face-first onto the floor, he went through a silly phase. That's when he usually made an ass of himself. The meanest desperado in the territory could be pointing a gun at his head, and he'd laugh until his sides split, until he puked.

Now he sprawled in the armchair across the room from the bed and laughed like a braying donkey, slapping his knee and joggling the glass in his other hand. The golden champagne slopped over the rim and wet his wrist. Chaz had said something that struck him as hilarious; damned if he could remember what it was. She said it again, making no more sense than the first time, and he roared with laughter.

"Dillon," she said, licking her lips and looking cross-eyed at her empty glass, way past the one drink she'd agreed to, "I think I need more. I believe you have been drinking my bubbly."

He hooted so hard he got the hiccups. Untangling himself from the chair, he made his unsteady way to the table and tried to open the second bottle—no the third. *The fourth?* It slipped out of his hands and clunked to the floor. He dropped down cross-legged and braced the bottle on the floor to tug at the cork. Chuckles rumbled up from his throat. Then he made a fatal mistake when his gaze swung to Chaz. She lay on her side on the bed, the golden gown scrunched up around her knees and one strap hanging off her shoulder. The light from the lantern cast a glow over her dusky skin, and she seemed to draw the illumination like the sun drew the planets.

Dillon set aside the bottle and crawled across the floor to her on his hands and knees.

"What?" Chaz asked, looking down, a fine web of creases appearing at the corners of her eyes.

He came up on his knees, leaned over, and kissed her full on the lips. "Nothing, *mi corazón*, but I had this insane idea I wanted to trot past you." He grasped at the tiny bit of sobriety that lingered on the edge of his consciousness, and no longer did everything seem so amusing.

"Ummm, I had an idea too." Her voice was low, sexy, and thick from the wine.

Even in his state of intoxication, Dillon grew long and hard, but he considered her veiled invitation for only two shakes of a mare's tail. "Not that kind of an idea. Something a little more novel."

She brushed her hair out of her eyes. "Novel? What do you mean by that? I know nothing about novel lovemaking."

Visions of tying Chaz to the bedposts and licking every inch of her body came to his mind. He drove them away with a shake of his head. "No. Not lovemaking. I know it's plumb crazy, but I was thinking we might get hitched." He reckoned his mouth had run away with him.

Confusion flowed across her face. "Hitched?"

"You know, married." There, he said it again. What was he thinking?

"Married?" Peals of laughter sprang from her lips, and she fell back on the bed, hugging her belly.

Dillon allowed her laughter to subside before saying, "I love you, *mi corazón*. I want to marry you, tonight. How about it, will you marry me? Let's drink to it." When he upended the bottle beside him, only a few drops landed on his tongue. *Oh yes, that one was empty.* As he transferred his attention from Chaz to the location of the full bottle, he was dimly aware of a great stillness that had come over her.

"I will belong to no man," she said with a harsh intake of breath, her words slurred. "I will not be any man's property,"

"You've got it all wrong," he ran on, head swinging back to her and digging himself in deeper, voice thickening again as the wine took possession. "I'll belong to you. I'll willingly be your property, your slave."

She pulled her brows together over a wrinkled nose and looked at him as if pine branches had grown from his ears. Another laugh exploded from her, and she hiccupped at the end of it. "*You* will belong to *me*? *You* will be *my* property? You will be my slave?"

A sloppy grin stretched his lips. "That's what I said, and I'm sticking by it."

"This is *estúpido*." When she shook her head, her unbound hair swayed back and forth. "*You* are *estúpido*. Bring me some more of that wine. I will need it to hear the rest of this ridiculous proposal."

Always obedient, Dillon pulled himself up, using the edge of the bed for leverage, and weaved away across the floor. He caught his hip on the edge of a table. "Ouch," he said and peered at the table as if it had sprung from the ether. "Who put that there?" At Chaz's laughter, he straightened his line of approach and made it to the bottle of champagne he'd left on the floor. When he bent over, his head swam. "Whoa," he said, straightening with a lurch. This time, he managed to pop the cork and pour two glasses, but he lost much of the contents on his way to Chaz. He handed them to her and returned for the bottle. By the time he made it back, Chaz had drunk his glass and hers. She took the bottle from his hands and poured herself another, only slightly missing the glass rim.

"That's me, all right," he said, "*estúpido* and *estúpido* in love." When he plopped down on the edge of the mattress, he bounced her about and spilled her wine.

"*¡Eh!*" she said. The mattress springs protested as loudly as she did.

"Sorry, darlin'." He slid off the bed onto his knees and pulled on her hands, bringing her to the edge of the mattress. "Let's find a priest tonight before I come to my senses, I mean change my mind, I mean change your mind."

Giggling, she swung her legs off the bed, reached down for the champagne bottle, and slopped more wine into the glass. "You are drunk, Dillon. We cannot be wed now. It is the middle of the night, and the priest will be asleep."

He clambered clumsily to his feet, gripped her hand, and tugged her off the bed. "Then we'll wake him. If he wants to go back to sleep, I'll march him to the altar at gunpoint. Even drunk, I can hold a gun. May not be able to shoot straight, but I can hold it."

She sipped on her wine, and light from the lantern reflected from her eyes. "I have not yet said yes, señor West. Will you also hold me at gunpoint?"

Dillon sank down on one knee in front of her and grasped her hands. Both their hands were shaking from their state of intoxication and the gravity of the moment. "No, *mi amore*, I'd never make you do something against your will, but if you say yes, you'll make my heart sing."

Her eyes narrowed on him. Dillon couldn't tell if it was the wine or if she was assessing his character. "Such a poet for a gun hand."

"The better to please you. The better to love you. I can even quote Shakespeare if you like." He tilted his head to one side. "'Who ever loved that loved not at first sight?'"

She tilted back her head, laughed, and her white throat beckoned.

He leaned forward, tried to place a kiss on the slim column of that throat, and missed. Still laughing, she caught him before he fell over, and righted him. He shook away his dizziness and pressed, "Will you, Chaz? Will you consent to be my wife and let me cherish you for all our days?"

She looked around the sparse room as her laughter subsided to hiccups. "Even if I said yes, I have nothing to wear."

His knees wobbled as Dillon fought his way to his feet. "Just like a woman."

"Are you of the faith?" the priest asked Dillon. Dillon, who still couldn't quite figure out how he'd gotten here, rested his gaze on Chaz and shrugged, flummoxed as to what he should answer. He was still more than a little drunk, subject to sudden and inappropriate hiccups, as was Chaz, and they both had shown more frivolity than was appropriate for the setting and event. The priest had displayed reluctance to marry them on such short notice, but now he seemed resigned to it. Dillon didn't want to muck it up, but to lie to a priest... He wasn't a religious man, but he liked to keep all his options open.

"Well, Padre," Dillon said slowly, "I have some faith, but—"

"I am with child, Padre," Chaz said.

Dillon whipped his head toward her, and his bloodshot eyes nearly bugged from his head. "With *child?*"

Chaz smiled sickly at the priest. "Forgive me, Padre. I had not yet told him. Please allow us a moment alone." She tugged hard on Dillon's arm and hauled him to a corner, well away from the priest.

"With *child*?" he said again, his brain numb and not just with wine. "With *child*? How? When? Is it Alec's? I'm damned sure it's not mine. With *child*?"

"*Silencio*," she said and giggled and hiccupped. "You sound like a parrot."

"But...but—"

"Of course I am not *embrazado*. I said that so the priest would marry us now. If we are to do this, I want to do it quickly, before I think too much about it."

Dillon goggled at her. "You *lied* to a *priest*...in a *church*?"

She shrugged. "*Una mentira pequeña.*"

Dillon shook his head, but it made him dizzy, so he abruptly stopped the motion and steadied himself with a hand flat on the wall. "That was no small lie. That was a whopper. You're going to hell for sure."

She chuckled. "Then you are going with me. Where I go, you go. You are my *marido*."

"*Marido*, eh? Your husband." A sloppy, lazy grin tugged up the corners of his mouth. "I like the ring of that."

He looked back at the priest, who yawned and covered his open mouth with a hand. Behind him, a few candles lit the altar and flung golden light into the apse. "Okay," he said, "might as well add lying to our sins. We're already in hell for robbery and arson." He tugged on her hand, and they came back to kneel at the chancel railing.

"Will thou..." The priest looked down at Chaz's bowed head when she remained silent. "My child, I must have your name."

She raised her head and glanced at Dillon before answering, "Charissa Marguerite Elena Gutierrez deSilva." In her intoxicated state, she stumbled over the words but managed to spit out all of them.

Dillon's mouth dropped open. Then he couldn't help

it. He laughed so hard he nearly fell over, hugged his sides and thought he'd never catch his breath again. With a stern expression, the priest turned to him.

"Dillon Charles West," Dillon said as he gasped through the tears running down his cheeks.

"I am not sure about this," Chaz said once they wended their way back to the hotel in an unsteady amble, weaving from one side of the street to the other, and Dillon made a ham-fisted attempt at undressing her. "How can I trust you?" She sent her gaze about the room, eyes unfocused and the flush of alcohol on her cheeks. "No trees in here." When her gaze came to the bed, she said, "I suppose the bedposts will have to do."

His mouth took a turn southward. "Aw, Chaz, please don't tell me you want to tie me up again? I mean, I'm always game for a little variety, but we've already done that. Besides, we're married."

Her smile came slowly, sweetly. "No, not if you promise to be a gentleman."

"Well, I've been called worse," he said with a chuckle and a grin. "If you want a gentleman, that's okay with me. I won't touch you unless you give me permission." His grin dissolved into a wry frown. "Guess you'll want to take the top again."

The wine had dulled her fears, but at the thought of his lying on top of her and holding her down, her stomach went into a sickening slide. It must have shown on her face.

He held up his hands. "Okay, that's fine. I like the bottom. Don't get all nervous filly on me. May I undress you?" he then asked, becoming serious.

She cast her gaze to the tips of her slippers peeking out from the hem of her gown. "I don't think I'm ready for that yet."

"Then will you undress me?" She looked up and

moved forward with only a little reluctance, but Dillon stopped her and walked to the lamp, glancing back. "First, some atmosphere." He bent over, blew out the flame, and opened the curtains, letting in the pale moonlight. Its hoary beams touched his hair, softening the wheat-blond hue to an ethereal silver. He was a pleasant man to look at, never more than now. Whereas Alec had a dark, devilish charm, Dillon's looks spoke more of angels, roguish angels. Notwithstanding his agreeable, nonthreatening appearance and captivating smile, he was no angel. Chaz had to remind herself he was a gun hand, a renegade, and a wanted man. *And my husband.* A sudden shiver crept up her spine. *Why? Why did you do this?* Was it solely the wine? Sobriety quickly surged back in, and she regretted finishing the champagne earlier. She could use its numbing comfort.

Dillon came back over and stood before her. Once again, hands trembling and fingers fumbling with the buttons and snaps, she managed to remove his clothing. He lay down on the bed, making a production of stacking his hands beneath his head.

"There they stay, darlin', until you say otherwise."

He was turgid, obviously ready for her, but she took care with her clothing, removing it slowly, piece by piece. She stopped at the long chemise that drifted down to her knees. When the past intruded, she tried to banish it. This man was not Thorne. He was Dillon, her husband, and he had never shown violence against her. She was unaware of the seductiveness of her languid movements, and her lack of haste and unhurried undressing pulled a groan from Dillon.

"Come on, darlin', you're killing me," he said. "I'm gonna lose it just watching you."

Regardless of his caressing words, his pleas, his attempts at logic — they were now married, and she had nothing to fear from him — she could not drop that last barrier, the chemise — the armor that barred his eyes from her body. However, she still felt nude, for she wore nothing beneath the silky covering.

This time, astride his hips, chemise raised to her waist, her bare flesh rode against his. The wine and the wedding ceremony lowered her inhibitions, and she found it easy to slip him inside her. A sweet heat rose between her legs, and the cream of her longing allowed the thrusting granite length of him to fill the center of her. With the whole of him thick within her, Chaz moved up and down, pressed against him, filled herself with him, and strained to reach some out-of-reach goal of which she was obviously ignorant. As frustration twisted her guts, his voice echoed softly in the moonlit room.

"Let me touch you, please. One hand, no, one finger," he pleaded. "That's all I need. Please, let me, Chaz."

At a loss as to what else she could do to relieve this emptiness inside her, she nodded.

Dillon's hand came out from behind his head, as quick as it ever was when drawing his gun, and he pressed one finger against the place where they joined. A jolt of sensation, unlike anything she'd ever felt before, ran through the core of her body and radiated out through the muscles in her thighs, making them twitch. Instinctively, she moved against his finger, seeking firmer contact. He turned his hand around, palm up, and slipped the finger inside her alongside his shaft. His finger pad pressed hard and rhythmically against a patch of tissue inside her passage. At the same time, a spot of exquisite sensitivity rose up and down against the base of his finger. The swelling flesh inside her stretched the walls of her channel, and hot, slick moisture dribbled out from between the lips of her sex to allow him greater, deeper access.

"Okay, darlin'," Dillon said through a tight jaw, "let's dance."

She braced her hands on the tense, rock-hard muscles

of his belly and eased back her head. Her hair flowed down her back, sweeping against her shoulder blades and the cheeks of her backside. When she closed her eyes, multicolored lights swirled behind her lids, and she rose higher and higher on a wave of euphoria. His finger against her and inside her, his shaft deeply buried, the heat generated by the friction of their bodies burning her, made her sweat inside and out. The pleasure gradually increased until it evolved into near pain.

Chaz wanted to stop. She could not.

In a sudden burst of white light and unbearable heat, pain, and pleasure, the tension released, breaking like a waterfall over a cliff, and surged through her belly, chest, arms, and legs. She all but screamed with the intensity of it. For endless seconds, languorous waves lapped through her nerves and muscles, and her cleft throbbed in spasms against his staff. As she fell forward onto Dillon's chest, unable to maintain her upright position any longer, he poured his hot essence into her.

Catorce

He was married, hitched, harnessed to the wagon, leg-shackled, had jumped the broom. After Patricia's death, Dillon never thought he'd end up this way again. He'd plowed a path through all the Pennsylvania debutantes, the independent Texicans, the fiery señoritas, and the sultry mademoiselles of New Orleans, and never come close. All on her own, this tragic, scarred mestizo with a teenaged son roped his heart and corralled him into marriage. No, she didn't corral him; he corralled her.

Would he have married her if he hadn't been drunk? Would she? Somehow, it didn't matter. Dillon was glad he'd done it. He really did love Chaz, even if it turned out she didn't love him. She'd given herself to him — her passion and her body that another man had abused. He had only one good point in his favor. He'd taught her that allowing a man to love her, physically, wasn't all bad. Eventually she would learn about his connection to Thorne, why this particular gun hand came into her life. She'd be furious with him. But Chaz, being Catholic, she couldn't divorce him.

Thoughts of Patricia and Grace surfaced. *'Til death do us part. It certainly turned out that way, didn't it?* Had he been sober, this marriage would have entailed the same commitment, and deep inside him, it already did, no matter his state of mind when he made his vows. Course, he'd be the one apt to die this time. She couldn't divorce him, but she could sure as shootin' kill him, and likely would when she learned his secrets. A furious Ghost Wolf could be a deadly adversary.

While she slept, warm and soft beside him, Dillon made his move toward the edge of the mattress. Demons pounded at his temples, reminding him of the three or more bottles of champagne that preceded the impromptu wedding. He groaned and held in his brains with one hand as he rolled off the bed. His knees hit the rag rug with a sickening thud that almost shattered his kneecaps.

"Damn," he said softly, as much to keep his head on his shoulders as to prevent wakening Chaz.

Movements stiff, head as sore as the haunch of a branded steer, he dressed and made his way to the telegraph office. More than likely, Thorne was already storming toward Mexico, but the train would have to stop at the border in El Paso, and there, Dillon hoped, his telegram would catch up with the powerful man, and he could put his plan in action.

A smile stretched the corners of his mouth, a smile he seemed unable to wipe from his face. Chaz was really something. Last night she'd overcome her fears and allowed herself to experience the pleasure a woman could feel only from letting go of her inhibitions during lovemaking. She was one plucky woman, and he had no business messing with her. She deserved a good man, a settled man, not one who'd wormed his way into her life and heart on false pretenses. Not a no-good roustabout like him.

At that thought, his smile waned. Wedding or no wedding, he should leave now. To hell with Thorne and Chaz's plans for revenge. He would, too, if he didn't have this feeling Thorne would find a way to kill Chaz before she had a chance to put that silver bullet in his heart. She needed him to protect her. *Really, she did.* He wasn't sticking around simply for the sex. Not that he would turn back the clock if he could.

Heart lighter, intentions firmly in place, conscience tossed in the dust where it seemed to spend most of its time, Dillon strolled the streets of Zacatecas and picked up a warm, sugar-dusted tortilla for breakfast from a street vendor.

Thorne arrived in Zacatecas two weeks later in his private Pullman car hitched to the rear of a Thorne Railroad passenger train. As Dillon stood on the platform, steam blew from beneath the engine to form heated clouds that drifted past the station, and brakes squealed with a sound not unlike cattle being slaughtered. He walked to the back of the train and waited for the great man outside the ornate, brass-bound door. The lawyer, Giles, his mustache and goatee wilting in the steam, opened the door and gestured to Dillon.

The car's interior was awash in bad taste, bordello style. Crimson velvet swags hung on the windows, red-flocked wallpaper covered the walls, and blood-red brocade sedans sat about in cozy groupings. Highly polished brass figured everywhere, even on the posts at the doors and the handrails, and brass cupids leered out from every corner. It lacked only a bosomy lady of the line in low-cut satin. Dillon wanted to hold his nose.

Thorne occupied a seat at a table in the rear. Dillon knew it was Thorne because the other passengers fawned like lackeys as they hovered over the man. He'd envisioned a corpulent figure, but Thorne was fit and hard. A big man but far from fat. Handsome in a way only wealthy men could be handsome, with an air of riches clothing him in consequence and superiority. A touch of coarseness touched his features here and there, as if a Welsh miner had slipped between the thighs of some recent ancestor. Red hair, which Dillon expected, since he was Raúl's father and Raúl got that auburn hair from someone other than Chaz, and mutton chops, which were less expected, although the trend in facial hair was all the rage in America. His eyes were most notable, a blue so pale they could have been carved from an Arctic iceberg.

This man was one mean snake. One rich, powerful, mean snake. Dillon felt it, knew it. When he thought about Thorne's raping Chaz, he wanted to blow a hole right through the man's face...or groin, mess up those expensive duds with a little blood. No, a whole hell of a lot of blood.

Thorne looked up with sharp eyes and half rose from his chair. With a wave of his hand, he indicated a seat across the table. "Mr. West," he said and settled back down when Dillon moved toward the chair, "at last we meet, though I had my doubts about ever seeing your face. From your lack of success thus far, I'd decided you were either the most inept railroad detective in the system, or you found The Ghost Wolf long ago and absconded with my silver for digs in Argentina."

Dillon forced a smile and eased into the seat, settling on one hip so he could reach the gun on his other. "Neither, Mr. Thorne. As I told you in my wire, I found The Ghost Wolf all right, but the silver has yet to surface. He's got it hidden away somewhere in the mountains. The only way we're going to find its location is by force. I'm just one lone cowboy with one little ole gun. I need your men and firepower."

Thorne nodded like a magnanimous despot. "You've got them. I swore to bring this wolf to bay, and I'm going to do it." He motioned to one of his men, who scurried to a rack of cut-crystal decanters. "Drink, Mr. West? Good whiskey, not the rotgut you get down here."

"Don't mind if I do."

The man slopped the amber liquor into a glass that probably cost more than Dillon's gun, horse, and saddle combined, and passed it over. He sipped and savored the smooth, smoky taste of aged Scotch whiskey. Must have cost Thorne a bundle, this imported stuff. Sure beat *aguardiente*. The whiskey ran through his bones and blood and settled a stomach queasy with the stench of Thorne's cologne.

"What's your plan, West?" Thorne asked. "Your wire was pretty sketchy on details."

Thorne had dropped the "mister." *Guess the pleasantries are over.* Dillon slouched back and crossed an ankle over his knee. "I can deliver The Ghost Wolf, but it has to be out of town."

"I'm must admit I'm surprised he's still here after his little stunt at the mint. I'd have thought he'd have scurried off to hide back under his rock."

"He's still here because he has friends. You'll never get within a mile of him in Zacatecas."

Thorne's smile was blatantly suspicious, and he leaned forward. "And how did you get within a mile of him?"

Dillon smiled back and sipped the whiskey again. "That's my job. I'm a gun hand. He needs gun hands."

Thorne eased against the chair's thick padding, and a brow lifted over a pale eye. "You're working for him?"

"You got that right. Have been for six months now."

Thorne took a cigar out of his waistcoat pocket. One of his men jumped like a startled deer and clipped off the end of the cigar. Another whipped out a match, lit it on a brass striker bolted to the side of the table, and offered the flame to Thorne. Thorne put the cigar in his mouth, held it to the flame, and drew deeply. The cigar end glowing, he blew out a stream of blue smoke and regarded Dillon through slitted eyes.

"Let me get this straight," he said. "You've been robbing my trains for six months?"

"That's what I said. And let me tell you, they're about

as safe and secure as a virgin at a convention of rapists."

The barb went nowhere; it didn't even elicit a flicker. But then Dillon didn't really expect a confession, some expression of remorse. The man was cold, as cold as a high desert night.

Thorne laughed and slapped his knee with one hand decorated with heavy diamond and onyx rings. "I like you, West. You've got balls."

"So the ladies say," Dillon replied.

"He's here, in Zacatecas," Dillon said.

Chaz strode about the room with a feral smile. Her skirt twined about her ankles like a bullwhip of silk. "I knew he would come. The mint was the last straw. I knew it would draw him to Mexico." She halted and slanted him a suspicious look from beneath her lashes. "How do you know?"

"I saw his train car at the station. It must belong to Thorne, because only God himself could afford a car like that."

"What were you doing at the station?"

His brows arched. "The schedule, remember? I heard you saying we needed the train schedule." He pulled a paper from his pocket and handed it to her. "Well, there I was, jawing with the clerk and minding my own business, when a train pulled in towing this fancy car. Knew it had to be Thorne's. The clerk confirmed it."

A frown tightened the line of her mouth. "Perhaps his car, but he could have sent someone else."

"Is he tall and broad with red hair and mutton chops?"

A shiver trembled her shoulders. "Yes. The last time I saw him, he didn't have the facial hair, but yes, that's him."

He held out his hands, and she went to him. He pulled her down onto his knee, and she rested her hands on his shoulders. "I hung around," he said, "and overheard him talking to a fat man with chin hair and a mustache."

"Giles," she said.

"Yes, I think that's what Thorne called him. Anyway, Thorne plans to meet with the magistrate, the *juez*, take him to task concerning the lack of suspects from the burning of the mint. Seems Thorne has a fancy hacienda on the edge of town. They'll be there tomorrow night. If the *juez* is lucky, Thorne won't string him up in a cottonwood."

"How many men did he bring with him?"

"I saw about a dozen, all hard cases, mean guns, other than Giles and a few others who look like businessmen."

She rested her head in the crook of his neck and sighed. "At last. At last I will have him. After all these years, he will be at my mercy. I will gut him like a deer."

"Aw, *querida*, I surely love it when you talk sweet like that. Gets me all hot and hard."

They made love that night, as they did every night, and Chaz took another small step toward putting the past behind her. Without his having to ask, she removed her chemise, slipping it off over her head and giving Dillon his first eyeful of her trim, toned body. He sat in a chair and coaxed her to sit on his lap, legs astride him, the core of her femininity resting right where he wanted it, hot and wet around him. While she rose and fell on his swelling cock, she allowed him to smooth his hands over her back and shoulders, down her arms and legs. As long as he didn't try to restrain her, she remained compliant to his wishes. Her silky skin warmed beneath his palms, and a fine sheen of moisture coated her body. His hands glided on the nectar with no resistance. Her legs twitched, breath came in great gasps, and heart thundered so hard he swore he could hear it. His own heart raced like a herd of wild mustangs. She clasped his shoulders so fiercely she pinched the nerves by his collarbone, and his arms grew numb. He rolled his shoulders to persuade her to release her grip, but she only held on tighter.

Dillon encouraged her frenzied motion by flexing his hips and driving deeply upward. He wanted to hold her closer, but she flinched when he tried to put his arms around her. He swore beneath his breath and braced the heels of his hands on the seat of the chair for leverage. Her passion sprang up like a wildfire, burning him with blazing flames. He leaned forward and caught her mouth beneath his, plunging his tongue into that fragrant cavity, twining and dueling. Going deeper, harder, mouth and tongue in sultry rhythm to his urgent movements below. His head was gonna blow clean off from trying to hold back.

At the end, when Chaz's body quaked and her sweet canal squeezed him tight, Dillon put his hands on her waist and pushed down, seating her more firmly so he could reach her womb. She stiffened at first, at his firm grasp, but then relaxed and let go. Her scream of pleasure was purely the sweetest music he'd ever heard.

Dillon had an idea and had cinched it by sending the telegram to Thorne. Not much of an idea, but the best he could do while under fire. He made a deal with Thorne, a deal with the devil, though he really didn't expect Thorne to keep his end of the bargain. Deals with the devil were fraught with deception; then again, so was Dillon.

Thorne, posing as a railroad competitor, thought he would be meeting with The Ghost Wolf. Dillon stipulated he bring only three men with him. The others would remain down along the creek a quarter mile from the hacienda. Thorne would cheat, of course, and his men would be close behind, but Dillon had every intention of working fast and decisively. Chaz thought by burning the mint and luring Thorne to Zacatecas she was setting a trap for Thorne, and she feverishly made plans to capture him at the hacienda. She didn't know that by then, Thorne would already be in Dillon's hands. He'd lied, told her the meeting was the night after the one during which *he* had a rendezvous with Thorne.

If all went well, he would take out Thorne's bodyguards by himself and spirit away the great man, deliver him to Chaz like a side of beef. *How?* That part he hadn't quite worked out yet. *But three on one?* Dillon had faced worse odds and was still walking around to talk about it. Thorne didn't carry a gun out in the open, but he probably had one of those little pepperbox gnat swatters in his waistcoat pocket, sitting alongside the expensive cigars.

A breeze sprang up, a hot, dry zephyr, agitating the dust and rolling tumbleweeds across Dillon's path. In the moon's glow, the spheres of prickly vegetation looked like ball lightning. He rode beside Thorne and continually scanned the washes and hills. His nape pricked, the hairs standing up, but he attributed it to the ghostly cacti, arms raised as though waving at them, and the occasional bat clipping his sombrero.

A mile out from the hacienda, before Dillon could make his move, all hell broke loose. Shooting came from a dry wash behind them, and Thorne's men pivoted their horses about, whipping them into a run. A bad feeling kicking around in his gut—a *really* bad feeling—Dillon crouched over Victory and allowed the chestnut to stretch out into a gallop. When he reached the lip of the wash, he hauled back on the reins and pulled up beside Thorne.

"Aw, hell," he muttered as he looked down at the men milling about in the hollow. Acid burning etched its way up from his gut to a point under his heart. Thorne's gunfighters had caught themselves some stragglers as neatly as flies in amber, stragglers who'd evidently followed him: Raúl and Salvatore. Raúl lay on the ground next to his horse. Salvatore stood beside an exposed chunk of sandstone, arms in the air, while one of Thorne's gun hands rode circles around him and two others lay facedown in the sand.

"I got him," the man covering Salvatore yelled up at Thorne.

Thorne pulled out a snowy handkerchief and mopped the sweat and fine sand from his face. "Bring him here," he called out.

When one of the men kicked him in the side, Raúl moved on the ground, and Dillon sucked in a breath. *The boy was alive.* Raúl climbed to his feet, a gun barrel stuck in his kidneys, and one man tied Raúl's hands behind his back. Then, at the pressure of a hand on his shoulder, he sat back down, legs crossed in front of him.

Escorted by men on horseback, Salvatore trudged across the wash and struggled up the incline to Thorne and Dillon. The *indito* had a wound in his arm that left a trail of blood, black in the moonlight, behind him in the sand.

Salvatore's eyes rose to the two men, and his jaw locked with anger when his gaze lit on Dillon. The look in the Yaqui's eyes, colored by pure hatred, could have peeled the hide off a steer. Though he remained silent— one mercy—Dillon thanked his stars Chaz's lieutenant was unarmed. "I got him," Thorne's man said again and pushed Salvatore forward.

With eyes as mean as a viper's, Thorne looked down on the *indito*. *"La Lobo Fantasma?"* he asked softly.

Salvatore nodded. *"Sí,"* he said in a voice as bitter as bile and a gaze that burned like a prairie wildfire on Dillon's skin.

With a satisfied smile, Thorne turned to Dillon. "Good work, West." He reached into his coat, withdrew an envelope, and held it out. "Here's the balance of the ten thousand we agreed on. Once you deliver the silver this bandit stole from me, you'll get your percentage." What could he do? Dillon took the envelope fat with dollar bills. He wanted to signal Salvatore in some fashion, let him know he hadn't planned it this way… that he was really on Chaz's side, but he didn't have the chance, and this wasn't the time or place. *Probably best this way.* If Salvatore said anything to Raúl, the boy's recklessness and immaturity would probably give him away. Then who would rescue him? Dillon didn't have to think hard to figure out what had happened. Raúl saw him leave and followed him, and Salvatore came after Raúl. Hell, for all he knew, he'd led an army of Chaz's men into the desert like a goddamn, fucking parade.

At the exchange of money and the damning words, Salvatore spat on the ground. If Salvatore had been a few feet closer, that spittle would have reached Dillon's eye.

"Take this one to the hacienda and the other to the presidio," Thorne said with a dismissive gesture. As Thorne's gunmen hauled Salvatore toward his horse and the men below did the same to Raúl, Thorne came back to Dillon. This time, he didn't look as pleased, as though his previous amiability had been show for Salvatore's benefit.

"How did this happen?" Thorne asked in a quiet, deadly voice.

Dillon lifted one shoulder in a casual shrug. "What do you care? You got your man, and I brought him to you. Don't matter whether I hogtied him to a horse or he followed me."

Thorne looked thoughtful and a bit amused, like a kindly tyrant showing tolerance for an unruly, dimwitted subject. "Yes, I suppose that's true."

"You bet your ass it is."

Thorne reined his horse around and walked him toward the men in the distance, who were pulling away. He spoke again but didn't bother to look at Dillon. "I still don't have my silver, West. You won't get another penny until I do."

Dillon fell in behind Thorne. That was fine with him. He didn't want the silver any longer. What he wanted now was Thorne's heart on the point of a cavalry sword. Nonetheless, some protest was indicated if he was to keep Thorne's trust and help Raúl and Salvatore.

"That's going to be difficult now," he said, "what with The Ghost Wolf captured and my cover blown. Any advantage I had is lost. The banditos will scatter and take the silver with them."

"Well, West," Thorne said, deigning to send a glance over his shoulder. "It's up to you to make sure that doesn't happen."

"And how do you figure I'll do that?"

Thorne turned back around. "That's your problem."

Sure as hell was.

Quince

When Dillon returned to the hotel, several of Chaz's men were hanging out in front of the building and were all abuzz with the news. A short while ago, *soldados* had ridden into town with Raúl and locked him up in the presidio. No one seemed to know what had happened to Salvatore. With Raúl taken directly to the prison, chances were, Thorne didn't get a good look at the boy... yet. Dillon hoped so. After turning Victory over at the livery stable, Dillon trudged up the stairs. He dreaded the confrontation with Chaz. Her men surely would have told her about Raúl. If he was lucky, she wouldn't be aware of his role.

"How did this happen?" Chaz all but shrieked while her booted feet stomped across the floor of the room.

Dillon dropped into a chair, expelled a weary sigh, and reached forward to pull off his boots. "I reckon Raúl followed me to the meeting with Thorne, and Salvatore followed him." Dumping the sand out of his boots, he tossed them aside then leaned back in the chair and looked over at her.

"He followed you? That makes no sense. The meeting was tomorr—" She went as still as a prairie

chicken under a coyote's gaze. Her hand lashed
out across his cheek as suddenly as the strike of a
sidewinder. Dillon caught her wrist in one hand before
she could hit him again. She struggled, and he came to
his feet, grabbing her other wrist when she made a move
for the gun on his hip. Hair thrashing about, she spit at
him, twisted and screamed invectives in Spanish. Her
face glowed as red as a wood stove in winter.

"*¡Silencio!*" he shouted and shook her, hard.

She stopped fighting. With eyes as cold as a Dakota
ice storm, she hissed, "You lied to me."

"You're damn right I lied, and I'd do it again. I
wasn't about to let you go up against Thorne and his
guns. I had it all planned out. I could have taken him and
delivered him to you, but Raúl and Salvatore showed up
before I had the chance."

"Raúl," she said, choking. Her eyes gleamed bright
with fear. "Did Thorne…"

He shook his head. "I don't think so. He was too
far away. Thorne is interested in only one person, The
Ghost Wolf. Salvatore admitted he was the bandito, and
Thorne's men took Raúl away before Thorne got a good
look at him. Anyway, Thorne and Raúl aren't the only
red-haired men in the world, not even in Mexico. Even
if he saw Raúl, he wouldn't see anything that would
interest him. Raúl favors you more than Thorne."

Chaz shivered, and Dillon released her wrists,
bringing her into his arms. "He would know," she said.
Her voice trembled as much as her body. "He is the
devil. He would know."

"I'll get him back before Thorne sees him," he
murmured into the part in her hair. "I promise. I'll get
him back."

He held her close, and his pesky cock sprang to
attention in spite of his attempt to tame it. That wasn't
what she required right now. She didn't fight him, his
tight embrace, even though their bodies nestled together

as closely as quail in a covey. She trusted him, accepted his comfort. This was what Dillon had wanted from her — more than sex — trust, though he didn't deserve it. He held her with one arm and ran his hand across her silky hair, pulling her head down on his shoulder. His conscience hurt him as much as Raúl's capture wounded her. He should be strung up at sunrise with a rope made of cactus and rattlesnakes striking at his feet.

"Hold me, Dillon," she whispered. "I need you now, your strength and comfort."

Another arrow in his heart, piercing as deeply as his guilt. Could he make her love him? Yes, he supposed he could, if he came clean and followed the straight and narrow road from here on out. But he wasn't quite ready to come clean yet; their relationship was still too fragile.

"I'm here, Chaz. I'm here for you. I won't let you go."

"Promise. Promise you'll rescue Raúl."

He sighed into her hair, stirring the black strands, dampening them with the moisture of his exhalation. "I promise, *querida*. On my life, I'll do my best."

Clinking metal woke Dillon. He opened his eyes, rolled over in the bed, and his gaze lit on Chaz dressed in leathers as she loaded her revolver. He came up on one elbow and glanced at the window. Night still reigned, and the streets were unusually hushed, indicating predawn.

"Are we riding out?" he asked.

"No. I'm riding out."

He yawned, swung his legs over the side of the bed, and sat on the edge. His bare skin was hot and sweaty, and he smelled of sex. He needed a bath, a shave, and a mountain of bacon and potatoes. He had the feeling he wasn't going to get any of those.

"Where?" he asked, and his stomach tightened at her set countenance.

"The presidio. I'm getting Raúl."

Combing a weary hand through his sleep-messed hair, he said, "Like hell you are. You're not going anywhere near the presidio. One jail break I can manage, but two will strain my limited store of brilliance."

"He is my son," she said as she strapped on the gun belt and tied down the holster to her thigh. "My only child."

Her voice had thickened, as though coated with tears. Dillon held out his hand, and she took it. He pulled her to him to stand between his spread knees. To keep her from going, he'd have to tie her to a chair, and he didn't have that right. He was the one who'd put Raúl in this predicament.

"Do you have a strategy, or were you just planning on busting in with guns blazing and dropping fifty or more *soldados*? Your bleeding out in the dirt of the presidio courtyard isn't going to help Raúl."

Her gaze feathered over his face. "You won't stop me?"

He shook his head slightly. "Not if you have a plan that has a chance in Hades of working. Of course, you go nowhere without me," he added with a grim smile. "Remember, I'm the gun hand, and I got the feeling you're gonna need one."

Chaz returned to the room with her plan—a nun's habit and a priest's cassock.

Dillon groaned and rubbed a hand over his head, ruffling his yellow hair. "This and the color of my eyes might be a problem. In fact, I'd be willing to bet we won't get through the gates."

A tiny frown puckered her smooth brow, and she nodded. "We'll dye your hair, and you'll keep your eyes directed downward."

"Dye my hair?" He grimaced. "I gotta tell you, I'm mighty fond of it just as it is."

She crossed her arms over her breasts. "Then I'll go alone or take Alec with me."

"No you won't!" He snatched the cassock from her hands and walked away. "So I'll dye it, but I'll look like a piebald when it starts growing back in." He stopped and turned, face creased with a worried frown. "Chaz, I can see how this could get us in, maybe even allow us to see Raúl, but how do you plan to get him out? You gonna hide him under that habit?"

"I want only to see him now, speak with him and make sure he is well. This will also give us the opportunity to find out where they are keeping him and assess the presidio's defenses."

Dillon didn't want to ask, but he did. "And Salvatore? Has anyone seen or heard from him?"

"No. He was *estúpido* to admit he was The Ghost Wolf. I cannot imagine what he was thinking."

"I can. He was thinking about saving your hide and Raúl's."

Chaz dashed a knuckle against the corner of one eye, catching nonexistent tears. In all their time together, Dillon had never seen her cry, unusual enough for a woman. Guess she'd shed enough tears in her life to last forever.

"We will find him," she said. "I am sure of that."

Dillon was sure, too, and he had to do something about Chaz, about what was happening between them before they found Salvatore and the man denounced him as one of Thorne's collaborators. He doubted she would give him the opportunity to explain before she filled him full of lead.

As they stood on a hill overlooking the presidio, Dillon sweated and cursed in his cassock. But Chaz, in her nun's habit, felt as cool as a columbine in a mountain breeze.

"Be still," she said. "Priests do not fidgit so."

"This damned thing is sticking to my skin and suffocating me. A hair shirt would have been more comfortable."

She vented an impatient sigh. Dillon was a superb gun hand and had become a joy to her heart, but he complained more than any man she knew. "Then you can remain here, and I shall go on alone." She tucked her hands into the habit's wide sleeves and started down the hill.

He trotted to catch up with her. "No you don't."

Her head bowed reverentially, Chaz smiled when the cassock wrapped around his legs and tripped him. He said, "Christ!" but softer, as they were drawing near the presidio's gates.

"Act dignified, refrain from taking the Lord's name in vain, and keep your head down," she said. "We're nearly there."

A fortified castle from the days of the conquest, the presidio rose above them. Its thick, square curtain wall of sandstone, anchored by towers in the corners, ascended to more than fifty feet high, and the four-foot-thick walls widened out into an overhanging wedge at the top. A gate of iron topped by a gatehouse guarded the entrance. When *soldados* stopped them and asked for their papers, Chaz produced the documents Largo had obtained from a sympathizer at the church. Once through the gate and into the outer ward, they faced another curtain wall and gatehouse, this one more heavily guarded.

Chaz began to sweat inside the habit while the guard examined the papers and ran his gaze over them as though he divined their true mission.

"Raúl Gutierrez?" he asked. His eyes held a wary look as he peered at Dillon.

"*Sí*," she replied. "Padre Estevez wishes to say the mass for his young soul."

Dillon tucked his chin tighter into the hollow of his throat.

"Can the padre not speak for himself?" the guard asked.

She said, "He has taken a vow to speak only the sacraments."

Head still downcast, Dillon raised one hand and made the sign of the cross.

The man grunted and waved them through.

Dillon stumbled again on his cassock, and Chaz held her breath until he righted himself. "A vow of silence?" he mumbled. "Wishful thinking."

A smile tugged at her mouth, but she composed her features when another *soldado* in front of the barracks barred their way. After glancing over their papers, he directed them to a door leading to the underground cells.

The stone steps wound down, deep into the bedrock beneath the castle, and the air grew cooler and damper. Moans came from far below, and Chaz's shoulders trembled. Dillon must have sensed her anxiety, because he gripped her arm and gave it a squeeze. She turned her head, and the taut muscles of her jaw relaxed with a smile.

"*Gracias*," she whispered.

"*De nada*." His return smile smoothed the worried furrows from her brow. His support lit up the dank spaces like a torch and made her glad she had agreed to his coming with her. Not that she could have stopped him. He was as stubborn as Delicia's old mule, Juanito.

A final stop at the prison guardroom and they were in, walking past barred cells with only straw on the cold stone floors. Beseeching hands reached out into the corridor, and pleas for succor filled the close, fetid air.

"Padre, *santa*, pray for my soul!"

"*Hermana*, I am innocent! I beg of you, tell the *soldados* I am innocent!"

Chaz closed her ears to the voices.

Raúl occupied a cell on the lowest level, the one with the least light and air, indicating his disfavor with the *soldados*. It was a mean cell, small and filthy, but when Chaz gripped the bars and called out his name, Raúl sprang to his feet. A wide smile cracked his face.

"Chaz! What are you doing here? And with this

priest? He need not pray over my body yet."

Dillon lifted his head. "When I get through with you, you'll wish to God you were dead and in hell."

Raúl sucked in a gasp, then his grin reappeared, wider than ever. "If you wish to play a priest, señor Dillon, you had better learn how to speak to penitents like one."

"What fucking impulse made you follow me—?"

"Are you well? Did they beat you—?"

"*Por favor*," Raúl said with a laugh, "one at a time."

Chaz and Dillon glanced at each other, and Dillon dipped his head. "You first," he said, "but then I get a crack at him."

She turned back to Raúl and took his head between her hands. "Are you well? Have they mistreated you in any way?"

"I am fine, *mi madre*. The food is meager and full of bugs, but I am well otherwise."

She let out her breath. "We will release you. Do not despair. You will be here but a short while." She pulled up the skirt of her habit and untied a sack around her waist. Handing it to Raúl, she watched him extract bread, cheese, smoked sausage, and a canteen of water.

"I thought you looked a little pregnant," Dillon said from beside her, "but I was afraid to ask."

She sent him a warning look. "This is no time for levity, señor West."

"I thought to bring along something a little more useful than bread," Dillon said to Raúl. From beneath his cassock, he produced two pistols and passed them to the boy. "Don't try anything stupid, like trying to shoot your guards," he warned. "Hide these in the straw and wait for us to come back with reinforcements."

Raúl nodded, an easy grin on his face. "I will do that, but don't take too long. I heard them talking about sending me to the silver mines."

"Good news. If they do," Dillon said, "leave the guns

behind and go along quietly. It'll be easier to spring you from the mines than from this fortress." He lifted his head, and his gaze scanned the rock overhead and on all sides of them.

"Do you know what happened to Salvatore?" Chaz asked.

"No, but the guards are chattering hens. They say he is *La Lobo Fantasma*. Thorne's men took him away before I could speak with him. The guards also say he is being held in isolation in an impregnable place, awaiting Thorne's pleasure." When he cast a look at Dillon, his expression sharpened. "What were you doing meeting with Thorne? The guards say an *Americano* pistolero helped capture *La Lobo Fantasma*."

"Your guards talk too much," Dillon said gruffly. "I had a plan to capture Thorne until you and Salvatore blundered in like a pair of dogies into quicksand. If not for your stupidity, I'd have wrapped up this whole revenge scheme of your ma's."

Raúl's grin appeared again. "I was in need of some entertainment, and when I saw you leave, I knew you would provide it."

"Hush, *niño*," Chaz said. "Show some respect and understanding of your situation. Señor West is correct. Had you minded your own business, as you should have, we would not be facing the dangerous task of extracting you from your own foolishness."

"*Dispénseme, madre.* Forgive me."

A smile smoothed the lines of stress from her face. "*Usted no tiene la culpa.*"

"Not his fault?" Dillon replied, incredulity in his voice. "Then whose is it?"

Snapping around, she drilled him with her gaze. "Yours. It is your fault."

His jaw dropped, and he braced his fists on his hips. "Mine? How in hell is it my fault when you can't control your child?"

"You should never have gone after Thorne without telling me."

"Shhh," Raúl said. "You will draw the guards."

She lowered her voice. "Raúl is right. This is no time to discuss fault."

"Señora," Dillon said, "you have a mind to discuss this again, and I'm liable to wring your neck."

The sound of footsteps tapping on the rock alerted them, and Dillon lowered his head once again. As the guard approached, Dillon described the sign of the cross before the bars. "Bless you, my son," he said. "*In nomine Patris, et Filii, et Spiritus Sancti. Amen.*"

Dieciséis

The bandits dribbled into the area surrounding the
mines and stood watch on a hillside while Dillon and
Chaz rode closer. Chaz had donned men's clothing: pants
and chaps, and a wide sombrero. After arguing with
Dillon for a week about storming the prison, she'd finally
kicked him out of their bed, and he'd spent the rest of his
nights half in, half out of the room's armchair. Whenever
he'd changed his uncomfortable position, snorts and
curses interrupted his loud snoring. After a week of
sleepless nights and the two of them snapping at each
other, her nerves were as knotted as a hanging noose.
Once word filtered out of the presidio that a contingent
of slaves had been sent to the mines, including a boy
from The Ghost Wolf's band, Chaz could wait no longer
to retrieve her son.

They paused before reaching the gates. Guards
with rifles held position beside the wooden doors, and a
stockade of sharpened saplings driven into the ground
surrounded the area. Through the gaps in the fence, Chaz
scrutinized the mine.

It gouged a broad hole, like a wound, in the
mountainside. Tracks for carts led into the gaping

entrance, and a constant stream of prisoners in rags shuffled in and out. Several dozen guards with whips moved the workers, the snap of the lashes like pistol shots in the still, heavy air. No conversation came from the men, no laughter, no smiles; only despair clothed emaciated bodies, and the occasional groan or cry rang out when a whip met its mark.

She stared, scarcely able to breathe. She could not imagine Raúl, her child, being subjected to such treatment. She had seen the mines before, not this one, but others, felt the misery of the poor unfortunates, but never had it come quite so close to her and her family. The mines and their forced labor were one of the reasons she fought so hard to win the freedom of her people. Her revenge on Thorne was only one vital battle in that war.

Her gaze skipped from worker to worker, looking for Raúl, but nowhere did she see his slim body. Even at a distance and were he in rags, she would recognize him.

"We must get inside," she said to Dillon, who sat beside her on his chestnut horse.

He leaned toward her, the points of his cheekbones as sharp as the picks the workers carried over their shoulders and as hard as the bounty of silver they wrested from the mountain. "We will. But I doubt they allow visitors beyond that gate. We'll have to go in after dark."

When a cart rumbled up to the gate, the guards stopped it and sifted through the contents before allowing it access. "It will be difficult," she said. "If this mine is like the others I've seen, the palisade is less heavily guarded after the sun sets, but they lock the prisoners inside the mine." She pointed to iron gates folded back against the mountain beside the hole. "They chain the men to the rock walls then close and lock the gates."

"Does it have another entrance?"

"I would not think so," she said with a brief shake of

her head. "The other mines have only the one entrance and exit."

"As they dig the mine deeper," he reasoned, "they have to have fresh air to breathe. The older the mine, the farther inside the mountain it goes and the more likely it has an air inlet. This looks like an old mine."

"I believe it has been in operation about seven years. However, Thorne does not care if his slaves breathe bad air. He can easily replace them."

"Every castle has a back door," he said.

"*¿Qué?*"

"Every castle has a back door. Every entrance has an exit. Every inlet has an outlet. Yin meets yang. It's my motto."

A crease pleated her forehead. "You have a motto?"

He lifted a brow. "Don't you?"

Bewilderment made her shake her head.

When Dillon reined his horse around, she followed suit. "I'd still like to check the backside of that mountain," he said, "and see if we can find a way in that doesn't involve gunning down twenty or thirty well-armed men and cutting through iron gates."

She shrugged with the smallest movement of her shoulder. "As you wish, but I will grant you only a few hours. Then we must penetrate the palisade. I will not leave Raúl in this mine any longer than that."

It took two hours to make their way to the other side of the mountain. Once there, Chaz ordered her men to fan out and search for caves or other openings in the rock. The sun was winging its way westward, and she was ready to call off the search, when Largo called out from behind a cairn of boulders.

"I have found something," he said, beckoning with an arm.

"See," Dillon said with a grin as they scrambled over the rock rubble and pushed their way through ocotillo bushes. "I told you there'd be another way in."

Chaz frowned. "It is not a way in, yet, señor West, merely something, and will probably turn out to be nothing."

"That's the difference between us," he said, still grinning. "I'm an optimist, and you're a pessimist. An optimist sees a light where there's none, and a pessimist always looks for one to blow out."

A glimmer of a smile flickered across her mouth. "Then truly, I am a pessimist."

"That you are, darlin'. That you are."

Largo had found a low hole no higher than Chaz's knees. "This is useless," she said. "We cannot—"

Dillon dropped onto his belly and squirmed into the hole.

Heart tumbling against her ribs, Chaz went down on her knees and grabbed the heel of one of his boots before it disappeared. "Do not!" she cried out. "You could be bitten. There will be snakes and other creatures inside. You have no light to see your way."

"If I did," his voice came back, muffled, "you'd only blow it out."

She latched onto his ankle, tugged, and nodded to Largo to take the other foot. "Come back now. We will find a light and go together. I promise you I will not blow it out if you will only come back."

With Chaz and Largo pulling on his legs and Dillon slithering backward on his belly, they managed to extricate him from the hole. He sat up once he was all the way out. Fuerte nosed over his body, as though to make sure all of him was still there.

"Whew," he said as he wiped the dirt from his forehead and cheeks, brushed it from his hair, and pushed the dog out of his face. "That's a tight fit."

"Did you see anything?" Chaz asked.

When he looked up, a crooked smile tugged at the corner of his mouth. "Yep. A whole lot of black. I need a light, remember?"

Alec supervised the men who hacked thick branches from the bushes and wrapped them with strips of cloth they cut from the blankets of their bedrolls. Striking a flint, he nursed small flames in a nest of dry grass, and lit the makeshift torches from the fire. He then smothered the flames on the ground.

Chaz took one of the torches from Alec. "I will go first," she said, "then Dillon, Largo, and Rafael. Alec will remain out here in case we need help. If the ceiling caves in, the men will have to dig us out." Her gaze went to Fuertes, who was trying to squirm into the hole. "Keep Fuertes with you. Tie him, if you must. He may bark if he smells Raúl."

Alec hauled the dog from the hole by his collar and kept hold of it.

Dillon clambered to his feet and wrenched the torch from her hand. "This is my hole. I'll lead. Chaz, you can follow me, and Largo, you follow up with the second torch. The rest of you, do what Chaz said."

Chaz braced a hand on his chest. "You do not give orders to my men."

He sent her a cocky grin. "Sorry, *querida*, but it *is* my hole. I'm the one who said there'd be one, didn't I?"

She vacillated between aggravation and capitulation.

"Don't make this difficult, darlin'" he said, still grinning. "Keep the goal in mind."

The breath leaking out of her in a harsh sigh, she yielded. "You are right. You may go first."

Dropping back down on his knees and onto his belly with the torch held in front of him, Dillon squirmed forward. Chaz followed, and Largo came behind her with his torch. In the close, dark confines, she blessed its illumination.

* * *

Dillon moved deeper into the hole, and as he inched along and cursed beneath his breath, he questioned the good sense of this move. Rocks cut into his elbows, and the dry bones of small creatures crunched under his chest and hips. The torch lit the way ahead, but the hole twisted and turned, so he saw only a few yards at a time. All he needed now was a mountain lion who'd made her den in the mountainside. A buzzing rattle alerted him, and he crept forward slowly. Around the next turn, a rattlesnake sat coiled on the rock. At the light of the torch, it uncoiled and slithered off into a crack in the side of the tunnel. That was the only wildlife he encountered, and at last, the tunnel gave way into a larger chamber where he could get off his belly and stand.

He reached around and pulled Chaz into the chamber, then helped Largo. They had entered a natural cavern made from the violent folding that formed the mountain. Different veins of rock ran diagonally on the walls, indicating an upthrusting of the earth beneath. He tilted his head backward. The ceiling appeared sturdy, but that observation was pure speculation.

Another tunnel led out of the chamber, this one tall and thin, more like a slit. By shuffling sideways and squeezing through tight sections, they moved upright along it. They came across few intersections, but at each, Dillon dropped a cartridge from his gun belt so they could find their way back. By the aching in his legs, he figured they'd gone a mile or so when the sound of picks resounding off rock echoed through the stagnant air.

"The mine," Chaz whispered from behind him. "You were right."

He declined from reminding her he was always right. "Douse those torches," he whispered and handed his torch to her to extinguish. The area they occupied plunged into darkness. Once his eyes adjusted, he perceived a faint gleam coming from a crack in the rock in front of him. Dillon edged over to it and peered inside.

A tunnel stretched beyond the barrier, and far down that tunnel, lanterns glimmered. The shadows of men wielding picks leapt on the walls.

Chaz crowded up behind him, bumping against his back. "Let me see," she hissed.

He moved aside and let her take his place.

"This is it," she said beneath her breath.

"Yes," he whispered in her ear. "All we have to do is break through this rock and unchain them."

When she turned, the faint radiance from the crack illuminated the side of her face, touching and softening the scars, and her eyes glistened with hope. "You believe we can do that?"

"Don't see why not. Course we need picks. Do they post guards inside the mine?"

She shook her head. "The *soldados* imprisoned Manuelo in just such a mine as this. With the palisade, the gate, and the chains, he said there was no need for guards inside."

"Then we come back with picks tomorrow after dark and get them out."

Her face fell. "Not until tomorrow?"

"Sorry, *querida*, it's the best I can offer."

After a moment's hesitation, an expression of pain chasing frustration across her face, she nodded. "*Sí.*"

They stumbled backward and felt along the walls until they were well out of sight of the crack, then Dillon struck a flint and relit the torches. They then made their way back to the waiting men.

In the softness of the ebony night, Dillon held Chaz in his arms, her moist, slim body curled around his limbs, and his conscience rode him like a bronc-breaker on a cayuse. Earlier, once again, he'd moved to undress her. Once again, she wouldn't let him. She'd stepped back and pulled off her own clothes.

"Still afraid?" he whispered.

"*Un poco*. Please do not become discouraged, *mi esposo*. My fear is not of you, you know that. I have a lot of memories to bury. Only one man has ever undressed me — Thorne — and then he tore the nightdress from my body. He liked to see the fabric shredded about me —"

"Hush," he said. "Don't speak of him. Don't even think about him. This is me, Dillon."

"Then I want to do this by myself...I need to."

She shed the pieces of clothing one by one, and eventually they lay skin to skin. Dillon turned her so her back nestled against his chest and groin. He ached with wanting her; lust rode heavily between his legs, and he wanted to take her hard and fast. Nevertheless, like always, he had to take it easy. He caressed her stomach and the fronts of her thighs, rubbing his hands in circles, building up heat from the friction until her skin warmed as though from a hidden fire. She reached for him, her hand brushing his groin, and he nearly exploded. He managed to stay his orgasm only by biting down hard on his tongue until the pain distracted him.

This time, Chaz's hesitation, her fear, failed to materialize. Against all her wishes, even her instincts, she was beginning to love this man, this man who professed his love for her. She'd never believed a man could be so gentle, so tender, his heart so open. Her muscles softened, like dawn creeping through fog, and her legs trembled.

He rolled her onto her stomach and looped an arm around her waist, easing her up onto her hands and knees. As he settled on his knees behind her, his fingers weaved into her hair, and he tugged lightly then released. The palm of his other hand smoothed down her spine and around her hip until he buried his fingers in the cleft of her thighs. Her head dropped to the side, to one shoulder, and she touched him with a lingering glance. Dillon smiled, sweet and kind of lopsided, and then gradually, a look of intensity hardened his jaw, stiffened his smile.

He spread her legs apart on the bed, stroked her with his fingers, dipped inside the heart of her. Her moisture coated his digits, making them slippery, and before long, Chaz moved of her own volition against his hand. He grasped her hips with both hands and slipped easily inside her. Hooking one arm about her waist, he brought her hips up into his thighs to meet the deep thrust of his penetration.

While still heavy inside her, he tugged her upright onto her knees. One hand splayed against her abdomen. He spread her to his touch, opening her for his caress, the fingers of his other hand moving down to stroke the petals of her sex. Her tender folds felt slick and distended, pulsing and heated with arousal. As Dillon pumped strongly inside her, his mouth moved across her shoulders and neck in wet, openmouthed kisses.

His breath became ragged, and he tucked his chin into the hollow between her neck and shoulder. His harsh exhalations bathed her skin with wet heat. At the hot center of her femininity, a liquid fire unfurled deep inside. His hand pressed more firmly against her lower stomach, and his thrusting became more urgent. At the steady thrust and drag, the driving rhythm, the rush of fire through her veins, Chaz let out a gasp.

A sudden wetness flooded between her legs, and she let out a little sob then a muffled scream. His hand left her font and turned her head to the side. His mouth closed over hers and took her whimpers into his throat. Heat ignited in her core and moved upward, pulsing through her body. She arched her back with the convulsing grip of the contractions, and he held her tighter and grunted, spilling his white-hot orgasm deep inside her. His teeth closed over her plump lower lip and bit down lightly. That last, small sensation brought her to full orgasm, and she nearly burst into flames from the explosion of light and searing fire.

As Chaz sagged back against Dillon's chest, he kept one hand against her abdomen, still pressing her firmly against his heated body. His other hand he let slip down the side of her neck, across her chest in a meandering path, along the side of her hip and the outside of her thigh, gliding through the moisture springing from her pores and smoothing it across her skin.

She murmured, voice muted and sleepy, and he lowered her to the bed, turned her on her side, and moved in behind her. His chest pressed against her back, and his knees nestled in the crook of hers. As he cuddled her, his fingers lightly traced the scars on her face. They were old, the skin nearly smooth. Only faint lines indicated her imperfections. Nevertheless, she winced at his light touch.

"How did you get these? I asked once before, but you wouldn't answer," he whispered then nibbled on the silky flesh of her neck.

"You do not want to know."

Dillon wasn't willing to accept that. Until she fully confronted the horror of her past, it would continue to haunt her.

"I do. Please, *querida*, tell me."

"I fought back." Her voice was very small, and he imagined it was almost the voice of the child she was at that time. "I decided I would kill him. I had a small hunting knife. It was not very long or sharp. I hid it beneath my pillow, and when he came to me and climbed on top of me, I stabbed him in the side."

"You must have been frightened."

"I was terrified. I knew if I did not kill him, he would kill me." She sighed, a shuddery release of breath. "I did not kill him. The knife was too small to inflict any real harm. He pulled it out and held me down."

His heart ached for her. "You don't need to tell me any more."

"No. You wanted to know, and now you should hear everything so you can understand Thorne's true evil." Her breath became rapid and shallow, as though she was trying to master her fear. "His words are burned into my memory. He said, 'I will teach you. When I am through, I will be the only man who will ever want you, ever have you. Your ugliness will provoke disgust and pity.' Then he took the knife and carved on me. Not deeply enough to sever muscle, only enough to scar."

"Your mother, the servants?" he asked.

"My mother died the year before, and the servants were all petrified of him. He told them I tripped and fell into the cheval mirror, cutting myself by accident. He shattered the mirror to back up his story. Only Mariposa suspected the truth. She was my mother's nursemaid and then mine. But there was nothing she could do. Thorne has more power over the police and politicians than you can imagine. None would have stood with me against him."

"Did you fight him again?" he asked.

"Every time." She released a short, humorless laugh. "For what good it did."

Dillon wrapped his arms around her and hugged her tight to him. Her chest hitched, as though with dry sobbing. Her silence and lack of tears were eerie, and he suspected she needed to release those tears to be truly free of Thorne.

Diecisiete

Chaz pressed for retrieving her son immediately, but
Dillon talked her into waiting until the dark of the moon,
saying he feared attracting the unwanted attention of
anyone who might question the presence of a group of
riders on the mountain. Though stars splayed brightly
across the heavens, that meager light helped them little,
if at all, as it failed to penetrate the tunnel. A long, dirty
night of hard work with the picks lay ahead, straining
muscles, and the torches seemed to suck all the air from
the small space in which Chaz's men worked. They kept
a constant eye on the cavern ceiling, as though expecting
it to crash down on their heads at any time. Other than
a sifting of rock dust, it held. Mindful the guards out in
front of the mine might hear the ringing of the picks, they
wrapped the iron heads in cloth, rendering them quieter
but less effective.

After hours of backbreaking labor, they broke
through and made a gap large enough for a man to
squeeze past if he sucked in his belly. Taking into
account that guards might still be inside or close to the
gates at the entrance, they extinguished the torches. They
climbed through the hole and groped their way along

the tunnel, for the lanterns inside the mine were dark. Only by keeping one hand on the side of the tunnel did they keep from running into the wall, although they often bumped into one another. They remained silent, wary of unnecessary noise, despite they'd already made a commotion worthy of awakening Satan in the bowels of hell. After what seemed to Chaz an endless span of time fumbling around in the dark, they found the prisoners.

The workers' prison lay well back from the entrance, but not so far back light from outside could not penetrate were the moon full. Chaz realized she had reached the prisoners when she stumbled over a soft object and wrenched a moan from it. She swung out an arm to halt Dillon, who trod silently a few feet behind her.

Crouching down, she whispered, "*¿Cómo se llama usted?*"

"Pietro," the man replied. "*¿Quiénes son tú?*"

"*La Lobo Fantasma.*"

"Ahhh," he sighed as though with his last breath.

Chaz wanted to ask about Raúl, but this was not the time. First, they had to release these men to lead them out through the caverns and tunnels. She reached up, placed her hands on the iron bracelets around the man's wrists, and slid her fingers up the chains to where they fastened into the wall. Scuffling on the rock came from her men fanning out among the other prisoners. The walls absorbed the soft whispers of exchanged names and muted conversation.

From beneath her jacket, Chaz withdrew one of the items Dillon had showed her men how to make. During the three days they'd waited to attack the mine, he had the men busy making these tools to cut the chains. They looked like heavy scissors but had thick blades as sharp as a saber edge. The men shaped and hardened them over fires built in rock ovens so the flames would burn as hotly as a blacksmith's forge. Dillon told her he'd learned about such tools back East in the United States.

She situated the blades around a chain link close to the man's cuff and bore down on the handles. It took all her strength, but the hardened steel blades finally cut through the iron with a soft snick. All around her, a similar sound came from the locations of other prisoners. After cutting through the chain on the man's other wrist, she whispered to him to remain where he was and moved on to the next man. She asked a few others about Raúl. It was a common name, and many among their number bore it. However, she could not make out faces in the darkness and did not hear a familiar voice. Each time she freed a prisoner and that man was not her son, she sank deeper into despair.

A hand landed on her shoulder, gripped it lightly. "Leave it," Dillon whispered into her ear. "Let's get out of here first."

They worked feverishly for nearly the entire night until a line of over a hundred prisoners followed Chaz and Dillon out the back of the mine and into the predawn. They shuffled and stumbled on shaky legs, and some could not walk at all without the aid of a steadying arm or bracing shoulder. It took more than a dozen trips to move all of them through the tunnel. Chaz stood at the exit. With the aid of a torch she held in one hand and a sky lightening with pinkish gray, she scrutinized every face that came through the hole. Her heart grew heavier when Raúl failed to emerge. Eventually, Largo came out, bringing up the rear.

The hillside was thick with swaying bodies, and her men helped mount the prisoners double on the remuda of horses they'd brought with them. As soon as they were horsed, they rode off in different directions in groups of a dozen or so, each guided by one of Chaz's men, to make their way to a hidden arroyo where Alec had stored food and water and medical supplies. Chaz remained beside the crevice. The wind coming up off the valley floor stung her eyes, and Fuerte pressed tightly against her legs, gazing mournfully up into her face. He looked as lost as she felt.

Dillon walked to them. "Come on," he said with a tug on her arm. "It'll be light soon. We have to make tracks before the guards find their guests missing." When she didn't respond, he stopped and cupped her chin, lifting her face. "We'll find him, Chaz. I swear we will. Soon as we have the chance, we'll question every man who was in that mine."

She could not answer him; her throat was too tight. Enfolding her in his arms, he hugged her tightly. "You know I won't rest until we've found him. But your being caught out here in the open won't help us find him."

An echo of gunfire came on the wind from over the mountain. Dillon was right. The guards had entered and found an empty mine.

They sprinted for their horses, leaped into the saddles, and pounded off the mountainside, the horses' shod hooves drawing sparks from the rocky ground, and the wolf-dog coursing silently behind.

Raúl walked into the gaudy railroad car with his hands secured behind his back. The mestizo guard pushed down on his shoulders, and he slumped onto a red, velvet-covered bench. The guards had told him they were taking him to the mine with the others, but they'd brought him here instead, to this railroad car on a siding outside Zacatecas. Raúl questioned the action only until he saw the railroad car. He now had a good idea why he was here: to meet Justus Thorne. The railroad owner had a mind to question him about *La Lobo Fantasma*. Because he was younger than Salvatore, Thorne thought he would be easier to bully. Raúl straightened his shoulders, firmed his chin. *Thorne was wrong.*

His gaze lit on a knot of men who congregated around a drink cart at the back of the car. One stood out from the others—a big man with red hair and expensive clothes. When the big man gestured, the others nodded. This was the bull in the herd, all right—Thorne.

"You should not flaunt such wealth in a poor country," Raúl said loudly with only a bit of tremor in his voice. "Someone less fortunate could be tempted to rob you."

The conversation among the men died like an expended dust devil. The man Raúl had identified as Thorne turned his head, and a glacial blue gaze pierced him as chillingly as an icicle to the spine. An involuntary shudder rippled across his shoulders, but he managed to make it look as though he were merely shrugging.

The man's eyes narrowed to slits, lines crinkling the outer corners, and he set his crystal glass on a table. Still watching Raúl with intensity, he slowly removed a cigar from his coat pocket, cut off the end with a silver clipper, and leaned over to allow one of the men to light it. He took a drag, released a halo of smoke, and then smiled without warmth. Raúl had never seen a polar bear, but he imagined one might smile in just such a way.

"Like you?" Thorne asked with a voice as low as the hiss of a gila monster. "Like you or your brother would rob me?"

Raúl returned the smile, the curve of his lips as false as the other's. "Not me, señor Justus Thorne. I merely said *someone* and implied it is impolite to live like a king where others starve. Someone could become jealous of such riches." When Thorne moved toward him, managing to convey menace in the strolling steps, Raúl added, "And you have mistaken me for someone else. I have no brother."

Thorne moved closer, only a few feet away, stood there with a look of concentration, and drew slowly on the cigar. Raúl studied him as he was being studied, measuring the height and breadth of the man, and thinking if his hands were free and they were alone, he could take Thorne. Some feature in the man's face looked familiar, but Raúl didn't dwell on it. He couldn't recall ever seeing a picture of Thorne, but perhaps he had. Chaz could have shown him one at some time in the past. Lord knows, this obsession had been with her as long as he could remember.

"No brother," Thorne repeated, his gaze growing sharper. "But perhaps a...mother?"

Raúl swallowed thickly. "A *madre*? Of course, señor Thorne, even a downtrodden campesino such as I has a *madre*." The sudden glint of interest in Thorne's eyes made him add, "She died a long time ago."

"A shame. That's a real shame, boy. I think I once knew your mother."

Behind his back, Raúl's hands knotted into fists. He despised this snake's words, their innuendo, the oiliness in his voice. Thorne must be thinking of someone else; he couldn't know Chaz. As far as Raúl knew, Chaz and Thorne had never met. Then again... He'd asked Chaz a thousand times why, of all the *Norteamericanos* operating in Mexico, she hated Thorne so much. Why she chose this particular man to destroy. She said he represented the worst of what was happening to their country through foreign investment. Raúl had believed her. But perhaps there was another reason why she was so diligent in pursuing Thorne. Why she robbed only his trains, stole only his silver. Perhaps there did exist a history and bad blood between her and Thorne.

"And if she's who I think she is," Thorne continued, "she was a real looker before someone took a knife to her face."

Raúl vibrated with the force of containing his anger, fought to keep it in check, to give this vulture no satisfaction that his words had hit with the force of a cannon shell.

Thorne flicked a hand toward one of the men, and the man scurried off, out of the car. A few moments later, while Raúl sat still, uncomfortable under Thorne's stare, his spine jerked as the car moved.

Thorne nodded to another man, a powerfully built specimen with no neck, and shoulders as wide as the Sierra Madres. His body seemed poised to burst the seams of his tweed suit. The man leaned sideways to take Thorne's words directly into his ear, as if the great man's utterances were too precious to be said aloud.

The man then came to Raúl, yanked him forward, and removed the cuffs from his wrists. Raúl rubbed the red rings on his skin, while the mountain of a man walked to the drink cart and poured two drinks.

"Whiskey?" Thorne asked as he accepted one of the crystal glasses holding amber liquid.

Raúl lifted his head, met squarely those Arctic blue eyes. "Don't mind if I do." Leaning back, spine sinking into the plush horsehair fabric, he crossed one ankle over his other knee. He took the glass and sipped at the smooth, potent libation.

"I suspect," Thorne said, "were I to strip the hide from your flesh, you wouldn't give me any information about The Ghost Wolf."

Raúl opened up one hand. "Señor Thorne, a man cannot tell what he does not know. Stripping off my skin might provide amusement for you, but it would gain you nothing other than a bloodied corpse. I know no more of this bandito than any other campesino."

"Your friend, the Yaqui, he confessed before he died that he was not, in fact, The Ghost Wolf, but a member of the bandit's band."

Raúl's gut took the news with a vicious blow. He held in his reaction. "I am astonished. He seemed like an honest man. He was not my friend, however, only a riding companion. We met at a cantina in Zacatecas and rode out together for protection. Word is, there are banditos in these parts. It is dangerous for a man to ride alone through wild country."

"You fired on my men," Thorne said, pressing.

"I beg to differ with you. Your men, they fired on us. We returned fire, as any man would do under similar circumstances. We only defended ourselves."

"What is your name? Who are your parents? We heard the other man call you Raúl."

"I told you my mother died when I was very young. I have known no name other than Raúl."

"Your father?"

Raúl shrugged.

"Someone must have raised you. A grandparent? Cousins?"

"Señor Thorne, I cannot understand why you have such an interest in my ancestry. It is of no consequence. I grew up in the homes of many families in a poor *edjido*. None were related to me. I told you, I have no family."

A short bark of laughter came from Thorne. "For a moment there, I thought you would say you were raised by a wolf."

Raúl's mouth curved derisively at the corner. "That would be far-fetched, would it not?"

"Yes, I suppose it would." Thorne's eyes held a nuance of respect for Raúl's coolness. "If nothing else, you're in possession of all your faculties. Glib and coolheaded but not foolish."

"It was foolish of me to pick a bandito to ride with."

"You may discover your unfortunate choice was not so unfortunate."

Raúl's gaze wandered to the railway-car window. As the train gathered speed, the plains outside Zacatecas blurred increasingly, streaming lines of gray, brown, and the occasional blob of green. "Where are we going, señor Thorne?" he asked, coming about to face forward again.

Thorne's expression reflected a touch of awe, as though he were truly seeing a ghost. A slow smile spread across his wide face. "Why, my boy, we're going home, and I expect this trip will be very illuminating for you."

Dieciocho

The dark indigo of the sky gave way to the faintest glimmer of light, revealing shadows ringing Chaz's eyes and a fine web of creases across her brow. An errant whisper of wind brought the *weerrrrr* of Montezuma quail and the low grunt of a foraging javelin from the spreading cover of cholla cactus.

Dillon and Chaz had rendezvoused with the freed prisoners in the arroyo, miles from the mine. As the sun came up, they, along with Alec and Largo, questioned the men one by one. None knew anything about Salvatore. *Not a surprising development*, Dillon thought. Thorne would have stashed the man he imagined to be The Ghost Wolf somewhere safe until he had time to deal personally with the bandito. *Raúl?* Also no information, which Dillon had more difficultly figuring out. He supposed Thorne could have recognized the family resemblance, enough so he'd keep the boy close until he found out for sure. Although Dillon wasn't convinced Thorne would suspect his relationship to Raúl, Chaz insisted that was what occurred.

After sending the prisoners on to Asilo, Chaz persisted in returning to Zacatecas, because the city was the last place she had seen her son. She could not be dissuaded, even though Dillon and Largo pointed out the dangers of remaining in the location where she'd not only blown up the Royal Mint but also liberated over a hundred prisoners.

Dillon had never seen Chaz so distraught. She was falling apart fast, and no words from Dillon or her family could calm her. She wouldn't take comfort, and she wouldn't listen to reason.

Once back in the Zacatecas hotel room, she could not remain at rest, and her rapid steps were the wind howling through a canyon. "Where are they? He took everything from me. He cannot have Raúl. Raúl is mine!" She kicked savagely at a ladder-back chair and sent it tumbling across the floor.

Dillon tried to bring her up against his chest, to calm her, still her restless motion, but she shoved him back. "Keep away from me," she shouted. "You men are all the same. Devils, all of you. I want nothing to do with you!"

He moved to a low sofa and sat on the padded arm, folding his arms over his chest. He knew what she must be going through and didn't take her words as a personal affront. He had an intimate familiarity with fear and frustration, as well as grief. He could wait. When her anger and worry ran its course, then they could approach the situation logically.

In the meantime, he *could* find out if Thorne had Raúl. As far as Thorne and Giles knew, Dillon was still a spy entrenched in the bandito band. He said in an aside to Alec, who sat on the sofa next to Largo, "Get her out of Zacatecas. I don't care if you have to drug her, tie her up, or hit her over the head with your gun. Take her back to the mountains before she does something stupid. I'll be a couple of days behind you. I have a task to take care of first."

Leaving Chaz with the men and exiting the hotel, he made his way to the railroad office. Why hadn't he thought of this earlier? Guess he was too wrapped up in trying to knock some sense into Chaz's hard head. The walk comprised about a mile of narrow streets filled with vendors selling mantillas, *huraches*, and all manner of fruits and vegetables. He strode past to the calls and cries of enterprising campesinos bent on trading his pesos for goods. Pigeons waddled beneath and around the stalls, cooing and pecking at crumbs from tortillas dropped to the stones.

Steam from the trains cloaked the platform, and the squeal of brakes pierced the morning air. Vendors with small carts lined the walls of the building and sold small, hard loaves of bread, the aroma of freshly baked goods mingling with the heavy odor of coal dust. A few travelers, their luggage sitting on the platform, wandered about in small groups. They gestured and talked loudly to be heard over the noise of the trains. Others, carting their bags, moved purposefully toward the metal steps and open doors of the cars.

Thorne's railway car had left the siding, and with a large handful of pesos, Dillon learned it had been coupled to a Thorne Railway passenger train bound for the border. With more money passing hands, he found out the time of departure and the stops the train would make as it headed for El Paso. The agent knew nothing more, not even where the train would go once it passed into *Los Estados Unidos*, but Dillon had a pretty good hunch. If Thorne had Raúl, he was going home, home to Chicago. If he had Raúl and suspected the boy was his son, he also believed he knew the identity of Raúl's mother. Thorne wanted his playmate back, and he would use Raúl as bait. Dillon couldn't believe Thorne actually had tender feelings for his son. He hadn't gotten the impression Thorne would make a doting father. The man was a selfish son of a bitch.

Dillon next stopped at the telegraph office where he sent wires to Corralitos and Chihuahua, two of the places the train would pause to load and disembark passengers and freight. He addressed the messages to Giles and said he had information regarding Raúl but had heard the boy escaped. Giles would let him know if he was wrong. Giles was like that. The lawyer wallowed in self-importance and would demand Dillon tell him what he knew about Raúl, because indeed, the boy had *not* escaped but rested comfortably in the bosom of Thorne. In hopes of a reward or other consideration, Giles would want to be the person to take any significant news to the magnate.

The hardest part would be waiting for a reply. Meanwhile, Dillon had to keep Chaz sane and out of trouble. He couldn't tell her what he was up to because, naturally, she had no idea he worked — had worked — for Thorne. The only people with that damning bit of information were Thorne, Giles, Thorne's suited thugs… and Salvatore, who saw Dillon take the envelope of blood money from Thorne. He had to assume Thorne had told Raúl about Dillon's true role in all this, so Dillon added the boy to the list. The only ones likely to carry the tale to Chaz were the latter two — and both were missing.

Once back in Asilo, Chaz sought out Alec and found him in the barn, saddling his horse. His possessions lay on the straw-sprinkled dirt beside him.

"You are leaving me?" she asked.

Alec rested one hand on the horse's mane, and a sad smile wreathed his handsome face. "*Sí, corazón,* you no longer need me."

She stepped forward and captured his hand in hers. "What do you mean? I have much need of you. We have been friends forever. I have always been able to count on you. How can you leave me now, with Raúl gone?"

He laid a hand on top of hers and pressed gently. "Charissa, when I first came to your hacienda, I met a beautiful, frightened young girl who was *muy embarazado*. The birth of Raúl filled my heart with joy because, for a time, the fear left you. I watched you grow from a girl into a woman, and Raúl become a man. And yes, all that time I was your friend."

"Then why do you leave me now, when I rely on your friendship?"

Alec shook his head. "You do not need me. Now you have Dillon. It is no longer my task." He paused to look away and came back to her face, his eyes reflecting a deep sadness. "No, that is not the correct word. It is no longer my right to look after you and watch you grow. Dillon now has that right." A small laugh tumbled from his lips. "Ah, you say friendship. Perhaps that is the problem, *corazón*, I always hoped for more."

"I know, Alec, and I am sorry for that."

"No, never be sorry for what we shared. I will always keep the moments we had together close to my heart. But I see now there will never be more, and remaining here would not be fair to you, to your husband, or to me. It is time for me to leave. Dillon will rescue your son. I had little trust in him at first, due to jealousy, I will admit. However, he has proven himself, and I have no doubt he will help you find and bring back Raúl."

A sick, heavy sense of loss gathered in the pit of her stomach, and tears burned the backs of her eyes. Alec caressed her cheek with the pads of his fingers, his touch light and lingering. "No sorrow now, *mi corazón*. That I cannot bear."

"Where will you go? Will I see you again?"

A rueful smile tugged at his lips. "Surely you will. I am joining with Venustiano in his campaign against the rich *hacendados* and Díaz's foreign friends. I will always be close by. Call for me if you need me."

Dropping her hands, he bent to pick up his saddle and tossed it onto the horse's back. As he cinched up the girth and tied on his bedroll and saddlebags, Chaz stood helplessly by. She wanted to rip the saddle off the horse and beg Alec to remain. Bitter, hollow pain invaded her heart, but she acknowledged the truth of his words. Friendship was not what Alec wanted...needed, and she could give him nothing more. To see her daily with Dillon must be heartbreaking for the man who had loved her in vain for so long.

Chaz moved to his side and circled her arms around his neck. She hugged him tightly and rested her head on his shoulder. "*Vaya con Dios*, Alec," she whispered.

"You will always be my *corazón*," he returned, kissed her on the cheek, and disengaged from her arms. Swinging up on his horse, he rode away, out into the dusky day.

"And you will always be my friend," she said softly.

Thorne's men stuffed Salvatore in a cattle car and trussed him like a pig for the fire. Hours later — could have been days for all he knew — three men forced their way into the car, gunned down his guards, slid open the door, and tossed Salvatore out into the desert. As the train continued away, gunfire still echoed from the car. Salvatore watched it retreat and saw one body tumble out the open door. A second man jumped and rolled across the ground in a boneless tumble. Salvatore dug his fingers into the sandy ground. He pulled his body across the hot surface, groaning with the effort and the pain in his leg, which had snapped in his hard fall from the train. When he reached the first man, he rolled him onto his back. A Yaqui, but his face one Salvatore had never seen. This man was not one of his captors and must have been one of the trio who rescued him. The man's eyes opened, and he grimaced up at Salvatore from a face filled with agony. "*Sí*," he said, managing a small, painful smile before taking his last breath. Salvatore inched over to the second man, who lay on his side, mouth slack in death, head lolling at an unnatural angle. The third man must have died and still be lying in the car.

Salvatore crawled away, alone in the harsh landscape of the high desert. The sun thrust sharp fingers of light through a bright blue sky, and a fiery wind whisked up from the desert floor to strike his body like whip lashes. Sand abraded his face and exposed skin and cut like tiny knives.

The distant peaks of Sierra de los Organos, the sheltering peaks that hid Asilo, stabbed the sky and shimmered like a mirage, but they lay miles away. He would never make it without help. He took a searing breath and pulled his body along by scrabbling into the gravely sand. The yellow disk of the sun bore down on him, sucking the moisture from his lungs and skin. When he reached the shade of a grouping of mesquite bushes, his broken leg would allow him to crawl no farther. Rolling into a depression by the roots, he waited and saved his strength for nighttime.

The ever-present wind in the valley blew Delicia across the yard toward the hacienda. Her long, fat black braid whipped back and forth, slapping against her shoulders. She wiped at her streaming eyes with her apron.

"They found Salvatore!" she shouted, *huraches*-shod feet pounding the ground and kicking up a streamer of dust that followed her.

Though relieved to hear Delicia's news, Chaz's main thought was for her son. She burst out of the house, saying, "Raúl?"

Delicia came to a stop, still crying, although they were obviously tears of joy. "No, *niña*, they did not yet find Raúl. But once Salvatore can speak again, we should learn what happened to Raúl. I have prayed nightly. You must believe *la Santísima Virgen* looks over him and will keep him safe."

Chaz put more faith in her gun than she did in

prayers. Since they'd returned to the mountain retreat and Alec had left, Largo and the others monitored her every move. "Wait for Dillon," they said, but she had no desire to wait for anyone. The only reason she remained was in the hope Raúl would find his way home. At first, she imagined him to be with Salvatore, but that now seemed a vain wish.

She fled across the yard to where Largo and two other men unloaded Salvatore from the back of a wagon pulled by a pair of burros. Breathless by the time she reached him, she managed only, "Salvatore!"

Largo's head shook repeatedly. "He cannot hear you. The desert almost killed him. A campesino found him crawling with a broken leg across the rocky heights northwest of Fresnillo, out of his mind with heat and thirst."

Her gaze lingered on her cousin's burned, pain-racked face and cracked, peeling lips. She wanted to shake him awake, make him tell her what had happened to her son. She allowed herself several long, deep breaths to calm her breast and organize her thoughts. "Get him inside," she said, "so we can set that leg."

For four days, Salvatore lay near death, fevered, his leg infected. On the morning of the fifth day, while Delicia bathed his face with a cool cloth, he opened his eyes and called for Chaz.

During Salvatore's illness, Chaz had haunted the room beyond Salvatore's sick bed. She beseeched God to spare his life, although on some level, she almost wished him dead, knowing she would go to hell for her thoughts. But if he were dead, he couldn't tell her Raúl was beyond her reach, that he shared that same fate. When Delicia called her, Chaz's stomach cramped, and she felt as if she might be sick. She placed one hand on her chest to control the wild, erratic fluttering of her heart, and walked into the room.

When she went down on her knees beside the bed and grasped Salvatore's hand, she was unable to overlook the weakness of his grip. If such a strong man could be brought to this state, what might happen to a boy of sixteen?

"He is alive," Salvatore whispered as he tried to raise his head, the words hoarse and barely audible.

Her heart leapt, accelerated into a fast, steady beat. She clutched his hand tighter. "Where is he? What happened to him?"

What he said next turned her blood to ice.

"With Thorne."

The short conversation exhausted him, and his head fell back to the pillow. She thought he had fallen asleep again and started to release his hand.

He would not let go. "Something else," he croaked out.

She strained forward to hear him. "What?"

"Dillon," he said on a faint breath.

"What about Dillon? Did Thorne capture him?" She had neither seen nor heard from Dillon in more than a week. She regretted the words they'd parted on, and as soon as he'd left, she'd wanted him to come back to her, to hold her...to help her. If he were dead and Raúl with Thorne—she did not know if she could go on. "What about him?" she asked again. "Is he hurt? Is he dead? Please, tell me."

Salvatore's head moved from side to side. "*Importante*," he whispered. "Watch out. Thorne's man."

"What do you mean? Watch out for what? What about Thorne's man and Dillon?" His hand went limp, and in a panic, Chaz clutched his shoulders and began to shake him. "No, do not do this to me. What are you talking about? Watch out for Thorne's men? Tell me."

"Stop it, Charissa!" Delicia said and pulled on Chaz's arms. "He can say no more. Leave him to heal. If the infection does not kill him, you will."

Chaz's head came about swiftly. "Do you know what he meant? Did he tell you?"

Delicia shook her head. Her gaze still rested with tenderness and concern on her husband. "He said nothing before he asked for you. Now go. You must let him rest."

Delicia shooed her out of the room and closed the door with a loud bang.

Chaz backed up to the wall and slid down until she was sitting on the floor. She pulled up her knees, rested her forearms on them, dropped her face in her palms, and examined Salvatore's words from every angle. He must have been trying to warn her that Thorne's men had somehow discovered her hidden valley. It seemed to be the only explanation.

She checked back hourly for a chance to question Salvatore further, but he remained asleep, and Delicia scolded her, banning her from the sickroom. Worried about the safety of Asilo, she ordered Largo to double the guards at the mountain passes and told the women to pack the essentials and be ready to move out at a moment's notice. She sent men ahead to Venustiano's camp, secreted away like hers, and asked for sanctuary in the event she needed it. Those tasks taken care of, she could only fret and wait for Salvatore to regain consciousness.

Six days ago, riders had left for the revolutionaries' camp, and when they returned, a dusty, road-worn Alec rode at the head of twenty of the rebel's men.

He dismounted and gathered Chaz into the shelter of his arms. She nestled against his chest, into the familiar scent of his body. Like a big brother, Alec always had the ability to soothe her.

"Raúl?" he said. "Have you word yet?"

"None," she replied in a voice worn ragged with

worry, and pulled back to peer into his dear face. Lines carved deeply into it, attesting to his concern for her and her child.

"I heard from our spies who were watching the train station in Zacatecas," Alec said. "Before Thorne's men locked Salvatore in a cattle car, Sanchos saw Raúl board the parlor car with Thorne. At that time, Raúl was alive and unharmed."

"Salvatore said as much, that Raúl was with Thorne," she said grimly.

"Yes, Charissa, but he is alive."

"Sí. I am, of course, relieved he is alive. And Raúl will tell Thorne nothing, certainly not about me or our family. My worry is that Thorne might notice the resemblance and guess at the relationship."

A frown wrinkled his brow. "What relationship?"

Chaz tasted bitterness at, once again, having to reveal her past, secrets she'd hidden for a lifetime. Alec had often questioned why she'd targeted Thorne for destruction. She'd never told him Thorne was her stepfather—only Delicia and Salvatore knew all her secrets. But to his credit, he had not pressed her for answers. Now he had earned the right to know, and, after all, Alec was family.

"Thorne is Raúl's father. He raped me many years ago."

Alec's chest hitched with a deeply inhaled breath. "I suspected as much but dared not accept it. I will kill him for you."

Her head came up, and she stepped back. "No, I will kill him. You or no man will take that from me. But first I must find my child." As she walked back and forth in front of him, boots whisking up dust and stones, Alec hitched a thumb into his hip pocket and shifted his weight to one leg. His eyes narrowed, and the muscles in his face became tight and hard. She sent him a questioning look. "Could Thorne possibly deduce that Raúl is his son, like you did?"

"How could he?"

"He must have a suspicion," she continued, speaking as much to herself as to him. "Otherwise, why would he take Raúl away? Why not put him in the mine with the others? He cannot possibly know about me. A man as depraved as Thorne must have raped dozens of women and would have to have a prodigious memory to keep them all straight in his mind. If it were not for Dillon being missing and Salvatore's words, I would be miles away by now, pursuing Thorne and Raúl."

Alec reached out to take hold of her arm and stop her agitated movement. "What words from Salvatore?"

Chaz told him what Salvatore had said, and a thoughtful expression came down over his face, as though he were silently chewing it over.

Finally, he said, "You can afford to wait a few more days, until Salvatore can explain what he meant. It must be significant. You know where to find Thorne and Raúl—in Chicago. When you go after them, we will ride with you."

She shook her head. "This is my responsibility. I must confront Thorne alone."

"My *chiquita*, you will not go alone. I will not allow it. I will follow you, if necessary. I will not let that man get his hands on you again."

While Alec settled the men in the bunkhouse and took himself off to wash the dust of the road from his skin, the soughing wind spun down out of the mountains to kindle a dust devil in the yard, and the sun dipped, hiding its face behind the tallest peaks of the Western Mother. Chaz sat on the steps of the hacienda, braced her elbows on her knees, and rested her chin on her fisted hands.

A corner of her mind, one she found unable to completely quiet, wondered whether Dillon had found his way into some señorita's bed. Largo had reported only that Dillon had business to tend to in Zacatecas before joining them. Largo knew nothing more, not the nature of that business or when Dillon would return. Perhaps he'd found tedious her reticence in lovemaking and what he saw as—no doubt—her irrational fears. Perhaps that elusive señorita could willingly give him what his wife could not.

"Where are you, Dillon?" she asked the wind, a touch of desperation in her voice. "Always you are underfoot, and now when I need you most, you are missing."

Two days later in the first pink traces of sunset over the valley, Dillon rode into the hideaway and up to the hacienda. As he swung down off a tired and lathered-up Victory, Chaz burst out the door and ran down the steps. He held out his arms to catch her.

Her face was pale, and exhaustion etched her features. His heart contracted painfully. He realized how much he truly loved her, though he knew his time with her was short. Once she found out about him, he would be gone…or dead.

She said, "Thorne has Raúl."

He hugged her close. "I know." Dillon had finally received the wire from Giles, confirming Raúl was on Thorne's train and headed for Chicago.

She pushed back, but he kept her in the circle of his arms. "How do you know?"

As he looked into her face, he hoped his expression was…expressionless and she couldn't read the panic that surely lurked in his eyes. "How did you know?" he asked, turning her question about.

"Salvatore. He escaped, and a campesino found him close to death in the desert. Now how did you know?"

Dillon's heart picked up its beat, and fear sucked the spit from his mouth. He welcomed the news of Salvatore's escaping certain death at the hands of Thorne, but he knew what it meant. *The end of my secret.* The trapdoor creaked, about to open, and he was plunging to the end of the hangman's rope. Chaz's cousin must not have disclosed the information, yet, or else she would have greeted him with a loaded gun rather than open arms.

"How's he doing?" he asked.

"Still feverish and falling in and out of consciousness. A couple of days ago, he recovered only long enough to tell me Raúl was alive and with Thorne. He also said something about you, but it made no sense."

"What'd he say?" Dillon asked carefully. It couldn't have been too damning, or he'd be dead already.

Her head shook. "No. I asked you a question. Tell me how you knew about Raúl."

He exhaled with a sigh and released her, moving to Victory's side to loosen the cinch. He pulled off the saddle and blanket, and draped them across the hitching post. "I talked to the railroad agent who saw them board Thorne's car. Took me a couple of days to find the man who was on duty at the time."

"Oh." She seemed to accept his answer, and his heart slowed down.

He stripped off his bandana and used it to wipe the sweat from the horse's coat. "Now, what did Salvatore say that's got you so addled?"

"Since you are still alive, I'm sure it is nothing. He said your name and told me to watch out. Then he said something about Thorne's man or men. I assumed they'd found their way to Asilo, but we haven't seen them."

Dillon held his tongue. He didn't know what to say. *You're wrong? I'm Thorne's man? That's what Salvatore meant?* He'd have to tell her before Salvatore did, but not now. Now he simply wanted to hold her, love her, perhaps for the last time before she measured him for a pine box. No, he doubted he'd merit that courtesy. She'd simply see him rolled up in his saddle blanket and dumped in a rocky chasm in the mountains.

Alec emerged from the soft evening shadows beneath a locust tree, eyes distinctly hostile when his gaze lit on Dillon.

Dillon forced a smile and offered his hand. *Ah, shit! The prodigal cousin returns, as pert as a rutting buck!* "I ran into some of Venustiano's men in Zacatecas. I thought you were with him."

Alec cracked a careless grin. "I was, señor West, but my Charissa had need of me. It seems her husband was missing. We assumed either Thorne captured you or his men had found the valley."

Again, Dillon bit down on his tongue to keep it from wagging. Swapping words with Alec right now wouldn't win him any favors. Once Chaz heard what Salvatore had to say, he'd need all the favors he could get. He conjured up a smile. "Thanks. I guess that's what cousins are for. But her husband is here now, so she doesn't need your help any longer."

"I shall be content to leave when *mí prima* tells me so." His stance and words were prickly with challenge.

Chaz stepped between them. "Please. No more of this." She turned to Alec. "Dillon is right. Venustiano needs you now more than I do. I am grateful you came to my assistance, but you may leave tomorrow and take your men with you."

Alec's gaze remained on Dillon, and he inclined his head. "If you say so, *mí corazón*. Nevertheless, if you call again, no one will keep me from riding back to Asilo."

She patted his arm. "I know, *Primo*. You are a true friend, and I can always count on you."

Dillon released an impatient huff. Why couldn't she send Alec out now? He knew his way home, even in the dark. If Salvatore improved enough to tell his tale tonight, tomorrow might be too late. The last thing Dillon wanted was a gunfight with the arrogant Spaniard. Dealing with Chaz and her men was going to be difficult enough.

Alec tipped his hat and walked off toward the bunkhouse.

"We have to leave in the morning to intercept the train," she said once Alec's figure vanished into the dark shadows beneath the trees. "Thorne has gone too far by kidnapping my son. The time has come to end this vendetta the way I always meant for it to end…with the devil's death."

Dillon silently agreed. Once Salvatore revealed Dillon's deception, not only would Chaz's men be gunning for him, but Alec would come riding back. The door would be wide open for the Spaniard to saunter in and take Dillon's place in her affections. He caught her shoulders in his hands. He hated to say this, because it would hurt her. However, she had a right to know.

"Something I gotta tell you, *querida*. Thorne may have kidnapped Raúl, but the boy's now with him willingly."

Her forehead puckered in a frown, and her eyes narrowed. "That can't be true. Raúl hates Thorne as much as I do."

"The agent said Raúl was handcuffed when he was taken aboard in Zacatecas. I had him wire ahead to Chihuahua, to make sure Raúl was still aboard. Thorne and Raúl exited the train together — no handcuffs — and had dinner in the hotel. They were laughing and thick as thieves when they boarded again later that night. Thorne must have said something to Raúl to make him so amenable."

Pain spurted across Chaz's face, transferring that same deep pain to Dillon's gut. He could only imagine what was running through her mind. Thorne, the man who raped her, had won over her only child, truly taken him away from her.

"He couldn't," she whispered, and Dillon embraced her, holding her against his chest. Her body trembled in his arms.

"Shhh," he said. "Raúl couldn't know the truth about

what happened to you, or he would have killed Thorne with his bare hands. Even if he now knows Thorne's his father, he'll forgive you for lying to him."

"What he thinks of me is of no matter. Raúl was all I had before I met you, the only person who gave me joy. I do not care if he knows Thorne is his father or that I lied. I only pray he does not know how he was conceived. He must never find out he is a child of rape."

Later in their bedroom, Chaz seemed possessed by the need to climb into Dillon's skin. She allowed him to do whatever he wanted. He took the advantage she gave him, pretty sure this was the last time he would receive her love.

Dillon stripped her for the first time, pulling off her clothes as easily as if they were nothing more than gossamer webs. Chaz wound her hands in his hair to tug painfully, and ravished his mouth. His shirt and pants disappeared as though a magician had uttered enigmatic words and waved a wand. His cock stood out, hard, with an excruciating erection, and begged for attention. It nudged up against her belly, looking for the way in.

As their tongues dueled in wet, openmouthed kisses, Dillon backed her up, step by step, until her buttocks hit the wall. He writhed against her hot body, and his hands were everywhere, on her breasts, kneading them and playing with the hard nipples, caressing her hips and thighs and dipping into the crevice between them. He dragged his kiss down the side of her neck, and the blood in her veins pulsed fiery against his lips. For the first time, Chaz made no protest, did not cringe away, no matter how rough he became, how demanding. It should have plucked his heartstrings, how much she fully trusted him. Instead, it withered his soul. She'd soon find out how she'd misplaced that trust. If he could only reverse time, do it over, meet her in some other way, some other situation. *But you can't.* He'd done what he'd done, and before too many more hours or days passed, he would reap hell for his deception.

Diecinueve

Chaz could not get enough of him. She wanted Dillon, really wanted him, around her, beneath her, inside her. He was blistering drink, spicy food, a soft bed, serenity, and solace. She loved him with all her heart and soul.

She shuffled backward, ever backward, until the adobe wall fetched up against her spine and she could go no farther. She wanted to move him to the bed, but he seemed to have no desire to take her direction. Rather than frightening her, this new, forceful personality she released in him made her feel cherished, desired. His hands touched, pressed, held — no longer Thorne's hands shackling her, holding her down, but Dillon's hands, worshipping her, fanning the flames inside her.

"Your leg," he said, his voice throaty, breath panting.

The words, seeming so out of context, pulled her from her sexual haze. "My leg?"

"Around me." He hooked a hand beneath her left leg and lifted it. "Bring it up. Put it around me."

She wrapped her leg about his waist, opening herself up to him. When he eased back his hips, cool air from the open window and the breeze outside teased the lips of her sex and wormed its way inside, sending a shiver through her body.

He came into her in a strong penetration that thrilled
rather than alarmed. Her liquid essence sucked him in
deeper, and he glided along its path.

"God, Chaz," he moaned. "You are so sweet, so
fucking sweet. I want more than this. I want it all." After
two or three deep plunges, he withdrew and dropped
to his knees. Her leg fell to the floor, and she leaned
back against the wall, mourning the loss of the thrilling
sensations and closing her eyes.

With his arms spreading her legs as far apart as
they would go, his thumbs parted her, and his mouth
pressed against her opening. Her mind in a fog, unable
to comprehend what he thought he was doing, Chaz
suppressed her startled reaction and let him in. His
tongue darted out, touched, licked, insinuated itself
inside and swirled about in a rhythm that got her hips
going. The heat became unbearable, and moisture poured
from her in a flood of juices. Dillon lapped them up,
his busy tongue driving her crazy. When he found that
sweet spot, the wellspring of all her desire, and dragged
his teeth across it, the muscles in her thighs contracted,
twitched, made her legs weak and barely able to hold
her up. He latched on to her feminine flesh, and sucked
and nibbled. His arms went around her, hands gripping
and kneading her buttocks, the press of his face and arms
keeping her on her feet. She exploded in a cataclysm of
pleasure, throbbing ecstasy and near pain, rapture and
virtual oblivion. Dillon milked her orgasm, kept her
coming and coming until she thought she could take no
more.

His mouth left her, and he came to his feet. He
grasped both her legs, lifted her, pulled her limbs around
him, and entered her with such thrilling strength Chaz
feared she would lose consciousness. This time, as he
pinned her to the wall, her legs about him and his hands
cradling her bottom, he dictated the pace, and a furious

pace it was. He took the dominant role and drove into her again and again, each rousing stroke pushing her against the wall and hurling her higher into the sky, beyond the heavens, beyond anything in experience. Chaz had never imagined what it would be like if she let Dillon take control, if she let him love her the way he wanted to. Now she knew and reveled in his intensity, in the feelings pouring through her, through body and heart. Heat and wetness, powerful thrusts, tortuous withdrawal, sensitive flesh dancing to the tune his body played against hers. All the stars in the heavens burst behind her closed eyelids, myriad colors and shapes, festival fireworks, and she bore down on his hard male flesh, inner muscles tightening around his thick width and long length. The wave gushed forth, washed over her, leaving flames dancing across her skin and fire lapping through her blood.

Dillon shouted and pumped one last time. His eruption doused her flames and cooled them into embers.

Morning came too soon, with sunlight spilling across the window's wide stone embrasure and spreading into the darkest corners of their room. The songs of sparrows and meadowlarks rose with the sun and roused Dillon from a deep sleep. He rolled onto his side, bent his head, and kissed the curve of Chaz's shoulder. When she stirred against him, he drew her into his arms and loved her again. He drank in the sweetness of her mouth as he eased into her tightness. This could be the last time she gave herself to him, and that thought made their lovemaking all the sweeter.

This morning they were to make ready to leave and chase Thorne's train. As of last night, Salvatore was still out of his head, and Dillon had hopes for a clean getaway. However, as Dillon tied the bedrolls to Victory's and Niebla's saddles and Chaz loaded two pack horses with supplies, Delicia came out of the hacienda onto the porch. Before she descended the steps, her gaze arrowed to Dillon, and his heart stumbled. From the woman's razor-sharp glare and the storm of fury on her face, Salvatore knew "Thorne's man" had returned, and her husband had spilled his story of the viper within their nest.

When Delicia approached, Chaz looked up. "How is Salvatore this morning? I dislike leaving with him so ill, but Dillon and I must go after Raúl before the train travels too far ahead of us."

"He is awake and wants to speak with you."

"Is it important? I am eager to get away."

"*Muy importante*. You must come now."

Chaz tied off the load and dusted off her hands. "If it is that important," she said, turning to Dillon, "perhaps you should come too."

Delicia's icy gaze froze his marrow. "Perhaps I should," he said carefully. What he really should do is get on his horse and spur him out of the valley before he left tied facedown across his saddle. In spite of his better instincts urging him to *git*, he followed Chaz up the steps and across the porch with resignation. He removed his hat at the doorway and combed the fingers of one hand through his shaggy hair. At least he'd be a well-groomed corpse.

Alec waited outside the door to the bedroom, arms crossed over his chest, a dark scowl sitting on his face. Sharp black eyes flayed Dillon to the bone. Dillon lowered his eyes and brushed past the man. When he turned his back on the Spaniard, he half-expected a knife to part his spine.

When they entered the sickroom, Alec stepped inside behind them and took up position against the wall. Salvatore's gaze fixed on Dillon, and in a voice weak but harsh, asked, "What is *he* doing here?"

Chaz glanced at Dillon, and she cast him a sideways

smile. "*Mi esposo* arrived yesterday."

"Did you not listen to what I said?" Salvatore's words could have sawed bone.

Bemusement carved lines in her brow. "When?"

His face reddened, and his features twisted into a mask of wrath. "I told you to watch out, that he was Thorne's man."

Her brows climbed slowly upward. "Surely you do not mean Dillon. You must be mistaken." A little frown took up residence on her lips and, with a plea on her face, she looked at Dillon. "Tell him. Tell him he is wrong."

Dillon wet his lips with his tongue. *How you gonna get out of this?* No hope for it; Salvatore had backed him into a mess of cactus. "He's right, Chaz. I'm Thorne's man, that is, I was, but not anymore."

She stared at him with slowly widening eyes. "I do not understand."

He had to be truthful. She deserved that much. "Sure you do."

"You mean you have been spying on me, on my family? You have been helping Thorne?" Her voice hissed like the sibilance of a rattlesnake. Underneath it lay a world of hurt.

Dillon opened his hands. "Only in the beginning, *querida*. As soon as I found out—"

"Do not dare to call me *querida*," she spat. Her body quaked as though in the grip of the same fever that had claimed Salvatore for so many days. "You have exactly five minutes to leave my *aidea*. When that time has passed, I will order my men to shoot you on sight."

"Let me shoot him now," Alec said, shifting a hand to the gun on his hip.

She raised a palm. "No. I gave him permission to leave. I keep my word."

Dillon's mouth flattened. She wasn't going to listen, and nothing he could do, nothing he could say, would make her listen. "You ain't gonna let me explain, are you? I love you, you love me, and you won't give me a chance to prove it."

"Give you a chance? When I think of what I did to you, what you did to me, what we did together… For all of my life, I thought Thorne was the devil, but you are worse than he. At least he was honest. He did not pretend to love me to get into my bed."

Dillon shifted his stance and slapped his hat against his leg. "Right. If you can't admit what I feel for you is love, I reckon this conversation is going nowhere fast. I'm leaving, darlin', and I'm going after Raúl. I'll bring him back to you, dead or alive, and dump him right on your doorstep. Then I'll get the hell out of your life forever, if you're still of a mind for me to do so. If we should happen to cross paths between here and Chicago, I'd advise you" — he nodded at Alec — "and your *amante* to keep your guns in your holsters. I may not be as mean and ornery as you, but I'm a damned sight faster."

As she pointed to the door, her hand shook. "You have little time left, señor West. I suggest you leave now. And you stay away from Raúl. I will bring him back without you."

He shoved his hands in his back pockets and leaned in toward her. "That'll be a damn cold day, señora West. Nobody tells me what I can or can't do, and I don't take kindly to anyone, much less my wife, handing me my hat and telling me to git."

" *¡Salir!* I never want to see you again!"

Her last words nearly blasted him out the door. "Damned stubborn woman," he muttered on his way through the *sala*. Fuerte met him at the front door. The wolf-dog wagged his tail and bumped his head against Dillon's leg. He reached down to scratch the creature's head. "Guess you're the only one here not mad at me. Want to come along? I could use some company."

Fuerte plopped down on his backside and cocked his head to one side.

Dillon pursed his lips and blew out a stream of air.

"I suppose not. Anyway, your mistress would accuse me of kidnapping you." He trotted down the steps, took up the lead of one of the pack horses, mounted Victory, and sped toward the pass in the mountains.

Veinte

Spears of sunlight fell from the egg-white sky and pierced the desert floor. Chaz's head ached fiercely from the raging heat, the storm of her emotions, and the lingering memory of her argument with Alec over his accompanying her. But mostly, she seethed inside and out over Dillon...a traitor to her and her people. After the years of anguish and caution, she'd put her trust in a man, and he'd thrown it back in her face. He'd wounded her as much as Thorne ever had. Never again would she make such a mistake. As she pushed Niebla into a gallop, she looked forward to crossing paths with her detestable husband. Her gun still held six silver bullets: she could spare one for him.

The day passed in a blur of chaparral-covered hills, sandstone outcroppings, and acacias. The Sierra Madre Mountains with their cool groves of hickory beckoned from her left, but the mountains would slow her down. She could make better time on the hardpan floor of the desert. Niebla's hooves scattered jackrabbits and roadrunners, scared up coveys of quail, and above her, the clear blue expanse of the sky stretched from the western mountains to merge with a shimmering border on the eastern horizon.

She had followed Dillon's tracks and those of his pack horse and was about half a day behind them but moving fast. Niebla and her pack horse were born in this furnace landscape, giving them an edge over his Texas-bred mount. The gray was accustomed to the desert heat and sandy ground, and she carried a lighter load than Dillon's horse. Fuerte ran alongside, his long legs and tireless muscles keeping stride with her. She had no intention of confronting her husband, yet, but she did not want to fall too far behind him. If he was Thorne's man, what might he do when he caught up with the train? *Tell Thorne I'm The Ghost Wolf? Confirm that Raúl is my son?* He might do anything. Regardless of his professions of love, she could not trust him. When he reached the train, she had to be there or within rifle range.

The sun dropped from the sky in a sudden eclipse typical to the desert, and she continued on by starlight for another hour before setting up camp beside a waterhole. Doves called with soft cooing from the bushes, and a coyote sang in the hills beyond. She made a smokeless fire from greasewood, heated coffee over the flames, and sat on the ground with her back against her saddle. The air grew chill, and she wrapped the blanket around her shoulders. She planned to be awake before sunrise and close in on Dillon's heels. Tossing the bitter dregs of the coffee on the ground, she smothered the fire and rolled up in the blanket, her saddle her pillow.

Morning came with the soft snorting of the horses and a fierce crick in her neck from the awkward position of her head on the saddle all night. She sat up and massaged her nape with one hand. As the blanket slipped to her waist, cool air nipped at her arms. She reached for her leather duster and slipped into it. To the East, swaths of struggling purple sage glowed, backlit from a slip of rising sun. Chaz quickly rose, packed her bedroll, and set out.

Three hours later, she came across the remains of Dillon's campfire. As Fuerte sniffed the ground, his tail wagging like a flag at the man's familiar, lingering scent, she dismounted and kicked apart the ashes. A frown tightened her lips at the message he'd left behind — a heart traced in the sandy ground beside the campfire. Inside the heart he inscribed the words: *Te amo.* So he knew she was following. She snorted. Love. As though he would recognize love. He knew nothing about love, but she did — the emotion she felt for Raúl, a mother's love for her son, the only true love that existed. Cold fear for Raúl roiled like a serpent in the pit of her stomach. And now, time was like a drum preceding a battle. When the drum stopped, her child would die.

"Come," she said to the wolf-dog and mounted her horse. Fuerte lifted his head from the sand, sneezed, and trotted after her.

Chaz could see from Dillon's tracks he was now about two hours ahead, managing to keep her close but not too close. Every few miles, she ran across another of his offerings — more hearts drawn on the ground, a word or two in each, *querida, corazón, mi esposa,* other endearments, or a bouquet of flowers — creamy yuccas, blood red paintbrush, fragrant blue-green sage.

At first, she destroyed the hearts, kicking at them with savage thrusts of her booted feet. After the fifth one, she found herself reluctantly smiling and looking forward to the next message. Dillon was nothing if not persistent. She admonished herself for allowing his tricks to lower her guard and vowed they would not melt her heart. He mocked the feelings she'd allowed to surface after years of loneliness, though she had not recognized the emotion as such until he touched her soul. Now her heart and soul were as hard as they were before she'd met the gringo. Dillon's treachery had sliced open the wounds she had, for some time now, thought might heal. Pain poured through her, like an escaping river from a broken dam. "Once I rescue my son," she muttered into the dry desert air, "I will teach Dillon West a thing or two about love." At the sound of Chaz's voice, silent for so long, Neibla flicked back an ear and tossed her head. Chaz smoothed a hand along the gray's moist, silky neck. "Yes, Niebla, he will learn better than to play with hearts."

She followed the trail of hearts along the edge of the mountains, through the center of Mexico, and ever northward. At the end, she would find the boy she loved, the man she would kill, and the man who betrayed her.

With evening close to stealing the daylight, Chaz angled toward a baldheaded rock that rose up from the land ahead and promised shelter for the night. Over the years of chasing Thorne and his silver, she'd developed the habit of preferring to sleep with her back protected. Thorne was ahead of her, not behind, so she felt she need not worry about him or his men pursuing her. Nevertheless, Manzanita's *rurales* could come across her trail at any point and decide to investigate.

She tethered Niebla and the pack horse, a skittish bay gelding, to a low, spreading jojoba tree. Its oval yellow leaves in a broad crown provided some shade from the punishing rays of the westering sun. She then pulled off Niebla's saddle and the bay's pack, and rubbed down the horses. After feeding out the grain in her saddlebags and watering the animals from the skins the pack horse carried, she started a fire and threw together a pot of beans and rice.

As the day melted into the declining sun, Chaz ate and lay back on her pallet. Then the pack horse snorted and stomped his feet. When Niebla followed with a shrill neigh and Fuerte barked, something he seldom did, she came up from her reclining position, the rifle in her hands, and swung the barrel toward the rock. In the last dim glow of the dipping sun, a puma stood out, silhouetted against the sky. It crouched low on its haunches, gaze on the horses, and a high, keening yowl came from its throat.

Fuerte's fur went up on his back, and he growled.

"No," she said and motioned to the dog to lie down. Fuerte would be a fair match for the cat. Even so, she could not bear the possibility of losing someone else dear to her.

The horses yanked on the reins anchoring them to the tree, in a panic at the predator's scent. Chaz spared them a quick look, torn between calming and securing her mounts and taking care of the cat. She doubted it would attack. Pumas were wary of humans and preferred lone, easy prey. She came back to the cat and fired off a round, chipping the rock close to its feet. The puma swung its head at her, hissed, whirled around, and slipped away.

She scrambled to her feet and spun toward the horses just as the pack horse broke its rein and wheeled about, pounding off into the dusky shadows. Niebla followed suit, eyes wild and rolling, and thundered past Chaz.

"Niebla!" She ran after the mare, but she had no chance of catching the horses until they ran out their fear. Come morning, she would have to track them. "*Merde*," she swore and returned to her campsite. Now she was afoot, and her hopes of catching up with Dillon and Raúl dwindled.

When sunlight spilled over the eastern plain, Chaz left the saddle and packs next to the rock, loaded up with water, and trekked out into the wild land, following the hoof prints of the two horses. She sent Fuerte ahead in hopes he would find the wayward animals and lead her to them. For two days, she strode across the sand and rocks, scared up jackrabbits, quail, and armadillos, and cursed Niebla, the pack horse, the puma, and Dillon in equal measure. The arid heat seared her throat, and the dust raised by her boots coated her with a fine film of silvery powder.

A low grove of cottonwoods in the distance signaled a possible water hole. "Thank the Blessed Virgin for mercy," she mumbled through a dry throat and a mouth that felt filled with pebbles. "At least I may now fill my water skins." *And thank the Lord, most likely find my horses.* She headed for the trees, her pace picking up in anticipation of coming upon Niebla and the pack horse filling their bellies with sweet water and tough grass.

Horse hooves, large canine paws, and the prints of deer muddied the ground along the banks of the small depression. The animals had stopped here, and Chaz knew they would not wander far from the water. She dropped to her knees and drank. The alkaline taste of the water and the grit of mud filled her throat, but she swallowed. Slowly, her thirst eased.

"Lose something?"

Chaz jerked up her head and sat back on her heels. Dillon sat on Victory in the shadows beneath the cottonwood branches, Niebla and her pack horse beside him, their reins held in his right hand. His own pack horse stood behind him. Fuerte came out of the dusky gloom and wagged his tail, an idiotic grin on his furry face.

"Traitor," she mumbled, the indictment directed equally at the man and the dog.

Dillon's slow smile did queer things to her stomach. Nonetheless, she drew her revolver and got slowly to her feet. "Turn them over."

He glanced at the horses to one side of him, and his gaze returned to her. "These? I found them wandering wild in the desert. Couldn't find a brand, so I figure they belong to me." He directed a look at Fuerte. "I also ran across this oversized dog, and he attached himself to my heels. But if he's yours, you can have him back."

Chaz slapped the side of her leg. "Fuerte," she said sharply.

Fuerte looked up at Dillon and whined. *Blasted*

dog. Though Fuerte was friendly with those in Asilo, he usually stayed close enough to Chaz for her to stumble over him. His friendship did not extend to strangers... as a rule. Nevertheless, he'd developed this aggravating bond with Dillon, and at times, seemed to listen better to the gun hand than to her. He could also sense her moods and often disappeared when she was in a foul temper... as she was now.

Dillon dropped his gaze, sent the dog a look. "Guess you'd better. She looks mighty angry."

Fuerte sighed and loped around the waterhole to Chaz, dropping into a sit at her side.

After sending the dog a sharp glare, causing him to hang his head, she turned back to Dillon. "I will not play games with you, señor West. Return my horses and go on your way."

When he grinned, anger rose hotly in her veins.

"They're right pretty ponies, especially the gray mare," he said. "Spirited, too. Had to chase her for a mile or two before I caught her. Reckon I could sell them. I don't really have much use for four horses. Seeing as you're afoot, I suppose I can set my own price. That is, unless you have a mind to walk all the way to Chicago or the next hacienda where you can buy or steal a mount. Closest one's about sixty miles in that direction." He lifted a hand and pointed east, then his gaze came back to the gun in her hand. "You wouldn't shoot me, would you, darlin'? I caught these wild horses fair and square, and you got your dog back. A reasonable price for my trouble, that's all I ask."

Her palm sweated as it tightened on her gun, and she glared at him from beneath half-closed lids. "How much do you want? I have silver."

His grin never wavered. "I'll bet you do, but I have no use for silver."

She snorted. "Since when? Silver is all you *ever* wanted."

His grin slowly melted, and his voice dropped to a low, caressing tone, a nuance of hurt behind his words. "You're wrong, *querida*. Sure, I was after the silver at first, but you changed my mind, you and Raúl and Salvatore and Delicia, and the rest of your goddamn bloodthirsty family. For the first time in my life, I found something I craved more than money."

"You lie," she spat.

"Never, least not lately."

"Your price," she said again. "I have urgent business with a train and another snake."

His hand went to his chest. "Ah, *mi esposa*, you wound me." He leaned forward, hands braced on the saddle horn, and his gaze tangled with hers. "A truce. My price is a truce between us until we find and rescue Raúl."

A truce? A truce between her and the man who'd stolen her heart, lied to her? *Never!*

"Your price is too high, señor."

His breath came out in a long, noisy sigh. "In that case, I'm right sorry we couldn't come to an agreement." He reined the horses about. "Have a nice walk."

"You would not leave me here!" she called to his back.

Dillon pulled up on Victory's reins, twisted at the waist, and rested one hand on his horse's rump. "Wouldn't I? According to you, I'm about the lowest reptile that ever slithered across the Mexican wasteland. Want to reconsider my price?" He turned Victory to face her. "Use your head, Chaz. It's gonna take both of us to rescue Raúl. On your own, you don't have a chance. You need me, and I need you. Afterward...well, that's up to you."

"*Jesu,*" she muttered. As much as she hated to admit the truth of his words, he was right, and she was damned sick of his being right. "*A bien.* A truce, then, but only until I have Raúl back."

* * *

Wheels clacked on the tracks, and trees whipped by.
The desert plain and occasional pueblo blurred into a
yellow-white landscape outside the window.

Raúl laid his hand of cards on the table and smiled
at Justus Thorne. As the train took a curve, the railway
car listed to one side, and Raúl grabbed the cards to keep
them from sliding off the table.

"A straight," Thorne said, peering at Raúl's hand.
He lowered his brows and puffed hard on his cigar. "A
damned straight, jack high." With a sigh, he tossed his
cards face up on the table and picked up his glass of
whiskey, taking a long swallow. "Three tens. Once again,
Son, you've managed to take my money."

"Yes," Raúl said, smugness in his voice. He slid the
silver eagles to his side of the table and grinned. He had
formulated a plan, of sorts, though he hadn't found the
chance to carry it out. His hands were now free, but he
was allowed to move no more than a few steps without
an armed guard.

*First, gain Thorne's trust, agree with him and get him
to lower his vigilance. Second, get my hands on a gun.*
Unfortunately, the only guns in the car sat holstered on
the hips of Thorne's men who stood beside the doors
at either end of the car. *Last, blast my way out, preferably
through Thorne, and leap off the train.*

Since first meeting Thorne, Raúl had thought a
lot about what the man disclosed with some glee. He
recalled the stories Chaz had spun about his father being
a Yaqui revolutionary. However, he'd always suspected
she was untruthful, that his father was instead a gringo.
Yaqui Indians didn't have red hair and blue eyes. It
seemed important to his mother that her son accept her
words, and to make her happy, he'd complied. But in his
wildest dreams, he'd never supposed that gringo would
be Thorne. And now the thought made him queasy. The

railroad man even knew Chaz's real name. *Okay, I'm Thorne's son.* He could live with that. His mother had lied, but Raúl was smart enough to know she had a good reason for lying. Although he acknowledged Thorne as his father, he couldn't swallow the remainder of what Thorne had told him—the rest of Thorne's story was a pack of lies.

"She was so beautiful," Thorne had said with a sigh that sounded as convincing as the bluff of a greenhorn at a poker table. "She worked in the Chicago house as a maid. Charissa was younger than me, but she had about her a seductiveness greater than that of the most practiced *puta*. She believed I would put aside my wife and marry her. Unable to resist her advances, I fell under her spell. I cannot completely fault her for what happened. I was as much to blame as she. When my wife discovered the affair, she turned out Charissa, giving her the funds to return to her relatives in Mexico. I had no idea the girl was carrying my child, or I never would have let her go. You see, I truly loved her, but I doubt she ever loved me."

You're right, you slimy bastard. She hated you, and now I have a good idea why. Despite his blood boiling at the lies Thorne spouted, Raúl had nodded, careful not to challenge the man's words. He knew he was in a precarious situation and fought the urge to strike out in anger. His mother was no seductress. For as many years as Raúl could remember, Chaz had rebuffed all men, other than Dillon. She even rejected Alec, and Alec was as good a man as Raúl ever met. Although he knew nothing about his mother's real past—only what she'd told him—he'd had no reason to defend her honor…until now.

The train rocked along the track, *clackity-clack, clackity-clack*, hurtling toward the border, and Raúl stared out the window against his right shoulder. A team of mules on the road alongside the tracks pulled a heavily laden wagon, and a row of white-clad campesinos trudged behind it in a dusty line. Cacti and mesquite formed scattered patterns of silvery green amongst the stony gray, sandy yellow, and white quartz of the desert floor.

At the thought of what this man — *his father* — must have done to Chaz to make her hate him so, Raúl could barely restrain himself from flying at Thorne and pounding him into the wood and brass of the car. Instead, he swallowed his anger, smiled like a simpleton, and played along. *My chance will come, and when it does, I will take it.*

They progressed in stony silence by day, Dillon pulling his sombrero far down on his forehead, shoulders slumped and hands holding the reins resting loosely on the saddle horn. Chaz rode off to one side, spine straight, hands tense and clutching the reins, eyes directed ahead and never wandering to her husband.

At night they rolled into cold bedrolls, the fire between them. Fuerte divided his time and attentions between the two. Dillon made no more professions of love, and remained as moody and taciturn in his solitary companionship as Chaz.

The rainy season had come to the *altoplano*, which usually meant sporadic light sprinkles and dense morning mist. The fates this year seemed to conspire to slow their journey. Downpours of gray rain drenched them for days, causing them to huddle beneath slickers. Torrents tumbled off the mountains and roared into small, mostly dry-bed gulches, creating ephemeral streams of increasing strength that swept across their path. The horses struggled through the waters, having difficulty finding their footing. Victory showed greater trepidation than Niebla, the Mexican horse having more experience with the capriciousness of the weather in the northern high desert. Once the rain ceased, a blistering yellow sun followed that could fry tortillas on the mountains' rocky foothills.

The furious rushing of the river reached them before they arrived at the banks of the Rio Conchos, the only major waterway in Northern Mexico south of the Rio Bravos. The river originated in the Sierra Madres and flowed sedately northeastward to empty into the Rio Bravos along the Texas border. It lay in a canyon with a low, gentle southern bank and cliffs rising steeply on the northern side. After the unusual amount of rain, the green water ran fast and deep, and spilled over the southern banks to double the width of the river. White foam beat against the cliffs on the other side.

Dillon looked warily at the river. "We're gonna have to head eastward to where the railroad crosses the river. The water's too deep and swift here."

"No," Chaz said, stubborn as a sitting jackass. "I will not lose a week tracking east. Our path is north, across this river."

"You're plumb crazy." He reined Victory around and walked away along the bank. "I'm in no mood to drown myself and my horses."

When he looked back at Chaz, his heart hammered in the hollow cavity of his chest. Niebla was sliding down the bank into the water, Fuerte on her heels and the pack horse following. His thoughts fled back to when he was ten and his brother pulled him from the Allegheny River. He could still taste the dark water closing over his head and filling his mouth. Pain settled deep in his gut, and he swallowed with difficulty. *Caleb died that day, drowning in my place. I should have been able to save him.*

"Get back here!"

She made no response and moved farther into the water.

Aw, hell! Dillon whirled Victory about on his back legs and sped back to the river where Chaz had entered. The swirling water had risen to her stirrups, and she was urging her horse onward. Fuerte passed Niebla and swam strongly for the far bank.

"Turn around! Come back," he shouted. "You're one senseless woman."

She ignored him and pushed Niebla deeper. When the gray mare leapt forward and began to swim, the swift current pulled her downstream away from Dillon. He wasn't about to let her kill herself. Course, if he went in after her, they were both likely to drown.

I can't lose someone else I love to the river! Before he could talk himself out of it, he nudged Victory forward and into the water. The mustang balked, but with further urging, waded in. Soon Victory was swimming, drifting downstream, and coming closer to Chaz.

"When I catch you," he called out, "I'm gonna wring your neck."

A thick tree branch swept out of nowhere and slammed into Victory's haunch. The horse panicked and disappeared beneath the fast-flowing water. Dillon, caught unaware, lost his hold on the saddle and spilled into the river. In his surprise, he sucked in a lungful of water and sank. He kicked strongly, broke the surface, and flailed his arms, fighting to keep his head above water.

Damn it, West! This was a fucking stupid move, especially when you can't swim!

Veintiuno

Chaz slipped out of the saddle and held onto the saddle horn to swim beside Niebla. Out of the corner of her eye, she caught the movement of a dark object bearing down on her. She turned her head as it swept by, missing her and her horse. Behind the branch came another object, a wildly splashing figure. *Dillon!*

Her stomach gave a violent heave. She'd expected him to follow her, but she'd thought he would have the good sense to hold onto his horse. Without truly thinking about it, she grabbed the reata hooked to her saddle and flung it out toward him as he rushed by. The loop landed over his head. She jerked, hard, and she prayed. *Por favor, la Santísima Virgen.* Thankfully, her silent prayer was answered when Dillon brought up his hands and grasped the rope before it tightened completely around his neck.

Niebla's hooves found solid ground on a low bank of sand in front of the cliffs, and the horse surged forward, pulling Chaz and Dillon behind her. Chaz drank in air to catch her breath, dropped her hold on the rope, and stumbled back to Dillon. He lay limp, still in the water. She hauled him up onto the sand and removed the noose.

He rolled onto his stomach and spit up water.

When he finished coughing up the river and flopped onto his back, he peered up at her, fury darkening his eyes. "Where are my blasted horses?"

She searched the river. Victory had come ashore on another sandbar about a hundred yards downstream. The mustang looked tired but uninjured. She had untied her pack horse after entering the river, and now neither horse was anywhere in sight.

"Your chestnut horse is fine, but I cannot see the pack horses. They must have landed at some other point on the river's bank."

"Lucky for you Victory is alive," he said as he sat up and swept his wet hair back and out of his eyes. "That damned mustang means more to me than an inside straight, and it's your fault I nearly lost him."

She got to her feet. "I did not force you to cross the river. That was your decision."

Fuerte joined them, standing between them and shaking the water off his coat.

Dillon shrugged off the extra soaking from the dog's vigorous action and rose beside her, his hands in fists at his sides. "I had no choice. What a damn fool thing to do. You could have drowned."

"I was not the one to nearly drown, señor West. The river is still rising, and if you do not move now, you will find yourself underwater again."

He peered down the length of the river to where it curved in a bend and flowed out of sight. "Them pack horses had all our supplies. This is gonna be a damn long, hungry journey without them."

"I have no time to search for them. They will find their way home." She took up Niebla's reins and moved off along the sand. Dillon tracked behind her, muttering beneath his breath incoherent words whose tone, nonetheless, seemed mingled with fear and anger. When they reached the end of the sand, they waded into the water again.

They retrieved Victory, found a cut in the cliff, and climbed the twisting path to the top. Earth softened by the recent rain crumbled beneath the horses' hoofs, making the ascent precarious. When they reached the top and moved out on the plain, Dillon sent Chaz a grin.

"You saved my life back there."

A frown wrinkled the skin between her brows. "So?"

"You said you were gonna kill me, and you saved my life."

"Do you have a point, Dillon?"

"Yeah, I have a point. My lady doth protest too much."

"You are making no sense. You must have hit your head on a rock."

"No. It's Shakespeare. It means all your bluster disguises the fact that you're still in love with me."

"Now I know you hit your head. I am simply choosing my own time and place." She kicked Niebla into a gallop, and Fuerte flowed beside the horse like a gray ground fog, leaving Dillon, on his slower horse, far behind.

Chaz rode into an area beyond the river where the desert took up residence again and sloped down into an inferno of sand and rock. The mountains to the west dwindled into a haze, and the hardpan floor of the plain contained fewer plants, fewer animals, only the occasional lizard or snake, armadillo or roadrunner that scurried across her path. She and Dillon made fewer miles each day as the horses tired, and they rationed their water. Six days out, Chaz swore and dismounted.

"*¡Maldita sea!* Niebla is limping."

Dillon glanced back and pulled up on his reins, bringing Victory to a halt. "Let me see," he said and began to swing off his horse.

Chaz dismounted and held up a hand. "Do not touch

my horse."

He stopped, took off his dusty hat, and slapped it against his thigh.

Shrugging off his dark look, she went down on one knee and lifted Niebla's left foreleg. An inflamed area on the frog of the foot indicated a stone bruise. She dropped the hoof and straightened. "I will have to walk her until we reach water and I can pack the hoof with mud." She gathered up her reins and strode off across the sand.

Dillon mounted and waited until she drew alongside him. "No need to walk. We can make better time if you ride with me."

She slid him a wary look. "I do not care for that idea, señor."

His mouth slanted in a slow smile. "Scared to get too close to me, señora?"

She shook her head. He was truly beyond belief. Even Alec, with all his *macho* preening, had not an ounce of the assurance of his irresistibility as did Dillon West. "Of course not, but the weight of both of us will soon wear down your horse."

"I think Victory can take it. He's a Texas mustang. They're a hardy breed."

She shook her head again.

"Come on, Chaz. Don't be mulish about this." He extended a hand, crooked his fingers. "If you walk, Raúl will be an old man before we catch up with him."

He had said the one thing that could convince her. *Raúl*. They had to get to Raúl as soon as possible. And as galling as it was, he was right...again. They could make better time with her riding double. He had also been right about her not wanting to get too close to him. *¡Merde!* Chaz preferred to nurse her anger at his deceit, and the longer they remained in each other's company, the closer their physical proximity, the harder that became.

She accepted his hand, and he lifted her up in front

of him. She would have chosen to ride behind, but he did not give her a choice. Now she straddled his saddle, wedged between the saddle horn and his solid body. To free her hands, he took Niebla's reins and tied them to his saddle horn.

When his arm came loosely around her, she pushed at it.

"Gotta steer the horse, darlin'," he said.

"Then use your knees and heels, like the *Méjicanos* do."

"Don't work that way with Victory, he's a neck-reiner."

"Then give me the reins."

As he shook his head, his chest shifted. "Not gonna happen."

"If you must *steer* your horse, please refrain from touching me."

Dillon chuckled, his other arm circled her waist, and his hand settled on her belt buckle.

"Dillon, I am warning you."

"'Bout what? You got something in your pants that's gonna bite me?"

"No, but I may shoot you." He did not remove his hand, and heat built up in her abdomen. Friction from the saddle horn rubbed against the juncture of her legs. When she tried to scoot backward, she ran into hard, masculine muscle.

"You do much more of that, and I may have to stop this horse, pull you down, and make love to you," he said, his voice lower and huskier.

Her face burned as hotly as the sun. "You do, and I *will* shoot you."

"Will you?" he asked softly.

She bit her bottom lip, and Dillon moved Victory into a ground-eating lope. Without the weight of a rider, Niebla moved easily along beside them, and the dog ranged out in front.

Now the discomfort of her position evolved into itching that worked its way inside her. She squirmed on the saddle, and Dillon's hand inched downward, his fingers opening and splaying against the seam of her trousers. She grabbed his hand and swiveled her head to send him a blistering glare.

"What are you doing?"

"Let me," he said, his words more sultry than the breeze flowing over the desert floor. "You're coiled up tighter than a sidewinder."

She turned back around and tugged his hand up to rest on her stomach. "No," she said firmly.

He shifted on the saddle, and Victory dug in his heels, slowing to a hard, bone-jarring trot. She fell forward and seized the saddle horn to keep from losing her seating. His hand moved down again, and when she tried to pull it away, he said, "Can't have you tumbling off. You might break your neck."

"You keep that up, and it will not be *my* neck that is broken." But she released her hold on him. Why, she could not have said. She supposed because she wanted the release she knew he could give her. She dwelt on her current anger toward Dillon. Her capitulation had nothing to do with passion…with love, meant nothing other than release.

His chest hitched with a deep breath, and he inched his hand downward, found the point at which her body met the saddle. When he nudged Victory into a slow, rocking lope again, the hypnotic movement of the horse and Dillon's fingers alongside the center of her passion sent her reeling, catapulting into a storm of desire. She rocked back and forth, forward against the torturous pressure of his fingers, backward against the stirring hardness of his erection pressing on her buttocks. She wanted to turn around, slip him inside her, feel his steely male flesh filling her. She wanted to kiss him with lips and tongue and teeth, tangle her fingers in the hair on his chest. Before she could act on any of those imaginings, it was over. She imploded. Heat poured from her fingertips and toes, and the top of her head threatened to blow off. Dillon pressed harder, hung on to squeeze the last contraction from her. When she braced her hands on Victory's neck and panted like a horse that had run a five-mile race, Dillon slipped his hand back up to her stomach, leaving her slick and wet below.

"You can relax," he said. "You were as stiff as a fencepost. Now you're as limp as wet sheets."

"Do not think this changes anything," she managed to say.

"Wouldn't think of it."

After a week of riding northward, the mountains on their west and the railroad to the east, they began to see trees dotting the hard plain of the desert, along with the low adobe walls of *aideas* and small plots of cultivated fields. Long-horned cattle grazed on dusty gray grasses and bushes, and horses and mules wandered about unfettered. Now riding both horses again, they picked up a much-used road and joined the wagons, donkeys, and walking campesinos, baskets of goods balanced on their heads and on slings across their backs, that wended their way toward Cuidad Juarez.

From a distance, the town looked as mean as the desert surrounding it, and later, as Chaz rode through, the dusty streets revealed nothing to raise her spirits. Juarez was a wide-open town. Brothels and saloons lined the thoroughfares, and wood-fronted stores and businesses shared space with adobe buildings, tents, and wooden shacks. Cowboys and riders who looked like Mexican banditos clogged the streets and spilled out of the doors of the less-savory establishments. Respectable women in high-neck dresses and bonnets pushed their way down the plank boardwalks and wandered in and out of the stores. Ladies of the line in low-cut, gaudy gowns, all the colors of the rainbow, plied their trade from the corners and outside the saloon doors. Dogs and children and Indians darted in and out of the way of the horses and the wheels of the many wagons.

Fuerte drew many eyes, pointing hands, and whistles and yells from children as he trotted close to Niebla. As befitted his status as The Ghost Wolf's companion, he refused to acknowledge the furor he created.

Dillon led the way, obviously familiar with the maze of streets and alleys making up the border town, and gravitated toward the far end where the railroad tracks passed by a smoke-blackened wooden depot.

"I'll check on the train," he said, dismounting. "Best you stay here. Horses left unattended are an invitation to theft. If we missed the train, I wouldn't want to try to buy a horse. You'd pay a year's wages for a mount."

Chaz surveyed the street. Something had seemed strange, and that was it. No horses hitched to posts or wagons without rifle-wielding lookouts. She nodded, took Dillon's reins, and he disappeared into the building.

He was gone but a few minutes before he emerged into the sunlight again. From his pleated brows and the frown pulling down his mouth, the news was not good.

He approached with maddening slowness and draped an arm over Niebla's neck. His gaze drifted up, and he looked her straight in the eyes.

"Well?" she asked.

"Well, we missed the train by a day. It stopped in El Paso yesterday, around one in the afternoon. Thorne disconnected his car and hitched it to a freight train heading to Denver. We'll have to leave the horses here and catch the next train, day after tomorrow. It stops at Kansas City, and then it's on to Denver. There, we can pick up a train for Chicago."

"No," she said. "I will not wait here, and I will not ride a train behind Thorne. We will find a map and determine a point at which we can intercept the freight train. I will accede to spending one night, to rest the horses, but in the morning, I am riding out."

Dillon caught his bottom lip between his teeth and leveled a narrow-eyed look at her. "Chaz" — his words were slow and patient, as though speaking to someone hard of hearing— "where the hell you gonna find a map? They don't grow on cactus, you know. And even if we could cut across country and catch up with the train, it's bound to be moving fast and full of Thorne's gunmen."

She tossed Victory's reins to the ground. "I saw a mining office when we came into town. Surely they have maps. If you wish, you can remain here and take the next train, but I am riding out."

He muttered what sounded like an oath, picked up his reins from the dust, and mounted. Reining about, he headed back into Juarez. They left the horses at a livery stable in a relatively quiet part of town, away from the roughnecks and gunplay, and paid the stable manager well to take care of the animals and tack. Then with Fuerte following, Dillon directed them to a small hotel near the stable. He had to pay double for the dog.

"Ain't having no flea-bitten hound in my rooms," the proprietor said. His scrawny chin uplifted pugnaciously, and his Adam's apple bobbed.

Chaz pulled her gun half out of its holster before Dillon laid his hand on hers. "He's clean," he told the man and flipped an extra ten dollars in silver on the counter.

They found dinner at a diner down the street, and then Dillon left Chaz in her room and walked down the hallway to his. Sure, they were still married, but according to Chaz, "no way in heaven or hell was she going to share a room, much less a bed, with him. She preferred sleeping with the flea-bitten hound." In the washroom, he ran his hand over the beard he'd grown over the past weeks and scratched through the wiry hairs. When he looked into the cracked mirror above the washbasin, he didn't like what he saw. No wonder his wife had relegated him to a room six doors down from hers. *Perhaps if you spruced up a bit.* He searched through his saddlebags for his razor and cup, failed to locate them, and then recalled he'd transferred them to Chaz's bag to make room for some venison he'd smoked up halfway through their journey.

He left the washroom and knocked on Chaz's door. A soft woof answered. After the incident with Raúl in Sombrerete, Dillon had learned the value of requesting an extra key to Chaz's room. He used the key, turned the lock, and swung open the door. Her saddlebags lay on the bed, half their contents spewed across the chintz coverlet. Her guns hung on a ladderback chair by the window. Fuerte wagged his tail, greeted him with an eager tongue like a long-lost lover, and tried to climb up Dillon's chest. He scratched the dog's head and pushed him down. *Fuerte is here. Her belongings are here. Where in hell, then, is she? Gone!* Bile burned in his gut. He should have tied her up in his room. No, he had to play the role of gentleman. *Damn, you've messed up again.* What was the chance she'd gone back out after Raúl alone? He scratched his chin through his whiskers. *Not much.* She wouldn't have snuck off and left him with the dog. She sure as hell didn't trust him, and that damn dog figured in her affections right behind her son and way ahead of him. She had to still be in town.

No use in getting up a head of steam. He ground his teeth at his stupidity in acquiescing to separate rooms and Chaz's ability to drive him crazy. Then he scooped his shaving implements off the bed, told the dog to stay put, and slammed the door on his way out. After shaving with quick flicks of the razor, he rinsed off and changed into a clean shirt. His mouth set grimly, he trotted down the stairs into the lobby, pushing past the dusty potted ferns swaying in the ceiling fan turning overhead. When he reached the registration desk, he pounded on the counter. A wide-eyed young clerk emerged from the room behind the desk, lips pursed in a frown.

The clerk's eyes grew wider when Dillon dropped his revolver on the counter with a loud thud and began to strap on his holster. The young man swallowed convulsively. "May I help you, señor?"

"Did señora West check out of her room?" The man shook his head, and the muscles in his face relaxed when the gun left the counter to be deposited in Dillon's holster. "She went out earlier on foot." He tapped an empty wooden pigeon hole on the wall behind him. "She dropped off her key before leaving."

Muscles as fired up as a cowpoke on Saturday night, blood beating a tympani in his brain, Dillon barreled his way through the lobby and out the glass-inset doors to the street. A riot of music and stirring people met him. *Another fucking festival.* Seemed Mexico thrived on festivals, and though he usually could get into the spirit of the frivolity, right now, he was mad as hell at Chaz for slipping out without telling him, and it merely burned his craw. He knew the people endured their meager days only to experience the next Saint's Day or glorious celebration of the revolution, and they had a right to that, but the surrounding gaiety now fed his anger.

Dillon marched down the boardwalk, shouldering past campesinos in their Sunday best and señoritas in bright, flirtatious skirts and off-the-shoulder *camisas.* Mariachi bands played on street corners, surrounded by groups of clapping, foot-stomping onlookers, and street vendors hawked grilled *cerdo* and tortillas cooked over small, wood-fired griddles. His stomach growled at the delicious odors of bubbling pork fat and parched corn, and his nostrils flared at the strong scent of sweat from the flaminco dancers and the closeness of humanity.

A young woman with a golden complexion and flowing black hair danced up to him, clacked her castanets beneath his nose, rotated her hips, and gave him a smile filled with invitation. He turned away and brushed past her. She wasn't the woman he'd come to the streets to seek.

Where the hell is she?

When he elbowed through a large crowd arranged around the edges of the central square, he caught sight of her. Chaz wore the same red skirt, white *camisa,* and sash she'd had on at their first meeting in Asilo. She was one of a dozen dancers in the square, and her *huraches*-shod feet flew over the hard-packed dirt. Ebony hair spun free about her shoulders, and slim arms described sinuous movements in the air above her head. With castanets in each of her delicate hands, she kept time to the music, and her body swayed like a zephyr to the stirring strings of the guitars. The torchlight illuminating the square gleamed softly on her skin, creating shadows that fell kindly on the scars on her face, making them less pronounced.

In front of her danced a slim caballero in tight pants with silver conchos and a short embroidered jacket. *What the hell? Alec Cazadore!* How did that worm manage to get to Juarez before them? The man's eyes gleamed shoe black, his gaze riveted on Dillon's wife. With each movement of the dance, boots pounded against the street, the sombrero bounced on his back, dangling from the string around his neck, and his hips brushed against hers.

She lowered her arms and trailed her fingers across Alec's chest.

Dillon's hands fisted, and his brows dipped to a lethal level. He shoved the people in front of him out of the way and stomped out into the square. "Cutting in," Dillon said, gripping Alec by one shoulder and flinging him toward the people ringing the dancers. Some unfortunate campesino caught a chest full of caballero, and they fell to the ground.

Dillon looked over to where Alec was shaking off the other man and climbing to his feet. He combed back his black hair with one hand and pointed the other at Dillon. "Hey!" he shouted.

"Hey, *you*!" Dillon responded. The words roared from his throat. "That's *my* wife you're bumping groins with!"

Alec reached down, plucked his hat out of the dust, and slapped it on his leg. "You betrayed her!"

A red mist filled Dillon's vision. "I LOVE HER!"

Chaz kept her gaze on the interplay with no break in the rhythm of her dancing. She did, however, raise a staying hand at Alec when he reached to draw his gun. "Love, hah," she said, dancing between the sparring males. "Cease your crowing. You love only the sound of your own voice, señor West. I denounce our ill-conceived marriage. You lied to me, misled me. The marriage is not legal in the eyes of the Church. They look with disfavor on liars and cheats. I am no more your wife than Fuerte is my husband, and my feelings for him are more charitable than those I have for you."

"We'll discuss that in private," he said with one last black look at Alec and the people staring at them from their positions about the square. Chaz danced away, and Dillon took the place of her ousted partner, straightening his shoulders and stamping his feet as he followed her across the dusty ground.

"What the hell are you doing here anyway?" he hissed under his breath when he drew close to her again.

She tossed her head, and her glare withered him. "Dancing. What are you doing, other than making a spectacle of yourself?" As she circled around him, skirt coiling and uncoiling with the flair of an experienced flaminco dancer, she clacked together the castanets with the tips of her fingers against her palms.

He danced back around to face her, pulled her toward him with an arm around her waist, and bent her backward over one arm. "Looking for my wife. And where do I find her? Dancing shamelessly in the streets with that horn dog of a Spaniard." *Damn, I'm smitten with her!* With most women, he thought only about how to get between their legs; with Chaz, all he seemed to think about was how to get into her heart.

Sparks ignited in her blue eyes, turning them as dark as storm clouds. When Dillon brought her upright, she spun away and picked up her skirts, flipping them about her legs, showing her slim ankles. "I can dance if I wish to dance. In *Méjico*, married women do not give up all freedom. But it matters not, as you are no longer my husband."

"Of course I'm still your husband." He danced closer, feet beating out a furious rhythm, elbows bent, one hand against the small of his back, the other resting on his abdomen, following her movement across the ground. "And how did Cazadore get here?" he asked through a rigid jaw and nodded toward the man standing at the edge of the square with his hands on his hips and all the fires of hell in his eyes. "Where'd you find him? And how'd he find you?"

"He took the train. If I had not had to drag you along, I would have made better time."

Dillon clenched his teeth and bared them. "If you hadn't had me along, you'd still be looking for your horses."

She shrugged a bare shoulder. "Perhaps. Though you probably found them ten minutes after they ran off and had a great laugh at making me track them on foot for two days."

"Well, I'm not laughing now." He reached over and yanked the off-the-shoulder *camisa* up onto her shoulders. "Another few minutes, and your caballero would have dragged you off into a dark alley. Apparently, he's been angling to do that since before I met him."

Her hand came across his face, hard enough to sting but light enough to make it seem like a part of their dance. The crowd roared their approval. "You will not talk to me in such a way. If I had wanted Alec's attentions, I would have accepted them long before you came to Asilo."

"You're my wife, and I'll talk to you any way I damn well please. And what do you mean by 'accepting Alec's attentions'? Just how long *has* he been sniffing after you?"

They linked elbows and danced around each other. Then he took her hand and twirled her in place.

"That is none of your concern. Remember what you said when you begged me to marry you, that you would be my slave, and I would not be yours."

"Don't recall begging. Maybe I exaggerated a bit, but I still expect my wife to refrain from flirting with men in the street. Seems to me you've made a damn miraculous leap in record time, from being frightened of men to acting like a *puta*. Makes me wonder if it was all an act from the beginning."

Even as the words tumbled out, he knew he shouldn't have said them. But *hell*, the damning statement had simply sprung from his tongue.

This time she did slap him, hard enough to knock him back a couple of steps, and he had a hell of a time keeping his footing. Whirling about, she sped off through the crowds, Alec on her heels.

Dillon pressed one hand against his burning cheek and pursued them. He caught up a block away and came chest to chest with Alec.

"I'd suggest you find another señorita, *hombre*," Dillon said, his words low and harsh.

Alec met his gaze directly. "And if I don't?"

"Perhaps I shouldn't have phrased it as a suggestion. She's *my* wife, and she'll be coming with me. I'd hate to have to mess up your face."

Alec's gaze slewed to one side, where Chaz had stopped and was watching them. He came back to Dillon. "If you harm her in any way, I will come after you."

Dillon nodded. "Agreed."

Once Alec disappeared into the crowd, Dillon looked at Chaz, and his pulse raced at the amused expression on her face. "You coming with me now?"

She assessed him with narrowed eyes. "You should not have spoken to Alec so."

"He should learn to keep his hands off other men's women."

Her hands curled into fists, and her shoulders became rigid. "I am *not* your woman!"

He was through talking, and locking his hand around her wrist, he towed her off in the direction of the hotel. She twisted and yelled, drawing the attention of the men gathered on the boardwalk. One ugly, mean-looking *hombre* stepped in front of Dillon and blocked his path.

Dillon peered up into deadly black eyes. The man had to be six-six if he was an inch and as muscled as a Brahman bull. He didn't cotton a fight with this one, reckoning he'd come out on the worst end. "This is a private matter," he said in Spanish. "This woman is my wife."

The man's gaze swung to Chaz. "Is this man your husband?"

"No," she said. "I do not know him. He is abducting me against my will."

Before Dillon could retort, a fist the size of Texas caved in his stomach. He released Chaz to grab his guts before they spilled out over the boardwalk. "She *is* my wife," he managed to wheeze out before the fist knocked his jaw out of whack and finished him with a jab to the temple. He crumpled to his knees. "I swear it." He threw Chaz a desperate look, but she stood with her arms over her chest, one foot tapping the boards, and a half smile

on her lips. Meanwhile, this oversized longhorn was
going to kill him, beat him right into the ground, while
his wife looked on with an *amused* expression.

"Ouch. Ow. Stop!" he said with a groan, barely
managing to grate out the words. "She's my *wife!*"

When the man started back in on him again,
concentrating this time on his ribs with pointy-toed
boots, Chaz pushed her way between them. "¡*Alto!* He is
my husband. I was angry at him because he beats me."

Dillon lay curled up on his side, trying to protect his
manly parts from hard, pointed objects, and he couldn't
help but feel a sense of outrage at her words. The *hombre*
obviously felt the same and planted one more killing kick
into Dillon's kidneys. "Thanks, darlin'," Dillon said right
before he passed out.

Veintidós

As Chaz bathed the cuts and bruises on Dillon's face and torso with a bandana dipped in cool water, she suffered the sting of conscience He looked a sight, like he'd tangled with a bear, and she smiled. The sympathetic *hombre* had somewhat resembled an *oso*, like the golden-brown ones that roamed the Sierra Madre. When Dillon groaned, her smile wilted. She should not have let the beating go on for so long. However, that he should say what he had, even in anger, was not to be tolerated and crueler than she thought he ever could be. He had been angry before, but he had never been cruel. That she, of all women, should be called a *puta*.

He opened one eye. The other had swollen shut. "Why?" He fixed her with a one-eyed stare. "Why did you deny being my wife?"

"Because, at the time, I did not wish to acknowledge you as such. Do you forget that you came into my life through deceit? That you betrayed me and my family? That you impugned my honor? That you are a snake, and I wish to do nothing more than shoot your legs out from under you?"

"But you lied." His voice held almost a whine, like

a sulky *niño* who'd had a favorite toy taken from him.
"That's worse."

"Soon it will not be a lie." When he tried to sit up,
she moved back and picked up the bowl of water to keep
him from spilling it on the floor.

He moaned and pressed his hands against his ribs.
Then shaking his head, he said, "You're Catholic, Chaz.
You'll never divorce me."

She came down on her knees in front of him and
lifted his chin with one hand so he had to look directly
into her eyes, so he would see the truth of what she said.
"*Mi esposo*, divorce is not the only way to rid oneself of
an unwanted husband."

His lips curved wryly. "You mean kill me."

"Unless someone else kills you first."

"Well, darlin', you can sure try, but I wouldn't
take odds on your success." His smile expanded into a
painful-looking grin. "Anyway, you love me. You know
you do. Otherwise, you would have left my sorry ass
back on that boardwalk. You won't kill me unless I die of
heart failure between your thighs."

Is he right? Do I still love him in spite of his deceit? Why
hadn't she left him to tend to his own injuries? His low,
caressing voice and smile roiled up unwelcome feelings,
ones she didn't want to face but that, nonetheless, rose to
the surface, touched her heart. She found she could not
deny them this time.

"If that is your dying wish, señor." She leaned
forward and took his lips in a searing kiss.

"Did you mean it?" Chaz asked.

His brows came together over a gaze of perplexity.
"What?"

"What you said. Did you mean it?"

"You mean 'ouch'?"

"No, *stupido*, that you love me."

His chest rose and fell with a deep breath. "Honey, I meant it, truly mean it. If I didn't love you, would I stay and take this kind of abuse? I'd have trussed you up neater than a rodeo calf, handed you over to Thorne, and collected the rest of my pay."

"So you do love me?"

"Didn't I say so? Damn right I love you, Chaz. More than my life, more than my horse, hell, more than silver. I don't care if you say you hate me. I know you love me too. And even if you don't, you will."

"And how will you make me love you?"

A gentle light kindled in his eyes and warmed her soul. "By filling every day of your life with my kisses and caresses and lovemaking. And by never lying to you again."

She arched a brow. "Never?"

He made a half-assed attempt at looking earnest. "Never."

She sat up, astride his hips, and with a twist of her head, flung her hair back over one shoulder.

"Ouch, ow, ah, easy, darlin'," he said, "I think my ribs are broken."

"This will never work."

"That's because we're doing it wrong. Roll onto your back, I'm coming up on top. My knees and hands are about the only parts of me that *hombre* didn't mangle."

Her heart beat faster, and that old fear swirled from her chest downward into her gut. She struggled to swallow. "On top? On top of me?"

The corners of his mouth winged down. "Now, don't start up on me again, Chaz. You know me better than to think I'd hold you down and take you against your will. 'Member, darlin', you started this."

She supposed her frown mirrored his, because his grew deeper. Thoughts of Thorne and his brutality washed through her mind in fathomless, dark rollers. He'd always held her down, used his weight to keep

her captive beneath him so she couldn't flee. Dillon…
in those glorious times they made love, allowed her
freedom of movement, the chance to retreat if she became
uncomfortable. Considering what she now knew about
him, about his lies, his duplicity, could she still have
that same trust? Could she lay beneath him in perfect
surrender? Her body, the heat in her blood, the gathering
moisture between her legs, which seemed to emerge from
somewhere deep inside her despite her state of mind, her
anger at him, her lingering questions about his motives,
urged her to do just that, but…

"I *thought* I knew you. But if you could lie to me,
you—"

He looked at her as if fangs had popped out of her
mouth. "Could rape you? Is that what you think? Well
then, woman, get the hell off my cock. You lied too, and
I'm the one feeling abused right now. I'd like to get some
whiskey and sleep, preferably in that order."

Chaz slipped off him and moved back, assessing him
with a critical gaze. He folded his arms over his chest and
glowered, returning her look.

But his state belied his words. He was as hard as a
hickory trunk…and he didn't want her. Somehow, his
denial of his desire hurt more than his deceit. "Truly, you
would go to sleep now?" The moisture from her arousal
dribbled down the insides of her legs, and she ached
inside.

He nodded. "Sure will. I thought you didn't trust
me."

She tracked back on her trail. "I did not say that…
exactly."

"Sure sounded like it to me."

"I do trust you, in bed." *How did he coerce that
confession from her?* "Only in everything else do I not trust
you."

He grinned. "Okay, I'll accept your apology. Roll
over, darlin'."

"You are impossible," she muttered and shifted, stretching out on her back.

"But you love me," he murmured.

"I hate you."

"Can't argue with that." He tried to get up and groaned, cursed a moderate amount in Spanish and English, and finally hauled his body up and got to his feet. "Move over, into the center of the bed."

She scooted over.

Fuerte, who was watching them with an intent gaze, climbed onto the bed and lay down next to Chaz.

"Not you, you brainless hound." Dillon shoved against the shaggy back. "Get down."

Fuerte gave him a hurt look and left the bed with a hefty sigh to curl up on Dillon's shirt in the corner of the room.

Dillon sat on the bed beside her, leaned over and kissed her — deep, wet, and soft. When she opened her mouth, his tongue described circles around hers and over her teeth. His hand smoothed over her neck and collarbone and slid down to cover the peak of one breast, and her nerves twitched beneath her skin; a silent cry rose up in her throat: *Her breasts?* She fought to keep from voicing her terror. Thorne had played particular attention to that tender flesh, pinching and twisting and mauling. Dillon had held her before, caressed her body, but only once had he touched her breasts. She'd borne through the trepidation and soon realized, much to her relief, that Dillon's way was nothing like Thorne's. That recollection helped her now. When his palm rubbed soft, gentle circles over and around her nipple, the peak stiffened and strained toward the heat and pressure.

As the kiss went on, endless and stealing her mind and senses, she rubbed her thighs together to relieve the pulsing between them.

"Part those legs, darlin'," he said into her mouth between kisses.

The words and his breath on her sped up the throbbing in her veins, and she spread her legs apart.

"Now this may hurt," he said and chuckled when she stiffened. "I meant me, not you." Another spate of soft cursing followed as he swung over her onto his hands and knees. Slowly, ever so slowly, he lowered his pelvis and slipped into her heat and wetness.

When he filled her, she sighed, and her inner muscles clenched around him. As soon as she had a tight grip, he pulled up and almost out. The withdrawal nearly killed her, and she gripped harder with her passage to keep from losing him.

A soft laugh came from him, and his eyes twinkled as he looked down at her. "Don't worry, darlin', I'm not going anywhere. But I surely love that muscle action."

With a dip of his hips, he plunged back into her, deeper than the first time. Then out slowly, in fast and hard, out, in, until her head spun and she arched up into him with his every downward thrust. Their hips met above the mattress, flesh slapping on flesh, and he murmured his approval. An inferno built up in the walls of her cleft, and the muscles in her thighs and buttocks clenched and released. Her entire universe shrank to the room around her, the bed beneath her, and the rigid male flesh inside her, driving her to rapture.

"Oh, God," Dillon said, breaking the moment. His cock swelled and bucked inside her; his juices flooded her channel.

She strained once more while he was still coming and found the end of her journey in a glorious eruption of rapture, heat, and languor.

He collapsed on top of her and flattened her into the mattress. Her greatest terror, to be held down again by a man. This time, however, to her complete bewilderment, contentment took the place of fear. She gently embraced his torso and held him to her.

"Ouch," Dillon said softly. "Just pack me in a pine

box, darlin'. I reckon I'm dying."

Chaz shook him.

"Ow!"

Words sharp and tone impatient, she said, "We must leave soon, or the train will be too far ahead for us to catch it."

Dillon peeled open an eyeball. His entire body hurt, and even the low morning sunshine sifting through the window and landing on his skin felt like a hammer blow. "I'm coming, darlin', give me a few minutes to splint my arms and legs and wrap up my ribs."

She snorted. "You are only bruised. If you are not up and dressed in fifteen minutes, I'll leave without you." As she crossed the room, her boots tapped on the wooden floor, and he winced when she closed the door with a soft bang.

"Okay, up and at 'em," he said to himself and rolled to the edge of the bed. With every muscle screaming and bone grating against bone, he swung his legs off the bed and pulled himself into a sitting position. "Now," he said, carrying on his one-sided conversation, "where are my pants?"

Fuerte whined, picked up the clothing in his teeth, and carried it to Dillon.

While Dillon dressed, Chaz found a mining office that had a map showing the railroad route. Numerous stops and the changing of cars loaded with metal ore from Mexico's interior would slow the train's progress. Chaz and Dillon crossed the border, rode out of El Paso and twenty miles north of town before they came to a point where the map showed the train would pass them. Short-grass prairie ran alongside the tracks and stretched out in rolling low hills and depressions for miles in every direction.

"You have a plan?" Dillon asked as he tilted back his hat and looked at Chaz.

"Of course." Her gaze narrowed on the distant extent of the tracks, where smoke from the boiler would announce the coming train.

"And that would be?"

Her eyes met his. "To rescue Raúl."

He sighed and leaned back, draping one leg over the saddle horn. "Darlin', that's not a plan, it's a goal. And it's loco. I told you we should have left the horses behind and taken the next train. We'd be behind them, but I reckon taking Raúl from a house in Chicago would be easier than off a train stuffed as tight as a tick with bad-tempered gunmen."

She regarded him with the fire of stubbornness in her eyes. "I told you I could not wait that long."

He glanced away to a herd of pronghorn antelope grazing not far away on the tough prairie grass. "How about my second idea? Hightail it to Kansas City. With all the train stops, we can make better time and be there before the train pulls in. They'll have to uncouple the car and hook it onto another line. When they transfer Raúl, we'll have a half-assed chance of getting him away from them."

Her gaze drifted out over the landscape, down the length of the track, as though she were willing the train to appear. "I wish to do it now…here. I will not leave my son with that devil for another day. In any event, I cannot kill Thorne in a railway station."

He leaned over and seized her hand, bringing her attention back to him. "Okay, *querida*, I understand, truly I do, but we still have to have a plan."

She vetoed every other suggestion he made. She was determined to have her way in this, and he reckoned he agreed, seeing as Raúl was her son. Still, he insisted on a strategy that had a better chance of working than the devil would have in claiming a priest's soul, and he wouldn't budge. His skin and hers were at risk here. He wasn't about to let her commit suicide, and he wasn't ready to die yet, either.

A convocation of buzzards spiraling overhead alerted them to the carcass and provided Chaz with an idea. The rank odor let them know they were drawing near. The steer lay in a shallow gulch, its rotting body covered in black birds with beaks tearing at the meat.

"This will never work," Dillon said as he pulled up his bandana to cover his nose. "God, it smells like ass."

She stared in puzzling question. "*¿Qué?*"

"It's an expression. You'd know what I meant if you'd spent months in a bunkhouse full of bean-eating banditos."

She shrugged. The smell of the carcass didn't seem to affect her, but Niebla dug in her hoofs and refused to move any closer. "It will work. They will have to stop to move it. Then we can board the train."

He gave up on trying to convince her to come up with another plan. Trying to breathe through his mouth, he wrapped his rope around the steer's horns and secured the end to his saddle horn. Chaz did the same. It seemed like a good plan, but the horses wouldn't cooperate and shied away from the putrefying steer. Even Fuerte declined to investigate and backed away. With a few well-chosen curses, comparing Victory to every low-bellied creature he'd ever seen or heard of, Dillon dismounted, released the rope, and hauled it over his shoulder. Even half-eaten by buzzards and coyotes, the cow must have weighed over three hundred pounds. Chaz joined him, and they dragged the animal toward the tracks. The steer bounced and slid along on the ground behind them, catching on every stray rock and bush.

Dillon sent Victory — who followed upwind at a

respectable distance — a frosty glance. "You damned, swayback coyote bait," he said. "I should shoot your legs out from under you and leave you for the buzzards. That's all you're good for."

Victory flicked his ears and looked unimpressed by the threat.

"Save your breath," Chaz said, panting as she hauled on the rope, "and pull."

By the time they reached their goal, more than a mile across the prairie, sweat sheathed Dillon's face and poured down his back.

"Damn fool woman," he grumbled to no one in particular, a lament he'd found himself voicing more than once. The words came out in a dry, scratchy voice.

Once the carcass lay across the tracks, they retrieved the horses and retired to a gently sloped dry wash filled with stones, mesquite, and lizards to await the train. In the far distance, smoke from the train's wood-fired boiler drifted upward into the clear blue sky, rising sinewy and unraveling like a ribbon as it grew closer. When the train came alongside them, it would be moving fast.

"How will they even know that cow's there?" Dillon asked, his tone revealing his skepticism. "If they don't see it in time, they'll plow right through it. I doubt that stinking pile of bones and hide will do more than make one hell of a mess on the cowcatcher."

Chaz tilted back her head. "The buzzards."

He glanced up. Sure enough, the buzzards had followed them and were already circling downward toward their interrupted meal. "A shame we couldn't have convinced them to move it for us," he mumbled.

"The engineer will see them and slow down," she said. "He cannot be certain that what is on the tracks will not derail the train. Even if they do not stop, they will slow enough for our purpose."

"You're sure about that."

She nodded. "I am sure."

So they had a plan. Well, a hit-or-miss kind of plan.

The train came into sight, a black smudge on the horizon. To Dillon, it looked like it was moving pretty damned fast.

The train did not slow down, and true to Dillon's prediction, smashed through the steer carcass as neatly as a meat cleaver.

Blasted man! Can he not be wrong once? On that unlikely day, Chaz would make a plaster statue of him and hold a festival in Asilo.

She spurred Niebla from a standing start into a flat-out run, and Fuerte ran alongside. The wind tore the sombrero off her head. The string choked her when the hat filled with wind and flew like a sail behind her. She slipped the string over her head and tossed the annoyance aside.

Victory had longer legs than Niebla and ran a half stride in front of her. When he stumbled in a gopher hole, she pulled ahead. By the time they reached the back of the train, they were neck-and-neck. Chaz brought Niebla alongside the platform, jerked the repeating rifle out of the saddle boot, and leaned forward, kicking her feet out of the stirrups. She doubled her knees and sprang to her feet, balancing her weight on the saddle.

"Damn it!" Dillon shouted from beside her. "Stop that! You'll break your fool neck!"

She laughed and jumped for the platform, managing to catch the railing with her free hand and wedge her toes beneath the bottom rung. In a heartbeat, she was over the barrier and reaching out for Dillon.

"Grab my hand!"

"No! I'll pull you off!"

"Do it! Grab my hand!"

One last jab of his heels in Victory's sides, and Dillon was there within reach. He swung his left leg over the saddle, kicked his right foot out of the stirrup, and latched onto her hand. When she pulled, he pushed away from Victory with a shove of his left foot against the saddle and landed over the railing on his stomach.

"Ow!"

She hauled on his arms to bring him the rest of the way over. He slid to the platform, flat on his back, eyes closed, and breathing like a racehorse.

Slowly, his eyelids lifted, and his sharp glare cut her to ribbons. "You ever do something as thoughtless as that again, and I'll tan your hide but good, you damn, out-of-control woman. What if you'd fallen beneath the wheels of the train?"

"I never fall."

With a loud groan, he pushed himself to his feet. "Well, there's a first time for everything. Just don't do it again." He looked over the railing at Fuerte, who now ran behind the train. "What about the dog? Gonna pull him up here too?"

"He knows how to hunt. He will stay with the horses and lead them to grazing and water. We can pick them up on our way back."

"You're pretty sure we're coming back, aren't you?"

"Certainly."

When Chaz slammed through the door into the car, the space held two guards, mean eyed and well armed. She dove to the floor, rolled up onto her feet, and brought up the rifle. Working the lever action, she drilled one man through the throat. With a flying tackle, Dillon caught the other one in the back of the knees and sent him to the boards on his face. A well-placed gun butt against the side of the head put the guard to sleep.

Dillon rebuked her with a glower. "You shouldn't have fired. Now they know we're here."

She gave him a flippant shrug of her shoulder. "They would know eventually."

They knew.

Three men came through the far door like bulls bursting through a fence after a herd of cows. Guns blazed—pistols from Dillon and Thorne's men, the rapid report of Chaz's rifle—overpowering all other sound. When the smoke cleared, the guards sprawled on the floor, their limbs cockeyed and blood pouring from numerous holes.

Dillon swung toward Chaz. "You okay?"

She got up off her knees and bent over the rifle, feeding bullets into it in rapid motion. "Yes. But that ugly one"—she gestured at the stocky man lying nearest her—"put a bullet through my leathers." She examined a tear near the top of her left shoulder, which oozed blood, then swung a foot into the dead man's side.

"Let me look at that," Dillon said.

She gave him a quick shake of her head. "*De nada.* We have to advance." She locked eyes with him. Her jaw jutted forward in challenge, but anxiety creased her forehead. "How many more do you suppose?"

His shoulders lifted and fell in a shrug. "Three cars to go, and for all I know, they could be packed shoulder to shoulder with Thorne's gunmen."

"Then we should not waste any more time."

She moved toward the door, but he pushed her aside. "Me first. Remember, I'm the gun hand, and I'm faster than you." He took his skills seriously, but more than anything, he'd give it his best shot to keep her from getting killed. Chaz seemed to draw danger like lightning to a tall pine. He loved this woman. Damned if he would let Thorne or her own impatience take her away from him.

Cautiously, he opened the door.

Blue smoke and hot lead, and like a stinging hornet, one of them damn pieces of lead creased his temple.

"Aw shit," he mumbled, crumpling to his knees and tumbling into blackness.

* * *

When Dillon went down, a crushing weight squeezed Chaz. She pressed her lips together to keep them from trembling, and she swallowed down a knot of cold, stark fear. She rushed toward him, but rough hands grabbed her arms and jerked her against a massive body that smelled of rancid sweat and strong cigars. Her hand went to the knife at her waist, grasped the deer-antler hilt, and yanked it from the scabbard. Twisting it in her hand, she stabbed backward, deeply into fat and muscle. Blood spurted over her hand, and she found herself free.

She went down on one knee and swung the rifle around...fired, jacked in another cartridge, fired again, another cartridge, fired. Every shot found a target. They had caught the men gathered around a scarred table in the middle of a game of poker. Now, the table fell over onto its side, and coins and cards scattered like tumbleweeds. Three men—four counting the gutted one—lay on the floor of the car, bleeding out onto the wood.

The other four occupants reached Chaz before she sent the fifth one to hell. They nearly broke her wrists prying the rifle from her hands. A burly hand slapped her across the face, once, twice, first to one side and then the other, again and again, and she reeled from the blows. Before she lost consciousness, a guttural voice said, "You kill her, and Thorne will string you up by your pecker. He wants her alive."

Then nothing.

Veintitres

Dillon came to his senses when he hit the ground. He supposed the impact with the less-than-soft sand and prickly pear cactus in his lower spine had something to do with it. When he cleared his head, wiped the blood out of his eyes, and looked up, the train was already far in the distance. Fuerte towered over him and laved his face with a soggy tongue. Slowly he inched to his feet, yanked the cactus spines from his back, and dusted off his clothes. His hat perched on a grandfather cactus a couple of feet away, and he hobbled over there to retrieve it, and jammed it on his head. He winced when it rubbed against an oozing crease the bullet left behind.

He tilted back the hat so it no longer irritated his wound, and with his hands on his hips, turned and watched the back of the train growing smaller and smaller.

Jesus! Now Raúl was on the train, Chaz was on the train, and he was without a horse in the midst of the Texas prairie, miles from any town. *I should have seen this coming.* If he hadn't let himself be blindsided by his feelings for that irritating woman, he would have.

First things first. A horse. He needed a horse,

preferably, his own horse.

The last time Dillon saw Victory, the stallion was running alongside Niebla behind the train. Fuerte was with them. Now Fuerte was greeting him, all lolling tongue and hot, panting breath. The stallion and mare couldn't be too far away. Dillon took off, limping on a twisted knee as he trudged across the uneven, tough-grass land, whistling and calling out his mount's name. Fuerte surged ahead, coursing over the ground as if he were hunting rabbits.

"Thought you were supposed to watch the horses," he called out to the dog.

Fuerte's nose lifted from the ground, and he glanced back for a second before resuming his hunt. Soon, evening crept in on shadowy feet and enveloped the landscape in a silky dark cloak. Dillon's feet hurt like they were nothing but a mess of blisters, and his pucker had nearly dried up. Then a loud barking and a soft nicker came from the darker blackness of an isolated grove of cottonwoods. He halted, pursed his lips, and whistled again.

Victory trotted out from beneath the trees, Niebla followed on his heels, and Fuerte bounded through the weeds. "Took a shine to her, eh, boy?" Dillon said when Victory reached him. The horse shook his head and blew air from his nostrils. Dillon stroked the velvety nose. "Don't blame you, you horny old cayuse. She's a looker. Too bad her mistress is as *dadblamed* mad as a sun-struck rattler." Victory snorted and dipped his head, butting Dillon in the chest.

Dillon looked around. No sign of a town, the railroad tracks, or even a trail. The night was now too black to see much of anything. In his current situation, he had a better chance of drawing a queen when four were already on the table than beating the train to Kansas City. Best he could do was catch another train and follow behind, that is, once he found a town and a railroad station. He

gathered up the reins and mounted, sighing when his
weight came off his aching feet and settled on his butt.
After tying Niebla's reins to a ring on the back of his
saddle, he turned Victory, urged him into a steady lope,
whistled to the dog, and headed northwest.

"Charissa." Thorne's oily voice lubricated the word,
making it sound obscene.

She raised her head. Her wrists were tied to the arms
of a plush chair bolted to the floor of the car. She swayed
when the train took the curves, but the chair stayed put.
The room sat in gloom, even though the curtains were
pulled back from the windows. Night rushed by outside
with only the hint of shadowy hills and plains, blacker
than black against the dark landscape.

When she gingerly opened her mouth, pain speared
through the bones, as if the big man in the ill-fitting suit
had dislocated her jaw. She managed to speak, and it
came out rusty, as disconnected from her body as her jaw
felt. "Where is Raúl?"

She did not bother asking about Dillon. *What is the
use? He's dead.* Thorne would not leave a lethal gun hand
like his ex-employee alive to come after him…them. Her
heart ached unbearably, but her main concern had to be
for her son. He was only a boy. Dillon was a man and
well aware that the dangerous life he led could end in a
premature death. Only now she realized how much she
loved that stubborn, maddening man, now, when it was
too late.

A lantern flared and threw a sudden and startling
pool of light into the car. Thorne emerged in stark relief
against the gloom. Leaning back in a chair identical to
hers, he crossed his legs and clipped off the end of a
cigar. A man in a corner of the car rushed forward with
a match, and Thorne waved him away. "Leave us," he
said. "My stepdaughter and I have a lot of catching up

to do." He drew a match from a box mounted to the arm of the chair and scratched it across a brass striker. As he touched the flame to the cigar, his gaze remained steadily on her...slitted and reptilelike. The match illuminated his craggy features, making him look like a troll in the dim surroundings of his grotto. Then he shook out the flame, and the image dissipated.

She could admit, on some level, that a certain kind of woman might find Thorne attractive, the kind who valued money over morals and principles. The old memories surfaced, the ones Dillon had almost erased, and her stomach sickened.

"Where is my son?" she asked again.

Thorne drew on the cigar, and the end glowed a sharp red. All the while, he stared out at her from a wreathing of smoke. Then he lowered the cigar and leaned forward. "You mean Raúl...my son?" His smile was feral.

She spat at him, and he jerked backward. "He has nothing to do with you. He is my son, mine alone." At the malice in his narrowed eyes, she realized she should not have done that, shown him such disrespect. A man like Thorne was all about respect and power. But hearing her son's name come from his vile mouth had taken away her sense. Nonetheless, if she was to get out of this with her life and Raúl's, she would have to swallow her revulsion and keep her head clear.

"*My* son is being cared for," he said. "It was not well done of you to keep him from me for so long. If you cooperate, Charissa, I may allow you to see him."

Cooperate. He used to say that to her, time and again all those years ago. *Cooperate, and I won't hurt you. But he did.* Chaz knew what the word meant. Her mouth filled with a bitter, metallic taste, not unlike blood.

When he leaned toward her again, this time the challenging arch of his brow dared her to show her contempt. His large hand, bejeweled with ostentatious

rings on long fingers, rested on her knee and slid
upward. She knew that hand, those fingers, knew what
they could do to a young girl, the pain they could cause,
how they could stain one's soul forever. She closed her
eyes, determined not to fight him, for Raúl's sake. He
laughed and withdrew.

She opened her eyes and regarded him quizzically.

"You aren't the tender young girl I once knew," he
said.

"I am no longer a girl."

"That's not exactly what I meant." His face and eyes
had gone blank, unreadable. "This life you've chosen has
made you hard. If only you'd stayed with me. I could've
given you everything you ever wanted."

Again, her wits deserted her, and she yelled at him.
"What? What could you have given me? More pain, more
shame, more scars? You took an innocent girl and turned
her into your *puta*. You are a pig! You were a pig when I
was a child, and you will die a pig! I had to leave or slit
my own throat. I only wish I had been given the strength
and opportunity to do the same to you."

He extended his thick, saugagelike fingers and traced
the scars on her face. "You did have the opportunity,
Charissa. But I had the strength, the upper hand, and still
do."

She jerked her head to one side. "All you will do is
talk me to death. When can I see my son?"

"Soon." He got to his feet and stubbed out his cigar
in a crystal ashtray. "For now, you'll rest. We still have a
long journey, and Fremont treated you roughly. I'll see
he's punished for bruising your face."

*The man who scarred my face forever worried himself over
a few bruises? Perhaps because he was not the one to inflict
them.* Thorne had nothing more to say to her, because
before she could open her mouth and make her situation
even more dire, he crossed to the end door and left. For
a large man, he moved quickly. She remembered that

about him and told herself to keep it in mind for the time when she was free and had access to a weapon. *That time will come.* Then she would exact vengeance for what he had done to her, her son, and to Dillon, the only man to steal her heart.

Thorne's men removed her from the parlor car and locked her in a small, windowless compartment. Wall-mounted lanterns lit the room, but the rich, dark wood of the walls made the space seem even smaller. In a recessed niche behind a purple velvet curtain sat a bed with a thick, feather mattress. One of Thorne's thugs brought her dinner—duck in currant sauce, thinly sliced carrots candied in honey, boiled potatoes dusted with chives and parsley, and a crystal glass holding a rich red Madeira.

Her stomach had shrunk to the size of a walnut, and she picked at her food. Later, unable to sleep, she roamed back and forth across the thick carpet. *Ten steps to the wall, turn, ten steps back.* Building panic assailed her mind. Nothing in the room looked hard or sharp enough to use as a weapon, and she would need a weapon. Thorne would come back.

When Thorne made his entrance, soon after eleven o'clock by the brass clock bolted to the wall, Chaz lay down on the whore's bed with no protest and stared up at the ceiling. Raúl's life was at stake, and there was nothing left for her, for now, but surrender. Thorne may take her body, but this time, he could not touch her soul. She divorced herself from all feeling, serene at last, and allowed her consciousness to float outward... The green valley of Asilo stretched out before her. Dusky blue shadows clothed the mountain slopes. Horses shuffled their feet in the remuda. Delicia rang the large iron bell on the *pórtico* of the hacienda, signaling the men to come in from their labors for the evening meal. Raúl ran across the meadow with Fuerte at his heels. Dillon's smile, tender and loving, his arms embracing her, keeping her safe...

Thorne could not frighten her, he could not force a

reaction from her, he could not harm her, and he could not touch her, inside, where it mattered.

Thorne left her bed, stopped at the door and looked back, his brows knitted together in a perplexed frown. "I'm disappointed, Charissa. You've changed more than I realized. I would have gotten more satisfaction from fucking a corpse."

Suddenly, her heart beat wildly. *That was it, the secret he was hiding.* She wished she had known all those years ago. The sex was not what excited him, compelled him to seek her out. He wanted her terror, her struggles. Like she thrived on revenge, he thrived on pain and panic. Without them, the act was hollow, meaningless, not worth the great man's effort.

All that long journey into the snow- and mist-shrouded city of Chicago, Chaz remained locked in her compartment, and Thorne did not come to her again.

Cold sliced through Dillon like the blade of a Bowie knife. Winter had come hard to the city on the lake, and lacey flakes sluiced downward in white veils to shroud the mansions. Victory shook his head, scattering a sugar coating of ice that clung to his mane.

"Easy, boy," Dillon said as he took off his hat and banged it on his leg to dump its weight of snow. Some caught the dog on the head, and he shook it off with a vigorous motion.

Chaz had been with Thorne for over two weeks. Dillon knew Thorne, or more precisely, Thorne's kind. That he would leave her untouched wasn't an option. The ice that encased Dillon's heart chilled him more than the wind sweeping off the lake.

He'd taken the train north from the first station he reached after being tossed off Thorne's railroad, and now lagged nearly four days behind Thorne and Chaz. His hand itched to pull his gun and deposit some lead where it would do the most good. If he looked into her deep blue eyes and saw an ounce of pain, he wouldn't need his gun. He swore he'd squash Thorne like a scorpion.

He hadn't prayed in a long time. In his line of work, he and his Maker were bound to be on somewhat touchy terms. Now, for the first time in years, he prayed. He prayed Chaz was stronger today than she was as a girl. He prayed his love had helped her find that strength. He prayed she hadn't reverted to that scared, bitter woman he'd first met. Most of all, he prayed she was still alive. If she fought Thorne, the man wasn't above killing her.

The mansion sat on a pinnacle of land jutting out into the lake and was surrounded by a tall granite wall like a medieval castle. Boathouses and jetties ringed the shore. Dillon rode around the wall, searching for a chink in the castle's armor. The sheer stone blocks fitted snugly together, allowing no purchase for hands or feet. Iron spikes topped the wall, reaching for a gray sky pregnant with snow clouds.

"See anything promising?" he asked the dog.

Fuerte cocked up his head, peered into Dillon's eyes, and whimpered. The dog's concern for his mistress mirrored Dillon's.

"You reckon we're expected, or does Thorne think he took care of me, permanent like, back in Texas? Regardless, I imagine he's got his bodyguards on alert, just in case." He tilted back his head and examined the wall. "If I'm lucky, I could get a rope around one of those spikes and haul myself up." His gaze dropped to the dog. "But I suppose you're not gonna let me climb that wall alone, are you?"

Fuerte uttered a soft bark.

Dillon's breath issued as a frosty cloud. "Didn't think so.

The wall curved around and disappeared into a dark forest of spruce and fir clothed in snow, their sweeping branches beaten to the ground by the storm. Dillon and Fuerte followed the wall, entering the woods and ducking beneath the black-green needled boughs. In the farthest corner of the forest, emerging from the sheets of snow and drifting ice spicules, a rusty iron gate stood out as a black beacon against the bleak gray rock and blinding white landscape.

"Eureka," Dillon said softly. "Told you. Every castle's got a back door."

Veinticuatro

Her childhood bedroom had not changed
significantly from when she was a child and stirred
up old memories of being held captive here, a slave to
her stepfather's wishes and perverted desires. Lace-
embellished cream drapes and bed hangings, pale peach
walls, graceful furniture. One addition was bars on the
windows. So this time the princess was more than a
virtual prisoner. She was an actual prisoner.

Another change stood out more than the bars. Every
conceivable space on the walls held a mirror. The better
to view her disfigurement, she supposed. Thorne must
believe it to be the height of cruelty, a vindictiveness
that would break her. Since her flight from Thorne and
Chicago, she'd shunned mirrors, banning them from her
home. She needed no reminder of the past, no reason to
recall what Thorne had done to her. He'd scarred her
soul as well as her face, and she carried that with her
every day. Mirrors reflected only the outer girl she once
was, not the inner woman she'd become. Chaz made an
effort to break the mirrors to obtain a weapon. But they
were made of some shiny metal...not glass. Therefore,
she ignored the mirrors as she ignored her tormentor,

and in some way rejoiced at failing to succeed in fulfilling her first impulse to obliterate the reflective surfaces. To remove the mirrors would give Thorne satisfaction, proof he still held power over her emotions. He would get no such satisfaction from her.

Once Thorne locked her in her silken, mirrored prison, he resumed his visits. This time, her indifference had an effect she did not foresee. It unmanned him.

"You damned witch!" he screamed, naked and flaccid.

He often came to her drunk, spouting venom about what he would do to Raúl, demanding acts to bring back his virility that she refused to perform.

"Tell me where he is," she stipulated, "show him to me, and I will do what you ask. Until that time, demand nothing of me. If you do not produce my son, you can go to hell for all I care."

"I'll kill him. I'll bring him in here and slit his throat so he falls dead at your feet," he replied, spittle flying from his lips. "You'll be sorry you wouldn't cooperate."

Would he truly kill his own son? She didn't think so, regardless of how he tried to goad her and make her believe otherwise.

Would he kill me? That, no doubt, was where her apathy would eventually push him.

Regardless of her instincts and his volatile temper, after that first time when he did nothing but bluster, she bore his vitriolic words, threats, and demands in stoic silence. Not by the flicker of an eye did she show him how much his ranting affected her. Like always, he left in a rage. At some point, his fury would overcome him. Then he would put an end to it…to her.

Since her arrival in Chicago, she had seen no one she knew. The entire staff appeared to have been replaced over the years. His diligence in filling the mansion with strangers served his purpose. She had no allies, no one who cared about her situation and would come to her aid. When she left her room for dinner with Thorne each night in the formal dining room, no one spoke to her; no one approached her. The looks sent her way ranged from curious to haughty. She supposed they believed she was nothing more than Thorne's whore.

As a result, although she tried at every opportunity to quiz the staff, they refused to speak to her. She had no luck in finding out whether Raúl was close at hand or had been taken elsewhere. She had not seen him, not even on the train. Was he dead, like Dillon? If that was true, she welcomed her death at Thorne's hands. Each night she prayed her stepfather would cease playing with her and simply get on with the killing.

Once he removed his reata from the saddle and looped the coils over his shoulder, Dillon tied Victory to a tree and said, "Stay here. I have a feeling we'll be hauling leather when we leave, and I won't have time to track you down."

Victory snorted and pawed at the snow.

"Yeah, well just make sure you're here when I come back, or you'll be finding your oats on your own."

Dillon turned to where Fuerte had taken to digging at the frozen ground beneath the gate's bottom edge, as if he thought he could tunnel his way inside. If the ground beneath the snow hadn't been frozen and as hard as shoe iron, perhaps he could.

The gate had an old, rusty lock. When Dillon kicked through the snow beside the wall, he uncovered a chunk of granite, apparently left over from the construction. He stripped off his heavy coat and wrapped the stone in the cloth. Several bone-jarring swings at the lock, and it broke into three jagged pieces. By now, Fuerte had cleared a respectable portion of the snow away from the gate, which swung outward with a hard yank and a wrench of muscles. As soon as an opening appeared, the dog slipped through and tore across the snowy space toward the house.

"Come back," Dillon whispered as loudly as he dared. "You'll alert any guards." On second thought, he figured the guards, if any, would be roasting their toes at the kitchen hearth by now. If he'd had a choice, so would he. The storm had picked up, along with the wind off the lake, and he lost sight of Fuerte and the mansion within minutes. He cursed into the howling wind and tracked the dog's huge paw prints through the deepening snow. Man and dog joined up again at the entrance to the servants' quarters.

Once Dillon united with him, Fuerte took off again, moving to the right along the long eastern wing. The drifting snow became knee-deep, and Dillon slogged his way through it, following Fuerte. He figured the dog knew where he was going, even though he'd never been here before. *Perhaps he'd picked up her scent or has some kind of dog mind-link thing with Chaz.* Fuerte was one damned spooky dog. Dillon rounded the arm of the east wing and ran into thick shrubbery. He pressed his back to the wall of the house, between the greenery and the stones, and inched his way along. At last he reached a clear space where Fuerte ran in circles and whined, his golden eyes fixed on a balcony on the third floor.

"So she's up there, eh, boy?" Dillon said while studying the stone and scratching the dog behind the ears. "Guess this is where we part company. Smart as you are, I don't think you can make this climb."

He slipped the reata off his shoulder, played out a loop, and stepped back, circling the rope over his head. He tossed it out and up to catch an iron prong on the balcony. Bracing his feet on the side of the house, he worked his way upward, hand over hand. Regardless of the cold in his hands and the slippery rock wall, which allowed for precarious footing, within minutes he reached the jutting stones and swung over the railing onto the solid balcony.

He spared a glance for the dog. Fuerte had dropped onto his haunches in the snow and was silently watching his progress. Intermittent snow squalls obscured his vision and made the dog look like a ghostly wolf waiting for a warm meal to fall from the sky. Dillon grinned; fortunately he was on friendly terms with the wolf.

He swung around and stepped over to the window. Bars covered them, a detail he'd missed in the veil of snow. The barrier looked new, showing no rust or other weaknesses. Thorne had planned well for reluctant guests. Dillon gripped the icy iron and leaned as close to the window glass as the bars would allow.

"*Querida*," he whispered, then louder, "*Querida!*"

"Querida."

"Dillon?"

"*Querida!*"

"Dillon!" Chaz sped to the window and threw open the panes. Wind and snow whipped inside, stinging her eyes and making them tear, and icy air froze her limbs.

Gloved hands grabbed her face and pulled her forward. Lips as cold as Satan's heart landed on hers. She warmed them with her breath.

Words gushed forth from both as forcefully as the storm.

"Are you okay? Did Thorne harm you—"

"I thought you were dead. I saw the wound on your head—"

"I'll grind him up for buzzard bait if he touched you—"

"How did you get away from those men on the train—"

"Where's Raúl? Is he here with you? How do I get you out of there—"

She slapped a hand over his mouth. "*Silencio*. Unless

we speak one at a time, we will accomplish nothing."

"Come here, you," he murmured, and he caught her head between his palms again and pulled her in for another searing kiss. "But you're freezing in this wind. Quickly, tell me where Raúl is and what I can do to get you out of there."

She shook her head, and her unbound hair, now frosted with snow, slapped her cheeks. "I have not seen Raúl. I did not even see him on the train, and Thorne keeps me locked in this room."

He peered deeply into her eyes, and she dreaded the question he would surely ask.

"And Thorne," he said. "What has he done to you?"

"Nothing," she said with a smile as cold as the day. If he became enraged over Thorne's treatment of her, he would be less careful. The time would come when they could discuss such things, but later, not now. "He merely keeps me prisoner, for what purpose I cannot imagine. Perhaps he wishes for me to return his silver in exchange for Raúl. However, we have had little conversation." At least that part was true.

He moved away to the right then crossed to the left of the balcony.

"How do I get you out?" he asked when he came back. "Every window is covered with these bars."

"A recent addition, I suspect," she said bitterly.

"In any case, this place is a fortress. Any ideas?"

She thought hard. *How to get Dillon into the house?* Then she smiled. "A tunnel. I know of a tunnel. It is old and may be in disrepair. It may even have collapsed. I played in it as a child, but that was many years ago."

"Where?" he asked, teeth chattering.

"The icehouse by the boat shelters. The servants once used it to bring ice into the house during the summer without having to carry it outside in the heat of the day. It runs from the icehouse into the cellars. When Thorne found out I was playing down there, he had the caretaker board up both ends."

"Okay, darlin', I'm on my way. See you on the other side."

"Dillon!" she called out when his face disappeared into the white mist. He reappeared, and she pulled him to her for another kiss. "Just in case," she said softly. "In case you do not make it past Thorne's men."

"To hell with that," he replied gruffly. "You know me better than to question what I say. When I say I'll see you, I'll see you. When was I ever wrong about anything?"

He was gone in an instant, disappearing into a squall of snow.

"Never, *mi amante*, never," she whispered into the wind. "May the Blessed Mother be at your side."

Fuerte greeted Dillon with a wildly wagging tail, paws on the shoulders, and a full body sniffing. He whimpered when he caught Chaz's scent on Dillon's gloves and face.

"Yes, I know," he told the dog. "I miss her too. Follow me this time, and we'll all soon be reunited." He took off toward the gate, pushing his way through the towering drifts.

He didn't believe a word she'd said about Thorne leaving her alone. He knew better, and the momentary pain that flashed across her face told him all he needed to know. Thorne would suffer the agonies of the damned for that bit of work. Even with that, her spirits lifted his. Whatever Thorne did to her this time, she seemed to have weathered it. She was one damn strong woman, and he loved her beyond all reason. She would never suffer again, and Thorne would be eating his next meal in hell.

Dillon wasn't as worried about Raúl. Unless Thorne had reason to let her see her son, he would keep the boy hidden. More than likely, Raúl was the last chip in a game of hide-the-silver. If force didn't make her turn over Thorne's bounty, threatening her son would. Of course, Thorne wanted his silver, but evidently, he wasn't through with Chaz. The silver was only one reason, an excuse, for keeping her captive.

Man and dog stumbled through the gate and followed the wall toward the lake. The snow was now so thick Dillon had to keep one hand on the rough granite wall to keep from wandering off into a white nothingness. The closer they drew to the water, the more blinding the snow. He literally ran into the side of a building. When he worked his way around to the front, he found large double doors and a dock running into the wind off the lake, which proclaimed it as one of the boathouses.

He blundered about, once slipping and nearly falling into the water, before he found the icehouse. It had thick granite walls and a stout wooden door secured with a heavy lock. He banged on the lock for a while with the butt of his revolver. When he made no headway and realized his efforts were no less silent than if he used the gun for its intended purpose, he turned the gun around, stepped back a pace, aimed at the lock, and fired. It was a hell of a lock and took three bullets before it parted.

He glanced at Fuerte, who acted as his sentry, but the dog showed no indication of impending danger, merely eagerness for Dillon to finish whatever strange ritual he had decided to engage in so they could find his mistress.

Dillon used the stock of his rifle to dig at the snow blocking the door. Fuerte seemed to understand and joined in. Before long, they had a trench cleared, and Dillon hauled open the door.

Once inside, he lit a match and examined the space. In the middle of the wooden floor, steps led downward. He descended to a second level and then a third. On the lowest level, he found a granite floor, wooden pallets for stacking ice, and damp straw. He scooped up a broken piece of wood, wrapped the driest straw he could find around it, and lit it with another match, nursing the flames until they drove off the dampness and the torch burned steadily.

Now for the door to the tunnel.

Dillon pivoted in place, inspected the walls. Chaz said the caretaker had boarded up the tunnel, but everywhere he looked, granite blocks surrounded him. The caretaker had been more diligent in his duties than any man had a right to be. It seemed he'd walled off the entrance, not merely put up a few boards. A tour of the walls with careful study revealed no area where a door could have existed.

What now?

Fuerte stood by the steps with his head cocked to the side, as if to ask why Dillon was making this unproductive perusal of a wall that was obviously nothing more than a wall. When the dog barked, turned, and headed back up the stairs, Dillon followed. He'd suddenly reached the same conclusion as the dog.

On the second floor, Dillon found the door in one dusty corner. Cobwebs swathed it in frosted lace, and a crisscross of boards, bolted to the granite blocks, covered it. Fuerte pawed at the door.

"I think we'll need more than your claws to get through this," Dillon said. He used his rifle as a lever and applied pressure to a board. The dampness of the room had gotten into the wood, and the rotten center broke with less effort than he'd expected. Quickly, he worked on the other boards. His shoulder, applied vigorously to the door, proved its undoing, though he swore he'd dislocated something and vowed to be a bit more subtle when they reached the other end.

The tunnel had been unused for decades, and rocks from small cave-ins littered the floor. Spiders by the thousands had made the tunnel their winter home, and Dillon and Fuerte brushed past webs of all sizes. But they made good time, soon reaching the far door.

Chambers lined the tunnel at this end, casks and trunks covered the floors, and the spiderwebs were cleaned away. Someone had been down here and used the area recently. Although the door into the cellars beckoned, Dillon detoured into one of the chambers and opened a chest. Silver bars gleamed inside. *Why here?* A frown slid over his mouth. Why would Thorne hide his own silver? It made no sense. He shook his head, left the chamber, and walked over to the door.

Rather than bulling his way through, he tried the handle. His brows went up when it opened outward into the cellar. If it was ever boarded up, no evidence remained of that now. But with millions of dollars in silver—he estimated—behind this door, why wouldn't Thorne keep it locked? The sounds of footsteps and iron wheels ringing on rock from the far end of the cellar answered his silent question.

He hurried across the cellar and into the shadows of a stone arch, with Fuerte gliding silently beside him. There they waited while two broad-shouldered men wheeled a cart loaded with a large chest over to the door and inside the tunnel.

More loot. That's all that came to mind. It had to be stolen. Clarity came to him with the suddenness of a twister spiraling down from the depths of a thunderstorm. If Thorne was robbing his own trains and pinning the crimes on The Ghost Wolf, his partners in the mines and railroad would never know the difference.

The men had left the key to the door in the lock. Dillon sped over, closed the door, turned the key, and withdrew it, tossing it into a dark corner of the cellar. Before someone found the men, he and Chaz would be out of the mansion. He'd managed to pack away two men, out of gunshot range, but now this exit was closed to them.

He walked through the cellars, past enough casks

and bottles of wine and brandy to water a thirsty country. The storerooms burst with flour, bacon, lard, and beans. It looked as if Thorne was preparing for a siege. Then he recalled some gossip he'd heard about food promised by Díaz and meant for the campesinos not getting to its destination. Could Díaz have given Thorne the stores as tribute? Thorne could then sell it in Chicago for profit. Seemed like a probable explanation and just the sort of dirty scheme in which Thorne would be involved: make money by starving the peasants.

They met no one on their way through the cellar and then climbed the steps to the kitchen, but when Fuerte stopped and sniffed the air, tail stiffening, Dillon drew a revolver. The dog's tail began wagging, and he trotted across the flagstone floor to the side of one hearth. A Mexican woman about Chaz's age sat in a rocking chair as she mended a handkerchief. She looked up at the dog and gasped.

Dillon ran to her side and silenced her with a palm across her mouth. "Give no alarm," he said low in Spanish, "and I won't hurt you."

Her eyes wide, she nodded, and Dillon removed his hand.

"Where are Thorne's men? How many are in the house and on the grounds?"

"About a dozen," she replied in a shaking voice. "Eight in the house and the rest outside." Then the fear left her face, and she stared at him in dawning comprehension. "You have come for Charissa, have you not?"

"What do you know about Charissa?"

"My *madre* was her *duena*. Charissa is in this house, locked upstairs by señor Thorne." Disgust curled the corners of her mouth, and she shuddered. "May the devil take his soul."

"What about the boy?" he asked. "Where is he?"

"Boy?" Her brows drew lower. "No boy is here.

Mariposa may know more. She is *mi madre*. But she is not here now."

No Raúl. No surprise. Thorne would tell Chaz Raúl was here, and use that lie to keep her compliant. Dillon trusted the boy was still alive. *Would Thorne murder his own issue? His son? Probably not.* He would send the boy away, somewhere safe. *But where?*

He couldn't worry about Raúl now. First he had to get Chaz out of this prison. *Eight men inside and four outside.* The two men he'd locked in the cellar, had they been inside or come in from outside? Not knowing the answer, he had to assume he had eight more men in the house to deal with. Once the bullets started flying, they'd come at him fast.

He turned back to the woman. "Thorne?" he asked. "Is Thorne here?"

"*Sí*," she said with that same twisting disgust of her mouth.

"What's your name?"

"Veridad."

"Truth," he said. "*Gracias*, Veridad. Stay here, and you should be in no danger."

"Señor," she said, stopping him before he left the kitchen. He turned to look back at her. "Be careful. They are killers, and they have many guns."

He wasn't exactly carrying light. He had two revolvers in the holsters tied down to his thighs, two more handguns he now pulled from his waistband and cocked, and the shotgun in its sheath across his back. He didn't even count the rifle in its saddle boot, left behind with Victory. Bullets lined his belt, and shells for the shotgun rested in loops on the front of the bandoliers that crisscrossed his chest.

Fuerte slipped past him and made directly for one side of the grand staircase. His fur-covered feet slid on the polished marble floor as he took the corner. When he got his feet beneath him, he bounded silently up the stairs.

Dillon couldn't afford to be as unconcerned for his hide. Someone must have seen the dog, because when Dillon stepped into the hallway, a high, whining bullet tugged at the top of the sleeve of his brand-new sheepskin coat. *Where the hell is that damn dog when I need him? Could have stuck around long enough to warn me.* Another shot came from the opposite direction, but by then, he was already in motion. He fell into a forward roll, firing one gun as he tumbled, came up on a knee, and fired again. Both men went down. *Two more out of the way.* At a click behind him, he spun on his knee and pulled off two shots before the other man had a chance to squeeze the trigger. *Three.* If he was lucky, he had only three more in the house to tangle with, or not so lucky, five. Then there were more outside and the almighty Justus Thorne, himself.

He rose slowly to his feet and moved toward the nearest doorway, turning in a circle and looking to all sides as he went. There, a flash of silver from the dark of the room. Both Dillon's guns blazed. *Another thug out of my hair.* As he sidled around the room, he fed bullets into his revolvers and cocked them.

Where was Thorne? The house was enormous. He could spend all day looking for the man. Suddenly he knew, and he froze as though transformed into a statue of ice. Not bothering to watch his back, he turned and sprinted for the staircase. From the third floor, Fuerte had set up a mournful howl that had barely impinged on Dillon's senses while he was dealing with Thorne's gunmen. He'd associated the dog's distress with no more than a desire to be with his mistress. Now it sounded more like a death knell.

When a shot came from overhead, he took the stairs three at a time.

Veinticinco

When the gunfire began, Chaz's hand went to her chest. Her heart pounded against her palm so fiercely she feared the organ would break her ribs. Then the door flew open, and she knew it was time—time for her to die.

Thorne stood in the doorway, impeccable suit in disarray and face carmine red. He slammed the door and locked it with a key he held in one hand. His other hand gripped a derringer.

"Your friend has come for you, Charissa," he said, his voice deadly calm for all his harried appearance.

"He is my husband."

Thorne smiled a corpselike grimace. "Ah, yes, your husband. You know I can't let him have you. No man can have you, Charissa. You've always been mine and mine alone. I'd rather see you dead than have you give to another man what you withhold from me. Tell me, does he hold you down and hurt you? Do you kick and scream for him? Does he draw that delicious terror from you?"

Rather than disconcerting her, his words merely sickened. Truly he was a pathetic creature—evil, yes, but also pathetic. "Where is Raúl?" she fired back.

"Raúl?" A single crease formed between his brows, marking his befuddlement. Then he blinked and seemed to surface from whatever dark world his mind was wandering. "Oh, our son. He's safe. I'll join him soon. But first, I have to deal with you and your *husband*." He leveled the small gun at her chest.

Thorne had left her nothing with which to defend herself. However, now that she knew Dillon and Raúl were alive, she wanted to live. *I will not make it easy for Thorne. He will have to work to kill me.* She seized on the nearest object, a small rosewood tea table, and flung it at him. It hit his hand, and he fired in reflex, the bullet shattering panes in the balcony's glass door behind her. Cold wind and fat, wet wisps of snowflakes swirled through the hole into the room.

A howling arose from behind the door. Cerebus calling from the gates of hell could not have made such a frightful sound. A large body bounced repeatedly off the door's surface, and claws dug at the threshold. *Fuerte!*

Thorne whirled toward the sound and fired a bullet through the wood.

"No!" Chaz ran at him and hurled her body into his larger one, knocking him off balance.

He pushed her away with one arm and sent her to the floor on her hands and knees.

"Chaz!" The cry came from the hallway, barely audible above the lamentations of the dog.

"Dillon!" she screamed. "Thorne has a gun!"

"I've got him beat! Four kings and an ace. Hug the floor!"

She fell to her stomach, and the deafening blast of a double-barreled shotgun rang in her ears. Wood splintered into the room, and a hole the size of a man's head appeared in the door. When the second blast took out the bottom panel, Fuerte squirmed through and sped straight for the railroad magnate.

Thorne snapped off his third and last shot from the

derringer and creased the dog. Fuerte yelped and slid
to a halt, clearly stunned but not down. In the wake of
the gun's sharp report, Chaz saw what she'd missed
before—a weapon, of sorts, a brass letter opener peeking
out from under the green leather blotter on the desk.

She scrambled to her feet and lunged for the desk.
Seizing the letter opener, she threw herself on Thorne. He
had made it to the balcony windows, tossed them open,
and was fumbling with a key, trying to open the lock on
the iron bars. Hard pellets of ice and fat flakes of snow
whipped in from the storm outside, covering them in a
mantle of white and drifting into the room.

Thorne fought to fend off Chaz with one hand while
rattling the key in the lock with the other. She slipped
under his arm and slashed out. The brass weapon had
a dull edge, but it parted the flesh on his cheek, hitting
bone and spraying blood. He howled and spun toward
her, his face contorted with pain and purple with rage.
She gripped the letter opener, slippery with his blood,
and struck again, splitting the other side of his face from
the corner of his eye to the point of his chin. Dillon finally
broke down the door, and now he and Fuerte stood back,
the man silent and immobile, eyes wide as though unable
to believe what was happening, the dog still stunned.

Thorne stumbled backward, clearly taken aback by
the violence of her attack. "You bitch," he spat before
falling away from her and smashing his shoulder against
the bars. The lock gave way, and he tumbled out onto the
slippery, snow-covered balcony. The dog came out of his
trance and bounded outside, close on Thorne's tail. Chaz
and Dillon stumbled out behind the dog. Thorne gained
his feet, and man and dog grappled in the storm. For a
few minutes, the lashing snow obscured their images
from the onlookers. Then Thorne struck out with a foot
and knocked Fuerte down. He clambered onto the iron
railing and leapt into the air, flailing his arms and kicking
his legs, struggling to make it to the adjacent balcony.

Fuerte got his feet beneath him and stood on his hind legs. He braced his front paws on the railing, reached out for the man, and snagged a leg in his teeth. Thorne screamed. The wind tore the sound apart and carried it into the howl of the storm. His momentum arrested, he fell, and catapulted through the driving snow and sheeting ice. The sharp iron spikes on the garden fence cut off the last dying remnants of his scream.

Chaz stood sheltered in the comfort of Dillon's arms and gazed down on her enemy, her stepfather, the man she had sworn to destroy. Through the years, in her mind, Justus Thorne had grown into this godlike creature, an invincible man, some superhuman who was somehow above the ordinary concerns of life and death. A man who could not die other than with a silver bullet through the heart. Now he lay dead in the garden, impaled on an iron fence. He was mortal after all. *What a disappointment.*

"Raúl," she whispered. "Thorne did not tell me what he did with my son."

"We'll find him," Dillon murmured into her hair and pulled her closer to the warmth of his body. "I promise you we'll find him."

She searched his blue eyes, looking for any hint of equivocation. The strength of love and commitment in their depths made her knees weak. "I believe you," she said solemnly. "I believe you."

With the demise of their employer, the remainder of the guards deserted the house. Only Veridad and an older Mexican woman remained huddled in a shadowy corner of the kitchen. They stood when Chaz and Dillon entered the room, and Veridad introduced the older woman as her mother, Mariposa. Chaz needed no introduction. With a cry wrenched from her gut, she threw herself into the woman's arms.

Dillon caught only snatches of the conversation, in both English and Spanish, punctuated with sobbing from the older woman and cries of joy and sorrow from both.

"*Mi niña,*" Mariposa said, tears streaming down her face while she stroked a hand over Chaz's black hair. "I prayed for you every night, my heart torn apart by the dangers you faced."

"I am well, Mariposa. Salvatore and Delicia kept me from harm. Once I find my son, I will take you and Veridad back to Asilo. You will always have a home with me. Without your help, I would never have survived."

Mariposa framed Chaz's face between her hands, held her still. "I know of Raúl. Delicia wrote me to tell of your arrival and the birth of your child."

"Where is he?" Her voice held desperation. "Do you know what happened to him?"

Mariposa nodded. "*Sí, niña.* I overheard señor Thorne talking with a man. He sent Raúl back to Mexico, to Veracruz."

"Veracruz?" She sent Dillon a tortured look. "Thorne has amethyst mines in Veracruz. He must have sent Raúl to the mines. But why? Why send him back?"

Dillon came forward and gently pulled her away from Mariposa, bringing her into the shelter of his arms. He nodded to the woman over Chaz's head. "Pleased to meet you, señora. I'm Charissa's husband."

Her round face spread into a smile. "I know who you are, señor West. Delicia had much to say about you in her letters."

"Nothing good, I reckon."

She chuckled. "I do not know why you would think such a thing, señor West. Delicia says you ignited a light in Charissa's heart. We, all of Charissa's family, owe you a debt we can never repay."

"No one owes me nothing," he said gruffly, unused to such sentiment directed his way. Normally, people came after him with guns.

Fuerte, being ignored by the company, forced himself between Dillon and Chaz. He stood on his hind legs and rested his front paws on Dillon's shoulders to slaver his face with a slippery tongue. Dillon pushed him down.

"Right," Dillon said. "Guess we're headed to Veracruz."

Hope transformed Chaz's face. "Niebla? And my gun with the silver bullets?"

"Niebla's stabled nearby. No gun. No silver bullets. You don't need them, darlin'. You can shoot someone just as dead with lead as with silver."

Veintiseis

The sharp, briny smell of the sea swept in from the eastern bay and inspired memories of Raúl's first visit to Veracruz. His mother had pointed out the sights, told him the city was founded by Hernán Cortéz in 1519, and began as *La Villa Rica de la Veracruz*, The Rich Town of the True Cross. The city sat on the edge of the sapphire waters of the *Bahía de Campeche* in a deep curve nestled between the sweep of eastern Mexico running to the north and the jutting Yucatan Peninsula to the south. Veracruz boasted a natural harbor and quickly became New Spain's main port. There, silver and wares from the *Manila Galleons*, transported overland from Acapulco, were loaded onto the treasure fleets for shipment to Spain. In response to harassment by pirates and hostile powers, the Spaniards built the large fortress of San Juan de Ulúa on Gallega Island in the harbor. The fort provided defense and contained the prisons, situated in the middle section of the structure, surrounded by a deep moat and accessible only by a drawbridge. Gallega's location in the shark-infested waters of the bay made escape impossible.

At the time, through the perception of a boy of

only ten, who had seen nothing more impressive than the *aideas* in the *altoplano*, Raúl had viewed the city goggle-eyed. And now, as he rode with Giles in a carriage through the streets, the stately Spanish homes and businesses reached into the blue sky, and the sea beckoned.

He fully expected to occupy a cell in the dungeons of San Juan de Ulúa. Although he rode in a carriage and wore no handcuffs or rawhide bindings, he was a prisoner, nonetheless. Giles lolled beside him, ensconced comfortably in the horsehair squabs of the carriage, and drew on a cigar as he viewed the city passing by outside the curtained window. Every few minutes, he would glance at Raúl, as if making sure the boy hadn't escaped his vigilance.

The sound of the carriage wheels clattering over the stone streets prompted Raúl to gaze out the window into downtown Veracruz, across the large, marble-tiled *zócalo*, the Plaza Lerdo. Arcades, cantinas, and cafés lined the square, anchored by the magnificent eighteenth century Our Lady of Assumption cathedral and the tower and vaulted arcade of the seventeenth century Palacio Municipal. In the distance glistened the sparkling waters of the bay along the *malecón*, the boardwalk that rimmed the harbor.

In front of the cathedral and to one side of the town hall sat the Hotel Imperial, the same hotel where Raúl and his mother had stayed all those years ago. When the carriage stopped in front of the hotel, he saw his chance for escape. He swung open the door beside him and tumbled out onto the ground, but he took no more than two steps before muscular arms caught him in a bearlike grip. Hands jerked his arms up into the middle of his back, and iron snapped onto his wrists. He ceased his struggles, accepting the futility of further resistance.

The man tossed him into the carriage, and he landed painfully on one shoulder. Carrying clearly through

the sounds on the street came Giles's laughter. When
Raúl looked up from his position on the carriage floor,
Giles appeared at the window, icy blue eyes bright with
amusement.

"You didn't think it would be that easy, did you?"
He chomped on the cigar between his teeth. "Thorne left
you in my care, and I take that commission seriously.
Had you shown less inclination to flee my hospitality,
you could have shared a room at this palatial hotel. But
seeing as you're determined to escape, I'll have to deposit
you in less comfortable but more secure lodgings."

The face moved away from the window, and Raúl
heard the orders Giles gave to the driver and guards.
"Carry him to San Juan de Ulúa, and take care with
his person. No deep, dank cell for this boy. Mr. Thorne
would be displeased if you showed disrespect for his son.
Place him in the lodgings for political prisoners. He'll be
safe there until Mr. Thorne arrives."

So it was the prison island after all. As the carriage
lurched forward, Raúl groaned at the pain in his bruised
shoulder.

The express train from El Paso streamed southward
toward Veracruz, rocking on the tracks with the pace of
its passage across the flat, dry plains of Northern and
Central Mexico. It could not, however, move quickly
enough for Chaz. She restlessly haunted the passageways
and aisles of the passenger cars as though the momentum
of her swift, booted feet could push the train to accelerate
to a speed achieved only by a stooping falcon. She ate
little and slept even less, lying in Dillon's arms in their
small compartment bed, tense and alert to every nuance
of clacking wheels, every curve along the tracks, every
climb and dip or change of speed.

Dillon took a crack at engaging her interest in
formulating a plan for when they reached the port city by

spreading out a map on the small table that flipped down from the wall of the compartment. "Thorne's amethyst mines are located outside the city in the mountainous area around the *Cumbres de Maltrata*." He glanced up at her. Chaz sat with downcast eyes, hands lying in her lap, and fists clenched. The tension in her body filled the space between them. He leaned over, placed a hand atop hers, and squeezed lightly. She looked up, and his gaze collided with hers. The pools of pain he saw nearly broke his heart. "We'll need help," he said softly. "We can't free him alone. How can we get word to Asilo? How long will it take to get your men here?"

She took in a deep breath and seemed to shake off her depression. "Tino has a cousin who works at the telegraph office in Zacatecas, and at this time of year, the revolutionaries camp close to the town. They are nearer than Asilo and have more guns. Tino will come to my aid."

He agreed with a nod. "The train stops at Tampico to take on coal and water. You can send a wire from there."

Dillon lay on his side facing Chaz. His fingers feathered down the side of her face, and his gaze settled on her. "I'm sorry," he said.

She searched his face. "About what?"

"Thorne." The word caught in his throat, coming out rough. She had remained mute about what occurred between her and Thorne. He wanted to ask, because what he assumed pained him more than he could express. But he didn't ask. "That he hurt you again. That I wasn't there. That I didn't stop him, couldn't stop him." His fingers left her face, and he closed them into a fist. "I promised myself he would never, ever touch you again."

Her smile was tender as she caught his hand, uncurling his fingers and bringing them to her lips, where she laid kisses on the pads. "He did not, Dillon.

He did not touch me where it counts — inside my soul. For all his evil, I learned a valuable lesson from Thorne. He taught me I could be hurt only if I allowed it. But the love I have for you and for Raúl fills me up. There is no room for hurt. So what he did is, how do you say it? Rain off the feathers of a goose."

A smile came unbidden. "Water off a duck's back."

She cupped the nape of his neck and pulled his head toward her. "A duck's back, then. And, my love, we shall never speak of him again. He is no longer a part of our lives."

Dillon had loved with all his heart once before. He knew love could be rough and urgent, like a storm over the mountains, or soft and patient, like a leaf floating on a lake. That night, worried that Thorne had reignited her fears of being touched, despite her protestations, he took it slow and easy. As they lay face-to-face, he kissed her as gently as though it were the first time their lips had touched, and stroked her skin from neck to toes, his hand skimming the silk of her body with long, leisurely caresses. He whispered into the crook of her neck and the shell of her ear how good she felt and how much he loved her. When her breathing quickened, chest rising and falling rapidly, and sweat beaded her skin, he lifted her leg over his hip and slid into her silken depths. Long, deliberate, languorous strokes, gliding on her inner moisture, grazing the bud of her passion with every forward movement, and her clinging to him on the reverse.

A cloud of serenity settled over him, and he left his body, hovered over them, above that perfect tableau of lover and loved. His heart expanded with his emotion for this brave woman who'd experienced so much pain and sorrow in her life. He swore upon his own death he would never let pain touch her again. Sure, he'd said it before and failed. But this time... Chaz contracted around him and released a surprised exhalation. He rejoined his body, clasped her to him, and lost himself in her cream and fiery heat.

They took up residence at a small *pensión* in a narrow, stone-paved alley off the Plaza Lardo. An excursion to a *tienda de ropa* provided them with clothing suitable for a well-to-do city couple, Dillon in a brown worsted wool suit and derby hat, Chaz in a dress and mantilla rendered in subdued shades of gray. Then they rode the tramway in a ceaseless search, alert for Giles or Thorne's other men, and discreetly questioned shopkeepers and tram conductors for word of a young gringo with auburn hair and blue eyes. They continually returned to the train station, meeting every train coming from Zacatecas. On the third day, they saddled the horses and rode out to the amethyst mines, but they could draw no nearer than half a mile because of the men who guarded every chasm and winding passage in the thickly wooded mountains leading to the excavations. Chaz's patience wore thinner than a spiderweb.

"*¡Christo!*" she said into the foggy air coming off the steep mountainside. Dillon made an effort at comforting her, mouthing platitudes, but she shrugged off his words. "Tino had better arrive soon," she said bitterly, "or I will go in alone."

"You'll do no such thing." His words were hot. "We don't move until reinforcements arrive. I know I've said it before, but it's worth saying again. How can you help him if you're dead?"

Her better sense told her that, once again, Dillon was right. A dead mother could not free her son. She also recalled he had reminded her of that several times in the past, and she hadn't listened.

Six days passed before Carranza arrived on the 11:24 a.m. train from Zacatecas.

"Tino!" Chaz shouted, running into his arms and

hugging him tightly. He kissed the part in her dark hair and held her out at arms' length. With his trimmed beard and mustache and wearing a dark suit and hat, he was no more distinguishable from any other businessman departing the train.

"How many?" she asked as she drank in his beloved image.

Tino grinned, his teeth white in his swarthy face. "Twenty-seven plus me, and your *amigo*, Alec. Is that enough to rescue one *niño*, or should I go back for more?" His gaze wandered over her shoulder to Dillon, who stood on the edge of the crowded platform. "I see the gringo flea accompanies you. Do we need him, or may I squash him beneath my heel?"

She cast him a chastising smile. "Tino, he is my *esposo*, and you will be respectful."

"Husband? You are married?" A flicker of remorse crossed his face.

Not until that moment did she recognize the lifelong friendship between them had a much different meaning for Venustiano than for her. *First Alec, and now Tino.* Two men whose hearts she had broken. She rued the pain she'd caused them, but she would not trade either for Dillon. She relegated the thought to the back of her mind, linked her arm in his, and tugged him over to Dillon.

Dillon doffed his hat at the approach of the larger man. "*Buenos días*, señor Carranza. We welcome your assistance." He extended his hand.

Carranza huffed and shook the proffered hand. "I do this for Chaz and Raúl."

Dillon gave him a level look and tightened his grip. "As do I, señor."

They strained briefly, each obviously striving to gain an advantage over the other. Then Carranza released first, tilted back his head, and laughed. "*Felicidadas*, señor West, on your recent *matrimonio*. *Tener cuidado*, though. Chaz is as dear to me as a *hermana*."

Dillon chuckled and massaged his aching hand. "I accept the warning, señor. I assure you she can be no dearer to you than she is to me. I'll protect her with my life."

Carranza grinned and slapped Dillon on the back, making him stagger on his feet. And then he said to Chaz in Spanish, "I like this flea, *chica*, even though he is a gringo. You have my permission to marry him."

During the tense exchange between them, her heart had taken a plunge, now it rose again with hope. "*Gracias*," she replied with a wry smile.

The remainder of Carranza's men left the train in small groups, dressed in suits similar to their leader's, and resembled a conference of traveling drummers. Only the bulges of guns at their hips under the skirts of their suit coats hinted at their true profession. They wandered about on the fringes of the arriving and departing passengers, unobtrusive and alert for a sign from Carranza. The last man to exit the train was Alec. He smiled broadly at Chaz, and she returned his expression with one of warmth and tenderness. He came up to her, rested his hands on her upper arms, and kissed her on the cheek.

She smiled at Dillon's low, gruff muttering, ending with, "Okay, maybe he's no more than a beloved cousin, but *damn*, the man still gets beneath my skin."

"We are staying at Pension de Los Vino Rosado," she told Alec and Carranza. "It is on La Calle de Los Ángeles."

"I know it," Carranza said, nodding. "I will stay nearby. Tonight we meet at Dos Campana, a café three streets to the west of your *pensión*. The proprietors are friends of the cause. I will be there at *las ocho de la tarde*. Then we will decide how best to liberate Raúl from the clutches of these *cerdos*."

"Pigs they may be," Dillon said, "but they're well-armed pigs."

"And so are we," Carranza replied and inclined his head toward his formidable crew.

* * *

They failed to locate Raúl at the mines.

Two days of traveling through the mountains, following mere slivers of goat and deer trails instead of the roads the wagons used to transport the mines' bounty, took them into the heart of the operation. In a valley between two bare hills, Chaz watched men with pickaxes moving into and out of the darkness of the mine, a black cavity about one hundred yards high by fifty yards wide that split the earth. Those returning deposited their amethyst treasure in a gourd clutched in the grip of an overseer who held court at the mine entrance. As in the silver mines, the workers appeared ragged and tired, stooped over and squint-eyed from their labor in dark, cramped quarters. The skin hung loose on their frames from a lack of nourishment, and their hands would be scabbed over with blisters from wielding the pickaxe for long hours, days, and months.

After many hundreds of pesos passed to dozens of guards, no doubt remained in Chaz's mind. Giles had taken Raúl elsewhere. They camped that night high above a steep mountain escarpment and beneath a bright canopy of stars arcing through the black sky. Coyotes sang a mournful chorus in the scrubland far beyond the circle of their campfire, held at bay not only by the light but also by Fuerte's low, menacing growls. Chaz kept a calming hand on the fur of his neck and prevented him from pursuing the intruders. Meanwhile, she remained lost in thought. Raúl was not in the city; Carranza's spies had confirmed that. He was not at the mines; money had told them that. In a camaraderie born from long association, Chaz and Tino came to agreement. Only one place remained.

San Juan de Ulúa.

No matter the bribe, no word of those incarcerated ever came out of the island. The secure fort and prison lay nearly half a mile out in the harbor. It was constructed from thick stone block, fortified by cannons and heavily armed troops, and surrounded by shark-infested waters. All proclaimed it to be escape-proof.

"No place is impregnable," she said, "not even San Juan de Ulúa."

"It's gonna be pretty damn difficult," Dillon said.

"Chucho El Roto escaped from there."

Carranza smiled with a grimness that would raise the hackles of a jackal. "Chucho El Roto is a legend, Charissa, a myth, not a real *hermano*."

She remained determined to sway the others to her point of view. "Legends are based on truth. If Chucho El Roto could find his way out, we can find our way in."

"And then what?" Dillon mumbled.

"And then we find our way out," she stated firmly and sent Dillon a grin.

Veintisiete

Gallega Island was the largest of dozens of rocky
coral reefs that dotted the harbor of Veracruz. Being
opposite the town, it bordered a half-mile wide strait
that separated the fortress from the town and protected
the coast from the swell of the sea, especially during
the *Nortes*, the northerly winds that whipped up the
waters of the Gulf of Mexico in the season of storms,
from October to April, and made navigation perilous.
Ships attempting passage during this time found their
anchorage stranded on shoals or at the bottom of the
sea. The rocks on which the Spanish erected the fort
contained iron rings where ships could attach themselves
to prevent being swept away. The violent winds that
blew that October night had one saving grace: they
cleared the air of *vomito prieto*, the yellow fever that
invaded the city during the summer.

    The band of rescuers dared not approach the fort
directly from Veracruz under the gaze of the cannons
and the boats filled with *soldados*, which patrolled the
strait day and night in all manner of weather. Therefore,
only stars guided the way of the six ship's boats that
fought their way from a northerly shoal, Punta Gorda, to

the small reef of Galleguilla Island, due west of Gallega Island. There the men secured the boats and rested, exhausted from wrestling with the winds and waves. They built small fires in the shelter of the rocks, confident no one would be insane enough to be out on such a hellish night to catch their dim glow. Then they checked their ammunition and weapons for moisture, slung bandoliers across their chests, and stowed rifles and scatterguns in slings over their backs.

Beaten by the wind and surf again, they negotiated the stepping-stones between Galleguilla and Gallega. Strung out in a line, Carranza leading, followed by Alec and three of his men, then Chaz and Dillon, the remainder bringing up the rear, they trudged through waist-high water across shifting sandy shoals and razor-sharp coral. The high ramparts of the fort lay ahead, but in the pitch-blackness of the night and the wind playing devilishly with the sand, they caught no glimpse of their objective.

They crossed three-quarters of the length of the island before the fort appeared in front of them, a dim shadow that came and went between the squalls of sand lifted into the air and driven by the winds. This side of the fort, facing the vast Gulf, should be sparsely guarded, especially considering the weather. The men crossed themselves, and in nearly silent voices, whispered entreaties to the Lord that the approaching wall held few *soldados*. It was not as if they were frightened for their lives; they were merely pragmatic and always prayed before a battle. If they died, they wanted to make sure their souls were in good standing.

Carranza had explained that the prison complex housed fifty or so guards with another two hundred armed *Federales* in the fort proper. Their only chance was to slip inside swiftly and quietly, silencing all along the way, find Raúl, overcome his guards, and spirit him out the same way they'd entered. The guns they carried in such abundance were only in the event they raised the alarm, and in that case, they had little chance of leaving alive.

The main party hung back under cover of a jumbled cairn of broken coral while two men with ropes slung across their shoulders darted to the walls and flattened themselves to the stone. The blocks, nearly three hundred years old, had gaps where the wind had eaten away at the sand- and-crushed-shell mortar. The men remained motionless, as if part of the structure, then turned as one and clambered up the wall, using the chinks for hand- and footholds. At the top, they allowed the ropes to uncoil and tied off one end to curved iron bars on the rim.

"Now!" Carranza said urgently. "*¡Dale prisa! ¡Rápidamente!*"

Chaz sped across the rocks ahead of Dillon, and he ran to keep up with her. *Damn pesky woman!* He'd forbidden her from coming along on this suicide mission, even appealing to Carranza. Neither would have any part of it. The most he'd accomplished was to convince her to leave Fuerte behind at the boats with one of Carranza's men. So here Chaz was, as reckless and fearless as she ever was while robbing a train. *Goddamn it!* She twisted him around and tied him up in knots more than any woman he'd ever known. *But this is the woman I love, and her courage is an integral part of why I love her.*

When she grasped the rope, Dillon elbowed her aside and gave her a determined glare. Damned if he'd allow her to ascend before him and get her throat slit by some overzealous guard. In her eagerness to be with Raúl, her motherly instincts were likely to be stronger than her caution.

"No," she said with a sob in her throat when he took her place at the rope.

"Hush, Chaz. Like it or not, I'm going first. You can either come up after me or stay here." He turned his back and began to scale the wall. She clutched at his clothes, but he shook off her hands. "Damn you," he heard her say as he climbed up into the stinging wind and sand. When he dropped over the edge onto the stone walkway, turned and looked down, she was only a few feet behind him. He reached over the wall, caught her wrist, and hauled her up.

Wildly flickering torches, partially enclosed in iron cages to diminish the effect of the wind, cast dim pools of light that chased shadows across the stones of the walkway.

Although Carranza had expressed his desire to permanently silence the guards, Chaz had ordered otherwise.

"It has never been the way of The Ghost Wolf to kill without reason," she had said. "I will not start now. And if we kill the guards, the entire force of Díaz's army will be on our trail when we leave here. Even Asilo will not keep us safe from his vengeance. I only want my child back. There has been enough bloodshed, and God willing, we will not add to it here."

Therefore, using the deep pockets of shadows to their advantage, Carranza's men spread out across the wide parapet, came up silently behind the fort's guards, and knocked them senseless. They then tied them up like turkeys and gagged them with their own bandanas. They found the ramparts thinly populated, due to their eastern exposure to the coral reef and the force of the northerly gale. The inattentive guards had hunkered down behind the stones to protect their eyes and exposed skin from the sting of the flying sand and had failed to see the creeping intruders until it was too late. Not a cry of surprise or dismay passed their throats. Soon, small mounds of silent, bound bodies lay tucked into dark corners.

At last they faced the moat, a daunting obstacle but one they had to overcome. A raised drawbridge mocked them. It attached to the far side, and it soon became obvious it could be operated only from the inner edge of the moat and would be of no help to them until their retreat.

They removed the ropes and grappling hooks from the walls, and now Marisio, a revolutionary nearly as large and imposing as Carranza, swung one rope with a grappling hook at its end back and forth, letting out a bit more of the line with each forward sweep of the pendulum. When he released, the hook flew across the span and scraped at the stone on the other side. With a screech of metal on stone, it slid across the surface, failed to find purchase, and dropped into the murky waters of the moat.

Within a few seconds, the surface of the water broke with the scaly backs of blackish hides and lashing tails. The faint torchlight revealed rows of sharp teeth that gleamed from gaping maws and snapping jaws. Soon the moat boiled with the thrashing of hundreds of reptile bodies.

"Crocodiles," Chaz breathed in a low, unsteady voice. As she looked down into a scene worthy of hell, her eyes rounded, and for the first time since the beginning of this mission, her body trembled. "They will tear apart anyone entering that water. This is madness."

Dillon caught an arm around her waist and cradled her close to his side. "Then we won't swim across," he said with devilry in his eyes.

A frown marred the smoothness of her brow. "This is no time for wit, señor West."

"And it's no time for panic, señora West." His eyes held hers steadily. "Against all odds, we've made it this far. It's either go back now or cross that moat. I don't know about you, but I'm fixin' to try it, and I can't swim."

Marisio retrieved the grappling hook and made another toss, again failing to catch it on any chink in the rock that would hold firm. It dropped into the water once again, further stirring the voracious reptiles, some of which the torchlight showed to measure more than eight feet in length. They snapped at the rope and hook in a frenzy that caused Carranza to raise his voice. "Haul it in! If we lose that hook, Marisio, you are going in after it!"

His swarthy complexion bleached white by Carranza's threat, the young man pulled madly on the rope. Dillon, Alec, and two others joined him. As they dragged it to the edge of the moat, one determined crocodile latched onto the hook, whipped its body back and forth, and the men's feet slid on the stones, closer to the edge.

Carranza drew his gun and aimed it at the persistent reptile. Dillon stopped him with a raised hand and firm words. "No, we'll announce our presence to all if you fire that." He pointed at the assembled men. "Get on the rope and bring that creature to the rim." He lay down on the stones, upper body hanging out over the edge, turned his rifle around in his hands, and angled the stock toward the animal as the men tried to beach it. Another crocodile inched up beside its companion and made a try for Dillon's rifle. Twisting, he swung the stock at the animal's head. As his body slid halfway off the rock toward the water, Alec dropped to the ground behind him and latched onto his legs.

When the head of the crocodile rose from the water on the grappling hook, pulled upward by the rope, Dillon jabbed the stock of the rifle at it. After half-a-dozen vicious thuds on the primitive skull, the reptile let go and splashed back into the water amongst the agitated mob.

"Thanks," Dillon said to Alec as the two clambered to their feet.

"*De nada,*" the man replied with a good-natured grin. "Chaz would never speak to me again if I did not save her *marido*. And after you kill yourself through your impulsive actions, I shall be there. I must remain in her good graces if I wish her to turn to me in her grief."

"Good point," Dillon said with a deadpan expression. "But sorry to disappoint you. I have no intention of dying today."

Alec's grin inched wider. "There is always tomorrow, *mi amigo*."

"Stop it!" Chaz hissed, and smacked both Alec and Dillon none too lightly on the back of the head, the flat of her hand traversing from one head to the other.

Dillon's brows snapped together in a scowl. "Don't hit me, woman."

"Then shut up!"

"Hey, he started it. All I said was 'thanks.'"

She leaned forward into his face. "Dillon. Shut. Up."

Damn bossy woman.

Marisio held onto the dripping grappling hook, hands trembling, and sent a quick, tight-lipped look at Carranza.

The revolutionary leader gave him a brusque nod. "Again," he said.

Marisio swung the rope, reaching far out over the moat when he released. The hook clanged on the far side, slid toward the water, and dug itself into a groove between two stones. Marisio yanked on the rope, making sure it was secure, and quickly wrapped it around an iron stake embedded in the outer wall.

Carranza swept his hand toward the rope. "Over," he said, and motioned to three men to remain behind and guard their retreat.

One by one, the men traveled the rope, hand over hand, their boots dangling only feet above the snapping jaws of the leaping crocodiles. This time, Dillon let Chaz go first. He unsheathed his Bowie knife and clutched it in a sweaty palm while he held his breath and watched her. If she fell, he would dive in among the crocodiles and kill as many as he could before they devoured him. As she swung across the deadly space, his heart beat more loudly than the roar of a buffalo stampede. She made it without incident, and, *figures*, Alec caught her on the other side.

Giles crushed the telegram in his fist. Its words still burned his eyes. Justus Thorne had died accidentally, fallen from a snowy balcony and impaled himself on the garden fence. That piece of news disturbed Giles less than the second. In the week preceding his untimely death, Thorne had a new will drawn up. After the portion that went to his investors, he was leaving everything — *everything* — mines, railroads, houses and furnishings, silver and cash, to his illegitimate son, Raúl Gutierrez.

Giles stalked out of the telegraph office, his body stiff and heat burning his face. For fifteen years he was Thorne's toady. He stole for the man, killed for him, carried out any dirty, violent task required of him. Thorne had promised him a share of the silver coming from the Mexico mines. Now all of it was gone. *Nothing.* He would get nothing. He dropped the telegram on the street and ground it beneath the sole of his boot.

After a few minutes, Giles halted his angry strides and forced himself to calm down. He leaned against a porch railing, drew a cigar from his coat pocket, and lit it, drawing in the rich smoke in panting gasps. Slowly, his heart settled into a normal beat, and the tightness in his chest eased.

He had to think. When Thorne's investors learned about the railroad man's demise, they would descend on Thorne Enterprises like vultures on a corpse. But Giles had one thing they did not: Raúl, and through Raúl, his mother, The Ghost Wolf. The Ghost Wolf and her banditos had taken millions in silver off Thorne's trains. She'd hidden that silver somewhere in the mountains. Would she trade it for her son's life? And then there was

Raúl's legacy. Giles stroked his chin with his fingertips and thumb. *What will happen to all that wealth if Raúl dies?*

His carriage waited in the street, the horses restless in the rising wind, and his coachman huddled beneath his cloak. Giles rapped on the driver's perch with his gold-headed cane. The man's head snapped up. "Sir?"

"San Juan de Ulúa," he shouted. "And don't spare the horses."

By the time their boat fought the waves whipped up by the northerly gale and arrived at the fort, salt spray had soaked Giles to the bone. Nonetheless, an inner heat baked him, kept him from shivering. *Silver.* If other men sought gold because it resembled the glow of the sun, silver was, to him, the personification of the moon. It ignited his soul with its cold, shiny beauty. Down the stone staircases, beneath the arches, and through the damp tunnels, he traversed the route to Raúl's prison. In deference to the boy's status and Thorne's orders, Raúl languished, not in a lightless dungeon with the wretches who opposed Díaz's rule. No, the prodigal son occupied a luxurious aerie in the tower. It made bile rise in his throat. To think that dirty bandit bastard would inherit *all* Thorne had accumulated. Again he considered how that money and property would be distributed were Raúl to die. The lawyers would know. All he had to do was send a telegram to Chicago. *But first, the boy.* There was that little matter of stolen silver.

He climbed the tunnels sloping upward to the steep spiral staircase leading to the tower, his determination firming with every step, every scuff of his shoes on the rough stone. His heart beat with one thought: *Silver. Silver. Silver.* He had to get the silver, get to it before anyone else did.

Giles waved away the guard. The key rasped in the lock, and he swung open the door. Beneath gauze mosquito netting, Raúl lay on his back on the bed amidst soft cotton coverings. He had one leg bent, foot flat on the mattress, and an arm thrown across his eyes. The leaded glass windows flapped open on the casements, and wind howled through the room, whipping the drapes into a twisted frenzy and guttering the candles in the candelabrum occupying the center of a carved wooden table. Metal clanged against metal when Giles slammed the door, and Raúl started from his sleep, rising up on one elbow. Giles locked the door and strode to the northern wall to close the banging windows. Then he faced Raúl. The young man still had sleep in his face, but an alert wariness lurked in his eyes. *Aha,* the cub was not as tame as he'd pretended to be. He was, perchance, even dangerous.

For a second, the young man's gaze flitted to the gun at Giles's hip, and his eyes widened. The lawyer's face split with a smile. The boy didn't know he had taken the gun from The Ghost Wolf on the train. At the time, he'd thought he would be using it on the bandit and found the image ironic: to be killed by one's own gun. But when Thorne refused to allow his mistress to suffer harm, Giles kept the gun. Now, seeing the distress it caused Raúl, he was glad he'd succumbed to that impulse.

Raúl lowered his legs and sat on the edge of the bed. "Where is my father?" he asked, gaze direct and probing. *To impart the information of Thorne's death, or not?* This was a subject on which Giles had spent much thought. If he imagined Thorne's death would wound the boy more, he would oblige with glee. However, he knew Raúl harbored no fondness for his father. Curiosity perhaps, but not fondness.

"He'll be here in his own time," Giles said. "First, he instructed me to question you about a serious matter."

"What?" Raúl asked, his expression sullen.

Giles pulled out a cigar and grimaced at the soggy mess. The boat trip had ruined his expensive smokes. He strode over to the table, opened a rosewood box, and extracted a cigar. *Cubans. Jesus, these should be mine! Thorne spoiled the boy!* Never did Thorne treat his lackey so well. He clipped off the cigar end with his silver trimmer, lit the weed, and inhaled fragrant smoke.

"Well?" Raúl asked, clearly impatient and resenting Giles's intrusion. Raúl stood and walked to the windows, opened them again, and let the storm blow in past him.

Giles half sat on the table, perching one hip on its wooden edge. He drew in more of the tobacco, and it streamed from between his lips as he said, "Silver."

Raúl turned about and rested the heels of his hands on the windowsill. "Silver?" He cocked an eyebrow.

Feigned or actual? Giles couldn't tell. "Thorne wants the silver your bitch of a mother stole from him."

The boy stiffened. A black scowl pulled down his mouth and darkened his eyes. "There's none left. She gave it all away."

Giles barked a brief laugh of disbelief. *Truly, does the boy think I'm stupid?* "Gave it away? Don't mistake me for an idiot. I'm not playing games with you, Raúl. Thorne wants the silver. He has your mother and will release her only if you cooperate."

Raúl smirked. "Why doesn't he ask *her?*"

Giles shot off the table and advanced a step. "Because…because she *won't tell* him! She cares nothing for you. She won't tell him even to save your life! Thorne believes you might be more sensible, that is, if you want your mother back alive."

The boy strolled back to the bed and stretched out on his side. He considered Giles carefully. "I don't believe you. You're lying. In fact, I don't think you even have her. Or if you did, you've misplaced her." The boy's dark blue eyes held hate and…and death.

An involuntary shiver rolled across Giles's shoulders. *Good thing the boy was unarmed.* Then the wind snuffed out the candles in the candelabrum on the table, and he blessed the darkness that shadowed the boy's face. He raised his fisted hands and moved closer. "You arrogant bastard! Do you want me to have the guards drag her beaten body in here so you can see what happens to those who defy Mr. Thorne?"

"Yes, Giles," Raúl said, undaunted, leaning forward into the light of the candles in the sconces along the wall. "Why don't you do that?"

Rage rose so swiftly inside him, Giles could barely speak, but he managed to spit out the words, "The silver, Raúl! Where is it? Tell me now, or you'll be dead by tomorrow. I swear it!"

"I already told you—there *is no* silver. Believe me or not. You won't harm me, because then my father would see to it you were the one who would not live to see tomorrow."

"*Your father's dead!*" Giles shouted. In the same breath, he called, "*Guard!*"

"Dead?" Raúl murmured, and a single crease appeared on his forehead.

The guard burst through the door in a crouch, rifle at the ready.

"Take him outside," Giles said with a gesture at Raúl.

At that point, Raúl became aware of his perilous situation and that he was at the lawyer's mercy, for his complexion went ashen. "Who has the upper hand now?" Giles said smugly. The guard grabbed Raúl and hauled him off the bed, cuffed his hands in front of him, and hustled him out the door and down the spiral stairs.

"Take him to the moat!" Giles called after them. "We'll introduce him to our pets and then see how long he retains that insolent attitude!"

Veintiocho

Carranza and his men had left the area of the moat, going off in different directions to silence the guards and prepare the way to the dungeons for Chaz and Dillon. They'd had no luck finding out ahead of time Raúl's exact location. For just such a reason as possible escape attempts perpetrated by family members, compadres, and co-conspirators, the prison officials used no names for those they incarcerated. All the men, and even the women, were assigned numbers, and even the guards had no idea whom they guarded. The government had instituted this policy after the alleged escape of a notorious bandit legend some said was Chucho el Roto. Only a few officials saw political prisoners, and to prevent corruption, they changed the guards daily by lottery. To reveal the name or location of a prisoner, particularly a political prisoner, meant death by the most excruciating methods, methods the Inquisition would have envied. The guards were not only in danger, but their families too. Therefore, men would not talk, not even for large amounts of silver.

Chaz waited with Dillon in a hollow area between two stones in the lee of the storm, which showed no signs of weakening. When she started to follow Carranza, Dillon tugged her back with an arm around her waist. "This time, you'll damn well listen to me, woman," he said. "Let Carranza and his men do their job. Without knowing where Raúl is imprisoned, we could wander for hours, and the guards would catch us as easily as flies in honey."

She sputtered, but he would not let her go. She detested this waiting, this feeling of helplessness. She had to move and move fast, find Raúl, remove him from his cell, and leave this place of death. Because in some eerie way, she knew, just knew, someone would die this night.

"I must be there when they release him," she said as she strained against the hold Dillon had on her arms.

He tightened his grip and pulled her back against his chest, cinching his arms around her. "You will be. You have my promise."

Promises were all well and good, but he could not possibly make good on this one. Her eyes stung from the sand propelled by the tempest and swept over the walls. The wind tasted heavily of salt and grains of coral, wicking the moisture from her skin. She tried to wet her dry lips, but her mouth was as arid as the sand. In spite of her reservations, she managed to mutter, "I had better."

She squirmed and flexed her muscles to loosen his embracing hug. "Let me go. You have my word I will remain here. I wish only to see if any of the men have returned."

"Let me look," he said immediately, like the stubborn burro of a man he was. "You remain behind this wall."

"No." When she turned in the circle of his arms to look into his eyes, she saw little other than the occasional blue gleam. Like her, he was squinting to reduce the effects of the stinging sand. She suspected his view of her was as dim. Nonetheless, she leveled as stern a glare on him as she was capable. "*I* will look."

Even if he could not see her determination, he must
have sensed it, for his arms fell away. "Okay. Look. But
move one step around the corner of this wall, and I'm
taking you down. You'll bite the ground fast and hard."

She could not help but smile at the fierce quality of
his voice. Low and firm, nevertheless it held a quaver
that testified to his fear for her. *Jesu, I love this man.*

She shuffled to the edge of the niche protecting them
from the eyes of any guards and peeked around the
corner. Torches on the ramparts gave some aid to vision,
although the flames streamed in the wind and the sand
had extinguished several. She saw no guards; nor could
she see the few men Carranza had left behind to secure
their retreat. She could, however, hear the crocodiles,
still agitated by the banditos' passage and a missed meal,
as they slapped their tails on the water with bursts like
gunshot and whipped the moat into froth. Sand flowed
over the outside walls like a surging sea, a constant
stinging against her cheeks, and the wind howled,
whistling in a high, keening voice when it flew through
cracks in the sandstone blocks.

Sudden movement on their side of the moat drew
her eye, and she concentrated on the four men emerging
from a door to her left, one that led into the prison's
interior. She swiped at her tearing eyes to remove the
sand crystals. The men remained in shadow, and the low
rumble of voices carried through the wind. She could
not quite hear the words, but the tone came through. *An
argument.* One imperious voice then penetrated. "Leave!"
Droning again. One man seemed to shove two of the
others, and they stepped back and walked away, leaving
only two behind.

One of the men was obviously a prisoner. Chaz
discerned only dark outlines, but the man's hands
remained down, arms rigid, as if his wrists were bound
together. The other man pulled the bound man to the
edge of the moat, and she sucked in a gasp. She was

about to witness the prisoner's murder. Was this to have been Raúl's fate?

"See anything?" Dillon's words poured into her ear, and she jumped, so intent was she on the actions of the men by the moat.

She spoke low. "Yes. Look. You must see this."

As he moved up behind her and looked over her head and around the corner, his chest settled in a heavy weight on her back. He sucked in a deep breath, and his chest hitched, then, "Shit."

"We must help him."

"I understand your concern, sweetheart. But if we do, we're gonna show our hand, and right now, we're already trying to draw a royal flush from a deck with no tens. Are you willing to sacrifice Raúl's life for this man's?"

"Of course not. But I also know I cannot sit here and calmly watch cold-blooded murder." Leave it to Dillon to come up with reasons why she should not do what her gut told her she must do. Yes, Raúl was still a prisoner in this place. *But to witness murder and do nothing to prevent it...*

"You remain here," she said, "and I will help that man. He has only one guard. If something happens to me, they will know nothing about you. You will still be able to rescue Raúl."

"To hell with that," he growled, and his body against hers hardened like adobe. When she glanced back at him, she was thankful for the dim illumination, thankful she could not decipher the expression on his face. "You go anywhere, I'll be right on your tail," he added. His warm breath feathered over her face.

Shouts came from the direction of the two men, and Chaz turned back to the scene by the moat. The prisoner was fighting, pushing at the guard and grabbing at the man's side. To seize a gun the guard surely wore? But if this was purely murder, why would the guard leave his

gun in its holster? Why would he not simply shoot the
prisoner and push him into the moat to be devoured by
the crocodiles? Why had the one guard sent the others
away? Something about the situation, more than simply
impending murder, sent chill bumps across her skin.

The struggle became fierce, and both men moved
closer to the edge of the moat.

"Come," she said. "We may already be too late." And
she took off at a sprint, drawing her gun as she ran. Dillon
pounded beside her, the sound of his boots on the rock
strangely muted, as if he were treading on moss.

As she grew closer, the men shifted and broke apart.
The light from a torch fell on the prisoner.

"Raúl!" she screamed, running hard, cocking her gun
and firing at the guard. She missed, and the two came
back together. The gun was no longer of any use, for if she
shot at the guard, she might hit Raúl. The scene playing
out in front of her made no sense. Thorne could not have
ordered Raúl's murder, would not have. She came to that
conclusion in Chicago. Raúl was his son. Thorne may have
had no scruples about killing the mother of his son, but
even he would not wipe out his seed. *Who, then? And why?*

The who became clear when the fighting men, once
again, spun away from the moat and closer to the torches.
Giles! Did he know of Thorne's death? Even so, why
would he want to murder Raúl?

Dillon blew past her and slammed into the two men,
sending them flying apart and to the stones. Giles lay on
his back, winded and bloodied. Dillon stood over him,
legs braced apart, gun pointed at the lawyer's head.

Chaz fell to her knees beside her son. She lifted his
head and held it against her breast.

"Unlock these cuffs," Raúl said. He was alert and in
better shape than Giles. Despite the shackles around Raúl's
wrists, Giles seemed to have gotten the worst of the fight.
Raúl had battered the lawyer's face with the iron bracelets.

"Why?" Chaz asked.

"Forget that," Dillon said, his voice breaking the moment between mother and son. "You want this son of a bitch dead? I don't want to waste a shot, but I can throw him to the crocks."

The image of Thorne's impaled body and the bodies of all those who'd died recently swam through her mind. Her chest felt heavy, and her stomach lurched. *So much blood; so much waste of life. Will it ever end?* Not until Díaz's stranglehold on Mexico ended, and even then, much bitterness would remain.

"No, Dillon. Leave him."

"Leave him?" His head turned, eyes narrowed, and disbelief flowed across his features. "This piece of filth tried to kill your son. And you want to spare his life?"

"Yes," she said firmly. "There has been enough killing. Find the keys to these shackles, and then keep Giles from interfering in our escape. We must still wait for our compadres."

Within minutes, a dozen banditos emerged from the shadows, coming in from all directions. Carranza led them, his face a study in despair at having failed to find Raúl. Raúl pushed Chaz away, sat up, and waved at the revolutionary leader. Carranza trotted over, bent down, and took hold of the boy's shoulders.

"You little rooster," he said, elation in his voice though the tone was brusque. "Where were you hiding? We searched this place from its bowels to its towers."

Raúl grinned. "They kept me—"

"Later," Dillon snapped. "Let's get the hell out of here. We have what we came for."

Carranza nodded. "Señor West is correct. We must make haste before the *soldados* find the debris we left in the corridors."

Chaz interpreted his words to mean they'd left a string of bound, unconscious guards behind them, tucked into corners, doorways, and niches.

"Soon," Carranza added, "they will be looking for

us. I would strongly suggest we be far away by then." He waved to his men, and they lowered the drawbridge and swarmed across, headed for the seaward wall.

Chaz helped Raúl to his feet, and Dillon handed her the key he'd extracted from the lawyer's vest pocket. He still stood guard over Giles, who showed no sign of resistance.

"What do you want done with him?" Dillon asked and tilted his head at Giles.

She looked at Dillon and then down at Giles, and her mouth firmed. "Put him to sleep for awhile. By the time he wakes, we will be gone."

Dillon leaned over and smashed his gun butt against the side of the lawyer's head. With no sound, the man slumped and fell to one side.

Chaz pulled Raúl toward the drawbridge, and Dillon followed. Carranza and his men had gone over the wall and down the rope. As planned, they would spread out along the route to the boats, watching for pursuers. Two men remained by the wall, rifles in hand, their restless gazes intent on the entrances from the prison onto the open area by the moat. So far, the *soldados* had failed to appear, but their time in safety was surely limited.

Dillon made a curt signal to the banditos, and they scrambled over the wall, Alec and Carranza following. Chaz went next, then Raúl and Dillon. They shimmied quickly down the rope and out across the island's coral surface. They sped across the coral as fast as they could move with the injured Raúl.

"*¡Jesu!*" Raúl swore, pulling up before they had gone far.

Chaz stopped behind him. "What is wrong?"

"My foot," he said. He balanced on one foot and lifted the other to examine the sole. Not that anyone could see anything in the dark night and swirling sand.

Dillon, coming up from the rear, nearly ran into Chaz. He barely stopped himself in time. "What the hell's going on?" he shouted. "We have to move, or we'll be dead meat!"

Chaz took no notice of him and grasped Raúl's foot. She could see nothing in the dark night and storm, so she ran her hand over the skin of his sole. Only then did she realize Raúl wore no shoes, not even *huraches*. Wetness from a cut flowed over her hand and dripped from her fingers. Although she could not see the injury, from the amount of blood, it was deep.

She dropped his foot. "Sit," she said. "I wish I had known they would take your boots. I would have brought some with me." She eased him down on the coral and pulled out her shirttail, ripping off a section and kneeling to bind his foot.

"I would have sent you a telegram, but I was a prisoner," he replied, the words tinged with humor.

This was no time for jesting, even if it stemmed from fear. "Hush, *niño*," she said. "Remain still while I think of what we should do."

Dillon stood guard over them, looking back toward the prison, which had disappeared in the sand whipping about in the wind. "I can carry him," he said.

She snorted. "He is nearly as big as you. You could not carry him more than a few yards. We would need someone as large and strong as Tino. But he is far ahead of us, and I cannot see any of the other men. Curse this storm! Besides, I need your guns behind us." She tugged Raúl to his feet, and he limped forward. She wedged her shoulder under his arm, taking much of his weight. "I will help him until we catch up with Carranza."

"I don't think that's gonna be as easy as it sounds." Dillon's voice sounded strange, and she looked over her shoulder. He stood with his back to her. When the wind tore a momentary hole in the screening sand, a dark figure stood out from the greater darkness behind him.

* * *

Giles lifted his head off the stones. When blood ran into his eyes, he calmly extracted a snowy handkerchief from his pocket and pressed it to the side of his skull. He sat up and slumped back against the stone wall.

Dillon West. Who the hell thought West would show up here? Certainly not he. The railroad detective had turned out to be an exceeding disappointment, both to Thorne and to him. In hitting him, West thought, perhaps, the blow would kill him. Giles had heard Charissa tell West to leave him alive, but he suspected the ex-Texas Ranger had made up his own mind. Fortunately, Giles had an idea of what was coming. Only the darkness and his quick action in falling as the gun descended deflected the blow.

He felt the pain against his temple—then nothing. But he couldn't have been out long. It was still dark, and the storm still raged around him. No guards had yet arrived.

He reached out, dug his fingers into a crevice in the wall, and hauled himself to his feet. The extended drawbridge lay before him. So they didn't come in from the front gates. At first, naturally, he thought the bandits had bribed one of the guards. *But no.* If they crossed the moat, they came from the rear of the fort, over the wall. Then he noticed the rope stretched across the moat, the grappling hook. When he thought about it, it made sense. In the storm, the guards would be less attentive and seeking shelter. And fewer men would be needed to guard the rear wall, because from what he knew, no one had ever gained entry to the fort from that direction.

Nevertheless, even with surprise on their side, Charissa and West couldn't have dealt with the guards alone. The Ghost Wolf's band must have helped them.

His steps unsteady, he walked toward the drawbridge, gaining strength as he crossed it. Sure, he could call for the guards, but the silver propelled him on alone. He would not share it. The silver was his—his alone. He'd earned it.

When he reached the ramparts, he snatched up a torch and used it to search the wall. The sandstorm tore at his face and clothes and undermined his precarious balance, but he soon found what he sought...another grappling hook attached to a rope snaking over the rim of the wall and downward. The bleeding from the cut on his head had already slowed to a sluggish seeping, but he covered it with a bandage fashioned from the handkerchief. Then he extinguished the torch, tucked it into his gun belt, and made his way down the rope. Once on the surface of the coral reef, he crouched on his heels, put his back to the wind, and struggled to light the torch once again. The wind kept blowing out the matches, but he persisted. Stepping into the lee of a coral formation, he waited for a lull in the gusts, and before long, flames engulfed the torch.

He got to his feet and moved forward, relying on instinct to guide him. It was as if the silver the bandit was hiding called to him, steered his uneven steps. A hundred yards out, he ran across a wetness that looked like blood on the coral. It gleamed blackly in the torchlight, and he went down on one knee to confirm his suspicion, dipping his fingers in the liquid and bringing it to the tip of his tongue. *Sure enough, blood.* One of them was injured, and he was on the right track.

Once, he halted and pulled out Charissa's gun, checking to make sure the silver bullets still filled its chambers. He should have done it before he left the fort, but in some mysterious way, he sensed no one had touched it. After all, it held silver, and all the silver was his.

* * *

"Is it one of Carranza's men?" Chaz asked, having

stopped and turned around, Raúl still leaning on her for support.

"I don't think so." Dillon thought he saw the glittering light of a torch, but then it vanished. If the man was carrying one, he'd put it out. "If it was, he would have hailed us, not snuck up behind us." The man seemed to be alone.

"Then who?" she asked. "A *soldado* from the fort?"

"*¡Alto!*" he shouted at the man. "*¿Cómo se llama usted?*"

A shot rang out, and Dillon took it in the shoulder. The force of the blow spun him around and dropped him to the coral. He rolled, snapped off a shot in the man's direction. But the storm closed in around him again, and the man's figure disappeared in the sandstorm.

"Get down!" he yelled at Chaz and Raúl. Right about now, he could use some reinforcements. When he was in the Rangers, he always had men in reserve. He clung to the hope Carranza had heard the shots. With that thought, he fired off half a dozen more times, aiming toward where the man had been and to either side in case he'd moved. Another bullet sped out of the sand to the right of him. Quickly, he loaded the revolver and returned fire. Then rifle lead came from behind him. *Chaz.*

"Save those cartridges," he told her, "until you can see the bastard." The bullet wound hurt like the devil, and he couldn't do a damn thing about it. He probed it with his fingers. The bullet had skipped across the top of his shoulder, ripping clothing and gouging flesh. He'd be sore for awhile, but he'd live. *Question is: how the hell are we getting out of here?* The man had them pinned down. No sign yet of Carranza and his men. He could sure use some help here.

Two more shots came out of the sand and darkness, from the left this time, close but whizzing past him toward Chaz and Raúl, and his heart stuttered. "You okay?" he shouted.

"*Sí*," her voice came back. "Where is he?"

"Damned if I know," he muttered. The man went right then left. Dillon figured he'd be stupid to go right again. The next shot would come from farther left. He rolled onto his belly and crawled forward. Sharp coral shredded his jacket and dug into his shirt, drawing blood from his belly, but he went on. It seemed like hours before he crawled the twenty yards or so to where the man should have been. At a sudden lessening of the wind, the sand settled, drifting down like snowflakes. Dillon recalled Chicago and another storm, a cold, wet one rather than the hot sand now peppering his body. Someone died that time.

He scanned the cleared area and caught no sight of the elusive man. "Damn," he said under his breath.

"Dillon!" Chaz screamed, a note of terror in her voice he'd never heard before.

A cold hand gripped his heart and squeezed.

He flipped over, jumped to his feet, and turned about at the same time. In the break from the storm, the sight before him turned him to stone. A reluctant dawn was changing the night sky to a washed-out yellow, dimmed by the sand still in the air. The man he was searching for stood over Chaz and Raúl, his gun angled downward. In the sallow light, Dillon recognized their pursuer—Giles.

"Get rid of your guns, or I'll shoot them," Giles yelled. "I know you'll probably get me, but not before I kill at least one of them. I don't want to kill anyone. I'm no killer. Really, I'm not. All I want is the location of the silver. Enough people have died. Just tell me where you hid it, and I'll let all of you go."

Helplessness washed over Dillon, and he glanced about for any sign of Carranza, but they were still alone. He dropped his guns to the coral, removed the scattergun slung over his shoulder, and let it fall beside the revolvers. The wind picked up in a sudden gust, and the sand did its dance again, obscuring the three figures. *Well, if I can't see them, they can't see me.* Dillon scooped up a revolver and sprinted forward, stumbling on the uneven surface of the coral slippery with sand. He slowed down and silently implored the wind to continue. He'd be little use to Chaz and Raúl if he fell and cracked open his head.

The sand curtain parted again, the wind now coming in fitful bursts, but not before it filled his eyes with grittiness.

When Dillon could see again, Raúl had jumped Giles, and the two were struggling desperately for the gun. Chaz lay motionless on the surface of the reef, her guns nowhere in sight. The wind seemed to target them for special attention, and sand swirled about the scene in a rotating motion like a Panhandle cyclone.

His vision now clear enough to reveal his footing, he sprang into a desperate run, rushing Giles and Raúl. Before he reached them, the gun in Giles's hand erupted, shooting flame. The sand blanketed their images then, covered them completely. Nonetheless, Dillon maintained his pace. By the time he reached Giles and Raúl, Raúl had possession of the gun and was holding it on Giles.

"Keep him there," Dillon ordered Raúl, "and don't get it into your head to shoot him." He turned and squinted into the sand-drenched air as thick as fog about him. "Chaz!" he called out, "where are you? I can't see anything in this damn sand."

Silence, other than the whistling of the wind and sand scratching on coral.

Ice pricked his spine. "Chaz? You'll have to call out so I can follow the sound of your voice."

No response, and the ice spread throughout his veins and settled into his chest and gut.

"CHAZ!"

A small lighted area cleared in the sandstorm, and

her figure emerged, lying lifeless on the coral, a bloom of red in her midsection.

"Chaz!" Dillon ran to her, fell down beside her. The wound was mortal. He'd seen enough of them to know. Once again, he was back in Texas during the Mason County Wars, bloodied and dying men all around him. He shook his head repeatedly. "No! Chaz! Don't you die! You open your eyes and look at me!"

She stirred, lashes fluttering, lifting, revealing the dulling sheen of her once expressive blue eyes. "Dillon, *querido.*" The words sifted from her on a sigh. Then she laughed, a small laugh, and ended on a cough that racked her body.

"Save your breath, sweetheart, we'll get you some help," he replied, helpless to halt the tears that flowed from his eyes and dripped from his chin.

As she gazed into his face, she smiled. Her eyes held pain and bewilderment...and love. "Dillon," she murmured, "do you not think it funny? They were not meant for me."

"What?" he asked, his voice as quiet as hers.

Her smile curved into a painful grin. "The silver bullets. They were not meant for me. But now they are mine." She lifted a shaky hand and caressed the side of his face with her fingertips. "Dillon?"

"Yes, *querida.*" He choked on the words.

"*Te amo*, Dillon," she said. "Have I ever told you? I don't think so, but I do love you. You know that."

The tears came harder and faster until he could scarcely see her beautiful face. "Yes," he said.

"I suppose I thought if I said the words I would lose you, lose everything."

"No, darlin', you'll never lose me. And I refuse to lose you."

He attempted a smile, but it died a quick death when her eyes closed. He gathered her into his arms, and blood as cold as snow seeped into his chest. If only he could open his veins and give his blood to her, replace that leaving her body and draining her of life. As her heart beat against him, its vibrant throb grew fainter and fainter.

He raised his head to the heavens, looking up through a storm that had increased to the intensity of a hurricane. Swirling yellow grains, sharp and glittering in the hidden sun behind them. "God!" he screamed, "help her! Take me, not her!"

A shot exploded behind him, and he snapped his head around in time to see Giles go down with a hole in the center of his forehead and Raúl standing before him with the smoking gun. Giles now had his silver. Raúl had given the lawyer the final silver bullet. The boy dropped his arm to his side, fingers still gripping the gun. His head hung down, and then his figure vanished behind the storm of sand.

Dillon became dimly aware of other voices, Carranza and Alec, and bodies hovering over him, but he focused solely on the dying woman, the woman who meant the world to him. She had shied away from men, been afraid of them, and he'd gained her trust, her love. Now he knew he couldn't live without it.

"Chaz," he whispered and wept. "*Mi corazón*, my heart. Don't leave me. Please don't leave me. Come back to me. I love you. I need you. Please, oh, God, please. Come back."

Veintinueve

A soft breeze sighed down from the mountain slopes surrounding Asilo, rippling the meadow grass and bending the heads of the Indian paintbrush. Victory flirted with Niebla, pulling her tail with his teeth, and she lashed out at him with a back hoof. He tossed his head and tore around the corral at a full-out gallop. Fuerte sat on his haunches, a solemn look on his furry face, and watched the horses from the safety of the yard outside the pine poles.

"So, you're still planning to go through with it?" Dillon asked as he propped up a boot on the lowest pole of the corral and rested his elbows on the top rail beside the spot where Raúl sat.

"Yes." Raúl chewed thoughtfully on a twist of straw, his gaze fixed on the antics of the horses. "Carranza needs men. Mexico is changing, and Díaz will not rule much longer. The people are beginning to throw their support behind Carranza. When the new government comes, I want to be a part of it."

"He's agreed to that?"

"*Sí.* He needs good gunmen for now and cool heads for afterward."

"Chaz ain't gonna like it. She wants you to stay here in Asilo, run the place for her."

"I know. She won't admit to my having grown up. I'm a man now."

Dillon chuckled. "Well, maybe not quite yet a man, but close enough to one to be out from under your momma's skirts and on your own."

"Dillon!" The shout came from the *pórtico*.

He whirled toward the voice. "Chaz! What in hell you doing out of bed? You get right back in there. You know what the doc said." He crossed the yard in long, ground-eating strides.

She hugged the porch rail with one arm and pressed her other hand against the bandages swathing her chest. The silver bullet had missed her heart and lungs, cracked a few ribs, angled upward, and lodged in the muscle of her right shoulder. The doctor uttered every swear word he knew—even some Dillon never heard—during the tricky operation to recover the bullet. *Tricky but successful.*

"*El médico* is overcautious," she said with a pout. "I am tired of lying in bed. And I am bored. I have nothing to do."

Dillon reached the *pórtico*, rested one foot on the bottom step, and braced a hand on his knee. "What you can do is rest and recoup your strength. If you don't go back in right now, I'll carry you in and tie you to the bed."

"Ah, señor West," she said, smiling wistfully, "you promise much but you deliver nothing."

From the corral, a bray of laughter came from Raúl.

"If you don't get moving, señora West, I'll deliver a thrashing to your backside."

At his mistress's voice, Fuerte had bounded up the porch steps. He now stood on his hind legs and placed his front paws on her shoulders. His weight staggered her, and his tongue swept over her face.

"Hey!" Dillon shouted. "Get down you brainless

mutt! You'll knock her over and open her stitches."

As he pulled away the dog, Chaz laughed. "He is only happy to see me. He misses me since you banned him from the bedroom."

"That's because he keeps crawling up in the bed with you." He waved a hand at the top step of the porch. "If you're staying, take a seat. I don't want you falling on your face and tearing them stitches."

She eased down until she sat on the step. "Stop blustering, Dillon. It cannot be good for your digestion."

His mouth flattened in a scowl. "It's your stubbornness that gives me indigestion."

"Come here, Raúl," she called and motioned to her son.

"Now?" Raúl sent Dillon an accusatory look.

Dillon lifted a brow and shook his head. He'd said nothing to Chaz about the boy's leaving.

Raúl sauntered over to Chaz, dragging his feet and kicking up small puffs of dust from the yard. She patted the wood step beside her, and he sat, hanging his head.

"Look at me," she said.

He raised his head and turned toward her. "How did you find out? I told no one other than Dillon. And he promised. Did he tell you?"

Her eyes crinkled with puzzlement, and her mouth tightened. "Tell me what?"

"Ah…ah, nothing important. Just man stuff."

Her brows arched. "A girl?"

"*Sí*, a girl," he said with a sudden grin.

Chaz sensed her son's secret did not concern a girl, but whatever he had on his mind, it was nothing compared with what she planned to disclose. She drew in a deep breath to steady herself.

"Raúl, I must tell you something, something important. You are nearly a man now, and I trust you are mature enough to understand. It concerns your father, Justus Thorne."

He brushed away her words with a hand. "I already know, *Mamá*, you need not put yourself through this," he said softly.

She jerked backward as if she'd been stung. "You know? How could you know? No one here at Asilo would disclose my past." *Dillon!* Dillon was the only other person privy to her secret. She threw him a withering glare. "I trusted you, you *vibora*, you viperous snake, you *bastardo*. You pried my secrets from me and spilled them to Raúl when you promised you would not." Holding on to the porch column, she pulled herself to her feet and sucked in a sharp breath when the motion pulled at her stitches.

Dillon folded his arms over his chest and shifted his weight to one leg. Lines of tension stood out against his grim face. "I didn't tell him a damn thing. Whatever he knows, he must have gotten it from you or your family. Or maybe he's just smart enough to figure out things by himself. He's not a kid anymore, you know."

She swept an arm toward the corral. "Collect your horse, señor West, and leave Asilo. You are no longer welcome here."

The breath leaked out of him in a harsh sigh. "Haven't we been through this before, Chaz? Your telling me to git and then coming after me?"

"*¡Salir!*" She screamed it so loudly the sound rasped across her throat like a rusty saw across a piece of metal.

"Stop it!" Raúl shouted and sprang to his feet. "He's right. No one told me. I figured it out by myself. Once I found out you lied about my real father, I figured it out. I'm no genius at higher mathematics, but I can count pretty damn good. I'm sixteen. You're thirty-two. That means you were younger than me when Thorne...when Thorne. *Damn it*, I know what happened. You'd never have allowed him to touch you. He'd have to take you by force, and you'd have fought him like a cornered puma. That's how you got the scars. He gave them to you. If you hadn't killed him in Chicago, I'd have put a bullet in him as soon as I saw him again."

Her eyes watered and burned, and she sank down on the porch, covering her face with her hands. Tears leaked out from between her fingers. It was the first time she'd cried in over seventeen years, ever since she ran away from Thorne and his Chicago mansion. Now it seemed she could not stop the flood. "Oh, Raúl, I am so sorry."

"For what?" he asked softly. He took her hands and pulled them away from her face. He brushed at her tears with gentle fingers, the gesture oddly mature for a boy of sixteen.

"For lying to you for so long."

"*De nada.* Who my father is isn't as important as who my mother is. You loved me, and I had a happy life in Asilo. That's why it's so hard..."

She wiped her face with the back of her arm and peered at him. "What is hard? What do you want to tell me?"

The intensity of her gaze made his fall away. "I'm leaving, to join Alec and Carranza."

"Oh no, Raúl. It is much too dangerous. You must stay here. Asilo needs you."

"No, my Ghost Wolf mother." He brought his gaze back to hers and gave her a sad, tender smile. "Asilo has Salvatore and Delicia and Largo and all the others. Carranza needs me now, and I need to go."

She cradled his face in her hands. "You are sure? This is what you must do?"

"*Sí.*"

She pulled Raúl to her and placed a kiss on his forehead. "Then *vaya con Dios, mi hijo. Vaya con Dios.*"

That afternoon, Raúl packed his saddlebags and bedroll. Chaz watched from the *pórtico* as her only child mounted his white-footed bay and rode out of the yard, into the orange and crimson sunset. Over the mountains, where the sun was sinking to its nightly slumber, it slipped behind a bank of white clouds. They glowed as though imbued with God's light, and brilliant silver edges outlined their shape. *Silver. The symbol of her revenge.* It brought her Dillon and was now taking away her son.

When Raúl halted to give her a wave, his figure blurred from her tears. He put his heels to his horse and sped away at a gallop. Dillon walked up behind her and put his arms around her, drawing her back against his chest.

"You'll see him again soon," he said.

Her eyes lifted to him, the tears flowing freely again. "Will I? I am not so sure."

Treinta

The spinet was the last item, and Dillon had just the place to put it, wedged in between the dining-room table and the bedstead. He'd taken his time, packing the wagon as carefully as if he was packing a load of dynamite.

"Watch it!" Chaz called out to Dillon and Salvatore. She made her way over to them, struggling with an enormous rug that tripped her at every step. "Here," she said. "Wrap this around it so you will not scratch it."

"Goddamn it, woman, I know how to do it," he said with a growl, set down his half of the spinet, and took the rug from her. "Don't you know better than to interfere with a man when he's packing his wagon? Just leave me alone, or I'll never get this weight distributed right. What do you need this damned piano for anyway? We could have come back for it next spring, when we pick up the rest of the fixin's."

A faint scowl pinched her brow. "I do not *need* my spinet, I *want* it."

When he scooped up a handful of pine nuts from the ground and threw them at her, she squealed, laughed, and ducked, scampering for the *pórtico*.

He swathed the spinet with the rug and bent down to lift it again. "Okay, let's get it on," he said to Salvatore. "The lady *wants* her spinet."

Salvatore grunted as he hefted the piano. "*Caramba,* this is heavy."

"Yeah, but it's the last thing. This wagon will be dragging bottom by the time we get out of here, but it's worth it. I don't want to listen to Chaz jabbering in my ear the whole way to Colorado because she misses her piano."

"One more," Chaz said as she backed out of the front door, dragging a rocking chair. She grunted with each bang it made as she muscled it down the steps.

"No," Dillon said. "We got a full load, *mi amore.* No more."

"But I want—"

"No! As it is, one of us will have to ride a horse, and the dog will have to make his own way on foot. One more pound of furniture, and I'll have to get out in front and pull with the mules."

Saying good-bye to Salvatore and Delicia proved to be almost more than Chaz could bear. They had taken the place of her parents and been a vital part of her life since she was a girl. Delicia cried and wiped her face with her apron. Even big, gruff Salvatore had tears glistening in his eyes.

And, at last, the time came to leave. Chaz looked around once more at Asilo. Tall blue mountains in the distance, girding gentle meadows. The burbling stream and the wildflowers with spring blooms of carmine, purple blue, and rusty orange. The adobe homes of the men and their families, and the rambling hacienda with its sweeping *pórtico* and clinging clusters of flowering flame vine. *Will Colorado be as beautiful, as soothing to my soul? Will it feel like home, and will the memories they would make there be gentler to my heart than those of my Mexican hideaway?*

There was only one way to find out. She mounted Niebla and whistled to Fuerte. Dillon climbed up onto the wagon to drive the mules, and with the reins in his hands, he turned to smile at her. The love in his expression warmed her more than any Mexican sun in summer.

"Ready, *querida*?" he asked, brows arching over his brilliant blue eyes.

"*Sí, mi amor,*" she said with smile as bright as his, "I am ready."

Starlight & Promises
by Cat Lindler

During an 1892 voyage to the Furneaux Islands near Tasmania, Lord Richard Colchester finds a living saber-toothed tiger, his discovery will astonish the world...that is, if he ever makes it back to England.

When Lady Samantha learns that her uncle has disappeared under suspicious circumstances, she enlists the help of Christian Badia, a noted zoologist and animal tracker. Christian is a hot-tempered man and a notorious recluse, so the last scenario Samantha anticipates is a romantic interlude. But she is drawn unexpectedly into a world of physical passion, and she soon realizes this enigmatic man is her soul mate. When Christian embarks Tasmania

abruptly, leaving Samantha behind, she fears she may forever lose her newfound love.

Unable to sit idly by and wait for his return, Samantha launches her own investigation—and finds herself in grave danger. *Will Christian find her...before it's too late?*

Reviewers say: "A series of fortunate and unfortunate events take you on an incredible whirlwind ride..." "Lovers of historical and romantic thrillers that do not follow the usual formula will drink in the unexpected turn of events." "In this latest story, the author Cat Lindler does not disappoint her readers." "Starlight and Promises, in short, is fantastic. It has a feel of the older romances with the exotic locations and seafaring travel, but is fresh and fun."

Kiss of a Traitor
by Cat Lindler

You may have seen the movie *The Patriot*, a thinly veiled biography of the Revolutionary partisan leader, Francis Marion, known as the Swamp Fox. In her debut historical romance, *Kiss of a Traitor*, Cat Lindler reveals the true story of the Swamp Fox, weaving it seamlessly with the stormy romance between Brendan Ford, a patriot spy, and Willa Bellingham, a loyal Tory.

In this absorbing novel, as Willa chases the Swamp Fox, and Ford chases Willa, Lindler immerses the reader in the lush landscape and thrilling battles of the Revolutionary War in South Carolina. Praise for *Kiss of a Traitor* includes *"spellbinding,"* and *"a fabulous look at the American Revolution through the eyes of loving adversaries."*

www.ingramcontent.com/pod-product-compliance
Lightning Source LLC
Chambersburg PA
CBHW071305200626
46813CB00015B/42